Unbound

Unbound

Kay Danella

HEAT | NEW YORK

THE BERKLEY PUBLISHING GROUP
Published by the Penguin Group
Penguin Group (USA) Inc.
375 Hudson Street, New York, New York 10014, USA
Penguin Group (Canada), 90 Eglinton Avenue East, Suite 700, Toronto, Ontario M4P 2Y3, Canada
(a division of Pearson Penguin Canada Inc.)
Penguin Books Ltd., 80 Strand, London WC2R 0RL, England
Penguin Group Ireland, 25 St. Stephen's Green, Dublin 2, Ireland (a division of Penguin Books Ltd.)
Penguin Group (Australia), 250 Camberwell Road, Camberwell, Victoria 3124, Australia
(a division of Pearson Australia Group Pty. Ltd.)
Penguin Books India Pvt. Ltd., 11 Community Centre, Panchsheel Park, New Delhi—110 017, India
Penguin Group (NZ), 67 Apollo Drive, Rosedale, North Shore 0632, New Zealand
(a division of Pearson New Zealand Ltd.)
Penguin Books (South Africa) (Pty.) Ltd., 24 Sturdee Avenue, Rosebank, Johannesburg 2196,
South Africa

Penguin Books Ltd., Registered Offices: 80 Strand, London WC2R 0RL, England

This book is an original publication of The Berkley Publishing Group.

This is a work of fiction. Names, characters, places, and incidents either are the product of the author's imagination or are used fictitiously, and any resemblance to actual persons, living or dead, business establishments, events, or locales is entirely coincidental. The publisher does not have any control over and does not assume any responsibility for author or third-party websites or their content.

Text design by Laura K. Corless.

PRINTING HISTORY
Heat trade paperback edition / October 2010

Library of Congress Cataloging-in-Publication Data

Danella, Kay.
Unbound / Kay Danella. — Heat trade pbk. ed.
p. cm.
ISBN 978-0-425-23444-0
I. Title.
PS3604.A513F53 2010
813'.6—dc22

2010013193

PRINTED IN THE UNITED STATES OF AMERICA

10 9 8 7 6 5 4 3 2 1

For my family—for ignoring my crazy hours,
for your uncomplaining bemusement at my writing music,
for your continued support.
I couldn't have finished Unbound *without you.*
And especially for Zia Veronica,
for not killing my laptop during this period.
Also, for the members of the writers_warren Yahoo! *group*
for all the smiles.

One

Pink sky parted at her approach, glowing banks of clouds fleeing her fiery descent, giving way to a view of dark blue water and the leading edge of brown land—the main continent on this side of the planet coming up fast. A beautiful sight that didn't pall, no matter how many times she'd seen its like. Too bad she didn't have time to appreciate it.

Asrial tapped the retros, adrenaline setting her heart racing. She really needed to slow down before the plasma shields overloaded—the last near miss was proof she couldn't ride her entries down, shields flaring, the way she used to. She'd kept putting off repairs; this was the price for the delays. The shock harness snapped tight around her, its straps biting into her shoulders with each jolt. By the time she'd shed enough speed to be safe, she'd left the ocean behind.

The planet Maj—WNX362948 in the Astrographic Record—was even eerier than she remembered. It spun beneath the *Castel*, its desolate terrain scarred with large glass plains—flat, fused glass, not obsidian flow—where nothing grew, their borders dismayingly circular. She'd worried about them on her first visit to Maj, but the instruments hadn't reported any unusual radioactivity.

Now she just ignored them, intent on reaching the mountains with their ruins. The planetary coordinates were already punched into the navputer.

A shudder rocked the *Castel*, several lights on her board turning amber as one of the thrusters lost power. The shock harness tightened as her ship veered off course with a stomach-rolling shimmy.

"Frigging crap." She ignored a twinge of old guilt at her language—language inappropriate for a sovreine, her mother would have chided her had she been alive. But then Asrial hadn't been a sovreine since before she learned to walk, not since Jamyl Kharym Rashad of House Dilaryn was forced to abdicate and take his family from Lomida. These days she was a Rim rat scurrying along the space lanes in search of treasure, not some pampered princess navigating Inner World halls of diplomacy.

Her hands flew across the board, tweaking power loads, jigging the secondaries, dumping speed. She coaxed the *Castel* back to stable flight, a grin on her face and her heart in her throat. Her ship was old, past its prime even when her parents bought it, so old it came with a hydroponics suite, but she knew its quirks better than she knew her own backside. Hopefully, the problem with the thruster wasn't anything major—nothing she couldn't fix with spit and a promise.

Come on, Cassie, *work with me!*

Amber turned back to green, though the lights continued to blink warning. *Ha!* She could live with that. Power stuttered back to acceptable levels, and none too soon.

The board flashed the coordinates of her destination coming up. Shortly after, mountains filled her primary display.

Not all of those peaks were natural. The ruins she was aiming for were rife with structures nearly as tall as the windswept summits. The city was perched on the lip of an upper valley above a broader, river-carved valley. Its long-vanished builders apparently attached much importance to panoramic views.

Typical grounders.

Switching to antigrav, she silenced the roaring thrusters, glided in the rest of the way, and came down in a small clearing tucked in the shoulder of a mountain beyond the city—right where the Astrographic Record's map said it would be. Downloading that old memory cube had been a good decision.

The *Castel* landed as though it were a feather, belying the earlier technical difficulty. Its arrival sent hundreds of flying creatures into the air, screeching in protest.

Asrial tilted her seat back as her ship whined to rest around her. Her body hummed, adrenaline and exhilaration mixing in a potent fizz in her blood. She squirmed, pressing her legs together as the throbbing homed in on her breasts and between her thighs. Spirit of space, that felt so good. There were times when she suspected she lived for these heart-racing moments. Sighing, she lay for a while longer to savor the decadent sensations.

Before she could take it any further, her upbringing caught up with her, and guilt raised its head.

She really ought to be more careful. Amin relied on her. Her mother's cousin had been badly injured when a cargo ship crashed into Lyrel 9, and the miserly disability pay the credit crunchers of the Paxis conglomerate granted him barely supported his family. He now acted as her agent, a polite fiction that let him keep his pride.

Asrial didn't regret her decision. Helping him out was only right, as he'd helped her parents when she was younger.

But something in her craved excitement. She didn't feel alive without it—probably one reason why she remained a Rim rat instead of selling off the *Castel* and going grounder in one of the Inner Worlds. Sure there were easier ways to make a living, but none of the alternatives appealed.

These days the galaxy, particularly the Inner Worlds, was dominated by corporations—huge conglomerates like Dareh and Paxis—whose reach spanned multiple star systems. They controlled much of interstellar trade through the rings that connected the various galactic sectors. The obvious resort for a former sovreine turned grounder in the Inner Worlds was a corporate job, trading on the Dilaryn name to get ahead in a narcissistic world.

Not for her. Not in this lifetime.

Space was in her blood, and the Rim was perfect for nomads like her who couldn't stand the corporations. No planet drew her so strongly that she was willing to set down roots and give up the stars. Perhaps she would have felt differently if she'd grown up on Lomida, sovreine in more than name, but even her parents' home world was just another planet.

Of course, if she wanted the stars, she needed funds, and just sitting here accomplished nothing.

Asrial pressed the release for the shock harness and bounced to her feet. Time to get to work. Relics needed hunting.

Gray fog surrounded him, thick and silent, roiling yet constant. An eternal death that was not death. The fate of all weavers with the misfortune to survive capture: to become djinn.

Betimes he had thought he had gone mad, seeing the faces of family and friends in the shifting mist—but not his betrothed. He could not recall her features anymore, the lips he had kissed, her eyes, her smooth brow, all blurred, her memory replaced by scenes of battle after battle, of carnage and slaughter, of genocide. By his hands.

Forced to weave attacks for his enemies.

Condemned to utter wretched betrayal.

No matter how many times Asrial had been to Maj, its structures still filled her with awe. Despite thousands of years—Standard—the towering stone spires continued to rake the skies, the tallest disappearing into the clouds. How its inhabitants had managed without lift tubes, she couldn't imagine.

The walls were beginning to show the effects of weathering, but the forest kept its distance. Not a blade of the local analogue of weeds marred the abandoned streets, just like the other sites she'd worked. As was usual with Majian ruins, there was no sign of anyone having lived in the city—as if the people had run away. Simply abandoned everything they owned.

Even the planet?

Uncanny—and part of the mystique of Maj that made its relics popular with a certain class of collectors. Plump on the credits of interstellar conglomerates, the dozens of races that filled the galaxy shared a fascination for the Rim Worlds that provided the raw materials for many industries. A sophisticated fascination, enjoyed from one remove. They wouldn't think of going themselves. Her buyers had a preference for the beautiful and the bizarre—novel artifacts that made for good boasting. She didn't mind their reasons, as long as their credits were good.

Flying low to avoid the gusts, Asrial guided the grav sled along the edge of the city. Exploring the center would just be a waste of time. The Astrographic Record had mapped Maj more than a hundred years back. Other Rim rats had scavenged these ruins long ago, ransacking sealed chambers for their secrets. But the last time she was on the planet, a powerful ground quake had rocked this area. She hadn't explored then, not wanting to risk venturing into unstable ground, but if she was lucky, it could have uncovered new sites.

She was pinning her hopes on a big find this time. The Vogan relics had brought in just enough to cover her operating costs and resupply plus a little for Amin. Interest in the shattered colony wasn't that high—not enough blood or controversy, was her guess. Loss due to unusual tectonic motion was too ordinary.

A big find would let her upgrade the *Castel*, something she'd been putting off. Do it up right, not these cut-rate patch jobs with used parts. New thrusters, new grav plates, stronger plasma shields—so many things needed replacement—and enough funds to keep her and Amin's family afloat while her ship was in the dock. What she would do with herself while station-bound, she didn't know, but the refurbishment was long overdue. She couldn't keep putting it off. One of these days, it would be the jump drive that failed, and she'd never emerge back into normal space.

If this trip didn't bring in enough, she'd sell the Dilaryn jewels. Sentiment wasn't of much use in the Rim, and that part of her inheritance would be even less useful with her dead. Her parents would have understood.

At the heels of that decision, Asrial spotted fresh-looking rockfall, almost like an answer to her prayers. Soon after, she found more. Too bad they were by the vertical cliff faces, not the ruins.

She almost missed the fissure. It lay in the shadows, between an outlying tower and a spur from the mountain, a fracture of darker shadow behind a pile of rubble. Only the relative cleanness of the stones' faces, sharp and unweathered, hinted at change.

Aiming the grav sled at the opening, she triggered a probing pulse. The screen lit up with contradictory reports of *void/no void.*

Depending on which scanners she believed, she was either looking at a solid mountain or a network of caves. Talk about an inconvenient time for equipment to act up. On the off chance the problem would clear up, she set the sled on hover and repeated the pulse.

Solid mountain, partial cave, caves, mountain, mountain, caves. Excitement shot through her as she realized what she was seeing, a cold blast that had the hairs on her arms standing on end. The equipment was fine. Something was interfering with the return pulse, making the mountain appear solid. But the fissure broke continuity. When the probing pulses were aimed through the fissure, the illusion of through-and-through solidity failed.

A more thorough scan revealed that what lay behind the rugged facade of natural stone had the regularity of artificial construction. The proximity of the tower suggested a connection to the ruins.

Her heart skipped, irrepressible imagination taking flight. It was a cunningly hidden site. If this breach was as new as she suspected, if it gave access to pristine, unexplored territory, she would be the first one in. This could be big.

Asrial set the grav sled on its skids on the broad, flat slab that was the end of the Majian street. Heart picking up speed, she raised the canopy and slid out of her seat. Funneled by the artificial canyon between the narrow towers, warm wind kicked up sand as it swirled into the clearing that separated building from mountainside and stirred her short curls, its moan a lonely sound that made her shiver despite the sweat beading her upper lip. She didn't need reminding that she was the only person on the planet.

She adjusted the fit of her T-top—not that she had much to support up front, but comfort was important—then pulled on her battered jacket at the last possible moment. It was snug, but its protection was necessary on planet. The carbon silk of her pants would withstand the demands of scrambling around, but the sleeveless top she wore on the *Castel* covered just enough for decency. She checked her jacket's seals to make sure they were tight, then patted the pockets. Stunner, spare charge, head lamp, tool kit, med kit, comm, comp. Everything was where it was supposed to be, ready to grab as needed.

The tall fissure waited, exhaling a cool draft—as if she needed enticement. Sunlight reached only a few paces inside, but it reflected off finished stone walls. She froze at the sight, tempted to break out in a victory dance. *Not a cave, yes!*

Sand had gathered at the opening, seemingly undisturbed. If anyone else had been here, enough time had passed that the signs had been obliterated—unlikely, given how recent the quake was. Besides, the galaxy was huge, and Maj was an old strike. Most Rim rats would have moved on to easier pickings. She could afford the challenge of Maj because she worked solo and turned a profit on smaller finds. But if this was as big as she hoped, she'd make a bundle—maybe even enough to restart her emergency fund after upgrading the *Castel*. It'd be good to have a buffer and have some time off again.

Clicking on her lamp, Asrial set out to explore.

The chamber beyond didn't hold anything much of interest to a Rim rat. It seemed to have been a dormitory of some sort, judging from the rows of beds. Perhaps an archaeologist or a museum would slaver over the mattresses, but it wouldn't be worth the effort to load them on the *Castel*. They were too fragile, and none of the collectors she sold to would waste a glance at them.

A large, wooden door opened into a wide corridor. From the little debris, it looked like she could use the grav sled. That was a stroke of luck, since the last scan indicated a complex extending deep into the mountain.

It took Asrial several days to map her way to the upper levels, in part because she refused to camp inside and had to retrace her path each day. Though the quake hadn't wreaked much damage in the lower levels, she didn't want to risk getting trapped underground while she slept. But also because the complex was that large—practically an entire city in itself.

She started to search in earnest at the top. Majians seemed to associate altitude with power. The best pickings were invariably in the highest chambers. Though she kept an eye out for exceptions to the rule, going straight to the top was the most efficient use of her time. As she'd expected, the upper levels were a treasure trove, chamber upon chamber of artifacts, some tarnished by time, others gleaming like new.

Typical of those in power to hoard the good stuff. She'd always wondered if that was the reason her father had been deposed: because he hadn't been greedy. He'd chosen to abdicate the scepter rather than risk an internecine war pitting Lomidari against Lomidari that would devastate the planet. He'd allowed them to strip him of most of the Dilaryn holdings, which they claimed were lands of the *reis*, not his personal property. Too idealistic to survive in yfreet-infested skies, her mother would have said, smiling. Nasri had compared Lomidar politics to a feeding frenzy of those horrific flying scavengers often enough that Asrial had looked for a vid of such an occasion. Watching the blood fest where only the most vicious yfreet emerged victorious made her regret pandering to her curiosity.

She shrugged off her cynical mood. At least the Majians hadn't taken their pretties with them when they fled or died out or whatever had happened to them.

At the topmost level, Asrial left the grav sled in a large atrium that gave on to several floors. Here, the Majian ruling class's taste for lavish surroundings took front and center. The sled's lights revealed elaborate sculpture and statues with something of a conquering hero motif—dominant central figures overawing smaller, lesser, kneeling figures. Some archaeologists argued that they depicted worship of some deity, but she wasn't convinced. She didn't get a benevolent vibe from those scenes.

Even the walls were decorated with murals of fantastical beasts and bewildering cities, their colors still bright despite the passage of time. The pigments were probably baked on, except she couldn't find any seams. The murals looked to have been made as entire pieces—a monumental effort, if that was the case. And a pity, since a piece as wide as her hand would probably spark a bidding war.

Say what some people might about Rim rats, she drew the line at defacing artwork. Finding some already in pieces was one thing, but having a hand in their destruction was something else entirely; in that much she could be true to her upbringing.

She continued her exploration on foot. This stage required care. Too quick a passage could lead her to overlook some prize—or worse, unbalance and damage a rare pretty. Fortunately, her head lamp was strong enough to illuminate the darkest corners.

Movement out of the corner of her eye startled Asrial. She crouched, ready to jump to safety, only to relax with a laugh at herself. It was just one of the flying creatures that filled Maj's skies. Then her brain caught up and realized she was seeing spires, mountains, clouds . . . the *Castel*!

How could that be? She didn't feel any wind or cold. She hadn't seen any windows in her scans of the mountainsides—if there had been any, surely this complex would have been discovered sooner.

The opening was larger than an ordinary window, larger than the usual door. She walked up to it on tentative feet, testing each step for weakness, maybe a trap.

A tingling pressure met her fingers when she reached out. It felt like a force wall. She froze, her eyes darting in search of its source. Nothing in the literature about Maj indicated any capability of this sort. She should know; she'd had to study the Rim to learn what artifacts collectors were interested in and how to find and identify them. She couldn't spot what generated the force wall. When she aimed her comp at its edges, the scan turned up blank: unknown source. She took comfort from that—at least the force wall hadn't been installed by another Rim rat.

She pushed her head and a hand through and found the stinging wind she'd expected. And got a shock at seeing her disembodied hand emerge from apparently solid rock.

This was no ordinary force wall. None of the conglomerates used this kind of tech, especially not in the Rim. If they could build this advanced a force wall, they wouldn't waste it out here where there was no profit to be made, nor would they leave it behind.

Asrial stared at the mountains, an endless vista with countless valleys, and couldn't help but wonder if there were many more such complexes hidden in them, in the entire planet.

How long she was lost in her thoughts, she didn't know. It took the prickling of her nose to recall her to herself. Other hidden complexes had no bearing on the here and now. She could fit only so much in the *Castel*'s hold. This was probably a once-in-a-lifetime find. She could break her heart and her pocket trying to find another. Not a good idea.

At least with the force wall, she wouldn't have to thread the maze back to the fissure the way she'd been doing. She'd take her blessings wherever she found them. The Spirit of space knew, they were few enough—she could count them on one hand with fingers to spare.

But if this collection sold as well as she hoped, she might have to start on her other hand.

On that cheerful thought, she resumed her exploration.

Asrial found more force walls looking out into the mountains, convincing arguments that they were Majian work. The conglomerates wouldn't have made them permanent installations, which made it unlikely someone would come swooping in to grab her find from under her.

She turned a corner and stopped before she stepped on a long pool of glass roughly bisected by a metal groove. Gravity must have taken its toll. Had that been artwork?

The room beyond thrust her Rim rat's disappointment at lost profit right out the airlock and straight into amazement. Here, the quake had left its mark. Debris from broken walls and fallen shelves littered the floor, like the remnants of a giant's rampage. But untouched amid all the destruction was what looked like a vase or a flask of some sort. It had a wide base and a long, narrow neck topped by a heart-shaped lid. Just visible under the dust was a distinctive golden brown with some dark tracery around the thickest part.

Asrial inhaled sharply, stunned by her discovery. Majian pottery! And intact. The examples she'd seen in museum catalogs were typically shards. She could think of dozens of collectors who'd pay insane sums for an intact piece. She screwed her eyes shut, cautioning herself to throttle back on the enthusiasm. *Don't spend those credits before they're in the bank.* This was just one side. For all she knew, it could have suffered massive damage somewhere she couldn't see.

Excitement urged her to find out, one way or the other, but the rubble made an immediate inspection impossible. The uneven footing forced her to choose her approach carefully. Haste wasn't her friend. If she misstepped and broke a leg, no one would come to her aid.

Climbing over the remains of a wall, she slithered over the debris, holding her breath as she got nearer, dreading the sight of a crack or chip. She ignored the rough edges under her hands, the clatter of stones shifting from her weight, focused completely on her prize.

It was perfect.

Her breath left her in a rush of relief. Asrial circled the flask again, incredulous at her luck. Up close, she saw it was elaborately etched with strange designs that ringed the narrow neck. Its base wasn't as regular as she had first thought. A deep indentation bisected the base into two ovate gobs with the neck rising at one end.

She stopped in her tracks, struck by the most absurd notion. From that angle, it looked like an enormous, erect, stylized phallus. Had that been intentional?

Snorting in self-deprecation, Asrial shook her head. There she went, thinking about sex again. Obviously it'd been too long since she'd had a man between her thighs, but that went hand in glove with being a Rim rat. Her choice.

Propping her hands on her hips, Asrial visually quartered the *Castel*'s hold before conceding defeat. "That's it. Finis. You're done." Much though it pained her to leave so much behind, she was out of space.

The *Castel* was too large a ship for one person. Its quarters could accommodate a family—or a small crew, if they were friendly. But with everything she'd gathered over the past several days, it would take some fancy load juggling to fit the grav sled into the hold without breaking something. As it was, she'd have to move the more valuable pieces to the spare cabins in order to accommodate the items still in the sled.

Sunlight streaming in through the exterior hatch propped open glinted off her finds. She had to laugh. Despite her attempts at order, the hold looked like some treasure cave from her mother's stories. All it lacked was a djinn guarding it to complete the image.

Rank silliness. When she started entertaining nonsense, that was a sure sign it was time to leave.

The artifacts that needed cleaning she took to the work cabin and the bank of expensive equipment for that purpose. They could handle the preliminary work of freeing her finds from centuries of dirt while she readied the *Castel* for liftoff. That problematic thruster needed her attention more. Once she'd input the parameters, she left the brush bots to their task. At least those still functioned properly. If the *Castel* cooperated, she could be headed outsystem in a matter of hours.

The summons was strange. Formless. Lacking the hated compulsion he . . . remembered. It did not demand his presence in a storm of impatience. Almost, he ignored it. Almost. But the gray fog that was his prison had surrounded him for too long. He yearned for release from the damnation of eternal sameness.

This strange summons came almost as a relief.

The gray fog thinned, temporary escape from his prison. Only exhaustion stirred in his heart, knowing it would not last.

Weaving the energies around him, he took form—emerging to silence. No one held his prison. It sat on a ledge beside a command baton, a perfume vial, a scry glass, a carved askeiwood box, many more things that had no place beside his prison. He stood inside an ordinary storeroom. Had the Mughelis so many djinn now that his prison had been relegated to the fripperies?

He waited. Yet no one came.

Only slowly did he notice his surroundings. After so many masters, being summoned in too many places, he had long ago chosen not to look, not to see the ruins around him, the once bustling cities reduced to lakes of glass, some at his hands, if not his will. Ignorance was less painful.

But with no master to command his attention, he found his eyes drawn to the walls.

Though outwardly plain, they sparkled to his weaver's sight.

They were made not of stone, wood, nor cloth. Not precisely metal, either. He could not identify the material, but beneath the surface, he could see the energies woven into them, some threadbare, only a glimmer of potential, others flowing with purpose.

Curiosity woke sluggishly, reluctantly. It had been such a long time since he had felt the emotion that, at first, he did not recognize it for what it was—forlorn hope.

The walls perturbed him, not so much for their strangeness, though he had never seen such work among the Mugheli. The changing patterns lacked balance, crying for a weaver's touch to bring them into harmony. Almost, he reached out—save doing so would aid the enemy. He did not want to think he had fallen so low.

When still no one came, he left his position. As he was able to move, it seemed he was allowed, perhaps even expected to. He had been summoned, and he was never summoned for no purpose.

Tracing the flows of energy, he found a section where they curved, parting like a river around a sandbar. He reached out. It seemed as though it should—

A panel slid sideways, disappearing into the wall with a soft hiss of air. The opening revealed a chamber beyond. Stepping through, he discovered it was a corridor. He turned to the room of his summoning and saw the panel resume its original position—without need for any weaving.

Wonder pierced his apathy for the space of a heartbeat. Much had changed since he was last summoned.

He sought the greatest confluence of energies, for surely only dire need would have drawn his summoner away without terminating the summons. The vortex of primal energies he found was housed in an unimposing chamber, paling in comparison to the meanest of Mugheli halls.

An atypical setting. The Mughelis considered lavish surroundings the right of those with power. Any vyzier who could harness such a vortex could demand the most ostentatious of chambers and not be denied.

Yet this chamber lacked even the minimum a Mugheli would consider necessary comfort: no seats, no cushions, no rugs, no servants. The utilitarian lines of the pipes snaking around the room held no beauty, save for the sparkling flows of energy. And no one kept watch over the vortex.

He roamed the corridors, finding more doors to an extensive storeroom, a plant room, smaller rooms used for storage, and others whose purpose was not evident. Nothing made sense. All the walls were of that same not-metal and sparkled to his sight. He was caught in a basket of energies suspended within an impossible void.

And still he saw no one.

The last door would not open, but he sensed a bundle of energy flaring with the rhythm of life beyond. The only hint of life to be found.

His master?

It was a simple matter to mist and flow between the matrix of the door's fabric. He re-formed in yet another room. Like most of the others, it was small, mere paces wide in all directions. But unlike the others, it was dimly lit by impossibly tiny pinpricks of light along the edges of the ceiling.

The flaring came from the far wall, a niche made up into a narrow bed. The discovery that it was occupied filled him with a shameful sense of relief. He was not alone, summoned and abandoned, in some bizarre twist to his captivity.

Asleep, his enemy shifted on the bed, turning over, away from the wall, to face him.

He sucked in air he did not need.

The light was too weak to reveal the color of the short curls brushing high cheekbones, but it was enough for him to see delicate features: graceful brows, a straight nose, lips poised on the edge of a smile. A sleeping beauty.

A woman.

A quick glance downward confirmed his initial impression. Slender fingers curled into the pillow beneath her cheek. A sleeveless blouse hung loosely over modest breasts and ended well short of a trim waist. A slender leg bent at the knee hid the rest beyond the strange garb wrapped around her hips.

This was his new master?

Two

This sleeping beauty in her unusual clothes had to be the one who had summoned him. She was the only person to be found in this alien place.

She was a vyzier? A prodigy, then, for she looked too young, her smooth face lacking the deep lines of experience.

He drifted closer, drawn to her deceptive air of serenity, to the uncommon sight of her femininity, to the soft gleam of bare skin at her belly. It had been so long since he had touched a woman, since before he had been forced into hateful servitude and the eternal death of a djinn—and longer, before his capture at that last desperate fight. Inwardly, he railed against the injustice of the universe, against this treacherous attraction to his enemy, for enemy she must be to be his master.

Perhaps that was her game. A twist to the betrayals he had been compelled to commit.

If only he could resist. But he had been djinn for too long. He knew obedience was not a choice. The master's will was a djinn's abiding purpose. Nothing else existed. Nothing else mattered. Nothing else could be.

No djinn had ever been freed, despite all his people's efforts; even his betrothed had applied her sharp mind to unraveling the trap—to no avail. None had ever escaped.

Long ago, at the beginning of his hated servitude, before the bitter reality of his fate had sunk home, he had tried to break the Mughelis' control. For more important reasons than mere pride—to protect the innocents ranged against his masters. He had failed. By his failure, he had killed thousands upon thousands—friends and family. Nameless, countless others. His efforts to resist, to deny his masters' commands, might have been a drop of water in the desert for all the inconvenience he had caused.

All for naught.

Each failure had lessened him.

His greatest regret was that he had not died in that rearguard action. He had held his ground, fighting beyond hope of escape. He should have killed himself before capture. Now it was too late.

Only resignation was left.

If his master's will was for him to touch her, resistance was less than nothing. One who could harness that vortex he had seen could surely afford a djinn for a plaything. Who would dare deny her?

He had never served as a pleasure slave, his battle weavings too potent to be set aside, but surely that was better than attacking his own people. He was tired of war, sick of it to the very depths of his soul.

Kneeling by the side of the bed, he reached out. The soft skin beneath his fingers was bittersweet pleasure and a unique torment. To be so close to a woman, to take such delight—from the enemy.

The smooth warmth of her beguiled. Her serenity held him in silence. The lure of another person's presence fed a treacherous weakness inside him, one that would draw reassurance even from a Mugheli.

His hand moved of its own volition; no thought of his commanded it. His fingers glided as if on velvet, stroking, caressing, lingering—almost in mockery of his memories of courtship, the last that remained of his betrothed. The rising anticipation. The breathless excitement. The gradual unveiling.

Still, he could not stop himself, lost in wonder. He pushed the hem of her shirt up and discovered small breasts with large, puffy areolas. So delicate . . . and soft. A delight to touch. He wished he could laugh at the insidious seduction of his senses, but his chest was tight.

Again, his hand moved, hesitantly circled a breast. Apart from him. His fingers tingled, her warmth reaching out to him. Temptation given female flesh.

She made a sound, a murmur of approval, by which he took to mean he was to continue. Did she enjoy such games?

He traced the edges of those pretty circles, watched them darken as her nipples puckered and pouted. He could have sworn his heart skipped at her response.

A quiver swept her, a quiet sigh that pressed her breast into his palm. A tender firmness he had not thought to feel ever again. Such pleasures were not granted to djinn.

She was so soft, so delicate in his hand. It seemed impossible someone like her could be a vyzier, but it was foolishness to doubt. There was no one else to harness that vortex.

His new master arched her back, her body undulating, sinuous and graceful as a veil dancer under his hand. He stilled in shock. He had not thought of veil dancers since before his capture. They were part of happier times, peaceful times, now and forever lost to him.

Another curve of her body, a lazy sway, and his hand continued its meandering, following the hint of muscle down her belly to the strange, silky garment wrapped around her loins. Her hips rose, pressing the juncture of her thighs against his tingling fingers. The dampness there scorched him. Only thin fabric separated him from her folds. He traced the edges of her delicate flesh with disbelieving strokes. Her game was unlike any of the demands of his previous masters, yet the musk of her desire was undeniable.

An irritable grunt accompanied the next insistent thrust of her hips, her impatience obvious. In obedience, he strengthened his strokes, rubbing deeper, searing his fingers on her heat.

The shortening of her breath accompanied the increasing voluptuousness of her motions. No longer needing her direction, he pressed down, mindless in his obedience to her desire.

"Oh! Oh! Aaa—" The triumphant cry was cut short. Her eyes flashed open, then wide. She gasped and jerked upright, wresting away her heat, her arm sweeping to one side.

He curled his fingers against the treacherous ache of loss. How could he regret losing something that had never been his? Was he so lost to himself that he now embraced his enslavement?

"Back off." She thrust her hands at him, brandishing some object in threat, underscoring her command.

Shock held him in place. Not at her reaction, but at the complete absence of compulsion in her words. He felt no need to obey her. None of the relentless pressure, the automatic obedience, the absolute disregard of his will.

But that was impossible.

She was his master.

And yet . . . he *did not move*. The curse of his servitude should have forced his instantaneous obedience to her command—without thought or delay.

The thing in her fist spat energy at him.

* * *

The stunner beam crackled through empty air, the man vanishing as if he'd never been there.

"Lights, thirty percent."

The glow from the walls brightened in response to her command. No one crouched beside her bunk. No one hid in the shadows, not that there was much room in her small cabin for hiding. No man lay on the deck temporarily paralyzed by the blast.

Perplexed, Asrial lowered her stunner. Neither door had opened, yet she was alone with only the heat in her blood to attest to her awakening.

No one moved that fast.

With a huff of disgust, she dropped her head into her free hand. "Spirit of space, Asrial, now you're seeing things."

Her nipples throbbed, the soft drape of her top irritating the sensitive buds. The flesh between her thighs pulsed in concert. She could almost feel hard fingers stroking her folds.

Impossible. She was in space, headed outsystem toward the first of several Jumps to the Eskarion Ring, one of Xerex sector's gateways to the Inner Worlds. No one could have gotten past her security—the one system she made sure was up to date—and boarded the *Castel* without her knowledge. She'd learned her lesson from her parents' deaths and kept up with the latest security advances. Never again would pirates set foot on her ship.

Despite that, her paranoia forced her to double-check. "*Castel*, head count, number of sentients aboard?"

"One, identified as Asrial Dilaryn." The ship comp's voice was blandly anonymous, never having been programmed for emotion. She hadn't bothered with the preset profiles, deeming it unnecessary. Personality was for conversation, and she didn't want conversation. Anyway, the *Castel*'s comp wasn't an AI; it couldn't have handled the load.

"See, just a dream." The solitude was getting to her. Too many hours at the board or wrestling with the control runs of that thruster, not enough downtime. That had to be it. She'd promised herself and her cousins she'd make time to visit and relax when she brought the *Castel* in for its upgrade. Clearly that wasn't soon enough for her body.

Asrial swept the cabin with another glance. The storage compartments remained sealed, as were the door to the rest of the ship and the door to the bio unit. If any of them had opened, the indicators would have lit up. No one had used them to escape, certainly no one faster than a stunner blast.

But still her body throbbed, hungry for relief. She rubbed her breasts, the worst offenders, so sensitive the slightest pressure sent tingles sizzling through her.

Strange what her subconscious dreamed up. She'd never been drawn to the dark and brooding type, preferring lanky, gregarious blonds with friends in every bar. Pilots, not dockhands. Lighthearted fun. She couldn't afford anything more serious with her runs to the Rim and all her funds tied up in her ship or earmarked for Amin's family.

So why did her heart race at the thought of a dark stranger bending over her, his large hands roaming her body at will? Why did her breath catch at the imagined pressure of long fingers parting her tingling folds?

She cupped her wet and aching flesh, the contact sending her body shuddering with carnal hunger. Yearning flooded her veins, her very skin shivering from the strength of her need. No way she could go back to sleep feeling like this.

Frigging biology. Asrial shook her head in resignation.

She scrounged through the locker under her bunk for her pleasure wand. Best she release some of the tension humming in her veins. She couldn't afford to wait until she got to a station and found a willing partner. Being distracted in space was guaranteed to get someone killed—her, most likely.

There it was. The pleasure wand's hard, familiar lines filled her hand like a friend. She'd been using it rather frequently of late. Amin's medical expenses had wiped out her emergency funds, and she'd been cutting costs wherever she could since then. Shorter stops on stations, less convenient docking bays, fewer drinks, cheap food. Which came down to less time to meet a man to warm her sheets.

Impatient now, Asrial wriggled free of the constriction of her clothes. Lying back, she activated the pleasure wand, its barely audible hum waking anticipation. Here, with this, she was certain of satisfaction.

She pressed it to the side of her breast, quiet sparks leaping out to lick at her nerves as she laid it against the erogenous zones repeated practice had made familiar. The passionless stimulation performed as designed, however much she might dislike the clinical effect.

Shivering at the electrifying contact, she stretched out on her bunk and closed her eyes to shut out the sight of the device. The wand might bring her body release, but it couldn't give her the sweat and heat and exertion of real sex.

But as soon as she closed her eyes, that dark man she'd thought had been bending over her came to mind. A brooding presence more sensed than seen. Even now, it felt as though he watched her, watched her hands as she pleasured herself.

A gulp of air did little to ease the tightness of her chest. How perverse to envisage him instead of one of her previous lovers, men with whom she'd actually shared intimacy. But whatever worked. She wasn't choosy. Efficiency had been her byword since Amin's accident. The end was what mattered—release from the tension tying her in knots.

Asrial used that erotic awareness to build her desire, imagining a mysterious lover who watched her from the shadows, wanting to tempt him into joining her in her empty bunk. The fantasy added spice to her usual routine, heightening her excitement. Her heart leaped at the scene, cool tingles sweeping her body in ever stronger waves as need rose.

Each touch of the pleasure wand was a spark of delight that fed the humming tension within. The throb homed in on her core, the low thrum of thrusters preparing for launch. She abandoned her usual restraint, embraced the fever of need rising in her veins, allowed her body to arch and twist as the mood took her.

In her imagination, she watched her lover's eyes heat as he watched her in turn. The thought of it made her so wet her womb clenched in a fury of desire, emptiness demanding fulfillment.

She pressed the wand between her legs and into herself, gasping at the jolt of pleasure it wrenched from her body. The imagined pressure of long fingers stroking her intimately taunted her with what she didn't have. She drove the wand deeper, chasing guaranteed release. Caught up now in carnal hunger, she writhed, riding the wand, its electrifying touch winding her need ever tighter. But it wasn't enough. Spirit of space, to have a man inside her, pumping her to overflowing.

The peak came inexorably, rising higher and higher with each erotic spark. With a final thrust of the pleasure wand, she slipped over the edge, breaking the bonds of need. Pleasure fountained up, effervescent delight shimmering through her veins in sweet waves.

Asrial powered down the pleasure wand and set it aside, her body spent. She let her eyes drift shut, savoring the aftershocks of her orgasm. The cool breeze of the climate control's night setting dried her sweat, the contrast with her hot skin sending another shiver through her.

And still she couldn't shake the notion that someone was watching her.

Three

As mist, he found his prison tugging at his essence, a loose chain drawing slowly, inevitably taut. But the woman's fascinating performance gave him the strength to resist. That and his fear that succumbing to the grayness would lose him what little freedom he had somehow gained kept him in her room.

He was still djinn, still tied to this despicable existence. But for some inexplicable reason, the woman who should be his master had no power to command him. Even more perplexing: she was alone when no vyzier was ever left alone. She wielded an energy weapon instead of weaves. From her reaction, she did not even know what he was.

Impossible hope clutched at him, clawing at the cloak of apathy that protected him. Suddenly all the strangeness he observed felt significant. He had to know what it portended.

Re-forming by the bedside, he looked down at the woman. "What is this place?"

With a gasp, she scrambled away, clawing around her as she pressed her back to the wall. "Lights, full!"

Brown eyes rounded, irises narrowed to tiny black dots in the sudden brightness from the walls, she stared at him. "Who are you? Where'd you come from?" She spoke with an unfamiliar accent, her words tumbling together like flowing water, not the harsh, guttural tones of the hated Mugheli.

Not Mugheli.

She was not the enemy!

He returned her stare, stunned. He was not in enemy hands? How was that possible? A djinn was a prize among the highest vyziers, their mastery a recognition of rank and power.

And yet he had seen his prison standing among trifles . . . and she did not know what he was.

Without taking her eyes from him, she continued to claw the beddings around her.

Spotting that curious object she had brandished at him, he picked it up, turning it over in his hand. Yet another thing made of some material he had never encountered, the energies at its heart like harnessed starlight. "Is this what you seek?"

Her eyes widened further when he offered her the object. She scrubbed her face. "Spirit of space, I've lost it. I did *not* see that."

He set it down, since it seemed to upset her. He had frightened her with his unthinking reappearance. More emotions long unfelt woke inside him: awkwardness, embarrassment, remorse . . . and something else.

The urge to touch her filled him once again, to explore the bare, creamy skin before him. But if she could not command him, did that mean the desire . . . was *his*?

Had it been his all along?

She lowered her hands slowly, then groaned when she saw him

still there. Squeezing her eyes shut, she chanted in a low voice, "Wake up, wake up, wake up already."

He touched her face with disbelieving fingers. "You are awake," he assured her, hoping he was not the one who dreamed.

She was awake? Asrial opened her eyes to stare at the intruder standing within arm's reach. Grabbing distance. Kissing distance. She stifled a spurt of awareness at the observation. What a thing to notice when she was sitting here naked!

The incongruities of his appearance gradually registered. He didn't wear spacer gear—in fact, his chest was bare—and it was rather obvious he didn't bear any weapons. Yet he didn't have the desperate look of someone who'd been abandoned on Maj and had managed to stow away.

What man would enter her cabin uninvited, then give her stunner back? Besides, how could he have gotten aboard in the first place, and how had he disappeared? She had to be dreaming. His presence didn't make sense.

"*Castel*, head count, number of sentients aboard?"

"Two, identified as Asrial Dilaryn and—anomaly detected."

Asrial froze at the ship comp's response, her head jerking to the speaker panel on the wall. "*Castel*, identify anomaly."

"Unregistered sentient exceeds set parameters."

No way. There was no way anyone could have boarded in midflight, not without her knowing. They'd have had to match trajectories and velocities, run a boarding tube to the *Castel*, then force a hatch open. Just the magnetic seal of the tube would have set off the alarms.

Secure in her logic, she relaxed infinitesimally, the stunner under her hand reassuring her further. "What are you? How'd you get on board?"

A strange look crossed his face. More than discomfort. Almost . . . shame?

"Well?"

"I am—" He drew a deep breath, that magnificent bare chest expanding. "A djinn." He spat the word as though it were poison, disgust twisting his features. If it was pretense, he put on a good show.

Asrial nearly believed him but . . . a djinn? That was straight out of her mother's stories, the same ones she'd been thinking about recently. "And how'd you get on board?"

"Someone put my prison here."

Prison? That wasn't in the tales. Djinn were always fearsome spirits guarding fabulous treasure or in the service of evil sorcerers.

The tension inside her eased, relief letting her breathe easier. He wasn't real. Her subconscious was playing games, drawing inspiration from recent events. She must have fallen asleep after her session with the pleasure wand and was now dreaming. A continuation of her fantasy.

"Perhaps I can prove it." His voice rasped, like a rough velvet tongue on her skin. His touch on her shoulder was light and tentative, unlike the intimate caresses she'd imagined ranging over her body. But the implication was clear.

Sex. Of course, it would be sex. She'd had sex on the brain since before she'd undocked from Nudra 4 for Maj.

What would it hurt? This was a dream. Best to get it out of her system while she was in local space. Her brain was obviously telling her she needed some downtime. Still, she couldn't deny some alarm at having a tall stranger standing at her bedside and her all naked.

Asrial took a longer look at him and felt a tingle of response. Her subconscious had a lot to answer for.

Broad, corded shoulders above an equally broad, bare chest. A smattering of hair across his pectorals. Flat, lean belly. Thin line of hair below the navel. Loose pants hung low on narrow hips. Mouthwatering details.

His features gave her no cause for complaint, somewhat drawn but not gaunt. Rim rat stubble shadowed a stern jaw and upper lip. Straight nose, a bit on the long side. Level brows. Direct gaze, wary and unblinking. If he were truly a man, she'd have said he had a past—a chancy one—and given him a wide berth. Especially after seeing the dark tat on his left shoulder.

But he had long hair no self-respecting spacer would sport, what with vari-grav zones and all the nooks and crannies it could catch on. Worn straight and loose, it ended at mid-thigh and was so dark it held a sheen of midnight blue. What had prompted her to imagine that?

"D'you have a name?" Just because this was a dream didn't mean she was willing to spend some rack time with a nameless stranger. She still had standards—however low.

Silver eyes stared at her blankly, darkening to gray as his pupils widened. His mouth opened then closed repeatedly while he searched—seemed to search—his memory. Frowning, he thrust his fingers through his hair as if the motion would jog an answer loose. "R—Ro—Romir. Romir . . . Gadaña."

It made no sense to her. He actually looked like a Lomidari, but that didn't sound like a Lomidar name nor was it a name from Ruxil or Cyri or Hagnash or any of the dozen or so races she frequently encountered. Why would her subconscious come up with an unfamiliar name?

She snorted to herself. What did it matter? He wasn't real. *Satisfy the urge, and get it out of your system.*

"Romir." The name melted on the tongue like high-grade

xoclat. Dark, rich, exotic, and not exactly good for you. A guilty pleasure. To be taken in small bites.

Those silver eyes sharpened, focusing on her with the intensity of a laser cutter.

Asrial swallowed, her throat suddenly dry. "You can try." So she was dreaming. When she woke up, rested, she'd be fine. No harm in indulging her subconscious.

He didn't join her on the bed as she'd half expected, getting down on his knees instead, which put his head lower than hers. It somehow made him seem less imposing.

Watching her, he took her hand and raised it to his mouth, brushing his lips against the backs of her fingers. The gesture struck her as cautious . . . and courtly. None of the men she'd met at the station bars would have done that.

He turned her hand over and pressed a kiss into her palm, the heat of it sending a shiver streaking through her. Still, he held her gaze, and she couldn't look away despite the intense intimacy of his unswerving regard.

Her heart skipped a beat, then scrambled to triple time, banging away like a laboring torsion pump. He hadn't touched her anywhere else, but she was already more aroused than she could remember being in a long time. The hunger she'd thought sated by the session with the pleasure wand was back, magnified to a yawning chasm. Air was suddenly a precious commodity; she couldn't get enough of it into her heaving lungs. She pressed her thighs together against the throb that had sprung to sudden life between them.

He stared at her as though committing her features to memory, as if his life depended on it. His lips on the base of her thumb stirred her awareness, sensitizing her to the rasp of his stubbled cheek.

Spirit of space, when her subconscious cooked up a dream man, it didn't stint on the details.

"That all you're gonna do?" The words came out husky—a breathless invitation instead of the challenge she intended.

Emotion flared behind his eyes, unreadable, his jaw tensing under her hand. But despite her complete nudity, he merely placed his other hand on her hip, his touch tentative. He seemed to hold his breath—expecting her to object? He had a long wait coming, if that was the case. The innocent contact dazzled her senses like fireworks the magnitude of a stellar flare. She placed her hand on top of his, urging him into motion.

Those silver eyes widened, then released hers to transfer his gaze to where she touched him. His hair slid forward, a black curtain concealing his expression. He caressed her over and over from waist to hip, acting as flesh-starved as she felt, petting her with rapt attention. Slow and slower. Deliberate. His focus unwavering. This wasn't the grab and grope of the station bar scene, eagerness lubricated by a few drinks. It was more temptation, a seduction in measured steps—not that she had much experience in the latter for comparison.

Despite her growing excitement, she didn't feel any need to rush. The simple contact satisfied some unspoken need inside her, a craving she hadn't known was there.

Asrial had to marvel at the extent of her imagination. His grounder's tan—the golden brown of good caffe—was stark against her spacer's paleness. Did she harbor some proclivity toward grounders she'd never admitted to herself?

He leaned toward her, coming lower and closer, his approach gradual—like watching a flower bloom. Until his firm lips brushed her side, but only barely. More sensed than felt. His breath was heavier than his kiss. When he finally mouthed her skin, he was gentle, careful. Savoring her like a sip of expensive Nikralian brandy. Worshipping her as if she were truly a sovreine, not a Rim rat.

This was the sort of sensation no pleasure wand could give her. Another person's heat. Another person's touch. The dampness of a stealthy lick. A wave of shivers swept her, raising prickles on her skin.

She closed her eyes, but that only heightened the sensations. His large hand on her belly and along her hip and down her thigh. His mouth on her side. His stubbled cheeks. His hair sliding over her body in a silky caress.

Wanting his mouth on her breast, she twisted her hand free to sink her fingers into his hair, around the back of his head, and urge him higher. He hesitated before complying, the delay doing strange things to her breathing. When he nuzzled her, his lips were almost reverent in their attentions. Finally he set his mouth to her breast, took an aching tip between his teeth, and nibbled ever so gently.

The tiny bite kicked desire into overdrive, plasma hot and exhilarating, a wild ride through a lightning storm. A moan escaped her, thin and throaty. She arched into his caress, unable to help herself as he drew on her, sucking her nipple with clever lips, his tongue stroking hard and catching it against his palate.

Need grew, twisting and warping into a blood-boiling, bone-melting hunger, the deep throb like the *Castel*'s engines about to take off. Fractured starlight filled her veins, glittering with the promise of ecstasy.

Asrial ground her other hand against her mound, trying to soothe the tension gathering there. She couldn't take much more. These days she wasn't used to delaying her release, not when it could be had with a pleasure wand. "Finish me."

He stilled. For a long moment, he did nothing, merely held her, even his mouth on her breast unmoving. He stared hard at her, a piercing look of fulgent silver, all virile intensity.

She held her breath, the hand in his hair clenching.

When he finally moved, he tugged her legs over the edge of the bunk and spread them. Wide.

Heat rolled through her, anticipation making her wetter. *Oh, yes!* Him inside her, filling her.

To her surprise, he remained kneeling, hooking her legs over his shoulders and parting her curls to press his mouth between her thighs.

This was what her subconscious craved? She'd have thought it was the full cycle she missed: penetration and vigorous pumping and heavy breathing and—

He flicked his tongue over her nub.

Pleasure burst in her core, an explosion of raw sensation, and she didn't think at all.

Believing her the enemy, the first time he had touched her had been a guilty pleasure. This time there was no guilt, only pleasure: knowing he was not commanded, that the desire moving him was his, not another's—his choosing, his willing. Her pleasure was his gift to her; it was his choice to bestow it upon her.

Asrial, she called herself. A name of an angel, from the gods Romir thought had abandoned him. She had returned to him his name. This pleasure was small enough recompense.

Licking her intimately, he drew her scent into himself and the incredible information it communicated to him: female, alive, unharmed, healthy, free of pain and fear. Such a glorious scent he had not smelled in uncounted years.

He nibbled on her tender flesh, unable to believe the change in his fortune. The salty cream of her surpassed all tastes in his war-torn memory, tempting him to gorge his senses.

A soft mewl of surprise rewarded him, even as her hot dew

anointed his lips with a kiss of a different sort. She gave of herself, accepting vulnerability. It shook him, this generosity of hers. In his recent experience only those with overwhelming confidence in their power were so casual of their weakness.

Her slender legs tightened around him, squeezing his ribs as she arched into his kisses. Her hands caught his head, holding him to her, the touch—the urgent pressure—sending a breathtaking bolt of exultation through him. The constriction did not bother him, bereft as he had been of any contact for so long. The tight clasp of her legs was a pleasure in itself.

The approval inherent in her actions encouraged him to further liberties. He tested the entrance of her body with his tongue, wondering if she would now object. That thrust was almost more than he dared. In the back of his mind, he waited for the inevitable command to desist, for the flood of absolute compulsion that would prove his continued enslavement.

"Aaah!" The wordless exclamation replete with pleasure was the song of angels to his ears, her gasps and purrs pure delight of themselves. His heart raced at her response, filling him with an almost forgotten sense of power.

He sucked on the nub of her desire, rolled it over his tongue like the precious indulgence it was. Only the gods knew if he would have it again.

She cried out again, exultant, joyful. A sound he could never tire of hearing, so potent did it make him feel.

Driven to have more of her gasps and moans, he licked her delicate flesh, dipped his tongue again into her, thrilling at his temerity.

Asrial tossed her head in a frenzy of delight, her skin flushed a delicate pink. An angel on the cusp of ecstasy. She cupped her breasts, stroking herself in a breathtaking display of feminine seduction, revealing a depth of desire that shocked him.

How could she allow herself to be so vulnerable?

But Asrial did.

She surged against him, eagerness in every line of her body. She participated in her own seduction, leaving herself open to his wondering eyes. Unmindful of his scrutiny. Unafraid to display her pleasure.

And when her release came, she withheld none of her delight. Her body jerked and twisted and arched in a gratifying display of carnal satisfaction. And more. She screamed. She shuddered. She swore.

Romir soaked it all in, taking it into himself—her cries, her scent, her pleasure—immersing his soul in her ecstasy. The potent elixir of freedom.

A reminder of his manhood.

He could barely remember a time he had not been djinn, when he had been free to love and be loved, before he had been bound into unthinking, unwilling service. Asrial's generous display recalled the possibility of being more than a slave.

The lines on her face eased, going slack as the crest passed. Her body relaxed, losing the rigidity of transport, until she lay stretched out before him, panting. Her breaths slowed to sighs, the rise and fall of her breasts easing with every heartbeat. Until she slept. With a smile on her face.

Romir eased her legs back onto the bed, careful not to disturb her sleep. He kept watch, unable to tear his eyes away. Not wanting to.

In repose, her features softened, gaining an innocence that belied her sensuality. The air of peace about her was a sprinkling of water to a parched soul, crumbs to a starving man, air to a drowning one. Such fanciful comparisons should have been meaningless—his hateful existence eliminated the need for water, food, or air—but he could not deny the attraction.

Had he convinced her?

Likely not. He doubted she would have surrendered so readily to sleep if he had, in the arms of a strange man. But still the illusory display of trust warmed him, a thawing of the frozen emptiness where his heart used to be.

He had time to convince her. He had nothing but time.

Perhaps once he had convinced her, he could understand what had happened, how his prison had slipped from the hands of the Mughelis. All he knew for certain was, his rescue had not been deliberate.

Maybe then he could believe it was true.

Four

Asrial woke slowly, indulgently, her body humming with contentment. Her dream had been so vivid, the memory of it alone sent a thrill of sweet delight singing through her. Sighing, she stretched, awash in a buoyant sense of well-being she hadn't felt since she'd learned of Amin's accident.

What a lovely dream. She half regretted waking up. If tech heads could replicate the effect reliably, offices would rattle and there'd be a new conglomerate within three years. It would shake up interstellar economies.

She laughed at the whimsy.

At the top of her stretch, she opened her eyes and turned to get up. And froze.

A man sat on the floor of her cabin, long black hair flowing over a bare, broad shoulder, his arms resting across his knees like a wall. Silver eyes met her gaze, intent, alert, wary, and somehow . . . bewildered.

"R—Ro—Romir. Romir . . . Gadaña." The introduction in the dream returned to haunt her.

The dream hadn't been a dream?

Aghast, Asrial snatched her pillow to her chest; her stunner wasn't under it where it should have been. They stared at each other in silence, her heart doing its best to break her ribs, its triple time echoing in her ears like a laboring drive. In the limited space of her cabin, he was so close that she didn't dare look away to search for her stunner.

How could it be? She was well-rested. Her last physical—taken to reassure Amin before this trip—detected no illness nor abnormality. She couldn't be hallucinating.

"I am—a djinn."

Impossible. Djinn were children's tales.

"What is this place?" The same question he asked in her dream—which obviously hadn't been a dream. He sounded sincere, the same now as he had then. He didn't look stupid, he'd gotten past her security, so how could he not know?

"Someone put my prison here."

She thrust the memory away. Children's tales had no place in the real world. *But, Spirit of space, how did he get aboard?*

He—Romir—continued to stare at her, the weight of his silence demanding an answer.

Asrial decided to humor him. While he hadn't made any moves she'd consider aggressive—aside from being aboard the *Castel* and in her cabin—she didn't want to push her luck quite yet. Just because he'd handed back her stunner that time didn't mean he was safe.

Of course, the way he looked tempted her to throw caution out the airlock . . . although if last night wasn't a dream, she'd done that already.

Heat washed through her at the thought. He'd had his hands on her, used his mouth to bring her to orgasm . . . and unless he'd mounted her while she'd slept, he'd left her alone. She squirmed experimentally. Her inner thighs felt tender, but there was none of the ache that came with a man's penetration; the effect of a pleasure wand was different. She didn't know whether to be relieved or piqued. She'd been naked—and he hadn't been tempted?!

Focus on business, Asrial. He'd asked a question. "This is the *Castel.*"

"Castel?" He leaned forward, wrinkles forming across his brow, as though he were willing her to say more. From his reaction, her answer didn't mean anything to him. His shoulders bunched as his arms tensed across his knees. It was an awkward position, one that didn't allow him to rise quickly. Almost defensive.

"That's the name of my ship. I'm headed for Eskarion. If you want to go elsewhere, you're out of luck." She took heart at his posture. The narrow confines of her cabin didn't lend itself to evasion. If he decided to grapple, she was in trouble unless she found her stunner.

"Eskarion?" Confusion deepened the furrows of his brow.

Frustration roiled in her stomach at his deliberate obtuseness—and it had to be deliberate. He couldn't be that clueless. With Maj void of sentient life, that meant he had to have shipped in. He'd gotten to the planet somehow and probably been abandoned there—or jumped ship.

Well, let him pretend, if that's what he wants.

At least there were two things she could be certain of: he wasn't a pirate who'd forced his way past the *Castel*'s security while she slept, and he wasn't a djinn from children's tales, whatever he might claim.

She ignored the inconsistencies in his appearance to focus on the most important aspect—unless she was willing to space Romir, she could do nothing about him until she docked at a station. In which case, her time would be better spent getting to Eskarion. The *Castel* should be far enough outsystem to Jump. The sooner she started, the sooner they'd arrive.

But there lay another problem.

"I need to get up." She didn't want him to watch her dress. A rather silly sentiment when he'd already watched her sleep—naked—but that was when she'd thought him a figment of her imagination.

Despite his awkward pose, he got to his feet in a single, fluid motion, as if he were in a low grav zone. No stiffness. No pushing off the deck or off his knees. Then, before she realized what he intended, he'd put his hands under her elbows and raised her off the bed, onto her feet . . . and so very close to him.

He stood more than a head taller than her, his shoulders that much wider. She hadn't really noticed it last night, but he was no slack-bodied grounder. From the scars on his arms, those corded muscles had seen hard use. He generated so much masculine heat that she felt wrapped in warmth, as if he were touching her all over.

More conscious than ever of her nudity, Asrial clutched her pillow to her torso, a fragile shield he could so easily wrench away. "I meant—*Out!* I have to dress."

Romir jerked back, understanding and belated embarrassment flashing across his face. At least he wasn't that lost to propriety.

Without him doing anything, the door slid open.

How . . . ? She stared at the door, now closed with her stowaway on the other side, then shook her head impatiently. There was work to be done.

She scrambled into some clothes quickly, half worried what he might be up to out of her sight. But only half. She couldn't think of a plausible reason for a pirate to sit by her bunk, waiting for her to wake up, instead of taking over the *Castel*. If he were after her ship or her cargo, he'd have had an easier time if he hadn't delayed. Besides, he hadn't threatened her in any way, not even a hint.

Once dressed, she felt ready to face the wild storm the Spirit of space had dropped upon her.

Asrial's next view of her stowaway sent a shiver of awareness zinging through her nerves. It had been some time since she'd had a lover, but he bore his undress with an unselfconscious air of pride that wasn't without basis.

Romir stood in the middle of the corridor, his back to her, his head moving side to side restlessly. His shoulders filled her view, precisely at eye level. From this angle, their breadth looked more imposing, stretching like wings beyond that gorgeous fall of black hair. The arc and rays of dark blue on the ball of his left shoulder only added to her impression of toughness. But without the bright silver wariness of his eyes to distract her, she noticed the definition of his muscles, a leanness to his body. Not starved, but not unfamiliar with short rations, either.

Asrial fought down the urge to feed him up. She wasn't here to mother him. In fact, she might have to make a detour to replenish if he ate a lot. She'd planned on doing so when she got to Eskarion, but she wouldn't be able to stretch her supplies that far with two to feed.

Still, she couldn't prevent a question as she paused by his side. "Did you spend the night on the floor?"

Had he been in her cabin the whole time, or had he used one of the bunks in the other cabins? She didn't know which she preferred: that he'd watched her sleep or having him enter her cabin—twice—without her waking.

Romir continued to look around, as though starved for sight. Even the plain walls merited long stares, particularly the access panels to the control runs—the latter gave her a twinge of concern.

No good could come from that look, especially if he was truly as clueless as he acted. "I have no need for sleep."

If he was going to be cryptic, she had more important things to do. So long as he stayed where she could see him, she wouldn't have to worry about him fooling around with the *Castel*'s innards.

Asrial had called it a ship. But from the sparseness of the threads of power Romir sensed beyond the walls, it was not a sailing ship nor an airship. *A starship?* If what lay outside was the abyss between worlds, then perhaps it was a starship.

The wonder of voyaging through that vastness held him silent—that and the realization that he was far from any Mugheli vyzier. A distance that could not be spanned by a single person's will. Could he be truly free of his hated masters?

He followed Asrial down the corridor. With her back to him, he was free from observation to feast his eyes on this unusual woman. She walked lightly, balanced on her feet, almost dancing, but there was a tension about her shoulders, like a warrior's readiness. She wore her hair shorter than had the women that remained in his tattered memory. And yet she exuded this air of refinement, of delicate beauty. As though . . .

Romir shook his head, unable to define the inconsistency. She was a woman of a different world. Such comparisons were foolhardy. He had to be wary. While she was not a vyzier, he could not accept that her intent was benign solely on faith. However much he may wish otherwise, he had lost too much to extend his trust so easily.

Asrial led him to one of the rooms whose purpose he could not divine. There, a pair of seats faced a wall-mounted table embedded with strange devices.

When she sat down, the table before her brightened, its muted lights strengthening as if oil had been added to their fire, subtle weaves responding to her presence. She played her hands across the panel, pressing ciphers without hesitation, moving with the serene confidence of long practice.

More rectangles on the wall sprang to bright life, images appearing as if summoned. They were akin to a scry glass, he realized, though he could not understand what they showed. They looked like stars, but not the ones he vaguely remembered seeing in the night skies.

The sparkles embedded in the walls that so fascinated him shifted, apparently in response to what she was doing at the panel. Such manipulation was something no vyzier or weaver had done. This, more than anything else he had seen in this strange "ship," assured Romir that Asrial truly was not Mugheli.

"I'm about to Jump."

Wondering at the warning in her voice, he stayed by the wall, according to Asrial the space a weaver would need to perform a high-level working. While she was not a weaver or a vyzier, her actions hinted at preparations best left undisturbed.

"Sit down and buckle in." Without looking at him, she snapped a hand to the empty seat beside hers, her manner making it clear she expected instant obedience.

Asrial's peremptory tone tempted Romir to ignore her order. He had had too many of those, and hers did not carry any compulsion. But when she pulled straps from the sides of her seat, he realized she was simply concerned with safety. Her brusqueness seemed to be a result of distraction, not intention.

He obeyed, copying her actions. He did not need the straps. He could have misted instead, but he suspected this would be an inopportune moment. She acted as though his admission of being djinn had never happened. If he were to mist, the surprise might be dangerous. He did not blame her for her skepticism; he, too, preferred to ignore the truth of his captivity and did not want to dwell on it.

Her hands danced over the panel, altering the patterns of the sparkles, but not in the familiar ways of weavers. The panel's lights changed, the orange ones shifting to green.

A square with a red ring *flashed*, *flushed*, *flashed*, turned blue. She slapped the square.

The ship lurched. Energies flared around them, the strands warping in a familiar pattern, forming—

A portal?

Romir stared. If he had breath, he would have lost it. The magnitude of this working! He could sense the weave drawing on that powerful vortex he had seen in the bowels of the ship, vast energies raging against his consciousness as they swept past him into the shining weave . . . and yet he could not feel Asrial manipulating the vortex. No vyzier could hope to accomplish this by himself—not and survive. Only once before had he himself experienced such power.

The next moment, it all became madness. For an endless heartbeat the universe exploded in myriads of colors—too many to count, too many to name, colors he had never imagined. The strands of existence stretched and warped.

Another lurch. The universe resolved itself, and the weave collapsed, unraveling faster than he could follow.

The glass revealed a different set of stars.

Asrial bent her attention to the panel, pressing ciphers as though nothing of significance had happened.

"That was—"

She turned a mild frown to him. "That was Jump." Clearly she did consider it nothing of significance. After a few more taps, she leaned back and released her straps.

"It is safe now?" He could not forget the madness of the universe exploding around him. It played before his mind's eye like the fluttering of wind-borne petals, a furious storm of incandescent possibilities whirling free before resolving into a single reality. What sort of world had he been summoned into that she could shrug off such a feat of power?

The question earned him another frown, puzzlement shadowing her brown eyes. "The autopilot's engaged. Anyway, we can't Jump any distance until the drive's coils are fully recharged."

Five

Romir trailed after Asrial, feeling as extraneous as a fifth limb, a loose thread dangling from a weave. Purposeless. A strange emotion for one such as he. A djinn had no purpose. It did not matter if a djinn supported the vyzier's goal. The only reason for their existence was obedience to the master's will. He had known that even before his capture and enslavement and had thought himself inured to the loss.

No hopes. No dreams. Those were for the fortunate free.

Yet now he felt the lack keenly. Cool air on a shallow wound, not fatal but more painful than a deeper cut. Was this the result of his peculiar freedom? Unbound yet constrained by his prison's tugging.

Deep in the heart of him, he feared that freedom would not last. The time would come when that line ran out; then he would be drawn back.

Carrying a tablet, Asrial entered the room with his prison, an air of purpose about her. From the ledge, she chose an ostentatious trifle box carved from askeiwood and covered with gold and deep red marjan stones. She examined it with great care, according it more attention than such frippery deserved. Only the soft taps of her stylus on the tablet broke the humming silence. Seeming to have come to some conclusions of her own, she asked him no questions, her lack of curiosity suggesting she had given no credence to his admission to being djinn. She treated him as if he were some hapless stowaway the gods had thrust upon her. If only that were truth.

Unlike in times past when vyziers demanded his attendance, this silence oppressed, weighing on Romir's spirit like the gray mists of his prison. To be ignored as a matter of habit felt worse than the deliberate malice of his Mugheli masters. Simply watching Asrial did not suffice to keep loneliness at bay. "What are you doing?"

"Logging an inventory of what I got." She did not look up from her task as she answered, her attention bent entirely on the trifle box. Short, tawny curls clung to high, pale cheekbones, tempting his fingers to do the same.

Her thumb skimmed over the carving in slow, gentle strokes that captured his gaze—such a contrast from her usual purposeful manner. The repetitive motion was hypnotic, stirring formless, nameless urges within him. He could not look away. "For what purpose?"

"My mother's cousin serves as my agent. He needs a list of what's available for sale," she answered absently, her stylus clicking on the tablet.

"For sale?"

"I don't collect for myself. These will go up on auction. People pay good creds for Majian artifacts." Smiling, she held up the box for his admiration. "Pretty, isn't it? I wonder what it was for."

"Likely just trinkets. It *is* a trifle box."

Stylus upraised, Asrial glanced at him finally, blinking in

obvious surprise. Amber chips glinted in her brown eyes, a detail he had overlooked before. "You've studied Majian artifacts?"

"Not at all. I just know what I know." The implications of a collector's market for such common, everyday objects and the fact that they were considered worthy of study troubled Romir. Those went against everything he knew of the Mughelis. Was this universe so different from the last time he had been summoned to serve? Did the Mughelis, too, voyage through the abyss between worlds? Was the hard-won haven of his people no longer secure? Surprised by the prospect of travel in a starship, he had not contemplated the possibility that his enemies might be closer than he had thought.

She made a face at him, clearly unconvinced by his protest. "You sounded so certain."

"It was just trivia I . . . picked up." Telling her he had seen it used in daily life might prompt the sort of questions he did not want to answer. If she sought knowledge of Mughelis, might she not seek them out?

He had been foolish. If he was not more careful, he could find himself back in the hands of the enemy. Perhaps for the moment, silence was the better strategy, no matter how oppressive he found it.

When he did not expound on his statement, Asrial did not pursue the matter, returning instead to the artifacts before her. "This is sure to be the centerpiece of the auction." She picked up his prison with careful hands, holding it as if it were precious. Raising it to the light, she traced a finger over the etching.

He *felt* it!

Sweet delight eddied within him, seeping through the mark on his shoulder as she explored his prison, slowly rotating it while her finger glided over its base. Romir stiffened, horror and unwelcome pleasure coursing through him in equal measures. It was the same—as if he had been summoned. A touch to his prison was like a touch to his essence. Only she did it gently, a caress instead of a strangling grip. But still the weave was sinking its hooks deeper into him. Perhaps that gentleness was worse—more seductive, inviting him to embrace his enslavement.

The sensation confirmed his deepest fear: if his prison succeeded in drawing him back, he could once again be summoned out and commanded.

He wanted to shout, to demand Asrial stop what she was doing. He choked down the protest for fear the knowledge would be used against him. Though he was certain she was not Mugheli, his hatred of their mastery was too ingrained; revealing the weakness could lose him what little independence he had gained.

"Why the centerpiece?" He forced the question past the evanescent fluttering against his insides, the breathtaking sensations made more arousing by their ephemeral nature.

Cradling his prison against her breasts, she turned to him. "Most examples of Majian pottery are broken shards. A rarity like this flask?" Her smile was bright with expectation, the glint in her eyes adding a sharp edge to her beauty. "Even the museums would sit up and pay attention, if only for this. Collectors will cross the galaxy just to see it."

His prison was destined to be auctioned off?

To Romir's relief, she set it back on the ledge. Those unnerving sensations stopped, confirming his suspicions. This was proof he was not as free as he had hoped. Only chance had given him a measure of independence. The Mugheli weave still held him bound, still a djinn trapped in this deathless servitude.

Shaken, he stood silent as Asrial continued her work, handing down the pieces she requested and replacing them when she was done. If he was not careful, he would lose his fight and return to the madness of the gray mists.

* * *

Performing inventory of her finds with Romir beside her had been an exercise in self-control. Asrial rubbed a hand on her thigh, drying its damp palm on her pants, as she laid the data logger on the comp. She'd been so conscious of his quiet presence she'd taken twice as long to inventory the items in the work cabin. Moreover, her heart insisted on making itself felt, its beat fluttering at her throat, on her wrists, and even between her legs, especially when he came within arm's reach.

The bio unit was the one place on the *Castel* where she could have privacy. Of course, she had only herself to blame for that, since she was the one who hadn't wanted him out of her sight. She undressed and dumped her sweaty clothes in the presser for washing. Stepping under the shower, she wrestled against temptation.

The warm stream of water reawakened her skin's distracting sensitivity. She could feel his hands on her again, the rasp of his stubble, his mouth between her thighs.

Asrial groaned as a frisson of delight streaked up her spine. She touched herself, trying to ease the ache, but her swollen flesh only throbbed all the more. She'd thought that need satisfied for the time being after the session with the pleasure wand, then the dream that hadn't been a dream. She usually went decs between sessions. Even when she found someone on station to warm her sheets, one time generally sufficed to satisfy her. So why was it that the simple presence of a man roused this acute carnal hunger?

Romir with his lean body. The carved planes of flowing muscle. The caffe brown skin that tempted her to lick and drink him up. The long hair that more than anything else marked him as a grounder. Even that dark blue tat of a stylized flaring star on his shoulder only added to his attractiveness, making him more exotic. Quite unlike the spacers she was accustomed to seeing on the stations.

Was that novelty why she responded so strongly to him? He did nothing to invite her attention—save to stand there.

The shower was replaced by hard jets of air that pushed the lingering beads of water off her skin and threw her hair into messy curls. The change made no difference to her carnal hunger.

Another throb of need had her pressing her thighs together. Her body didn't care about reasons. It ached, and she couldn't think of a good reason to deny herself.

Romir was here for the duration. He'd already seen her naked. He'd already pleasured her once. Why not take him to her bed? He hadn't acted in any way suspicious; he didn't behave as if that one night of pleasure earned him the right to her. And he seemed genuinely grounder-muddled about space travel—the astonishment on his face when they exited from Jump was too extreme an expression for such a guarded man—so she was safe, since he needed her to pilot the *Castel*.

Besides, there was still the inventory of the other cabins and the hold to do and two decs—twenty Standard days—to the Eskarion Ring. She really couldn't imagine keeping him at a distance for no good reason for all that time. She'd never been one for senseless self-denial. The Spirit of space only knew what the future would bring, and she of all people knew how life could be cut tragically short. Why not make the most of what time she had with Romir?

Anticipation washed through her, sweet seduction all by itself. Her fingers tingled with the need to touch, to stroke, to tease. To feel that hard body under her hands and explore it to her heart's content. To share his heat and take him into herself. Her skin prickled with the knowledge that satisfaction lay only a few short steps away, on the other side of the door. She reached for her robe, her body melting with need, more than ready to close the distance between her and Romir.

Six

Asrial emerged from the small chamber she called a bio unit. From her improved cleanliness, he understood it to be a bathing place, something else he did not have need for—another mark of his servitude. All she wore was a thin robe that fell to the tops of her thighs. It was obvious she was naked under it.

Romir straightened off the wall, suddenly acutely aware he was still alive—by certain definitions of living. He certainly remained in possession of his male instincts and one in particular, the one that knew when a woman wanted him.

Asrial was looking at him the way no woman had in a long time—with carnal hunger and open desire. As though he were a man in truth. An ordinary man, free to choose his fate.

How he wished that were the truth.

The pretense was folly. Djinn were barred from choice, existing only to serve their master's will. When the pretense ended, as it inevitably would, the reality would only bring more pain. But the urge to forget, if only for a moment, remained unchanged, undiminished.

Angel though she may be, the look of desire in Asrial's eyes seduced. He could not look away.

She smiled, free and unshadowed. So certain of her reception. So beautiful in her confidence. "Want to warm the sheets? There's no need to deprive ourselves." Her robe fell open, one side sliding off her shoulder and down her arm, baring pale skin he knew to be smooth, skin he wanted to feel and taste once more with every drop of his being. Lithe temptation, sleek and slender and strong, dared him to reach out and touch her.

Though there was no question of what she wanted, Romir hesitated, taken aback by the turn of events. Unlike before, Asrial knew full well he was no dream. And yet she still wanted him? He kept silent, torn between self-preservation and the hunger of his starved senses.

Asrial placed strong hands on his shoulders, pulling him down and herself to her toes. Her lips grazed the base of his throat, then traced the line of his collarbone. Such soft contact—gentle, irresistible, and utterly devastating. Overcoming his better judgment without compulsion.

Then those hands moved higher, wrapping her arms around his shoulders and drawing her body along . . . closer. The hard tips of her breasts scorched his awareness.

Though he was djinn, he still had a man's sensibilities. Her sure caresses woke dim memories of making love and of need. They woke his body, and it responded—erupting in flames like silk floss touched with fire.

Romir raised his arms slowly, for fear a more aggressive motion would set her to flight. He did not want that. He would give anything to avoid that. This second chance was more precious for not being stolen nor given unwittingly. Freely and knowingly offered, it was a gift from the gods that had forsaken him so long ago.

A murmur of approval greeted his embrace, a feminine welcome and music to a soul starved of kindness. It encouraged him to risk more—a tighter hug, a kiss, surely nothing she would find objectionable.

She slid her fingers under his waistband, her short nails scraping the line of his hip. The delicate contact shivered through him, a whisper of reckless delight tantalizingly sweet. She pushed his pants down his legs and off, baring all of him to her golden gaze.

The secretive smile that curved the corners of her mouth hinted at approval withheld and dared him to win it. Her hands touched him with hunger, caressed his length slowly. Boldly. Deliberately. Her fingers traced little circles of sensual torment on the base of his shaft, lingering on his turgid flesh with maddening thoroughness. With her other hand, she teased the head, tracing the slit and the sensitive ridge around the crown with nimble strokes.

He groaned, a vulnerable sound he did not recognize as coming from his throat. An unfamiliar sound, rusty with disuse. It had been a long time since he had felt this much. The sensations verged on overwhelming.

Bending down, he planted hungry kisses across her small breasts, taking her hard nipples in turn into his mouth. Sweet. So sweet. She gasped again and again as he drew on her, and he relished the sound.

Here he was not djinn, merely a man pleasuring a woman. Surely that was little enough to hope for?

The heat of him surrounded her, his weight pinning her down on the bed, a living blanket of resilient muscle—sensations no pleasure wand could provide. Asrial groaned, reveling in Romir's hard body spreading her thighs wide. The contact, the closeness with a man—no device could duplicate those.

This was a rare indulgence, one she intended to savor to the fullest of her ability. But that was only because the schedule she'd adopted after Amin's accident made it difficult to meet suitable men to warm her sheets.

And if she craved the reassurance of skin on skin, if only on occasion, surely that didn't make her weak? Surely it was only natural? It wasn't as if she wanted something permanent.

This was simply pleasure given and received, a commonplace exchange, nothing more. Nothing to worry about.

In the next moment, Asrial's worries fled, driven away by sensation. Romir cupped her breasts, pushing them together and burying his face in the shallow valley he created. His lips fluttered over her, soft and gentle, so careful, sipping on her as if she were candy foam to disappear at the slightest breath.

"Harder. I'm not fragile, you know." She ran her hands over his shoulders, relishing the strength beneath her fingers. The tat registered as a slight roughness to the touch, as if the dark ink had left a scar.

He gasped, his breath warming the slopes of her breasts, a shudder rocking his body—and hers. Panting, he closed his eyes as she traced that fascinating roughness. Such an extreme response to a light touch, it enticed her to linger there and explore the possibilities.

A low moan caressed her skin, damp heat like velvet over the sensitized flesh. It sank into silence, muffled against her breasts. His stubble prickled, the abrasion a sweet ache that drew an answering throb from between her thighs.

His hot mouth closed over her left breast, sucking hard as though he sought to drink her down whole. The carnal heat of his suction flooded her veins, all melting seduction and virile power in that one contact. She shivered, feeling the pull to the tips of her toes. The pressure grew, a hunger for his touch, his care, his strength.

Delight was a tangible thing unfurling beneath her skin like an exotic flower opening for the sun. Here was a man who could pleasure her to the fullest, one who knew how to use his body as it was meant to be used.

Asrial moaned, her body writhing as she gave herself up to his expert touch. She pressed herself against him, her mound a rough caress as she clutched at him. Her hands tugged at his thighs, insistent. Did she want him to mount her?

It seemed that way. Her motions called to him, tempted him—almost like a living invitation to pleasure.

She quivered under his hands, her fingers digging into his shoulders with an urgency that seduced. What man could resist the sure knowledge of a woman's willing welcome?

But, no, he could not believe she wanted him to mount her—he dared not. He was djinn, not an ordinary man. He had failed too many times. One such as he was not worthy of such trust. If she knew what he had done, she would not want him. He could not betray her confidence.

"Romir, come on." Asrial urged him with voice and hands and mouth, a flood of sensual invitation that sapped his resolve.

Only she did not know what he was. The thought of her horror once she knew the truth prevented him from succumbing to sweetest temptation.

He could not bring himself to take that final step. All he could do was focus on bringing her to ecstasy. Surely she would allow him this gift.

Ignoring her protest, he dropped lower and kissed her belly, tracing the firm slopes and lines of muscle with his tongue. Strength and gentleness all in one woman. Too gentle for her own good. Unable to resist, he nibbled on her, capturing tender skin between his teeth.

She giggled, plunging her fingers into his hair and grasping the back of his head. "That tickles!"

Such a carefree sound. It lightened his heart and drove back the darkness lurking in tattered memory. He wanted to hear more of it. He rubbed his cheek on her inner hip, feeling the tug on his jaw as the stubble caught and rasped.

"Ah!" Though she flinched, another gurgle of laughter followed her gasp. "D-don't."

"How about this, then?" Spreading her thighs, he made a place for himself in their cradle, holding her wide with the span of his shoulders.

She murmured something incoherent that trailed off in a moan she muffled against her fist. The sight of her sprawled across the bed open and eager for his attentions, so beautiful in her vulnerability, sent a pang through Romir.

He delved between her wet folds to find the hard nub hidden in her curls. Further proof of her honest desire, a dark red jewel beyond price. He took it into his mouth, stroking it with his tongue and sucking down. She tasted so good, he couldn't resist licking her, nibbling on her, immersing his senses in her desire. The salty sweetness of her arousal was slick on his lips, and more spilled over his questing fingers. He slid a thumb over her folds, spreading her cream across that tender flesh.

The musk of Asrial's excitement spiced the air, a woman's perfume that was uniquely her own. It etched itself deep into his memory, into his very essence—so deeply that he feared she would be the one memory he could not bear to lose.

The possibility cut to the quick, shaking him to his soul.

Another moan escaped her, thready with need. Her hands grasped at him—his hair, his shoulders, his arms, everywhere she could reach—feverish touches that should have branded him.

If he drew out this pleasure, perhaps he would be branded in truth. That risk was too great. Already, he ached, carnal hunger a blunt force pounding inside him.

Circling her nub with his thumb, Romir slid a finger inside her, coaxing her to give him more of her sweetness. He added a second finger to thrust vigorously, augmenting the motion with his tongue and thumb around the entrance of her wet and willing body.

Achieving his goal did not take long.

With a shout of surprise, Asrial melted over him, spilling the cream of her pleasure, her tender flesh quivering against his mouth, sweet as festival candy. Her thighs gripped him tight as she cried out in ecstasy, arching up again and again, her hips rising off the bed from the strength of her release. She shook and shuddered in his arms, her heels digging into his sides.

Another wave of orgasm had her body rippling around his fingers. He closed his eyes, the better to savor her delight. Letting her pleasure seep into his senses. Impressing it into his memory.

This was enough.

It had to be enough.

Victory was a painful throb in his loins, the heavy drumbeat of desire, a mockery of life. Romir sucked in unnecessary air, calling on the habits of a lifetime lost in the gray mists to suppress the torment of carnal hunger.

Pleasure ebbed slowly, sinking deep into Asrial's cells and leaving her replete. Not a single muscle left tense in her body.

She sighed happily. What a difference a real lover made compared to a pleasure wand!

The weight between her thighs eased up.

Romir lowered himself to the floor, as if settling in for a long wait—or for the night. He did so quietly, behaving as though it were a matter of course. Were grounders so submissive?

He couldn't be serious! She couldn't imagine making the man who'd just pleasured her so well spend the night sitting on the floor beside her bunk. Only a slave would have accepted such treatment; no spacer would have stood for it. Asrial frowned down at him, uncomfortable that he'd done so without objection. "You can use a bunk in one of the other cabins."

He shook his head. "I have no need for sleep."

She stared at him, but he just sat there, as if it were nothing out of the ordinary. Rather like how she might imagine a slave would behave. He hadn't even mentioned the possibility of him taking release. "I can't sleep with you like that."

The silence stretched out, while cryptic thoughts flickered behind his silver eyes. "As you will." He came to his feet with that unnatural fluidity, his face blank of emotion. Once again, the door slid aside without him touching the lock panel.

Asrial made a mental note to add checking the electronics to her unending list of things to fix.

"Lights, off."

She snuggled down and tried to sleep. Though her body continued to hum, replete with pleasure, her mind was too busy to power off. It just felt awkward having a man in her cabin, much less one sitting on the floor like some frigging slave. But inviting him to share her bunk would have been just as awkward. Most times, when a man warmed her sheets, it was on station, and she made sure he left the *Castel* before she slept. Though insisting

Romir use one of the other cabins seemed callous when he hadn't even finished, it was the least distasteful of her options.

But his face haunted her, that lack of expression after their intimacies. There'd been no anger nor offense, all emotion carefully swept behind a wall of calm. His measured dispassion stood in sharp contrast to his shock at her invitation. That reinforced her impression of sincerity. Despite that other night, he clearly hadn't expected anything more from her. Certainly he didn't act like he believed it had given him a right to her bed.

But why hadn't he mounted her? She'd thought her invitation clear in that respect. She hadn't expected him to service her like some pleasure bod. What man wouldn't seek release for himself, especially when he'd already brought her to orgasm?

Was that a clue to his history? Had he acted that way because of training? Had he escaped service as a pleasure bod? Was that why he'd been on Maj? Her suspicions seemed to fit the pieces. It would explain why he knew nothing about space.

Had she mistaken his willingness to share pleasure with her? Had he serviced her simply because he'd thought she expected payment?

No, Romir welcomed her invitation. She hadn't read that wrong. He'd been shocked but not upset; she would have wagered the *Castel* on it. She pummeled her pillow in search of the proper softness to lure sleep, wishing it would silence the doubts, too.

Anyway, what was she supposed to do with him? She could understand why he stowed away on the *Castel*—it was his best chance to get off Maj—but he didn't seem to have any destination in mind. He didn't mention any plans for after he left the *Castel*.

Asrial turned over, troubled by the course of her thoughts. She couldn't simply dump him in the first station she stopped at. He looked like a grounder and acted just as clueless. Only the Spirit of space knew what would happen to him if she did that. Despite herself, she couldn't help feeling responsible for him. If she just abandoned him, he'd probably end up a pleasure bod in some backwater station or in the hands of slavers. Again?

He had that look of weary defeat of someone who'd hit a grav well and was falling into the star. Like he was struggling only because he didn't know what else to do. She knew the feeling well, having tangled with it a time or two.

She at least had Amin and her cousins to help pull her out. He didn't have anyone. That look tugged at her heart, another weight to that already burdened organ but one she couldn't seem to avoid.

The darkness pressed in, filled with only the normal noises of the *Castel* in flight. It didn't sound as if she wasn't alone. The night cycle sounded entirely normal. But the knowledge that Romir was out there leavened the solitude.

Sleep claimed her without her realizing.

Romir forced himself not to return to Asrial's side. He did not want to leave her—and that alien desire kept him where he was. He could not afford the weakness of preference, of emotional attachment. Of thinking his wishes could change this uncaring universe. Bitter experience had shown that to be a lie.

The walls winked at him seductively, hinting at hidden knowledge, at new horizons . . . at challenges to his skill—things that had long been lost to him. In truth, they were things that were still lost to him, trapped as he was in this existence.

Drawn to their mysteries, to the unfamiliar weaves within arm's reach, he walked the corridors with new eyes, no longer looking for the hand of the Mughelis. In the past, he might have given in to temptation, tested the limits of his knowledge. But the time when he was free to indulge his curiosity was gone.

He could not trust this dubious freedom. His prison continued to call to him. And if he should succumb, anyone who possessed his prison would master him.

So he walked the corridors, waiting for Asrial to wake. His feet led him to the plant room. Of all the rooms in the starship, the plant room was the only one that did not make him feel lost. Though most of the plants were nothing he recognized, the smell of green and growth was a reminder of familiar things. The abyss between worlds, the starship, the sparkling walls, the harnessing of that vortex—these were all beyond his ken.

This night the smell of the room was different.

Several plants bloomed in the low light, one of which offered a sweet fragrance. He filled his lungs with its scent, realizing only now how much he had missed such things. His prison was a deprivation of the senses. He walked down a row, trying to find the source of that fragrance.

So much had been taken from him; others he had surrendered. He had forced himself not to care; if he did not care, it would have no meaning. And yet he found he still cared, if only for his loss. The smallest things still mattered.

He touched a slender white petal, marveling at its bristly texture—another memory that would taunt him should he return to his prison. The flower snapped shut around the tip of his finger, its petals clinging tight. A surprise. Rather like the woman who flew this starship.

But this memory was better than the others that awaited him in the mists. The faces of the vyziers who had commanded him were blurs lost in a miasma of bitter self-disgust and helpless rage. If only he could forget the results of his betrayal.

Entire cities melted beneath his weaves, slain by their refusal to surrender. The graceful spires of Xabun, the ancient arches of Gavor, the stone lace of Yalixo, and countless others too many to name, the proud and ancient strongholds of Parvin all fell victim to his failure to resist his masters. He had destroyed them—them and the Parvinese who had remained, trapped within their walls.

Their deaths were a stain on his soul that could never be washed clean. A damned traitor such as he had no business touching someone like Asrial.

Seven

"**You don't have** to have sex with me, if you don't want to. I don't expect you to pay for your passage that way."

Asrial's pronouncement took Romir by surprise. Surely his enthusiasm last night had been plain? But her face was set, intent on distasteful duty.

"I—certainly not. That is not it at all."

His shocked protest did not seem to make an impression on her. She entered the larger storeroom with an air of purpose, her attention focused entirely on the contents of the shelves. If today was a repeat of the previous day, he could expect more silence while she took inventory, ignoring him as a matter of course. He did not want that.

The sudden realization stunned him: he *wanted* her attention . . . and he could *do something* about it. He was no longer trapped in the gray mists, subject to a vyzier's whims.

"May I help?" Romir stood deliberately close—too close for

her to ignore gracefully. Despite her abrupt manner, instinct told him grace was ingrained in her nature.

"You might as well make yourself useful." Her acceptance of his aid was less than gracious, but it was better than the alternative. He found an unwitting smile on his face, one that took conscious effort to erase.

Asrial was methodical in her undertaking, always starting on her right, working by sections, from the lowest shelf to the topmost. Her comments hinted at an inquisitive mind, yet she displayed no curiosity about him and his admission of being djinn. The dichotomy puzzled him, drew him in, made him watch her even more closely.

And what he saw made him want her more.

After several days, Asrial didn't know what to make of Romir. She could tell he wanted her; there was no denying his willingness. But he'd bring her to orgasm . . . and that was as far as he went! What man didn't want pleasure? He wasn't doing it to build her excitement; he gave her pleasure then just stopped. After several nights of that, he still held out.

What did that say about her as a woman, that he didn't want her that way? She shoved that thought into storage in the back of her mind and locked it down. That had nothing to do with anything!

Consider the fact that he didn't eat, not in her presence, and wasn't raiding her supplies behind her back. That was enough to throw any sentient for a loop. Plus he didn't use the bio unit, didn't seem to need to piss or crap. He didn't shave, but his stubble didn't get any darker or thicker. And he didn't share her bed.

That last peeved her. She was accustomed to her solitude, reveled in it to a certain extent. She wasn't used to sharing her space with other people any longer. Ever since her parents' deaths, she'd flown alone. *Face it, you've become a hermit.* Now, she was constantly tripping over him, worried about him when he wasn't around, didn't have any privacy unless she went to the bio unit, but he made no effort to share her bed, and that last was what really peeved her. How contrary was that?

Every night since she'd told him she couldn't sleep with him on her floor, he left her cabin once he'd finished pleasuring her. And each morning, the first thing she saw when she stepped out of her cabin was Romir standing in the corridor, waiting for her.

On top of those, there was the mystery of the doors: no amount of troubleshooting revealed why they opened to him without his touching the lock panel. She'd had to set that question aside to focus on the thruster problem, but it still bugged her.

Despite the perks of frequent sex, in her heart, Asrial suspected she'd cheer when Romir finally left the *Castel* for . . . wherever his destination. He posed too fascinating a distraction at a time when she couldn't afford one.

Beeeeee—

The sudden shrill interrupted her train of thought. She clicked the tester off, irritation driving her thumb harder on the button than necessary. Her frigging mind had wandered again.

At this rate, the *Castel* would be Jumping into the Xerex sector with a dodgy thruster. Not a good idea. Unlike entry into a deserted planet with all the atmosphere to maneuver in, Eskarion space was less forgiving. Constellation authorities and the Patrol frowned on sudden course corrections and fined erring ships accordingly. She couldn't blame them when lives and trillions of creds were on the line.

She jiggered with the contacts, adjusted the settings, and tried again.

Beeeeee—

The control run still didn't test stable.

Asrial kept up a stream of swearing, soft and steady, as she struggled to pinpoint the faulty circuit. Power words. Sometimes the *Castel*'s hardware responded to threats.

"Is there a problem?"

She started at the question, not having noticed Romir's reappearance from wherever he'd gone off to. He looked over her shoulder, making no comment when she pressed a hand over her bounding heart. "Don't do that."

Disgust at her lack of progress magnified the shock he'd given her. She exhaled sharply, willing her pulse steady. She'd be glad when she had the *Castel* to herself once again. "There's an intermittent signal somewhere that's causing a power drop. I can't isolate the frigging circuit." While it didn't pose any danger on Jumps, she preferred not to approach a station when a thruster might act up. With the volume of traffic in Eskarion space, sudden loss of fine control could be hazardous.

Asrial didn't hold out much hope for useful advice from him. Her stowaway seemed surprisingly clueless about spacer matters—witness his reaction to Jump. It was like he'd never experienced it before boarding the *Castel*. If he'd been drugged on the ship that had brought him to Maj, that might account for his ignorance, but that implied he'd been . . . cargo.

"Try here." He indicated a point in the wall, a different block of the control run from the one she'd been wrestling with.

To her surprise, the tester confirmed his suggestion, and a quick replacement of that block cleared up the fluctuation. Putting the tools she'd used back with the rest of the kit, she stared at him in perplexity. He'd simply looked at the wall then put his finger right on the problem. His performance only emphasized how little she knew about him. He never spoke of his past or how he'd gotten to Maj or why he'd been abandoned there—or had he escaped? "How did you know that?"

"The flow flickers there."

"Flow?"

"The flow of energy." Romir slid his fingers along the wall, tracing a pattern that—uncannily—matched the circuits she'd been troubleshooting. Only a thorough knowledge of the *Castel* would have let him do that; over the years, the *Castel*'s design had diverged from the specs for its class. His tracing of the circuits couldn't be explained by rote training from outdated technical manuals.

"What?"

"I am a weaver," he said—at least that's what she thought he said. He'd used an archaic word for *weaver* and given it a strange intonation that made her doubt her ears. "I weave energy, the threads of creation. It was why I was made a djinn."

Djinn, again.

"Please, I'm not a child to be fed children's tales." She turned away from him and stared hard at the wall. She slammed her hand into it, the sharp sting in her palm confirming its solidity. She was awake, not dreaming. She could not—*would not*—believe such a story. Djinn were children's tales, told by generations of Lomidar mothers to entertain offspring. He had to be an ordinary man, someone who'd managed to stow away on the *Castel*, no matter that he didn't look like he'd been abandoned on Maj, didn't act like it, either, and shouldn't have been able to get aboard in the first place.

Any other explanation was too fanciful for words. Life didn't work that way. There were no happily-ever-afters. The Spirit of space didn't play fair. Crap happened, then she had to clear the mess. Her parents' deaths and Amin's accident had taught her that.

"No!" The pained shout spun her around in surprise.

Asrial gasped, disbelief welding her feet to the deck. Romir was fading right before her eyes. She could see the wall through his body! "What's happening?"

Raw fear blazed in his eyes, desperation bordering on panic. "My prison. It is pulling me back. I cannot stop it." Clawing at his left shoulder, he struggled against an invisible towline, leaning so far forward he should have fallen on his face. Yet he didn't fall as he streamed backward down the corridor. His feet didn't slide on the deck—they didn't seem to touch it at all.

His gaze locked on her, wide and fixed. As if she were his one last hope. Infecting her with clawing desperation.

She'd thought she wanted to see the back of him, that she resented Romir's invasion of the *Castel*, that she would welcome a return to her solitude. But not like this. Not this way.

"No!" She lunged for him.

And missed.

Landing hard on the deck, Asrial gave chase, forearms stinging.

He disappeared, melting into the door of the work cabin.

Heart in her throat, she slapped the panel to open it, cursing the delay as the hatch slid aside.

In the half-light, that precious example of Majian pottery glowed, a shimmering gray mist winding about its narrow neck and up to the lid. A mist that led to a transparent, writhing Romir floating in midair.

She threw herself forward with some crazy thought of wrenching him away from the flask that was sucking him in, not knowing what else to do. She half expected her arms to go through him, certainly light already was.

Her fingers brushed something solid as she lost her balance. Romir was there. Despite what her eyes told her, he was there. She grasped at him, invisible muscles sliding over her falling body in a final sensual caress.

A hiss of surprise. Hard hands caught her waist, saving her from a rude landing on her face.

The gray of the worn carpet vanished, replaced by slabs of caffe brown flesh. Warm muscle tipped by small dark nipples.

Solid muscle.

Asrial clung to that beautiful sight as her knees folded under her. Her heart thundered in her chest, in her throat, in her head. Her skin throbbed, too tight, too empty.

Spirit of space, don't let me be too late.

Strength rushed into Romir, uncoiling the reel of his prison—snapping it loose. He was still bound, but no longer straitly. He had been so weak, the measure of freedom he had thought won spilling through his fingers like trickles of water. Yet just as his prison was about to reclaim him, this happened.

How?

With a choked sob, Asrial pressed her face to his chest, her small breasts soft against his belly as her arms tightened around him. Her rapid gasps warmed his chest, a damp heat that burned away the gray fog numbing his senses.

Pleasure and desire streaked through Romir, and he understood. Somehow the contact, the sensations, interfered with his prison's pull and weakened it enough that he could resist. Or perhaps it strengthened his resistance. Power had no effect against the Mugheli trap; neither did desperation nor the yearning for freedom. The sensations flooding him promised so much, promised life—and perhaps that was what weakened the reel of his prison.

He lifted Asrial up to kiss her cheek in gratitude.

She twisted around, twining her arms around his neck and meeting his lips with hers. Her kiss was hungry, frantic, salty with tears he had not realized she had shed, returning the pressure of his lips with ravenous intensity.

They had never kissed before, not mouth to mouth, though he had given her more intimate kisses when he pleasured her. This seemed more personal—a greater privilege.

Asrial opened her mouth, her tongue darting into his—there then gone. Sweet modesty, seductive beyond all measure. He wanted to immerse himself in it for as long as he was able. With each shy thrust, her warmth filled him, her kindness, her gentleness. She woke so much hope inside him—gave him a reason to hope. She reminded him of happier times, before he had become djinn.

Making him long to be simply a man once more.

He wanted her, now more than ever, this angel with her soft and generous heart. Wanted to give her everything she desired. Wanted to kiss away her tears and replace them with smiles.

Romir pressed his lips to her shoulder, gently, making no demand he was not entitled to make. He wanted to cherish her, to give her all the pleasure she deserved for her unstinting generosity, for the care she had given a nameless djinn who had given up hope.

Murmuring his name, she sank her fingers in his hair, twining the mass around them like a skein. She enfolded him in the circle of her arms, trapping him. But it was a sweet trap he had no wish to escape. He wanted to be caught in her silken embrace, wanted to remain there for as long as she would let him. There were far worse cages to be caught in than her arms.

Asrial used his hair to draw his head back so she could take his mouth again. This time the strokes of her tongue were bold, hungry, certain of her desire and confident of her welcome. She hooked a leg over his and rubbed her body against him, her soft mound etching a line of fire along his thigh.

The carnal friction inflamed his essence.

Heat filled him. Need. Hunger. They overflowed, burning away restraint and gentle desire. He kissed her back, returning heat for heat, lust for lust, thrust for thrust.

She tugged on her pants, shoved them down her hips, and kicked them off to stand before him half naked, the neat patch of brown curls at the juncture of her pale thighs already dewy. "I want all of you."

Romir hesitated. *All of him?* He had been owned, mastered, dismissed. Choice wrested from him. Reduced to a slave. Yet never had the Mughelis taken all of him. He had kept the core of himself, however much reduced. Even when pleasuring Asrial, he had held back part of himself.

Now she wanted all?

Doubts struggled for the upper hand.

But this was Asrial, and pleasure with her was not slavery. It was—

A giving and a taking.

A taking.

To take Asrial . . .

He could not deny her—nor could he deny himself.

His pants vanished, leaving him naked for the first time since . . . He could not finish the thought, could not remember ever having been naked. He had forced himself to unravel those memories of happier times. The loss ate at him, as if surrendering them had been a betrayal of her—his betrothed. But better the loss than to have clung to fine sentiment and still have failed; his sanity would not have survived that.

With a wordless exclamation, Asrial took him in her hand, her eyes blazing, her touch sure. Hooking her leg back over his hip, she held him to the entrance of her body, unwavering in her desire.

Trapping her against the wall, he took her slowly, taking care as he pushed into her, not wanting to rush this stolen moment.

Damp heat gripped him, firm yet yielding. Delight coursed through his veins like the potent wines of Mehr, an elixir made more precious by its rarity. A shudder ripped through him. He had forgotten what it was like to make love. He felt like a boy all over again, discovering the pleasures of the flesh and the mysteries of women.

It was a good thing he did not need to breathe. His chest was tight, all his senses focused on that one point of contact. He could not have gotten air past his heart in his throat.

Impatient for more, he lifted her by the thighs and sank even deeper until he was seated to the hilt. He stilled, the better to savor the hot clasp of her body.

Asrial wrapped her legs around his waist and locked them tight, a rapt smile curving her lips. "Finally. I've wanted this for so long."

She rode him leisurely, arching her back and raising her breasts to rub against him, strength and grace in her every move. The double friction felt too good to be true, twin lashes of delight to scorch his senses. She rolled her hips, her breath hitching on a gasp of need.

At that sound, his restraint snapped.

He drove back in, fast, forceful, grinding into her, glorying in the storm of raw sensation that blazed through him. The illusion of life and freedom was intoxicating.

Clinging to his shoulders, Asrial kept up with him, her strong body accepting his thrusts with a vigorous welcome, sweat trickling down her neck. Her breath came short and fast, blending with the wet slaps of their lovemaking.

Pleasure built with each thrust and her every quiver, gust upon gust of sensation fanning the flames of desire.

And yet . . .

Though she moved over him, around him, arousing him to

greater heights, the sensations only continued to build, adding fuel to the fire. Pressure grew in his balls, higher, tighter, sharper, until it was almost pain.

And still it built . . .

Romir finally understood. No amount of trying would span the gap to orgasm. There could be no release for him. That much was denied him.

All he had left was Asrial—her pleasure, her release, her ecstasy. That much he could share. He watched her face as he drove into her, watched the vital expressions displayed so openly, so honestly.

Asrial shuddered around him, her ripples of pleasure communicating flesh to flesh the ultimate in rapture. They rushed through her again and again, whetting the edge of his need. She cried out, joyful, triumphant. Without reservation. Her eyes went blind, her face slack, as she surrendered to it—to him.

The pounding in her ears quieted to a gentle beat as her heart slowed, no longer urgent. The shoulder under her cheek was firm, solid, whole. That was good, since Asrial felt exactly the opposite—all light and floaty, like she was in a zero grav zone. Free of all cares, as though nothing could go wrong.

She could get addicted to that sensation. It felt good. No, it felt better than good. It was fantastic.

Movement. She was moving. The bulkhead slid along her back as Romir sank to his knees. He moved inside her, still thick and eager, triggering another blast of delight through her veins.

Romir laid her on the deck, and she let him, too euphoric to help. She really should have insisted on the full cycle much sooner. They'd wasted decs in a holding pattern.

All her thoughts circled back to sex. No surprise after that prolonged orgasm that had blown through her like a supernova. It had wiped all other considerations from her mind. Taking a deep breath, she squeezed him with her inner muscles, encouraging him to take his release, but unfortunately those were the only parts of her that were up to the challenge.

Hunger throbbed, a clawing, bone-deep urgency that could never be relieved, never sated. Pain sang in his loins, the sweet flutters of Asrial's body keeping it honed, teetering one short impossible step from shattering.

Pressing against him, she moaned again, low and soft and blissful. The fast pace of her breathing eased and the urgency of her touch with it. And slowly, eventually, thankfully, so did his need.

Romir stretched out beside her on the hard floor, shaken to the depths of his soul. For the first time since his capture, he had truly made love to a woman—had performed as a man.

He had chosen to take Asrial and be taken.

This was one memory he would be hard-pressed to unravel, so deeply was it seared into his being, carnal pain and all.

Long moments later, Asrial smiled at him, like a contented *shera* after a successful hunt, temporarily sated. Her eyes sparkled with a lazy light, as though yellow stars hung in the dark brown depths.

Despite the ache of no release, Romir found he looked forward to once again being her prey with pleasure. Whenever she wanted him would be fine.

With a sigh, she stirred, raising her hand to his hip. "You didn't finish."

"I have no seed to give. This form mimics life, but it is not life. Release is impossible." He did not mind—too much. Bringing her pleasure was enough. And in any case, he deserved the pain; it was only his due.

She stilled. "What do you mean by that?"

He took her hand, set it on his chest where his heart did not beat, and waited.

"What?" Asrial frowned, confusion knitting her brows.

"Can you feel my heartbeat?" He released her, leaving her to touch and press where she would in search for what was not there.

Her eyes flared wide, her cheeks losing their color the longer she found silence. "But you breathe."

"Simply habit. I only need air to speak." It hurt to see the contentment in her face replaced by tension, but he could not look away. This was the reality the gods had cursed him with.

"You . . . disappeared. Turned into smoke." Her eyes grew wider, the irises thin rings of starless brown. "You're really a djinn."

Eight

Asrial pulled her clothes back into place, needing a semblance of propriety for this conversation. Sprawling naked on the floor of the work cabin wouldn't help. A reminder of her panic wasn't conducive to calm discussion.

Though Romir hadn't moved from where he lay, he wore his loose pants again. She couldn't avoid the truth any longer. However fantastic it might sound, he really was a djinn—she had to accept that, though he was nothing like she'd imagined djinn to look from her mother's stories.

Certainly she'd never imagined djinn doing what she'd been doing with Romir just now. Directing all her attention on smoothing her already wrinkle-free carbon silk pants, she fought down a flush. "You mentioned a prison. *That* is your prison?"

No longer glowing, the flask sat among the other relics in the work cabin, looking innocuous. Freed by the brush bots of the dust from the ruins, it was now a burnished brown that her fingers itched to touch.

Romir's glare at the flask bordered on hatred, diluted as it was by heavy measures of weariness and desolation. "Yes, I was captured by the Mughelis and forced to become . . . *this*." He flickered in place, gone for the space of a heartbeat, incontrovertible proof he was not the ordinary man she'd told herself he was.

She'd been so willfully blind, ignoring the evidence of her senses. No longer. She had to educate herself about this bizarre shift the universe had taken, approach it the way she approached new territory on the Rim. "Why did they do that?"

"Power. It is efficient, you see. In making djinn, they received a new weapon, reduced the risk to their vyziers, and weakened those forces resisting them." He recited the reasons as though narrating an educational vid.

"They made people into weapons?" Asrial's stomach threatened to rebel, lurching in protest at this talk of war. "Why?" What reason could justify such atrocity?

"For territory. The *padsha*, the Mugheli ruling class, are expansionist. When they invaded Parvin, we were just the next in a savage grab for territory. Despite everything we tried, they conquered much of our land, our world."

The story of lust for power resonated, striking close to home: an enemy that cared only about winning and didn't count the cost, that saw people as tools to be used and discarded. Her father had withdrawn from that game in the hopes of sparing his followers from retaliation from the Dareh.

Asrial rubbed the cold-prickled skin on her arms, reminding herself that this wasn't about her. The situations weren't comparable; technically, House Dilaryn and House Bintanan had been on the same side. "And you were captured?"

Romir stepped away from the flask, backed up until his back was against a bulkhead, as if he was afraid of standing too near.

Perhaps he was. "We were losing. The Mughelis were too powerful, too ruthless. We thought to escape."

"To where?"

"We found another world, benign and suitable for our needs—Omid, our hope." For a moment, his eyes brightened with happy memory, but she couldn't tune out his words.

Another world? Did he mean a planet other than Maj? Her breath caught at the scope of such a project. To be able to connect two points light-years apart . . . within atmospheres! Her first instinct was to scoff. None of the conglomerates was capable of such a feat. Even the most advanced ships couldn't perform long-distance Jumps with any degree of safety while within a planet's gravity well.

But then she remembered the force walls in that hidden complex that were far more advanced than anything in the market and had to admit the possibility. After all, a civilization that had djinn could have comparable achievements in other fields.

"It was our greatest working, a full thousand of our strongest weavers acting in concert. We wove a portal. But some of us had to stay behind to anchor it and to unravel the weave before the Mughelis could seize control of it." The muscles on his cheeks twitched almost into a smile—but they didn't make it that far.

Happiness faded. His face became bleak, his eyes distant, seeing some place other than the *Castel.* "We tried to hold them off, so as many as possible could escape. Fought too long. Unraveling the weave took too much out of me. They caught me . . . then they remade me into a weapon and used me against my people." He squeezed his hands into fists, his eyes tight, his mouth twisting bitterly. "I should have killed myself before then."

Suicide? Romir?

Shocked by the scathing heat in his last words, by his conviction, by the chance that he might still entertain thoughts of self-termination, Asrial grabbed his arm. She could sympathize. There was a time, shortly after pirates killed her parents, when she'd felt the same. Now she no longer had the latitude to indulge her whims, not with Amin relying on her, but she still remembered the despair that consumed her life, that black hole that swallowed all light and nearly swallowed her, too. She didn't want that for Romir. "They're dead now, these Mughelis you speak of. They've been gone for thousands of years. You won."

He gaped down at her without comprehension, his mouth working wordlessly.

"It's true. The complex where I found that"—she flicked her free hand at the flask—"was deserted. There are no people on Maj, only ruins."

"That is . . . impossible. The Mughelis, vanquished?" Romir looked lost, his eyes blank of all expression, his face slack with disbelief.

"I've gone there several times. I've flown over the whole planet, and the only sentients I ever saw there were other Rim rats. There are no *Mughelis*"—she stumbled over the word, trying to pronounce it the way Romir did—"left. According to the archaeologists, the Mougal civilization died out around two and a half thousand years ago."

"Then so are my people." He bowed his head, his hair falling forward and concealing his face. The desolation in his voice tore at her heart. Had he hoped to return to them?

Asrial knew the need for family, for connection—a link to something greater than herself. Amin and her cousins were what had kept her sane after the pirate attack. Though she saw them only infrequently, the knowledge that they were there if she needed them had carried her through some desolate times. "But didn't you say some of them escaped to another world? Omid was it?"

"By your account, that was thousands of years ago. There is no guarantee that they survive to this day. Less, in fact. Refugees in an unfamiliar world, lacking the resources the Mughelis had." His head stayed down, his shoulders curved. Hiding behind his hair, drowning in sorrow.

She bit her lip, foiled by his logic. What now? What could she say that would make a difference?

Frigging crap, she wasn't equipped to handle this. This was like heading into deep space without a star chart. She hated feeling so useless, and she hated seeing so vital a man despondent. The Romir who warmed her sheets was daring, seductive, reaching for what he wanted without giving thought to the cost. That first time, he'd seduced her in her sleep, not bothering with an introduction.

"That's no reason to give up. Just establishing that portal must have been a miracle, a chance in a lifetime. This is the same."

Silence was her answer. He didn't even bother replying.

Unable to stand the sight of Romir's despondence, Asrial stared instead at his prison. Now that she knew what it was, its semblance to an erect phallus was appalling. "This is barbaric. There has to be some way to free you."

One thing she had learned with the *Castel*: nothing was perfect; everything broke down, no matter how well made. Even stars died. Whatever the Mughelis did to make Romir a djinn, it could be broken. And somehow, someway, she'd do just that.

The numb look she got in return shouted his doubts. He'd lost all hope of ever escaping this coil. Despite the measure of freedom he'd attained, he'd resigned himself to remaining a djinn forever.

Unacceptable, absolutely unacceptable. Her horror flared against the sinking helplessness, transforming it to fury and commitment.

"We'll free you, whatever it takes."

Sure, the Spirit of space didn't play fair. But right then and there, she wanted happily-ever-after. If she couldn't have it for her parents nor for Amin, she wanted it for Romir.

Astonishment overwhelmed Romir's shock at the news of the Mughelis' defeat, flooding the emptiness in his heart. Asrial's outrage alone would have stunned him. But the determination on her face, as if his enslavement were a personal affront, confounded him.

"You do not know what you are saying." She could not have considered the implications of such a commitment. He had tried to unravel the weave both from outside and after his capture from inside. If indeed thousands of years had passed since his enslavement, how could she hope to free him?

Asrial caught his face between her hands and rose to her toes. Leaning into him, she stared into his eyes. "It doesn't matter. I'll free you, however long it takes."

Supremely conscious of her small breasts pressed to his chest, of her palms on his cheeks, he could not tear his gaze from the burning intensity of her determination. Such foolishness, but her will seared him, demanded he live. Demanded he believe.

"Surely there's some way to break this . . . binding."

"There is. If the flask shatters, the djinn can no longer be summoned."

"You go free?"

"No, merely that the djinn fails to respond to the vyzier. It was never proven conclusively, but the best guess is, the djinn is lost in the mists—or perhaps he dies."

She gasped, the whites around her irises widening. "I don't want to kill you! I meant reverse it. How did they do it, anyway?"

Romir closed his eyes against the memory and the fierce demand in hers. From the heights of lovemaking to the depths of shocking revelation to the distant impossibility of hope, the shifts demanded of him numbed the mind.

"I do not remember what the Mugheli vyzier did. Just pain." Such pain that it became his entire world and everything else faded to white. He did not know if he had ever known the weave and had simply chosen to forget or if the pain had ripped it from his memory. The only favor the gods had granted him was that his skill lay in battle weavings, which precluded his power being used to make other djinn. But because of that, he could not answer her question.

"When it was over, I was djinn and tied to that." He flicked a hand at the ordinary-seeming flask that was the bane of his deathless existence.

"But you've escaped."

Had he ever been so hopeful? The earnestness in Asrial's voice only drove home the extent of his enslavement. He had no hope. Even now he did not know what whim of the gods had granted him this measure of freedom. Should he ever return to the gray mists, it was likely he would lose that much. He had not escaped.

"For the moment. As you saw, my prison may draw me back at any time." It never changed: he had been helpless against its pull, his essence sucked away despite his struggles.

Asrial gripped his shoulder. The bite of her fingers drew his attention to her. She met his gaze without wavering, the amber chips in her brown eyes glinting bright, her determination unshaken despite what he had said. "How do we keep you out?"

He explained what he suspected. It would be easy for her to return him to his prison, but he could not—would not—force himself upon her. He also did not want her in ignorance of his purpose: he would be using her to remain free.

* * *

Asrial smiled, relieved that maintaining Romir's freedom could be that simple. "So you just need sex?" It was a temporary measure, but it would do for now.

"Just sex?" he repeated, staring at her with wondering eyes. The display of emotion was more life than she expected to see in him at this point.

Perhaps a little distraction would be good. His face had been so blank, his body so still, she wanted to make him react, to do something to break through that mask. To see the silver passion that had burned in his eyes when he'd taken her.

"To keep you out of there." She played her fingers across his bare chest, thrilling to the broad sweeps of golden muscle. His dark nipple hardened to a tight nub as she circled it, wonderfully responsive to her touch. His chest rose, muscles flexing as she traced them downward. Her fingers snagged on the waistband of the pants once again hanging low on his narrow hips.

Really, she should have realized long ago that he couldn't have been an ordinary grounder nor an escaped pleasure bod. His pants were unlike any style she'd seen in the Rim. His body and posture weren't those of a pleasure bod. And she'd never asked him how he'd come to be on Maj. Maybe she'd turned a blind eye to the indications because that meant getting involved.

"It's no problem if it's sex. That's easier than extracting a chunk of dazjanite, for example. Or murder." She stuck her tongue out at him and winked.

Romir shook his head, pressing his lips together as he fought back amusement. His hair spilled over a shoulder and down his chest, the motion snagging her eye. He'd used his hair on her before, but she'd never taken the time to appreciate it.

She took a strand, twining it through her fingers, drawn by its unusual length. His hair hung to mid-thigh with not a kink to mar its fall. It marked him as a grounder, and yet there was something alluring about that extravagant curtain of blue black framing such broad shoulders. "Was long hair the fashion for men, in your day?"

He touched the strand spanning the gap between them, his brows giving a twitch of surprise. "Not for all men, only weavers. By my time, long hair was as much a symbol of our ability as our badges. We grew our hair long because we could." He shook his head. "Such vanity. It was because of this hair that the Mughelis captured me, instead of killing me outright. If I had cut it, they would not have bothered." His expression turned distant, his thoughts going where she couldn't follow.

Asrial cursed her curiosity for waking yet another unhappy memory. She just couldn't leave well enough alone.

Nine

The *Castel* emerged from Jump on the outskirts of the approach lanes, far enough to be safe. The Eskarion Ring flashed steadily in the distance, the interstellar trade's heart disgorging ship after ship with each scintillating pulse. The enormous structure was the Xerex sector's gateway to the Inner Worlds, connecting the Rim to the Cyri sector, and the main booster of Xer and Cyrian wealth. Rings gave a corporation virtual control over interstellar trade in the sectors where the Rings were located. The cost of construction was more than any planetary government could justify.

As they got closer, a galaxy of lights became visible on the far side of the Ring—the inbound traffic headed for the Inner Worlds awaiting their turn. More light flashed farther out, ships headed toward one of the Ring's satellite stations that flourished around the Ring catering to the transit traffic.

Romir leaned toward the screen, lips parted, staring with unabashed wonder at the endless flow of galactic trade. Never had he looked more like a grounder than now.

How would he react to the sentients on the stations? Space held an odd assortment of races. Except for Tehld with their telepathic hive groups, most larger ships had mixed crews. Perhaps a word of warning was called for.

Asrial commed the Ring's admin to add the *Castel* to the inbound queue. They gave her a slot three days hence by Ring standard—not great, but she'd had longer waits. It was better than the alternative. With only the *Castel*'s jump drive, she couldn't hope to reach the Inner Worlds in her lifetime.

She changed course to head for Eskarion 14. Of the nine stations in the Eskarion constellation on the Rim side, it had the best mix of low docking fees, cheap food, and good security. There were cheaper docking bays on some of the other stations, but the ships patronizing those usually had crews that were . . . less than aboveboard. With her hold full of Majian relics, she preferred not to throw temptation in their path.

The approach to Eskarion 14 was the usual orderly chaos as cargo ships, traders, and personal craft converged on the sprawling station. Time and expansion had added to the original structure, obscuring the three-ringed cylinder favored by the designers of the iBor corporation. All the rings now sprouted irregular arms that stretched more than the cylinder's length.

A bay was immediately available, allowing Asrial to dock without undue delay. While the *Castel* wasn't as small as those sleek one-man ships, it fitted inside without difficulty, unlike the larger traders that required an outside slot with external hard points and boarding tubes.

Even before the bay door was sealed and the clamps and linkages were green, her focus had shifted to the supplies she needed.

The stations operated around the clock and always on "daytime." The commercial levels hadn't observed night cycles for as long as Asrial could remember. With all the ships passing through, their shipboard clocks set to different times, there was no lack of people wanting to buy something, and the stations were organized to sell it to them. Downtime was lost profit for the conglomerates that owned the constellations.

But before she could tackle replenishing her supplies, she had to do something about Romir. She considered his appearance carefully as she shrugged into her jacket. "You'll draw attention if you walk the station dressed like that."

It would be a pity to hide that chest, but only pleasure bods showed that much skin. She'd rather not spend her time fending off offers for his services, but the alternative would be to leave him on the *Castel* while she bought suitable attire. While she accepted that he was a djinn, the thought of leaving anyone alone on her ship turned her stomach.

"How should I dress?" Romir's calm acceptance of her decision only underscored the difference between him and most men of her acquaintance. His demeanor made the back of her neck itch. Pleasure bods were similarly complaisant.

Using the comp, she accessed the station net to check the clothes shops. She could have something delivered, but the fees for the service made her wince. "I think something like that." She settled on an ordinary pair of pants, a long-sleeved shirt, and boots—typical spacer gear and entirely unexceptionable.

She turned to him to gauge his size and stared.

Romir was now garbed exactly as the figure on the comp's screen, the loose pants he'd worn nowhere in sight. He ran a hand over a sleeve, smoothing down the bland, gray green fabric. "Better now?"

"Well," she temporized, trying to act as if nothing unusual had happened, "if you can do something about your hair, it'd be perfect."

Grimacing, he gathered the long tresses and plaited them into a thick, elaborate braid that ended halfway down his back—he still wouldn't pass for a spacer, but he was no longer quite so obviously a grounder. "I can alter my garb but not my hair. Part of my limits is this form. I cannot change so much as a strand from when I was made djinn."

Asrial stared at the result. Except for his dark skin, he looked just like any other spacer—at least from the front. "That will do."

Leaving the *Castel* with a man by her side felt strange. She'd been alone for so long that she didn't know how to treat Romir. More than acquaintance, not quite crew, less than family.

He watched her check and double-check the telltales of her security, confirming they were online and functioning properly. "Is there a problem?"

She flushed, embarrassed by her display of paranoia but not so much that she stopped. After all, the contents of the hold were sufficient justification. "Not really, just cautious."

Lockdown confirmed, they headed out, Asrial finding unlooked-for comfort in his companionship. A woman alone, even one who could defend herself, was always at risk, especially in the Rim. By his mere presence, Romir reduced that danger.

First, she needed a comm console to message Amin. He'd need the catalog of the contents of the *Castel*'s hold to contact interested buyers. If there was sufficient interest, he would arrange for an auction, and that required some travel time, since auctions included personal inspection of the goods by the buyers or their representatives. She used to handle those arrangements herself, but now that he was acting as her agent, she had to concede a portion of her independence. His pride was at stake. Anyway, she found she liked not having to handle that bit of business. Amin was also able to keep track of the market for relics while she was in the Rim; he could get a better price for her finds.

The *Castel* didn't have the capability for interstellar point-to-point communications—needle comm required power she couldn't spare, and the registration fee for a permanent comm address designation was steep. Asrial had to rely on the slower, less secure, but far more affordable bounce relays. Eskarion relays beamed data packets daily to inbound courier ships, which then passed the packets on to other couriers, until they got to their intended recipients.

Still, because she knew how easily messages in the bounce stream could be tapped and decrypted, she'd chosen to hold off sending a message to Amin until Eskarion 14. Her message would go out on the next courier, reaching Lyrel 9 at least a dec before she would.

She headed for the booth of a comm company she trusted, her senses on high as they threaded the crowd on the bridge to the commercial district, one ear to the babble of the avatars on the screens. The too-perfect-to-be-real heads blathered on, speculating about an alliance between iBor and NexulMed. Reports blasted on station channels were news of sectoral interest; smaller planetary clips didn't get much vid time. One word snagged her complete attention: Dareh. Something about contract negotiations falling through—or being postponed, she wasn't quite sure which—due to massive protests and civil unrest in some Lomidar colonies.

Asrial smiled to herself, taking malicious pleasure at the news. It seemed the power they schemed to grab was causing some problems. A few steps later, she realized she'd lost her companion while listening to the report. She turned back and found Romir still on the bridge.

He gripped the side rail tightly with both hands, as if afraid of losing his balance or that he'd step off the platform. He leaned forward, his weight on the low barrier, his gaze fixed on the bloom of fantastic color beyond the station's three-level glassteel windows. The view was framed by the black grid supporting the enormous windows, an older, almost obsolete technology dating back to the original construction of Eskarion 14 that didn't detract from its beauty.

The luminous gas cloud turned near space into swirls of milky rainbow with a star at its heart. It was such sights that kept her in space. How ironic that this time she'd walked past the viewing platform without stopping.

She rejoined him and drank in the sense of power beyond the grasp of puny politicians and corporations. Only silence seemed appropriate at this point.

"What is that?" Romir continued to stare in wonder, his pleasure there for all to see.

"That's the Dagaerin Field. It's the original reason iBor built the Eskarion Ring."

"To look at it?"

Asrial laughed, waving a hand in negation. The thought of a corporation spending creds for tourists to ogle something was too ridiculous for words, no matter how beautiful she found the Dagaerin Field. "Hardly. The rock field around the star is a rich source of dazjanite, which is used to power the Rings." There were no habitable planets within two jumps of Eskarion; however, mining dazjanite was profitable enough to justify the cost—for a corporation. Other sources had since been developed, reducing iBor's margin, but the transit fees had more than offset the difference.

Long moments passed while he remained lost in appreciation. Asrial got the impression he'd stand there for days if she let him.

"Let's go. It'll still be here on our return."

Though Romir followed obediently, he kept glancing back. Of course, it was his first time to witness such a phenomenon.

That the sight of the gas cloud could elicit such open wonder in him, breaking the guard he kept on his emotions, gave her hope. Perhaps the similarities she'd noted between his behavior and a pleasure bod's were off base. His reticence might just be innate, nothing for her to be concerned about.

She continued to the comm company in a better mood.

Romir trailed Asrial through the station, content to leave her to her thoughts. There was much to see all around them. He had thought they arrived at a busy time—much like a market day—but the station was just as crowded when they left the communications kiosk.

He followed her into another kiosk, this one emanating savory aromas, where a thin woman with glittering purple hair that swayed around her head—and covered most of her face—served dish after dish with barely a pause, her high voice calling out numbers with singsong regularity. A Cyrian, Asrial said simply, as if that explained why the hair moved in opposition to the rest of the woman's body or the granules of her hair that caused the glitter.

The Cyrian was just one of more than a handful of unusual races mingling in the kiosk. People with horns, with large eyes and slit pupils, with fur, balancing on strangely shaped limbs, all ate with steady purpose. Romir marveled at the variety that greeted him at every turn. Truly the universe held more than he had ever imagined. The existence of something in the abyss between worlds like that fantasy of brilliance he had witnessed on the path, much less one that was wedded to an intricate tangle of power, staggered his mind.

Asrial approached a vacant board and considered the images on display. "Are you sure you don't want to eat something?" The furrow between her brows hinted at unease.

"I have no need."

"Veg noodles, then." She touched the board, then moved to the counter. Her order came quickly, served by the Cyrian, and she took it to an empty table. As she ate, she watched him, questions darkening her brown eyes to the shade of askeiwood.

"Ask."

"Am I that transparent?" Her gaze drifted to one of the glasses on the wall, her attention momentarily caught by whatever the people in it were saying. He listened but came away just as ignorant; what he could understand of their speech still made no sense to him—speaking as they did of people or places he knew nothing of.

"Is this so very different from your world, your time?"

"Very, so much that I fear I am dreaming."

Curiosity sparkled in her eyes. "How?"

"No war, the variety of forms in people, voyaging in the abyss between worlds—there are too many differences to count." He spread his hands.

Her eyes rounded at his answer, but then she smiled self-deprecatingly. "I suppose that was a silly question. Majians were grounders, after all."

"Surely there are as many differences between grounders as there are races."

"Probably. I wouldn't really know." Asrial waved a hand, casually dismissing the matter. "One thing I've always wondered about: the spires in Maj are so high and they have only stairs; did people just climb all those steps the whole time?"

The innocence her question revealed made Romir shake his head in disbelief. She had such a generous soul that the answer that was obvious to him did not occur to her. "The highest spires are usually vyzier's towers. Among the Mughelis, those of privilege have djinn—"

"Had," she corrected him with a frown, pausing with her fork upraised. "The Mughelis are all gone now."

He nodded, acknowledging the reminder, an echo of the shock he had felt rippling through him anew. "So they are. I still find it difficult to conceive." The enemy of his people had been unstoppable, their forces relentless. The Mughelis respected only ruthlessness, using all means to achieve their goals—even defying nature to create djinn. "But back then, vyziers did not stint in their use of power. They thought nothing of commanding djinn to waft them where they wished to go, including up and down spires. The stairs were for menials and slaves."

Asrial did not linger at her meal, eating as steadily as the others around her, the food seeming to give her no pleasure. She treated it as a necessity, fuel for the body, nothing more. Had she always done so?

He himself had no use for food, but he remembered enjoying the flavors. Meals were some of the few memories he permitted himself to retain, lacking as they did any association to . . . the people he cared for.

As soon as they left the kiosk, they were accosted.

A group broke out of the flow of people, another example of variety in the universe. These had scales on every part of their bodies left bare—their arms, their chests, even their heads. Scales of blues on black covered most of them, no two patterns alike, though only one had scales of reds and yellows on white. Stones at the bases of their throats flared with the rhythm of life. Bright to his weaver's sight, all seven looked male yet female—too slender to be men, yet their forms could not be said to be women's. The scales on their faces were so fine they appeared to have tiny gems outlining their eyes and mouth, the patterns like tattoos.

The black eyes of the seven were fixed on Romir as they approached purposefully. The stares, lidless and devoid of white, made his back prickle. If his heart beat, it might have skipped at the pressure of those unswerving eyes.

One stepped forward, bending a look of inquiry to Asrial. "We wish to know. What is he?"

Romir needed a few moments to understand what had been said. The being sounded as though—he? she? it?—were gargling rocks and phrased the question in a halting pidgin.

Asrial shot Romir a startled glance. "I don't understand."

They answered her in a cascade of voices as they spread to surround the two of them.

"He shines."

"So bright."

"The consciousness is here."

"But his body is not."

As one, their heads tilted, their black eyes devoid of any white looking past the kiosks . . . toward the docking bays where Asrial and he had left the *Castel*.

"We wish to know." They reached for him all in unison, as though one mind ruled all seven bodies.

Romir flinched. Without thinking, he wove the air before him into a barrier, not wanting to be touched.

"Keep your hands to yourselves. He's not a pleasure bod for you to fondle." Face hard, Asrial flung up an arm, interposing herself between him and the inquisitive strangers. Shielding him with her body.

Shocked that she would protect a djinn, Romir grabbed her shoulder, intending to pull her aside.

"Ah!"

He could not tell which throat made the exclamation—they all stared at his hand, mouths agape.

"Apologies." They pulled their hands away with that eerie synchronism, then stepped back until they stood together arrayed like a matched set.

Asrial lowered her arm, but otherwise did not relax her guard, her shoulders tense where they pressed against Romir.

The one nearest her bowed. Performed alone, the stilted motion looked even more awkward, as if resisting some compulsion to remain vertical like his companions. "Apologies," he repeated. "Never have we seen a Lomidari so . . . gifted. We would trade for knowledge."

"Gifted," Asrial repeated in a dubious tone, ignoring the offer to trade.

The others jostled closer. "What purpose?"

"To walk separate?"

Irritation pleated her brow. "What d'you mean by that?"

One of them jerkily raised an arm to point away. "His body is there, not here."

Romir stiffened. How could they know he was not as he appeared, that this form was not truly his own?

Asrial darted a glance over her shoulder to him, a question in her eyes. He shook his head, not understanding what she wanted. Raising her chin, she straightened to her full height, regarding them sternly. "Our purpose is no concern of yours." And still she continued to shield him with her body.

The stones on their throats flashed and flickered in turn and at once, the only divergence in their appearance. It was as if they conversed; Romir had noticed something similar with the lights on the *Castel*'s panel when Asrial sat at the controls. "No trade?"

She said nothing, her silence speaking for her.

They bowed, murmuring "Forgive the intrusion." Again their motion, their voices were as one. They merged back into the flow of people, disappearing as though they had never been.

Asrial marched off in the opposite direction, the crowd parting before her like a flock of prastu fleeing a hungry yfreet.

"That was strange."

"Tehld." Snatching a glance over her shoulder, she pressed a hand to her chest. "That was a hive. They're telepaths."

"Telepaths?"

"Among themselves they communicate by thought."

He understood now why they had behaved as they had, acting in concert, speaking as though of one will. "They trade for knowledge?"

She shrugged. "They pay creds for information. What they do with it, no one knows."

"What kind of information?"

"I don't really know. I've never had much to do with the Tehld. They don't sell information, and I'm usually on the buying side, myself."

Romir eyed the tense line of her back. So had she held herself while shielding him, protecting him without a thought to her own safety. He kept the rest of his questions to himself. The day had given him much to think upon.

The Tehld had known he was not what he seemed. But gifted? He was tempted to laugh at their misapprehension. As though it were his choice to be djinn.

But what had they meant when they said his body was *there*? He had lost his body when he was made djinn.

Ten

After the strangeness of their encounter with the Tehld, buying supplies was a welcome breath of normalcy. Asrial's heart finally settled on a moderate beat, though her knees still threatened to knock together.

The meal kits didn't take long. Unless she splurged, the choices were limited. The only decisions necessary were how many of each to get and when to schedule delivery to the *Castel*.

That left her more time for the more important purchases. She headed down two levels, away from the food and recreation kiosks, into the arms assigned to the industrial section. While none of the stations in the Eskarion constellation hosted a shipyard, there was a brisk trade in micro parts, particularly in the Rim-side stations. She could never have enough spares. Maintenance on the *Castel*'s electronics was a never-ending chore, especially with its ancient control runs.

Unlike the entertainment section that catered to travelers and off-duty spacers, the industrial section didn't bother with flashy displays or expensive frills: bland, static signs or none at all were the norm. Here, iBor's station designers had done without the multilevel atriums and glassteel windows. Here, the colorful ceracrete floor tiles were replaced by rugged, gray plasteel, and any polish they acquired was due to foot traffic, not the efforts of maintenance bots. Here, the ventilation scrubbers struggled to filter out the acrid tang of hydraulic fluid, the pungent stench of solder scorch, and the smells of a dozen races; their failure left a heavy atmosphere of aggression and teeth-grinding labor.

Romir accompanied her quietly through the grungier corridors, a man-shaped chunk of watchful silence keeping station by her left shoulder. Away from the glitter, that mask of reserve settled back on his face.

Had he always been like that, or was that silence something he'd adopted as a djinn? Not wanting to stir up painful memories, she couldn't bring herself to ask.

Forcing her thoughts to a safer course, she explained to Romir what she was looking to buy as they walked. While she was accustomed to doing things by herself, it felt awkward to carry on as usual, as though he weren't with her.

"So you need to separate the good from the bad?"

She nodded, most of her attention given to the spacers around them. "The cheaper parts are usually cannibalized from decommissioned ships too old or damaged to fly or cranked out by Rim World shops with outdated equipment, so they're either used or of uncertain quality. Unfortunately, they're sold as is."

"You are not allowed to test them?"

"Out of the question."

"Perhaps I can help, then."

Asrial took him at his word. She couldn't tell what he based his decisions on; he just riffled through the parts available, plucking out those he deemed acceptable. She could only assume it had something to do with how he'd pinpointed the problem with the *Castel*'s control run.

With the two of them there, she bought more than she would have alone. When they finally set out for the *Castel*, they dragged two rented dollies piled high with her acquisitions plus some crates under their arms.

Romir glanced at her again, his brow furrowed with discomfort. Though his load contained the heavier cable runs, he made it look effortless. "I can carry those for you."

And have her walk alongside unladen, like some pampered sovreine too delicate to dirty her hands? Asrial shook her head, smiling when he wiggled his fingers in invitation. "There's no need."

She couldn't let herself become dependent on Romir. As a Rim rat, she worked alone. She preferred it that way. It was safer.

For her heart.

Once out of the commercial section and across the bridge, the lights were noticeably dimmer. One of the disadvantages of the cheaper docking bays was that the station admin cut costs where they could to maximize profits—which meant the lights were permanently on night setting. But usually it wasn't this dim.

Unease crawled across Asrial's shoulders with clammy suckers. She wasn't usually so jumpy, but the encounter with the Tehld hive left her uneasy.

Footsteps sounded ahead of them, echoing off the gray walls. Her back stiffened instinctively. With them both heavily laden, they were in a poor position to fend off an ambush. The shadows could hide all sorts of criminal activity from the security cams.

Irritated with herself, Asrial eased her stunner out of its holster. She'd gotten carried away with replenishing her supplies and forgotten caution. She shouldn't have bought so much when spare parts couldn't be delivered to the *Castel*'s bay.

"Is there a problem?" Romir's question drifted to her ears, barely louder than the rumble of the dollies' rollers.

"It's too dark."

Romir glanced up the corridor. The fingers of the hand on the dolly's guide bar flicked surreptitiously, little more than a tremor, a motion she caught out of the corner of her eye. The lights brightened to day strength, possibly for the first time in Eskarion 14's history. "Better now?"

Asrial gave him a sidelong look. Had he done that?

A soft curse floated on the air, the voice harsh and guttural—and nearby.

Her muscles tightened in readiness. Run or fight?

Simple robbery happened, even abduction and murder. It didn't have to be pirates targeting the *Castel*'s cargo. She didn't fool herself that slavers didn't transit at Eskarion. There were planets and colonies in the Inner Worlds that sustained their economies by not asking questions.

It wasn't just that curse that made her wary. Romir had pulled ahead, suddenly radiating menace, a willingness to do violence to whomever crossed his path. This was the grounder she'd been worried about?

She set her crates on top of her overloaded dolly, then tapped his arm. "Just don't block my line of fire."

With a nod, he continued, still carrying his load and pulling his dolly, an ordinary enough figure in the docking bays, only infinitely menacing. He exuded a confidence that said he could wipe out a horde of professional muscle without breaking his stride—no boast.

A Hagnashr and two Xers crouched in a nearby alcove doing a spot of gambling, the heavygrav worlder looming over his wiry companions. It was a normal enough scene, but Asrial didn't buy the pose. While stations attracted a mix of races, she didn't see any reason for them to be right there. Ship crew would head for the commercial districts if they had free time. Station locals had their own hangouts. If they were loafing off, they'd be better hidden using one of the maintenance hatches instead of a public corridor. Besides, Hagnash were fast for their bulk, especially in lighter gravities, and this one sported a jagged horn that added to his air of danger. Xers, on the other hand, evolved in low-light conditions; it made no sense for the Hagnashr to gamble with them in the shadows.

The trio made no attempt to attack as she and Romir passed; whether due to the brighter lights, the security cams, Romir's presence, or actual lack of criminal intent, she couldn't guess.

They regained the *Castel* without encountering any more suspicious characters. Either the trio had been responsible for the footsteps she'd heard or someone ahead of them had slipped into one of the bays before they'd reached the junction.

Asrial breathed out a sigh, the sight of her ship hunkered down on its belly in the middle of the bay calming her fears. She studied the *Castel*, wondering what it looked like to Romir. Old, with more replacement parts than original, it had none of the predatory sleekness of fast couriers, the gray, duraskin paint mottled from countless entries and repairs hiding minor dings. It made no pretense of being more than it was—a hard-worked, low-cred trader.

"Is there a problem?"

"No, I just thought someone might have tried to break in." She circled her ship anyway for a thorough inspection. The telltales on the dock clamps glowed green. The air and power linkages were solid. No odd marks to be seen around the hatches.

Romir considered the *Castel*, the look in his eyes distant as he duplicated her circuit around the ship. As if he were seeing beneath the surface—or beyond it. After how he'd manipulated the lights in the corridor, she couldn't dismiss the possibility that it was precisely what he was doing.

"It is intact. I do not see any damage."

"What about tampering?" Why anyone would attempt sabotage, she couldn't imagine, but she didn't take back the question. Better paranoid than dead. If her father had been more cautious, he and Nasri might be alive today.

"That is more difficult to ascertain." He set down his load in preparation for doing—something.

She grabbed his arm and pulled him toward the bay door, out of sight of the security cams. "Might be better here. You'll have fewer witnesses," she explained when he glanced at her askance.

"Spies?"

It was her turn to glance in surprise, abruptly reminded that he'd been captured in a war. "Something like that."

He accepted her vague answer with a nod. Raising his empty hands, he gestured quickly, his fingers flicking in an intricate dance, then laid his hand on the *Castel*. The result wasn't conspicuous. If she hadn't been looking for it, she wouldn't have noticed the shift in light. Tiny glints appeared around his hand then streaked off in various directions, crisscrossing the *Castel*'s surface in a grid. "No tampering. Everything is as we left it."

Asrial smiled, suddenly abashed by her paranoia. The Tehld hive must have unnerved her more than she'd thought for her to entertain such extreme suspicions. iBor wasn't affiliated with Dareh in any way; that was why she continued to transit through Eskarion. A route through the Sattar Ring, which connected Xerex with the Brauten sector where Lyrel 9 was located, was shorter and could have cut decs from her flight time, but that constellation was Dareh-controlled and therefore never an option. Although transiting through Eskarion made for a longer flight, because iBor competed directly with Dareh, their stations were less likely to give her trouble—they were safe enough that she really needn't have double-checked the *Castel.*

Sabotage? What was she thinking? Asrial exhaled in a silent huff. Just her imagination running wild.

They boarded the *Castel* without further delay, but her baseless fear didn't release its grip on her until the hatch was sealed behind them and the locks engaged.

"Do you have enemies here?" Romir's question was matter-of-fact, drifting over his shoulder as he continued into the service hold with the spare parts.

"N-no, why'd you ask?"

"You worried about spies." He unloaded the packs and stowed the electronics in the proper places—precisely where she kept such items. He'd taken the time to learn her system. "I need to know, if I am to protect you."

"I can protect myself." She'd flown alone for so long that her reply was automatic.

"But would not another set of eyes help? You cannot be on watch all the time. Even you need sleep." Despite the offer, his expression wasn't particularly enthusiastic—dutiful would've been the strongest term she'd use to describe it, but really he didn't let much emotion slip past his mask of ready menace.

She waved aside the question, scanning the hold to confirm that everything was where it ought to be and not because she was avoiding his gaze. "No enemies that I know of. I'm just careful that way." According to the latest comm dispatch from Amin, Dareh still had no affiliates on Eskarion. There was no reason for alarm . . . and no reason to talk about the Dareh.

"So you do have enemies to ward against." Lack of persistence definitely wasn't one of Romir's failings. Was that a flicker of concern that shadowed his eyes?

"Who doesn't?" Asrial didn't want to dwell on old news. Danger and enemies were facts of life, especially a spacer's life. She was more interested in what he'd done to the lights in the corridor and during his inspection of the *Castel*. Ready for a change in subject, she turned to fix a no-nonsense look on him over her shoulder, then stared for real.

Was Romir fading—again? Whatever he'd done had to have a price. How much had his efforts on her behalf cost him?

The memory of his struggle, of seeing the deck through his transparent body slammed to the front of her brain, and her heart skipped, the shock and fear of that time rushing back.

Not again, not if she could help it. She took his hand and slid it under her T-top, to her breast. His hand was so much larger than hers, hot and firm, easily cupping the small mound. She molded his palm against her, arching herself into him in a deliberate invitation even he should understand.

"Asrial," Romir protested, even as his fingers caressed her, teasing her nipple into aching stiffness. "You need not . . ."

"It's all right. If this gives you the strength to resist your prison, then I don't mind." She leaned back, resting her head on his chest as shivers of delight washed through her veins like a fiery sip of Nikralian brandy. He handled her with utmost gentleness to stunning effect. Something inside her melted at his delicate attentions. Such seductive gentleness. She didn't want it to end. "It's not as if it's a hardship."

"I should not abuse you this way."

"Abuse?" she repeated, reluctantly amused by his choice of words. She yanked up her T-top to give him better access. "You're not taking advantage of me. More like I'm the one taking advantage of you."

Another wave of shivers swept her, prickles of delight stealing her breath and filling her with frothy lightness. The thought of waking to find him gone, retaken by his prison, floated in the back of her mind—the specter of future loss. Each time Romir used whatever it was that let him manipulate the lights in the corridor, he probably weakened his ability to resist his prison. If making love helped keep him free, it was no burden.

No burden at all.

The nipple under his fingers grew taut and her breast, warmer and rosier, a firm weight in his palm. The unexpected pleasure of it was a blessing from the gods.

Romir could feel his prison tugging on his essence, his use of power strengthening its call. But Asrial's was stronger.

Her heart drummed under his hand, its beat pronounced and steadily faster. Arching against him like a lazy *shera*, she purred, a definite sound of pleasure. Her buttocks pressed back, stroking him firmly. Her motions woke the hunger of his senses, blowing on the embers and fanning the hesitant flames to life.

Asrial's generosity astonished him: to offer herself so freely, to allow him to touch her so intimately, to trust him this much . . .

He did not deserve such a gift, yet still she reached for him, her open desire honest and guileless. She argued that it was no hardship, yet how could that be? He was using her to maintain what little freedom he had. If he were a decent man, he would not.

Leaning into him, she exhaled softly, her breath warming the base of his throat.

Awareness bloomed, matching the throb from yielding heat in his palm. His entire being converged on those points, and all thoughts of decency and gallantry fled on angel wings.

She was woman, and he wanted her, wanted this. He could do nothing to stop it.

Twisting around in the circle of his arms, Asrial pulled her blouse over her head and flung it aside. With her hands on his shoulders, she pushed him back. A stack of crates cut off his retreat, hitting the backs of his knees and forcing him to sit. She straddled his lap, her strong calves gripping his hips, the long muscles of her back flexing against his palms.

Wrapping her arms around his neck, she tugged loose his braid and sank her hands in his hair, impatiently unraveling the strands—and for the first time that he could remember, it did not matter that his hair was long enough to be so handled. At that moment all that mattered was that she held him.

The uncounted years of servitude were the farthest things from Romir's mind as she tugged a thick handful of hair to her face and inhaled, her eyes falling shut in a look of bliss.

Just from that?

Then she bent over him with a lazy smile. Her breath warmed his lips, made them throb to the beat of an unbeating heart—impossible but undeniable. This form only mimicked life. Cut him, and he would not bleed. Yet his lips ached for her kiss, ached for the touch of her lips. Whether firm pressure or fleeting, it did not matter. Only that it was Asrial's.

Romir pushed up, eliminating the finger's breadth of air separating them. Sweet. A tenderness he had almost forgotten could exist, trapped as he was in this eternal death.

Her kiss filled him, spilling kindness and caring into his parched soul and unbidden generosity into his barren world. He yearned only to remain in this paradise.

She pushed his shirt off his shoulders, her intent obvious. Rather than release her, he let his clothes vanish back into the mists of power he had used to form them.

This dream that was no dream spun a cocoon of delight around his senses. Small, strong hands fondled him, held him. Fingertips roughened by honest effort explored his body. Soft curls tickled his chest, his belly, and lower . . . his inner thighs as she slid off his lap to kneel on the floor.

Asrial licked him slowly, leisurely, taking her time as she twirled the tip of her tongue up his length from the base to the tip and along the sensitive ridge. Pleasure flooded him in fiery waves, burning the hold of his prison to mere threads.

Romir groaned, grabbing the sides of the crate he sat on.

"Stay with me," she whispered against him, her warm breath ruffling his short hairs in a moist caress.

As though he could wish to be elsewhere!

She used her mouth on him, her lips impossibly soft as she kissed and nibbled and sucked along his shaft. As though she wanted to eat him—except she had never evinced this much enjoyment with food. Hot delight clawed and danced up his spine, uncontrollable shivers sweeping his body.

Asrial watched him intently, amber glinting in her brown eyes as the flat of her tongue slathered him with wet heat. She plied her tongue with a sure instinct for pleasure, gliding over and around him, swirling without pause.

There was no mistaking her exultation at his response or the smile she wore just before she took the tip of his head into her mouth. He watched her pink lips close around him, the heart he did not have racing impossibly.

Need burned, seared, scorched—a carnal hunger she fed with her intimate kisses. There was no mistaking her desire—for him, for this—and that knowledge made his need burn hotter.

Her agile fingers stroked his balls, playing teasing scratching games on the thin skin. When she took them into her mouth and sucked, he nearly went up in flames.

Romir jerked at the sharp lash of pleasure, his hips rising.

Shocked by the strength of his response, he did not feel the jolt when he landed back on the crate at her urging. A firestorm raged in his body, stoked by her avid encouragement.

Pleasure racked him, his shaft swollen almost to the point of pain. The flames of her making leaped high in his veins, ready to consume him.

"I—you—" His thoughts were scattered to the wind. He could not set them to words.

"That's right. That's it," Asrial crooned, her breath on his damp flesh sparking another wave of excitement. She crawled up his yearning body and cradled him with hers. With sure hands, she guided him to her entrance and sank down with a wordless cry of pleasure.

Whatever his doubts, he could have none about her desire. At this moment, he had to believe that for her this lovemaking was not hardship.

She was wet, the clasp of her body glove-tight yet yielding to his entry. The warmth of her, the slickness, the pressure around him combined to stimulating, nerve-blazing effect. But all too soon she reversed her direction, rocking to her knees and denying him her heat. She rode him in short, shallow digs, dipping and rising and taking barely more than his sensitive head. Too shallow.

He lunged up, needing more, needing her. She took him deeper, but it still was not enough. Hugging her close, he dropped to his knees and laid her out on the floor, the better to pleasure her.

Asrial gave a startled shout, her eyes bright with surprise, her arms locked on his shoulders. She paused, assimilating their new position, then she hooked her ankles behind his thighs, her strong legs clamping around his waist and driving him deep to their mutual delight.

Finally—*finally!*—she took all of him. All the way to the center of her being.

Each thrust drew a moan of approval from her, low and hoarse and exquisitely sweet. Exquisitely precious. The sound was reward enough.

Again!

Romir slowly withdrew, prolonging the delicious torture of his senses. Though he could take no release, that edge of pain was precious—sure proof that his prison was not held by Mugheli hands. Only with Asrial had he felt such excruciating delight.

It was too soon to end it.

He whetted the hunger, honing the fiery edge of pleasure until it bordered on agony. He savored the sensations racking his body, the pangs of delight cutting him with jagged teeth.

Asrial cried out—triumphant, exultant. A joyful shout of abandon, free of all cares. The voice of a woman thoroughly and properly pleasured. Her body shuddered around him, ecstasy rippling through her in savage waves.

Hungry for sensation, he coaxed it on, spinning out the aftermath until she fell into an exhausted sleep, a smile curving her lips. Nothing about her sated stretch belied the appearance of contentment. No tension knotted her muscles.

An unfamiliar sensation filled his chest, a lightness of the heart despite the continued ache in his loins. That she could lie there so blissfully and he was the one who had given her that was a source of wonder.

He was djinn. The gods did not smile on such as he.

Romir laid Asrial on her bed and—mindful of her dislike for his watching her while she slept—reluctantly left her cabin. Without her to occupy his mind, his thoughts circled back to the events of the day when he had pulled on the strands around him to brighten the lights in the corridor and to check for tampering.

It had been a long time since he had been called to weave power, but that minor tweaking of threads should not have wearied him so much that he began to fade. He remembered destroying entire cities, raining down fire from the sky, torrents of whirling blue flame melting everything before them, before succumbing to the call of his prison. Had that been because he had been commanded? Did the master's will somehow ease a djinn's chains?

If so, he could not be separated from Asrial for long, not if he wished to remain free. The conclusion left him with mixed emotions: while it offered him a measure of freedom, if she knew how much he depended on her, it would give her the shuttle hand in this weave between them.

He owed her his protection, but that was all he was willing to give her. Though he was in her debt for rescuing him from the mists, he could not bring himself to trust in her completely. If she knew the full extent of his betrayal, the millions of lives he had cost, surely she would gladly return him to his prison.

Eleven

The remainder of their stay at Eskarion 14 passed without incident, though Asrial couldn't throw off a persistent itch between her shoulder blades that claimed someone was staring at her. Nothing untoward happened. Even the Tehld kept their distance—though that might have been because she limited her excursions from the *Castel* to the cheaper vending kiosks in the docks to avoid the commercial district.

Once they transited, that nagging itch eased.

The Inner World half of the Eskarion Ring was noticeably busier than its Rim-side counterpart. Space traffic was heavier with more small craft, cargo ships, and passenger liners, and fewer freighters and traders than on the Rim. The traffic posed only a minor irritation; she'd transited through Eskarion so often she could have done it blindfolded with one ear to Ring control.

With supplies topped off, there was nothing to keep them hanging around the constellation. That left them almost two decs to make their way to Lyrel—and Amin and the auction.

Unfortunately, since she flew from Eskarion to Lyrel frequently and the course was regularly patrolled, the autopilot could readily handle most of the route between Jumps and stops at stations. That meant time hung heavy on her hands. However much she might want to make the most of having a man to warm her sheets, she could make love only so often before it became too much of a good thing.

The more time she spent with Romir, the more she wanted to know about him. And her heart railed against his slavery, that he was trapped in the "undying existence" of a djinn.

There had to be a way to free him.

Asrial stared at the rare example of Majian pottery. Intact. The only one of its kind, to her knowledge, which made it precious beyond belief. Glowing a golden brown, the flask represented so many possibilities. A complete and thorough upgrade for the *Castel*. Her promise to her cousins to visit. Seed capital for her emergency fund.

But no matter the cost, she couldn't sell Romir's prison. Selling it was unconscionable, and mourning the lost credits was a waste of time.

Despite her Rim rat's disappointment, she suspected her parents would have approved. Whatever her circumstances, however much she might try to forget, she'd been raised a sovreine, and a sovreine was supposed to consider what was best for those under her care. For Jamyl Kharym Rashad of House Dilaryn that had meant abdication; for her that meant freeing Romir.

Fact of the matter was, she probably wouldn't make enough on her cargo to refurbish the *Castel*, not if she was serious about freeing Romir. To do that, she needed more funds.

She'd have to sell the Dilaryn jewels. Though she'd steeled herself to the necessity, though she'd never worn them nor had any intention to do so, the decision still felt like a betrayal of her father. Her parents had worked so hard as traders—shuttling around a group of star systems while raising her in the *Castel.* They'd managed without selling a single piece. Despite his abdication, her father had considered it as much a sacred trust as Salima, House Dilaryn's hereditary domain on Lomida. She'd kept that in mind when repairing the *Castel* after the pirate attack that had killed them.

But searching for a way to free Romir meant extraordinary expenses over and above those she incurred as a Rim rat. There would be added costs in time and research. But she'd meant it, then and now, when she vowed to free him. She couldn't weld her hopes to another big find. She needed to secure funds now, not some nebulous point in the future.

Her heart shuddered like a failing thruster, laboring to move blood turned cold, but she'd never been one to avoid unpleasant duties. Best to catalog the jewels now and choose which to sell. Putting it off till later wouldn't make it any easier.

Entering the cabin where she'd stored her parents' belongings for safekeeping was unexpectedly difficult. The barren sterility of the space brought back the shock of their deaths and the disbelief of the succeeding days. Gathering their possessions and putting them away had been an exercise in tears and pain. She hadn't had the heart to dispose of anything, even though it cut into the *Castel*'s available storage space.

"Lights, full." With trembling fingers, Asrial keyed open the locker with her mother's finery. The gems sparkled in a blinding display of wealth—crowns, rings, pins, necklaces, earrings, bracelets, armlets, whatever-lets—many of which her mother had probably never worn, the gaudy and ancient designs, especially. Most had come to Nasri upon her marriage into House Dilaryn, but she never used them that Asrial could remember.

"Never forget that you were born a sovreine." Her mother had been insistent. But Asrial preferred to do precisely that. The accident of her birth had never done her any good.

There were more treasures—the priceless historical tracts that were her mother's delight, all loaded onto thousands of memory cubes, precisely cataloged. Nasri had been a historian at heart and by training. Asrial had lost count of the number of times she'd found a gem of information that had helped her with her relics. But those were tucked out of sight, their data accessible through the *Castel*'s comp.

Her eyes skimmed past an intricate earring with dangling swirls of gold and diamonds that looped and relooped in a three-dimensional replica of the symbol of Lomidar royalty. Nasri had worn it, but Asrial had no intention of taking up those airs. She didn't style herself a sovreine and saw no reason to pretend otherwise even in the privacy of her own ship.

From among the glittering array, she pulled out one of her mother's favorites, an ancient enameled square with a strange design and a chain apparently added so it could be worn as a pendant. Nasri had traced its provenance to the first decades of Lomidar history. Handed down within House Dilaryn, it was the only one she couldn't sell, bound as she was by the entail. It would be her daughter's should she ever have a daughter; as the last of House Dilaryn, she didn't have a niece nor a nephew's wife to receive it.

"Why, Mama?"

"It is a promise." Nasri's answer never changed, never wavered, even when Asrial was older. But what that promise was, her mother had never said—probably just another sacred trust, worded for a child's understanding.

Raising the square to the light, she took a moment to once again admire the colorful design that had attended her childhood. Happy memories. The fractals had always fascinated her, even as a child—Nasri had stories of using the necklace to lull her to sleep.

The cabin door's seals gave a soft hiss, the only hint that she was no longer alone. Still holding the necklace between her hands,

Asrial turned, certain she would see Romir. After more than two decs with him on board, she'd adjusted to his constant presence.

"Where did you get that?" His voice was weak, breathless, as though he'd taken a body blow. His gaze was locked on her hands, his eyes stricken, thin silver rings around circles of haunted black.

A roaring in her ears filled her with dread. What now? Why such an extreme reaction to an old necklace? Except for its age and the nostalgia invested in it, there was nothing special about the necklace. "I inherited it from my mother."

"Your mother?" His head jerked up, his eyes darting around the cabin as if expecting to see Nasri.

Her heart clenched, a sudden pang of guilt and loss. The reminder that she would never see her parents again made her lash out. "Don't worry, she's gone. Pirates killed her and my father."

"That was not what I meant." His eyes narrowed with sudden, unsuspected temper, silver sparks flaring beneath dark lashes.

Asrial closed her hands around the pendant protectively, clasping it to her chest. "What did you mean?"

"You are alone. I had not considered the existence of your family. For that discourtesy, you have my apology." Romir gave her a formal bow, absurdly proper in his half-dressed state, his loose pants hanging low on his hips and exposing taut ridges of muscle that drew her eyes to the juncture of his thighs; yet the gesture was fluid and unmistakably sincere. "I . . . would like to know how your mother came to possess such."

Caught up in his intensity, she swallowed down the thickness in her throat, fully aware of her pulse fluttering against her skin. "Through marriage. It's an heirloom of my father's family." House Dilaryn, which was no more. "Why?"

The weight of his gaze on her hands made her self-conscious, given her pose. He wasn't staring at her breasts, but the thing next to them. She uncovered the square and held it out for his inspection.

Sure enough, his attention followed. Despite her discomfort at his stare, the loss of his attention gave her a twinge of pique—an illogical response she couldn't understand.

He turned the pendant over with a finger to reveal an inscription on the back that she'd never noticed before. "This—this was my weaver's badge. I gave it to . . . my betrothed."

Romir had been engaged? The thought that he'd pledged himself to another woman made her heart clench inexplicably.

Without a doubt, it was his badge, given in faith and honor, to complete their troth to twine the skeins of their lives together. He recognized its presence now—a part of him resided in the badge, its design wrought from the pattern of his blood. The weave that bound it to his essence remained intact, a small knot of power amid the threads of creation that tied everything in the universe.

He clenched his hand to keep from touching it.

So many memories were tied to that small square of metal—his parents' joy at the ceremony celebrating his mastery, his lover's acceptance. He wanted none of it. He could not bear to remember what he had lost, those he had failed.

What a bizarre twist of fate for his prison to fall into the hands of the woman who possessed his badge. "An heirloom of your family?"

"It's been handed down through House Dilaryn for centuries," Asrial added with some heat, as if he had accused her of falsehood. She closed her fingers around his badge, protective, possessive, holding it as precious above the lavish display of jewelry behind her.

None of the other jewelry glowed with a power similar to the knot around his badge. That knot would have told anyone with a weaver's sight that he lived—and kept her bound to him. "I am certain it has. She must have wanted it so."

"She?"

"My betrothed." She would have known—or at least suspected—that he had been captured. The knot would have dissipated at his death, leaving her free of their troth, and she could set his badge aside in all honor to pledge to another. Had she wed after his capture, she could not have given his badge to be handed down.

Yet another betrayal on his part: to have bound her to him without hope of release. It had been selfish of him to do so in the midst of war with the Mughelis.

Averting his eyes, he bowed his head. "Forgive me, I do not remember her name." He could not bear to remember . . . and stir other memories best left forgotten.

"How could you forget something like that?" Asrial's voice lilted with shock and disbelief. As might be expected from one so openhearted.

"It was necessary." Romir bit his lip, choking down the scenes of death and devastation that fought to rise—the deaths and destruction he had wreaked. To remember what he had lost was the path to insanity.

Asrial stared at him, obvious disappointment thinning her lips, the golden sparks in her eyes muted to a dull brown. Her silence was sufficient condemnation. Of course she did not understand the necessity of forgetting; she would not be the woman she was if she did.

He was glad she did not understand, but still he fled the room and the bitter reminder of his many failures. Such cowardice was easier than seeing himself reduced in her estimation.

Asrial stared at the door of the work cabin, trying to sort out the bewildering storm of emotions Romir's disclosure had roused: confusion at his abrupt departure, shock that he didn't remember the name of a woman so important to him, relief that her rival had no name.

Rival? Wasn't Romir just another man who warmed her sheets? Why such an extreme reaction to a woman long dead? And what did he mean when he said forgetting his betrothed's name had been necessary?

Metal bit into her palm, the smooth edges digging hard lines into her hand. The enameled square pulsed with warmth, the inscription rasping her fingertips. Now that she knew it was there, her incessant curiosity wouldn't let her rest. She had to know what it meant.

She scanned the inscription on the necklace and set the comp to search her mother's library for similar scripts. Identifying a time period would give her a starting point. The search would take time, but time was something they had in abundance on the way to Lyrel 9.

After a short internal debate, Asrial slipped the enamel badge with its chain over her head and tucked it under her T-top. It didn't weigh much, but its invisible presence was warm reassurance. It was her mother's and . . . She huffed, bringing her wandering thoughts back under control. The connection to her mother was all that was important, nothing more.

Romir still hadn't rejoined her by the time she resumed the heart-rending task of cataloging the Dilaryn jewels. She would have welcomed a distraction, but he stayed away, which was unlike him. She usually had to ask him to leave her alone in order to have some privacy.

This was the first time she'd examined the Dilaryn jewels in their entirety. Nasri had never worn them in Asrial's presence, but her mother had researched their histories and told her about them, just as she'd shared with her the provenance of Romir's badge.

Every piece had a story attached to it, be it Nasri's or Jamyl's or some ancestor's or distant relation's. Great or small, those stories were the history of House Dilaryn.

And here she was, planning to sell them.

Guilt scraped her nerves yet again. But really, if she was an ordinary Rim rat, there was no reason for her to hang on to such things. Weren't they just excess weight that took up storage space? It was high time she disposed of them.

Time crept by on broken limbs, painful and unconscionably slow. Stubborn pride kept her tapping away on the data logger, determined to finally complete this one task before they reached Lyrel 9. After all, there was nothing else to do while waiting for the drive to power up between Jumps.

Four Jumps later, Romir was still avoiding her. He was around. Asrial sometimes caught glimpses of him out of the corner of her eye, but he played least in sight, appearing just when she began to worry that his prison had pulled him back. Puzzling over his unusual behavior got her through the catalog of the Dilaryn jewels, but it was a relief to finish.

So strange. She'd thought she preferred to be alone. Hadn't she been looking forward to regaining her solitude? Yet now, though Romir had been on the *Castel* for only decs, when she was alone, it felt wrong—lonely.

Asrial rubbed her eyes, trying to throw off the gloom. If this kept up, she might find herself in tears.

The flask called to her, the one connection to Romir in the cabin. Just holding it made her feel less alone. His prison fascinated her. Why this shape? Why the etchings? How could pottery contain a djinn? She studied the designs etched on its neck, wondering if they had some purpose other than decoration.

Though she knew how easily appearances could deceive, she still had difficulty viewing the rare piece of golden brown pottery as a prison. What did the blend of slavery and art say about the Mughelis? Was the shape a deliberate choice, or was it simply a result of whatever had been done to Romir to make him a djinn?

Despite the climate control's night setting, the flask was warm and seemed to invite her touch. The curve of the base and the stretch of long neck fit her hands as if made for them. The edges of the etching were smooth, lacking a burr. She traced the design with wondering fingers. It was almost as if it had been stamped on the flask, not etched, yet it seemed too fine for stamping.

"I wish you would not do that." The heated objection nearly jumped Asrial out of her skin. When had Romir joined her in the work cabin?

She fumbled for a better grip on the flask, finally clutching it to her chest to keep it from falling. "Do what?"

He swung his arm, waving at her hands, the gesture so violent she felt the wind of its passage. "Do not touch it."

Taken aback by his vehemence, she stared at him. "Why?"

His hands clenched, opened, then clenched again repeatedly as he glared at the flask, though he did nothing to remove it from her grasp. "I can feel it . . . like hands over me, inside me . . . touching me intimately."

"*What?*" He wasn't just glaring at the flask, he was glaring at—she started when she realized the focus of his fury: her fingers, which were stroking the flask as if they had minds of their own.

Romir turned on his heel and slammed his hands on the bulkhead. His nails gouged old paint off of the metal, gray flakes showering down amid hoarse gasps. His panting filled the work cabin, harsh, rapid and erratic. It hurt just to hear it.

"I can feel it," he repeated in a desperate whisper of horror and yearning, his head hanging down between his arms. He slumped there like a man on the brink of exhaustion or the edge of despair.

Alarmed, she hurriedly set the flask back on the worktable. *He can feel it?* The magnitude of his reaction shocked her, but in the depths of her heart, she was relieved—at least he wasn't avoiding her now.

Though she no longer touched his prison, he continued to pant, his back jerking in an unnerving display of loss of control in so guarded a man.

Asrial went to him, reached out—and stopped. Her hand hovered over his shoulder, indecision holding it back. She was at a loss how to handle him. Since her parents' deaths, she'd spent most of her time in the Rim. Alone.

Romir shuddered, his fists on the bulkhead so tight his knuckles were white. His long hair shielded his face, hanging down his chest in a straight fall of black that swayed to his pain.

Guilt scored her. She was the cause of his distress, however unintentional. She had to do something. Steeling her nerve, she wrapped her arms around his waist and pressed her cheek against his broad back.

His chest quaked under her hands as he struggled to regain control. And it was a struggle, she could tell. His chest's motion was proof of it: he'd forgotten he didn't need to breathe.

"Did it hurt?" Had her thoughtlessness contributed to his pain?

Romir flinched at her question. He wasn't one to put his vulnerability on display. "No, it did not. It felt . . . good. Too good."

Pleasure? "What's wrong with that? Make me understand."

Make her understand? He wanted to laugh. He could not make her do anything. A djinn had no such freedom.

A fleeting caress of soft lips on his nape sent a shiver through Romir. Her hands were flat on his belly, living heat branding him with Asrial's essence. She remained pressed against him. The heat of her body along his back did not shift, the softness against his shoulder blades an external delight unlike the sensations from his prison.

"Talk to me. Please."

Romir buried his face in his hands, ashamed to the depths of his soul by his outburst. He thought he had nothing more left in him, but this illusion of freedom proved him wrong: some shred of foolish hope remained. Nevertheless, his fraying control was no excuse. He owed her an explanation.

"It felt as when the Mughelis controlled me. Those unnatural sensations where no hands could touch. That they did not hurt only made it worse." When the vyziers commanded him, the touch on his prison bound his will, including the pleasure that swirled through him. His masters had used that pleasure against him, tormenting him for no reason other than that they could. He had not been a lover of men to welcome pleasure inflicted by their mastery. "And they did it while commanding me to destroy my people."

Asrial inhaled sharply. "I apologize. I didn't know."

He bowed his head, weary with futile anger. If this form could have cried, he would have. "I am not free. I am still bound to the eternal death of a djinn. I will always be bound."

Grabbing his shoulder, she pulled him toward her. When he resisted, she pushed forward to stand between him and the wall. "You mustn't think that."

"Must I not?" If the period of his enslavement could be counted in centuries—in millennia—as she said, freedom was a forlorn hope. The gods had abandoned him long ago.

Twelve

Asrial stretched her arms wide, her joints cracking as she worked through the tension from the last Jump. No matter how many times she'd brought the *Castel* through Jump, the suspense and the exhilaration remained the same. There was always the risk of something going wrong, especially in a ship as old as hers. She had yet to grow tired of it.

Beside her, Romir released the straps of his shock harness and got to his feet without any hesitation. He'd explained how such safety measures were unnecessary for a djinn but continued to use them—to placate her, she suspected. His face was bereft of expression, displaying none of the despair he harbored in his heart.

A green light on a corner of the board blinked to life: the comp notifying her of a task completed. She waited until Romir left; after each Jump, he went to the engine room without fail, to marvel at what he called a vortex. She couldn't tell what he found so interesting about staring at a motionless piece of equipment, but that was what he did. That was all he did—just stare—he didn't touch anything. Not that he needed to touch to do whatever he did to manipulate electronics.

Once the door of the pilot chamber sealed behind him, she accessed the comp, tilting her seat to lounge in comfort.

The translation of the badge's inscription had run its course. The search had taken a while, since the comp wasn't an AI and her mother's library was extensive, covering both Inner World and Rim planets, and she hadn't set any limits.

The comp had found similarities to first-century Lomidar script . . . and to Mougal script. From Majian texts. Two planets, one an Inner World, the other on the Rim, separated by nearly 25,000 light-years. What were the chances of that happening? Surely that was too small for coincidence.

Then there were the translations.

Lomidar: *Romir Gadaña. Weaver. Sixth skein. 45.6.2179. Promise.*

Mougal: *Romir Gadaña. Strand puller. Sixth level master. 45.6.2179. Vow.*

Almost exactly the same.

Her heart skipped a beat.

Two different planets separated by thousands of light-years. What were the odds of that? She hadn't expected to find confirmation of Romir's claim this easily.

"It was our greatest working."

Once again the magnitude of such a feat took her breath away. To bridge two points, not only separated by thousands of light-years but also located within the slopes of planetary gravity wells, and even more—within atmospheres—they should have failed. Yet here was evidence that they'd succeeded.

She slipped the badge from under her T-top and off her neck, turning it over to study the inscription on the reverse.

"It is a promise."

The slight roughness under her thumb didn't register as she pondered Nasri's words floating through the back of her mind. The entailment was a promise. Yet of all the Dilaryn jewels, the necklace with Romir's badge was the only one so entailed. Was it significant that it bore the same word?

She activated the comp and opened her mother's file on the necklace's provenance. As she'd thought, its history was unbroken, stretching back to the founding of Salima and always in the senior Dilaryn line—from mother to eldest son's wife or to firstborn daughter or niece. Nasri had been meticulous in her avocation; there could be no doubting her research.

So what could be so important that the badge alone of all the Dilaryn jewels was entailed?

Asrial still had not come to any conclusion when the door to the pilot chamber hissed open.

"What promise?"

Romir's slight smile faded, his face going blank with confusion as the door slid shut behind him. "I do not follow."

"Your badge." She flicked a hand at the scan on the comp, directing his attention to the image as she slipped the badge back under her T-top. "The inscription includes 'Promise.' What promise?"

He tipped his head to one side as he peered at the screen. "That was not there when I had it."

Asrial pressed her fist to her mouth, nibbling on a knuckle as she thought. It had been added later, after he'd given it to his betrothed? Did that make *Promise* in the inscription more significant?

"You think it is important."

"Don't you think it is?" It frustrated her that he wasn't more excited. The inscription might be a wild jump, but it was a definite link to his people and a better lead than nothing and just searching at random.

"What I think does not matter."

Her heart clenched at hearing such apathy couched in so simple an answer. She grimaced, irritated. Wanting to free him was one thing, just like using him to warm her sheets. She had to remember that was as far as it went. This heartache wasn't part of it; she wasn't going to get more involved. Once he was free, they would go their separate ways.

After all, she had other people to worry about.

But she was getting sidetracked. Convincing Romir of the importance of his opinion wasn't the point; freeing him was. Maybe she was going about her questioning in the wrong way.

"What was she like?" Almost before the words were said, Asrial wished she hadn't asked. She didn't want to hear Romir describe the woman he loved, the one he'd planned to share his life with, but she needed to know. Her nails bit into her palm as she fixed her gaze on the screen.

"I . . . do not remember what she looked like anymore." He closed his eyes at the admission.

Shock shattered her pretense of casualness, and she found herself staring across her shoulder at his tight face.

How could that be? Romir wasn't a shallow man who dispensed his affections wherever he would. The way he'd held off from the full cycle of intimacy proved it. How could he not remember the appearance of someone as important to him as his betrothed? And yet why would he lie?

Asrial bit her lip. She should have been relieved not to have competition, but her heart ached for his loss. "Not her appearance.

What kind of woman was she? Would she have done this as a joke?" She managed to summon a brisk tone from somewhere. Romir didn't look like he'd appreciate any sympathy right then.

His eyes turned distant, blurring with longing she didn't want to see—that she shouldn't have minded seeing. "No."

Looking away, Asrial cleared her throat impatiently. "Then what would this promise of hers be? What's so important that she'd have it engraved on your weaver's badge? Your engagement?" If it was that, then her hope was futile.

"It could not be our betrothal." His calm statement relieved her enough to allow her to look at Romir only to see him cross his arms, his shoulders hunching. Despite his control over his voice, he wasn't as unaffected by the discussion as he pretended to be.

"Then what?"

His brow furrowed in sudden thought, but then he shook his head, dismissing it. "Impossible."

"Tell me."

"She vowed to learn how the Mughelis made djinn . . . and how to break that weave." His right hand rose suddenly, going to his left shoulder to rub the tat adorning it, tracing the arc that gleamed dark blue against his golden skin with distracted strokes. No, not rub—scratch. He used his nails repeatedly as though he could dig out the ink. If he weren't djinn, she would have expected him to draw blood before too long.

Romir stopped when he noticed her looking, jerking his hand down into a self-conscious fist. But after she turned her gaze back to the screen, in the edge of her vision, she saw his hand creep back to his shoulder to resume scratching.

"What is it about that tat? Why do you keep doing that?"

A grim look twisted his face as he jerked his hand away again. "This tat, as you call it, is the mark the Mughelis place on djinn—or so we surmised. I did not have this black star before my capture."

She studied it carefully. There was nothing menacing about the design of the tat. When viewed from the front or back, all she could see was a dark blue arc with flares shooting out from it. She could see the complete design only when she stood on his left: a circle with wild flares in all directions. "Black star?"

"Yes, it is indigo, but *black star* is what we called the djinn mark. It seemed appropriate, a perversion of nature." He pressed his fists together, their trembling betraying a struggle for control—a struggle she would be better off ignoring if she wanted to keep some emotional distance between them.

Sidetracked again. Frigging crap, she couldn't seem to keep her mind on course. What were they talking about?

Promise, that was it.

"So she was trying to free djinn. No," Asrial corrected herself, raising a finger in emphasis, "she *promised* to free djinn?"

"She made it her life's work, after her brother was captured. She would have known I was . . . alive and likely in Mugheli hands. But for it to mean she succeeded—" Running his fingers through his hair, Romir shook his head. "That is impossible."

Frustration swelled at his hasty dismissal. "Why not? What if this promise really is the knowledge of how to break this djinn weave? Don't you think it's worth pursuing?"

"I would give anything to be free of this deathless servitude. But the best minds of the Academe spent years trying to unravel that cursed weave. We all tried—to no avail." The fear in his eyes, that weathered look of failure and old disappointments that shadowed the silver to gray, weighed on her heart. In his time as a djinn, what had happened that he behaved like this? From what little he had slipped about the Mughelis and what she'd seen on Maj, she wasn't sure she wanted to know.

But if Romir couldn't hope—was afraid to hope—she would

do so for both of them. It was better than the alternative. But now that she had a lead, what to do about it?

Asrial ground her hand on her chest, feeling the badge under her palm. Instinct said she had the right of it. She had until the auction on Lyrel 9 to decide her course.

Thirteen

"**It is different**—neater than the other stations." Leaning forward, Romir tipped his head to one side as he considered his screen. He had it set on visual as they approached Lyrel 9, and the station loomed large.

Little remained of the station of her childhood. Bubble cars replaced the speed seats that ferried people between the arms of the station. So much had been changed in the reconstruction. The maze of annex corridors she'd explored with her cousins were gone, relegated to history.

Asrial had to laugh at her nostalgia. And they wondered why she preferred the Rim where change came more slowly.

"Something amuses you?"

"It's not important." She shifted the *Castel* to a different space lane in obedience to Lyrel 9 control's instructions, passing below a passenger liner undocking from the station in preparation for departure. The liner was an entirely different ship from the *Castel*, with entire stretches of bulkhead made up of transparent sapphire—much like the new Lyrel 9, now that she thought of it. They must give passengers an exceptional view of space, though. "It's different because it's new construction."

"You do not approve."

The astute comment had her glancing at him in surprise. What had he seen that prompted that comment? "I prefer the system it had before."

His answer was a waiting silence—and he waited well with an expectant silence that was a demand in itself. All very polite . . . and something she couldn't seem to ignore. He was good at that. His silence was worth several cubes of scholarly tracts.

"I don't like the bubble cars. Sure, they're safer than the speed seats in the event of a catastrophic decompression, but they're slower, and you have to wait on their schedules. The speed seats were faster; you just got a seat and joined the flow in the tubes. The system zipped you to your destination and—it was fun." She and her cousins had delighted in zipping around Lyrel 9, back when Jamyl and Nasri were still alive. The thought woke a pang of old pain, and she continued in a subdued tone, "It was the closest you could get to feeling the wind in your hair, here in space."

The arms of Lyrel 9 stretched out like the radials of a spider's web she'd seen on Gehna with the aforementioned bubble cars traversing the spaces between them in concentric rings, like mobile beads of dew. The larger ships docked perpendicular to the arms, almost as though caught by the web.

Rather similar to her situation.

Except those ships could get away. She was tangled in a web of love and duty, fighting to get ahead.

"Asri-*ki*, you look well." Despite the deep scars across his cheeks and throat, Amin had a broad smile for her, greeting her the way he always had from toddling child to grown woman. It pained her to see him like this, a shell of his former stocky self. Now, only his floater kept his head at her height, and the smell of antiseptic constantly surrounded him.

He had been a large, vital man—a genial giant to a little girl—going about his duties with a spring in his stride, and as a deputy administrator of Lyrel 9, those duties had been many. Until a cargo ship crashed into the station. The credit crunchers of the Paxis conglomerate had retired him on permanent disability. They'd granted him lodgings on the rebuilt Lyrel 9, but the pittance of a stipend they paid didn't stretch to buying and maintaining his floater.

"And you." Asrial squeezed his hand, returning his smile automatically. His use of her pet name brought to mind happier memories, and anyway, railing at the whims of fortune and corporate bods wouldn't help him.

"Your cousins miss you. You should visit more often." She hadn't been able to stay long, after her last return from the Rim with the disappointing take from the Vogan relics. "You know there's a mug of xoclat waiting for you at home," Amin added, sweetening his bribe. Xoclat was a luxury she would never buy for herself, but Amin's wife indulged once in a while, though she kept an otherwise tight grip on the family's credits. He knew Asrial would have difficulty passing up the offer.

"I miss them, too. But it can't be helped."

Amin's children treated her more like an elder sister than a distant cousin. They'd been close in childhood, but every time she returned to Lyrel 9, there were changes. When she was younger, they were mostly physical changes—her cousins growing taller or developing breasts or a deeper voice. She'd accepted those as natural, but the more recent changes were traumatic: Jamyl's and Nasri's deaths, Amin's paralysis. Now, even minor changes seemed to foster more distance between her and her remaining family.

But it really couldn't be helped. She'd have to sell the *Castel* if she wanted to tie herself to the Lyrel constellation. No job in the area could support her as well as cover Amin's medical expenses. While his daughters, Ghala and Minu, had completed their apprenticeships, they were so junior in their trades that the pay wasn't much.

"Unfortunately, yes. Well, let us transfer your load to the vault so you can relax." Amin spun his floater around nimbly and nodded to the work gang he'd brought, trusted friends one and all and a mixed bag of races. He might no longer be an admin bod, but he still had his connections among the old dockhands.

Asrial waved them to the hold, equally eager to move the Majian relics to a more secure location. Inuoie, an old dockhand and one of Amin's oldest friends, straightened to his full height and swayed his arms through a stylized gesture of Honored Greeting that ended in a pose of Joyful Esteem, the Ruxilian's extra joints and elongated body adding a sinuous grace to the courtesy. Inuoie might have risen from dockhand to admin bod, but decades away from his home world hadn't erased his taste for the dance of manners, as he called it—a good thing, since the bony plates of Ruxilian faces denied them the mobility and expression of Lomidari.

She smiled and nodded in acknowledgment. A sovreine might attempt to match his greeting, but she was a Rim rat. No amount of training would let her answer with equal grace, and anything less would make a mockery of the courtesy.

Anyway, Inuoie didn't expect it of her, as he proved by dropping his pose and joining the rest of the work gang waiting for the hold's rising hatch to lock open. He'd taken the time to teach a young girl how to read something of Ruxilian manners, but the gestures were intended for more joints than she had, and she'd never mastered the performance of them.

"Who is that?" Amin's eyes shifted to a point over her shoulder.

She followed his gaze to the *Castel*'s hatch where Romir stood, watching the approaching work gang with rather obvious wariness. Thinking to divert Amin's attention, she'd gone ahead to greet him, leaving Romir to exit the *Castel* later. She should have known the older man would still take notice.

Despite Romir having his hair tied back and wearing spacer garb, he had an air about him that marked him as other. Not a port tough. Not quite grounder. But not an admin bod, either.

"That's Romir Gadaña, he's . . ." How to explain his presence? She couldn't say he was a djinn she hoped to free, and calling him her lover would make her sound like a galaxy-class idiot; either way Amin would think she'd taken leave of her senses. "He's crewing for me on this trip."

Her answer resulted in a sudden narrowing of eyes and a loss of easy humor.

"Crewing? You had not mentioned wanting crew. I could have recommended someone." Though he was her mother's cousin, he'd been like an uncle to her, doting on her whenever they'd stopped on Lyrel 9. He felt some responsibility for her with Nasri dead, even though Asrial had already reached adulthood when her parents were killed.

Asrial fought down a flush at his stare, feeling the weight of his disappointment. "It was a recent decision. Romir was available."

That answer earned Romir a longer look. "Are you sure he can be trusted?" The slack flesh around Amin's jaw emphasized his unease, quivering as he clenched his teeth. His enthusiastic greeting had blinded her to it until now, but he'd lost more weight since she'd last seen him. Yet his concern was all for her.

"Romir's fine. Don't worry."

"You cannot blame me for worrying, Asri-*ki*. Ever since your parents' deaths, you have flown alone. But now you appear with this *long-haired* crew hand." The grimace that accompanied his *long-haired* comment made his objection clear: only grounders wore their hair long. "Why him?"

Asrial waved a hand, dismissing all import. "It was just a matter of timing, convenience. Nothing much, really. I needed a hand, and he was there."

How could she explain Romir's situation to her mother's cousin? Amin himself had told her and his children stories of djinn and evil sorcerers and the heroes who triumphed over them. Without a demonstration of Romir's powers, he'd think her mad to believe Romir was a djinn.

"He's a big help with maintenance on the *Castel*."

"Eh?"

"He has a feel for the electronics," she added. That much was true. She wouldn't have dared any of the Rings if she hadn't been able to isolate the problem with the control runs. She had Romir to thank for that. "I'm lucky he's with me."

"The *Castel* is an old ship. I suppose there are not that many techs in the Inner Worlds that would be familiar with her class." Despite the conciliatory words, a frown still creased Amin's brow, one that cleared when he added, "But with this, you will be able to upgrade her. Finally."

Asrial only smiled, unwilling to commit herself. Guilt squirmed in her belly at misleading him even that much. Amin had been like a second father to her. The omission felt almost as bad as a lie.

She beckoned Romir to join them. He immediately straightened from his slouch against the hatch, his gaze sharpening with concern then flicking around the bay. She bit her cheek to suppress a smile. It looked like her paranoia had rubbed off on him.

Romir stalked through the chaos of dockhands unloading the *Castel*, seeming to pay them little more than a glance. But he reached her side with quick efficiency, while nimbly avoiding several would-be collisions. His performance was a joy to watch, the ripple of muscle and long, sure strides easy on the eyes. He walked with a confidence that sent a thrill up her spine.

Pride and delight mixed with bemusement in an unsettling brew of emotions. She'd never reacted like this to a man before and didn't know what to make of it.

Amin's face darkened at seeing the true length of Romir's bound hair, which marked him as grounder to most spacers. But after a sharp glance at her, he refrained from comment. She sensed the influence of one of her cousins behind his discretion. Perhaps a paternal lecture gone awry? Whatever the cause, she was grateful, unwilling to explain Romir's situation with so many ears around.

After the *Castel* was unloaded and the Majian relics secure in a station vacuum vault, Asrial went with Amin to his quarters, Romir a quiet shadow by her shoulder. The fog of antiseptic that accompanied Amin was more noticeable.

Her mother's cousin maneuvered his floater well, taking corners easily, but beneath the smile he kept on his face, he looked tired. She'd have to ask his wife, Hana, the results of his latest medical checkup.

"Asri-*ki*, you need not worry so about me."

"Of course." Asrial nodded, stretching an agreeable smile across her face. "But you know me. I'll worry all the same."

"Do not waste my breath, in other words?"

"Save it for more important things, like how Ghala, Minu, and Khayri are doing."

With a low laugh of surrender, Amin gave in, allowing her to divert the conversation to her cousins. The three were all younger than she. At nineteen, Khayri was the youngest and as the only boy somewhat spoiled by women's attentions; his antics made for good stories, and Amin related the latest with vigor.

Asrial sat back on the old couch in the living room, relaxing in the embrace of family. She'd missed this on the long ventures into the Rim. And if she wasn't mistaken, Romir enjoyed it as well; though he hadn't unbent so far as to slouch, his face had lost a measure of tension as Amin told his stories.

Soon enough it neared the end of shift for her cousins and Hana. After they got home, there would be no more talk of business. "How're the preparations for the auction coming along?"

Amin nodded to his worktable where a printout lay beside the comp. He had a voice-activated setup and server bots programmed to deal with those routine tasks he could no longer perform. "The list of interested buyers. Most of them have already arrived. The inspection is scheduled for tomorrow and the auction on the day after."

Picking up the sheet, she scanned the list, blinking at the length and some of the names. She ruffled her hair in thought, excitement bubbling through her veins and tempting her to laughter. The earnest money each name represented would be hefty additions to the coffers, but Amin had also attracted museum buyers.

"Who's Volsung?" She thought she knew the major collectors in the relics market. That was a new name.

Amin twitched his hand in place of a shrug. "Some Cyrian out of Diarid. He heard about the auction from somewhere and insisted on taking part. He even put up the earnest for a place in the auction without haggling. I ran a background check, but nothing suspicious came up, no conglomerate affiliation. His ship plies a trade route in Wainek."

An Inner Worlds trader, then. Lack of conglomerate backing would explain why he serviced one of the less affluent sectors. But why would he be bidding on Majian relics? Wainek trade wasn't that lucrative—as she well knew. Would a trader like this Volsung spend his own hard-earned funds on rarities that didn't have much of a market in the Wainek sector?

Asrial's fingers itched, instinct and curiosity humming alert to possible opportunity waiting to be exploited. If Volsung fronted a newbie, someone just beginning to amass a collection, perhaps he'd be willing to pay a premium to avoid an auction?

The long hall Amin had reserved for the inspection of the Majian relics echoed with the hurried footsteps of trusted dockhands overseen and commanded by Amin's old friend, Inuoie.

From the sidelines, Asrial watched with rapt attention the Ruxilian's writhing as he shifted from Respectful Disagreement with a subtle twist of Irritation to Tentative Approval to . . . a pose she couldn't read, all within a matter of heartbeats. "It's like he's dancing."

Beside her, Amin chuckled. "You were always fascinated by Ruxilians, even as a child."

The memory made her smile. The pageant of races never failed to entertain her. It was never the same; there was always something different: a change in the players, in their goals, in their priorities, in their spheres of influence. But for the most part, it had nothing to do with her. She was safe in her role as observer, so long as she avoided Dareh territory.

Amin glanced at Romir standing among the Majian artifacts waiting to be placed on display, then angled his floater to face her. "I still have my doubts about the wisdom of your having a grounder as crew."

"We'll have to agree to disagree. Anyway, there's something else I wanted to talk about." Her heart clenched, a sliver of pain sharp and sudden that made her lungs seize.

"I am all ears."

"I want you to explore the possibility of . . . selling the Dilaryn jewels." Now that she'd said it, she felt strange, as if she'd stepped out of an airlock into zero grav and the vacuum of deep space.

Dumbstruck silence spoke louder than any words Amin could have said. Though her mother's cousin had been a spacer since before she was born, he was still Lomidari. He understood—probably better than she did—the implications of the sale. Disposing of the Dilaryn jewels dispersed the history of House Dilaryn; it was another step in dissolving the house.

"But—ah—you, you are the *sraya*. As sovreine, even if not the enthroned *reis* . . ." The faltering words stumbled into renewed silence.

"Feelers only," she hurried to assure Amin, her cheeks going cold then hot in turns. "It might not be necessary, but I'd like to know my options."

Slumping in the floater, he stared at her with troubled eyes. "If that is what you wish."

"It is." She forced the words past gritted teeth, feeling like a traitor to all the Dilaryns who had gone before her. She laced her clammy hands behind her to hide their trembling. Best she get used to the idea. She would have to sell the jewels, sooner or later.

Amin closed his eyes, a pained expression crossing his face before he bowed his head in submission. "As you wish, *Sraya*."

She bit her cheek, catching her useless protest before it left her lips. No more was said as the setup was completed. Nothing more needed to be said. He'd addressed her as sovreine for the first time in her life, making his objection clear, and she had heard him.

The doors to the hall were opened, and the first of the buyers entered, a tall Ruxilian, his elongated body graceful in a dark blue rasteen tunic and a retinue of tiny Jenins swarming around him in a flurry of wings. The two races were native to Gehna and had some sort of codependent relationship. In space, Ruxilians were rarely seen alone, and Jenins were always in the company of a Ruxilian. Inuoie was the only Ruxilian she'd met who had no Jenin retinue.

The Ruxilian danced forward, his pose shifting from Polite Interest to Minor Doubt and Quiet Disagreement to Subtle Reprimand then another and another in continuous, fluid, silent conversation. The Jenins fluttered around him, leaving enough room for him to gesture and no farther.

Asrial left them to Amin, not wanting to undermine his role. This was just the preliminary stage where the buyers scrutinized the items on auction. Familiar faces circulated the room, wiped clean of all emotion. No one wanted to tip their hand on which relics interested them for fear of driving up the bidding, but the various reactions she caught confirmed her instincts: this was a major haul.

A robot clamp rotated the trifle box, displaying the underside for a buyer's inspection. Try though they might to disguise it, the close scrutiny and thorough examination hinted at strong interest.

Relief gave her heart wings. It was too early yet to bank the profits from the sales, but she could hope. Perhaps she wouldn't need to put the Dilaryn jewels up for sale. It would eliminate a point of contention with Amin.

A sway of electric blue at the edge of her vision gave her pause. The blue had been optic hair, but that was the only eye-catching thing about this Cyrian. He had the lanky physique of most of his race, and his attire was modest. Unlike many of the other buyers, he walked alone, unattended by a flock of hangers-on. Since she didn't recognize him, he had to be Volsung.

Remembering her speculation about the Inner Worlds trader, she smiled. Here was a potential source for additional creds. They needed all of those they could get.

Romir kept to the edges of the chamber, fascinated by the mix of races who had come to bid on the artifacts. That so many had come so far, crossing the abyss between worlds, simply to obtain such commonplace items like a trifle box, no matter how prettily decorated, was a constant source of astonishment.

To think he had lived to see such a sight. Yet he had seen a similar variety on the different stations en route to this one, and at no time had there been any hint of Mugheli presence. Slowly he was coming to believe that his people's enemy was truly gone from this universe.

None of the bidders were of the horned race Asrial called Hagnash, and he wondered at the lack. There were no Tehld, either, for which he was grateful. That one encounter with a hive had been disconcerting. But there were representatives of other races: dancerlike Ruxilians, large-eyed Xers, Cyrians with their bright hair, Lomidari, and others he could not name.

As Romir watched, a Cyrian swaggered by, barely paying any notice to the artifacts—unless he saw someone looking his way. He seemed distracted. If this had been Parvin, he would have suspected the Cyrian of spying for the enemy. The subterfuge hinted at dishonest motives.

He shook off the dread that threatened to spoil his enjoyment of the scene. There was no war here. At worst, the Cyrian might be a thief. However, the security around the artifacts precluded theft during the viewing, so there was no reason for him to be concerned.

Despite the spectacle before him, his attention returned once again to the levitating chair.

Asrial's kin had been a surprise in this new universe. Most of the people he had encountered appeared uncommonly healthy, however strange their form. This Amin with his wizened body in his levitating chair was the first he had seen who was not hale.

And yet Romir could not help but see the similarity in their situations. Both of them were trapped: he by the Mugheli weave and the other man in his body. Amin, however, would eventually escape, if only through death. Romir could not help but envy him. Even with his limitations, the other man had family and a purpose, friends, a future.

Again his mood threatened to turn dark. This self-pity would not do. In receiving Asrial's care, he was already fortunate beyond measure.

"Gadaña." The hail was accompanied by a pungent miasma of strange odors emanating from the levitating chair, a tangible cloud of wrongness that stained the very air.

To avoid giving offense, Romir schooled his face to blankness, his stomach queasy despite the impossibility of nausea as a djinn. He bowed to the other man and followed him to a side chamber hidden from the view of the visiting buyers.

"Have you seen Captain Dilaryn?" Asrial's kin treated Romir with extreme suspicion. Romir could not fault him for that, not when the object of his care was Asrial; but for the ailing man to approach him now implied great concern. "It is most unlike her to stay away during an auction."

"She went to speak with one of the buyers." Romir frowned at the door through which Asrial had left, the uneasy sensation of earlier deepening into dread. Now that he thought of it, she had been gone for some time. "She did not say which one, but she has not returned."

"She was not seen leaving. But with all the coming and going, it would be easy to miss one woman." The fingers on the chair's controls twitched, belying the attempt at confidence.

"Amin." The Ruxilian who had supervised the unloading of the *Castel* ran to them, gesturing strangely—not the wave for attracting attention nor the hand flick of a summons. Restless motion. Agitation with none of the grace he had displayed when Romir had first seen him.

"Inuoie." The ailing man turned a face of fearful hope to the newcomer, his concern plain for all to see. "Asrial?"

The bony plates of the Ruxilian's head were inexpressive, but his long fingers moved jerkily, the arms stiff with tension. "No, but a Jenin was found dead nearby. Killed by stunner blast. I have seen such before."

Romir realized this Inuoie meant one of the tiny winged beings that accompanied the Ruxilian buyer. One had been flitting around near Asrial earlier; he had noticed since the Jenins reminded him of the *mazzi* the Mughelis used for spying; such small, light creatures were easily overlooked, especially when they were motionless. Now one was dead, and Asrial was missing.

Fourteen

Her entire body ached—and not in a good way. Even her thumbs and cheeks hurt. As if all her muscles had suffered a massive cramp. Simultaneously. Total system meltdown. Asrial couldn't prevent a groan from escaping. She hated stunner hang-overs. Lucky for her, she hadn't bitten her tongue.

What had happened? A bar brawl? Bar jaunts were the only times she'd been stunned, but she hadn't taken part in one of those in ages. These days, she preferred to avoid the fines.

But wait . . . she was on Lyrel 9, and she made a point not to get into trouble on that station.

Memories started to trickle back. *The auction! That's right.* She'd been with Amin and . . .

Her head throbbed like it was going to shake itself to pieces, and her swollen fingers weren't far behind. She thrust back the darkness clinging to her thoughts. Even if she could do nothing about her situation at the moment, it was still better to know what she faced.

Pressure on her stomach and blood rushing to her head told her she was slung over something bony. She wasn't in the hands of station security, that was for certain. They used bots to handle stun cases.

"Put her there." The nasal voice combined with the awkward stress on the consonants identified the speaker to her ear: Volsung. The sneaky, spindly Cyrian bastard.

The one carrying her dumped her on the deck, the impact adding insult to injury—stars went nova inside her head. A Hagnashr. It figured. They usually forgot the other races weren't as tough as they were.

Feeling all too vulnerable lying on her back and unable to move, she glared at the Cyrian, silently cursing him and her temporary paralysis. She couldn't even get her throat to work properly.

"You're awake." Volsung smiled insincerely, electric blue optic hair waving about like a tangle of live cables. "Nothing personal. This is just business."

Another Hagnashr towered behind the bastard, as broad as the rest of his race. Three to one. Even if she could twitch a finger to fire a stunner, she was outnumbered.

They stood around her as though having a woman sprawled at their feet were nothing out of the ordinary. She had a bad feeling the Cyrian wouldn't cavil at slave running.

The Hagnashr who'd carried her pinched her arm between thick, blunt fingers, a contemplative look on his broad face. "Skinny, soft. Need to mark her up if you want good money." He flexed a thick arm thoroughly covered with livid, puckered scars.

"Hands off, *ga'go*," Volsung ordered in that short-of-breath manner of all Cyrians. Asrial could only wish she could make his shortness of breath a reality: a really tight chokehold would do it or even just two fingers, if one were determined enough—which she was. "She's not for the meat market. The client's paying good credits to get her alive and unharmed."

She went cold. They'd paid the auction earnest simply to get close to her? Who would go to such lengths to get their hands on her? She was a Rim rat. Just a Rim rat.

Several heartbeats passed before those thick fingers released her arm—an eternity to Asrial lying paralyzed on the cold floor. And even if she weren't stunned, she couldn't yet draw an easy breath: that delay suggested Volsung's command over his crew was shaky.

The other Hagnashr looked familiar. Though he stood more than a head taller than Volsung, he was small for his race. One of his horns looked like it had broken off in a fight, but the tip of the stump had been sharpened to a wicked point. When he turned to snarl at his companion, the new angle jarred her memory: Eskarion 14. One of the gamblers near the *Castel*'s bay. His presence there hadn't been a coincidence. They'd followed her from the Rim to Lyrel 9—which meant Volsung's history as an Inner Worlds trader was all a sham to get her to drop her guard.

Her abduction had to be part of some greater scheme. If just any Rim rat would do, they could have taken someone on Eskarion 14. But they hadn't. They wanted her—specifically.

"That is enough." Volsung jerked his chin toward the door, a unspoken order to precede him. The Hagnash obeyed with much grumbling and dark looks, a mismatched pair of hulking threat—as if her lying paralyzed on the floor wasn't enough.

The door hissed as they approached, then slid open. They were met by a tall Xer who came to the top of the shorter Hagnashr's shoulders and an otherwise empty corridor. Squinting large red eyes at the tablet he held at arm's length, the Xer started talking. "I got us moved to a slot in tomorrow's second transit. That was the earliest Rakel could fit us in."

Volsung made a strange sound halfway between a whistling chirp and a grunt. "It'll have to do. Recall the crew and—"

The door's closure cut off the rest of the conversation, but her situation was clear: she was on a ship, and they planned to depart within the next station cycle. An earlier departure because they had what they'd come for?

Asrial cursed and didn't bother to do it silently. Running her mouth and doing it properly helped to distract her from her situation—which didn't look good. Amin would wonder where she'd gone, but would it be in time? Station admin couldn't search a ship without strong evidence. Convincing them to lock down a ship would be even more difficult. While they were busy going through all the proper channels, this ship would have left already.

Taking her with it.

Volsung would get away with her kidnapping.

Her muscles twitched uncontrollably as they recovered from the stunner beam. The misery of the constant shivers only heightened her damnable helplessness. Even if she somehow got her hands on a stunner, she wouldn't be able to hold it—much less aim it.

She would fail Amin . . . and Romir.

No one knew to look for her. She'd gone off with Volsung to discuss business without word to anyone. A few clicks of her time, he'd said, mentioning a premium for acquisition of a particular Majian artifact, and was she interested in discussing a contract? She'd taken the bait like an idiot, not passing him on to Amin, since she wasn't certain she would accept.

His few clicks were shaping into the rest of her—probably short—life.

Frustration had Asrial at the point of tears, the walls blurring before her eyes. She could barely move her head. They must have blasted her several times for the paralysis to linger so long. At this rate, Volsung would leave the station before she got back on her feet.

* * *

The energies in the walls distracted his senses, interfering with the thin, gleaming strand Romir sought. He had difficulty singling out the one he wanted among all the threads of power. Asrial lay in that direction—somewhere beyond uncounted intervening barriers.

In danger. Instinct argued the likelihood as high, the thought giving him no peace. She would not have left of her own will without informing Amin. She held her kinsman in such high regard that she would not want him to worry unduly.

He cursed her kinsman's suspicion, understandable though it was. If Amin had sought him out earlier, the trail would not be so tangled. He tugged on the thread connecting him to his badge, the pulse of power he willed through it making it brighten temporarily.

The thread led to one of the dock arms. Unlike Eskarion 14, Lyrel 9 was easy to navigate, its corridors laid out in a discernible pattern. However, certain sections were clearly private: storerooms and the like.

Frustration bit deep into Romir with long, jagged fangs. Already, he had had to backtrack twice, faced with guards at junctions to limited access areas that lay between where he was and the weak pulse that marked Asrial's location. His lack of familiarity with the station's design hindered his search more than his ignorance of the ciphers on the walls. He knew where he had to go, but not which route would get him there. Not on foot. Since he did not know where his destination lay, he could not take one of those bubble cars Asrial derided.

His search would go faster if he did not have to thread his way through the station's corridors. The thought of watchers—spies—gave him only momentary pause. Asrial was more important.

In the next pool of shadow, he misted.

The anchor that was his prison suddenly loomed large in the distance, a tangible presence in the opposite direction to where he needed to go. He could feel it tugging on his essence, a throbbing wound like a beat in his blood.

If he remained as mist, it would only grow stronger.

Until he could no longer resist its call.

Time passed with the excruciating sluggishness of ignorance. How many hours had gone by? No sound penetrated the bulkheads. At least the engines weren't online yet. Given the size of this spare cabin, Volsung's ship had to be much larger than the *Castel*. His engines would need time to warm up before the ship could undock.

Asrial's nose twitched, picking up unfamiliar odors. Not the green from hydroponics. A whiff of sweat or molds or something equally rank underlay the reek of old cleaning agents. The scrubbers in the ventilation ducts needed new filters.

She snorted at the criticism. As if she had anything to say about that. But it was better than lying there feeling sorry for herself. Self-pity was just a waste of energy. She hadn't given up when her parents were killed; she wasn't about to give up now. She'd get a chance to escape—or make one.

Sooner or later.

But the thought that it might be later did unpleasant things to her stomach.

Something appeared on the bulkhead before her: gas, smoke, vapor? Whatever it was, it shimmered faintly but wasn't drawn into the ventilation grills. Asrial stared at it warily, clawing at the deck to try to drag herself away when it spread and thickened, rising up and flowing down to the floor. What now?

Before her disbelieving eyes, the vapor took form, taking on details and solidity, until Romir stood there, bare-chested, his long hair a black cape around his shoulders, once again wearing only those loose pants of his. "There you are."

Relief flooded her at his appearance, tears welling up despite herself. She'd thought she would never see him again.

"You are injured." He dropped to his knees beside her, outrage darkening his face and striking silver sparks in his gray eyes as he ran his hands over her.

"Got hit by a stunner." Even now she couldn't believe how easily Volsung had caught her. She'd walked into his trap like a clueless grounder. "I'll be fine in a few hours." As long as they got off this ship.

Romir wavered in her view and not just because he put an arm behind her back and raised her up. He cradled her head, supporting her when her neck proved too weak. His chest warmed her side, a welcome contrast to the cold deck. She must have been lying in the same position for hours; her muscles ached from the misery of stunner hangover. A gentle kiss on her forehead triggered more tears. He was being so careful.

Crap, she hated being so helpless. Frigging crap. And it was all her own fault.

He brushed another soft kiss across her lips, and her threadbare control snapped.

She gasped his name, incredulous at his sudden appearance, hope and fear bubbling over in a volatile brew of emotions. She heard herself repeating his name over and over like some sense-dulled idiot but couldn't stop. She'd thought she couldn't feel worse, but worse than lying helpless, trapped in her own body, was lying limp in the arms of her lover, unable to return his embrace. She needed to feel him against her, his familiar heat a promise of normalcy.

Romir kissed her again, this time a hot, urgent exchange that swallowed her cries. He kissed her with the desperation of a spacer down to his last bottle of air, craving more yet wanting to make it last.

She clung to his kiss, drawing on his strength as her tears spilled over. This had to be a dream. But if it was, she didn't want to wake just yet, not and find herself still trapped, paralyzed, alone, dreading the first tremors of the engines cycling up in preparation for undocking. She poured all those fears into the kiss.

The deck shuddered.

Asrial froze, adrenaline shredding the fog of desperation. It couldn't be. Surely it was too soon for Volsung's crew to have been recalled. The ship couldn't be preparing to undock already, not yet. Surely . . . ?

Holding her breath, she waited for confirmation.

Nothing followed. The silence preyed on her nerves, whispering of imminent discovery, the trap springing shut. No escape.

"Is your business here done?" The calm question shattered the humming tension that held her thoughts hostage.

What were they doing giving Volsung time to complete his plan? They had to get off the ship now while Volsung believed her to be helpless—before more of the crew returned, before it was too late.

"I-I can't s-stand." In truth, she could barely sit up. Her body still refused to obey her, her throat tight and inclined to stutter.

Romir slid an arm under her knees, cradling her with a gentleness that belied the fury blazing in his silver eyes. He regained his feet so smoothly she didn't register the change, as if she lay on a floater instead of a man's arms.

"They took my s-stunner." She didn't know why she said that. It would be utter stupidity to ask him to search the ship for it. But it was hers. Silly jill.

"That would be more difficult to retrieve." A small smile tipped the corners of his mouth, the only change in his manner.

"It doesn't matter." Her stunner hadn't been anything special. She could always buy another on any station. "But you'll attract attention d-dressed like this."

He glanced at himself, the fury in his eyes momentarily cooling with surprise. The space over his chest shimmered into a long-sleeved shirt, the loose pants becoming snug carbon silk. A heartbeat later, his hair was once again pulled back in an elaborate braid. "Now we may leave?" A look of long-suffering accompanied the question.

Asrial managed a smile. His uncharacteristic teasing was so obviously a deliberate attempt at relieving her fear that she had to respond. "Whenever you're ready."

In spite of the lit *Locked* indicator, the door slid aside at Romir's approach, offering no resistance to his strange powers. The corridor was empty, but how long that would last was anyone's guess. Her heart thundered in her ears, fluttered in her throat with every step Romir took. Any moment now one of those doors would open, and they'd be caught.

Pounding sounded from farther down—heavy pounding for it to be audible. Likely a Hagnashr.

She gasped, her hands clenching on Romir's shirt despite herself. Like a baby, she huddled closer. As if even he could stop a stunner beam.

"Be at ease. The doors are sealed." Romir walked on, in no apparent hurry as they passed the source of the noise. She stared over his shoulder as the pounding grew more vehement. That explained it. Hagnash had little tolerance for being locked in; she half expected the metal to buckle beneath that attack.

They reached an airlock without encountering any of the crew and no further alarms. As with other doors, the iris expanded at

Romir's approach, revealing a boarding tube to the station and safety.

He stepped through, launching them into zero grav. Stars flashed over his shoulder beyond the transparent tube, dwarfed into insignificance by the station's and ship's proximity. If their situation weren't so dire with discovery imminent, she might have enjoyed floating in his arms more. As it was, fear and her body's aches dominated her awareness.

The airlock at the other end of the tube opened on an empty corridor. The lights were off. Not just dim, but dead. The emergency strips glowed faintly, showing where the bulkheads stood but nothing more. Even the signs that depended on independent power were faint.

Powered by the docked ship, the airlock's iris sealed shut behind them, unaffected by the outage. Unfortunately, that also meant anyone could follow them from the ship. But it looked like pursuit was the least of their problems.

Small spots of light appeared in the distance, bobbing nearer. Disgruntled mutters echoed down the dark corridor, ominous and unsettling.

"Easy f'r you to say, Red Eyes. You don't mind caves."

Red Eyes? One of them was a Xer then, adapted to low-light conditions. This darkness would be no hindrance to a Xer. He'd be able to see them.

The sudden, metallic taste of blood on the tongue startled Asrial out of the trance of fear gripping her. She'd bitten her lip without knowing, the pain blending with the clamor of her aches.

"What's to be scared of? It's just like space. Safer, if you think of it. There's an atmosphere." The reply was louder, closer. The thumps of heavy boots grew louder, too—almost as loud as the pounding of her pulse.

"No, it ain't. There be no stars. Na enough light."

Romir walked toward the voices, seeming to float, so silent were his steps despite his burden. Asrial couldn't hear him, though her ears strained for the first dreaded shout of discovery.

Any moment now.

Any moment . . .

Xer eyes swiveled in their direction, glowing red in the faint light of handheld lamps. "Who's there?"

Asrial stiffened. They were outnumbered, but they couldn't escape. Romir couldn't make any speed carrying her.

One of the hand lamps turned their way, battling to pierce the darkness. A dark cloud swallowed the thin beam as it got closer, revealing little.

But it was enough for her to see the vapor surrounding them, thick and murky. It came from Romir, a shapeless cloud much like he'd come to her earlier. As if he spread himself thin, though the arms and chest around her felt solid.

Her heart skipped a few beats at the sight. She didn't look down for fear of what she might see—or not see.

"Nah, nothin' there."

What a coward she was. Romir was using his djinn powers to hide her from the bastards who'd tried to scoop her up, and all she could think of was him floating legless? The image might be spooky, but it gave her something else to think about besides impending discovery.

"Someone's there, I tell you." The beam slashed around, crisscrossing the corridor. It lit the gray bulkheads with their dead lights, the sealed airlocks, the brown tiles of industrial flooring, the lamp holder's wary companions standing in a loose circle.

Asrial darted a glance at Romir, waiting for him to do something. He only pressed his fingers over her lips, warning her to silence, as he continued down the corridor.

"Don't hear anything."

“Yer imagin’ things.”

She kept her eyes on Romir, clinging to his resolute expression. He betrayed no uncertainty, his confidence absolute, as he slipped past the first of the spacers. She didn’t think he would fade while he held her—physical contact seemed to give him strength. But after . . .

If he drained himself, his prison would draw him back.

And she wouldn’t be able to do anything about it.

As they passed the knot of arguing spacers, an airlock irised open behind them. At the hiss, hand lamps slashed the darkness, homing in on the sound.

The lights pinned the Hagnashr sporting a broken horn and bad temper. Raising a massive hand before his narrowed eyes, he broke out a freight load of swearing. “What’s the holdup? You lot lazing around still?”

“Power’s down, and Red Eyes here’s freaking.”

“I tell you—”

The Hagnashr drowned out the outraged protest. “’Nough of that. Get moving. We’re done here, and there’s work to do. Pain in the crack hatches . . .”

Distance reduced the complaints to unintelligible grumbles, but Asrial didn’t breathe easily until Romir turned into another corridor and she lost sight of the spacers.

Fifteen

The remainder of the walk to the *Castel* passed without incident. Romir kept to the side corridors, avoiding the bubble cars and the more brightly lit areas, even backtracking in order to do so. They eventually gained the *Castel*'s bay, still shrouded in a thick mist of anomalous darkness that extended from his body.

Asrial's heart thundered in her ears, dread an efficient amplifier. She couldn't imagine how much that expenditure of power cost him. His form was reminiscent of that time his prison had nearly reclaimed him. Only the solidity of the arms supporting her assured her of his continued freedom.

Once they were aboard the *Castel*, the mist disappeared, withdrawing into Romir and leaving him standing whole, once more clad only in loose pants. He brought her straight to her cabin, not releasing her until he laid her on her bunk.

Her limbs prickled, a barrage of excruciating sensation as the stunner's effect eased, her nerves protesting the return of mobility.

Gasping, she squeezed her eyes shut, fighting to hold back tears of relief. But they leaked out in spite of her.

"Asrial? What—" The dismay in Romir's voice forced her eyes open. His hands hovered above her, hesitant and trembling. "I have no skill with healing weaves. You must tell me what is wrong."

"I'm fine."

"Do not say that when even a blind man can tell you are in pain." The furrow between his slashing black brows deepened, his eyes glinting silver amid all the white.

A soft, breathless laugh escaped her at his fluster. He had suffered untold pain and loss yet worried over a minor matter like this. "This is normal." Volsung must have blasted her more than once, but stunner hangover wouldn't kill her—it only felt like it should.

Grimacing, Romir left her side to disappear into the bio unit. Her heart skipped a beat at his absence. *Spirit of space, keep him free.*

He returned with a wet rag and used it on her face, removing any evidence of tears. The dampness was welcome, as was the cleaning. From the black muck, Volsung's men must have stashed her some place dirty before they dumped her in that cabin.

Romir was gentle, his touch light, handling her as though she were some precious artifact he feared to scratch. He stripped her of her T-top with equal care and turned his attention to wiping her throat and shoulders.

"How'd you find me?" she finally thought to ask when he returned from rinsing out the rag yet again.

"This." He tapped the enameled square between her breasts.

Heat rushed to her cheeks at being discovered. Hopefully he'd think she wore it as a memento of her mother. "That's how you found me? How?"

"A weaver's badge is wrought with the blood of the weaver. This was mine, so I can sense it."

"You knew . . . I was wearing it?"

Romir nodded absently, intent on cleaning her. "It is good you wore it."

He'd known all this time? He hadn't said anything.

She stared at his impassive face, searching for a clue to interpret that *good*. Did he approve? Or was it merely convenient? Did he want her to continue wearing it? But he kept his attention on what his hands were doing, not once meeting her eyes, so she couldn't tell.

Flat on her back, Asrial shivered, suddenly beset by an uncomfortable sense of fragility, chilled and hollow to the bone. She fisted her fingers to stop their trembling, but that did little for her hands despite her tight knuckles. Crap, she hated being so weak. Where was the Rim rat who flew the space lanes and explored ancient ruins alone without a qualm?

The slap of the wet rag hitting the deck snapped her attention back to Romir. "You are cold. If I touch you, will that hurt you more?"

"I'm more sore than anything else. I just need to get my blood flowing." She wasn't dying; she just felt like it. Encouraging her circulation was the fastest way to recover from stunner hangover.

A sigh greeted her answer. Romir proceeded to chafe her arms as he muttered scathing phrases under his breath, a steady flow of growled outrage that made her smile through the pain. His hands felt solid enough as his biceps bunched and flexed with hypnotic regularity.

Asrial clung to the sight, unable to look away for fear his prison would steal him away in that moment of inattention. He had used so much power she didn't want to risk it.

"Hold me. Touch me. Make love to me." She raised trembling

arms to Romir, relieved she could manage that much. During that agonizing captivity, she'd been so afraid she'd never see him again. Even now, she could lose him so easily.

"You need to speak with your mother's cousin." Kneeling, he pressed his face against her, his lips busy with heart-stoppingly gentle caresses over her breasts. "He was worried when you disappeared."

Amin would have to wait; Romir couldn't. If he faded, she couldn't give chase. It pained her to realize she hadn't hesitated. Faced with a choice between the two men, the one not related to her by blood was the clear winner, not the man who was like an uncle to her. The decision had taken less than a heartbeat. She soothed her conscience with the thought that her present condition was unlikely to reassure Amin of her safety. She still couldn't sit up without Romir's support.

"I'll talk to him later." She fought the icy weight of her limbs to pull him closer. "I'm so cold."

Concern narrowing his eyes and creasing his brow, Romir took her hands and held them against his shoulders, sharing his heat and making her fingers tingle. He growled wordlessly in a tone fierce enough to sport claws and fangs. "Leave it to me."

He turned her so that she lay with her legs hanging off the edge of the bunk. He disposed of her boots and pants with a thorough solicitude that brought tears to her eyes. No one had cared for her like this in such a long time, not since her childhood. Being the recipient of it now undermined her determination to be strong.

"Not on my back." She might be on her own bunk, but it was too reminiscent of her time in Volsung's hands, heightening the feeling of vulnerability.

"Here." Romir twisted around until he lay on the bunk and she was sprawled on top of him. The new position let her touch him more easily: no longer did she have to fight the pull of gravity.

His body warmed her, his chest beneath her cheek, his belly against her breasts, his pelvis cradling hers, his legs tangled with hers, his arms embracing her. Such welcome male heat. She basked in it, an unspoken, unsuspected fear releasing its coils from around her heart. "Better. Much better."

Slowly, a sense of well-being seeped into her, even a measure of security. Though she hated to admit it, that was because of Romir. Because he was there. Because he was willing to risk his freedom for her.

She pressed her lips to his skin and licked. Her tongue found warmth . . . and nothing else—another reminder of his djinn state. He didn't sweat, didn't have dead hair or skin cells to lose, didn't ejaculate.

"Are you not too tired for that?" His hand combed through her hair with restful repetition. What expression he wore, she couldn't tell, too tired to raise her head to look.

No matter. Her answer remained the same.

Asrial kissed his chest again, ignoring the difference as part of what he was. "It'll make me feel better. I need to feel you inside me."

He took such exquisite care, making sure she was wet and ready for him, then filling her slowly. So comforting. But the aftereffects of the stunner blast left her nerve endings so sensitized that she gasped at the steady pressure. He rocked her to a gentle, undemanding release that sprinkled bliss through her veins like starlight.

She could only lie there accepting his ministrations, but she hoped the intimate contact was enough. She couldn't lose him, too.

Heaving a contented sigh, Asrial rested her head on his shoulder. Her heart drummed against his ribs, a rapid tattoo assuring him of her eventual recovery. "You're still here. That's good."

She fell silent, doing nothing for long enough that Romir thought she must have fallen asleep. He cherished her slight weight on top of him, the display of trust that let her share her bed with him. He even welcomed the painful ache in his loins, the insistent throb further proof of her return.

During the search through the station, when he thought he would not find her, he feared he would never know this pleasure again. He had feared he would fail yet another one who had placed their confidence in him. If that had happened, if he had failed, he did not know what he would have done.

The heart he did not have shuddered at the thought of losing Asrial.

As though she could read his mind, her next words were "If anything happens to me, you should take your prison and escape." She had not fallen asleep, after all. Even now, her thoughts were for him.

He smiled, his heart bleak. "I cannot. To touch it is to be captured. It will draw me inside." Back into the mists, into nothingness.

"You can't?" Asrial went still, holding her body so stiffly that he started to worry. Clearly she was thinking, and her thoughts did not seem to bring her any comfort. "So that cryptic inscription . . ." Her voice trailed off into a mumble. Her eyes remained stubbornly open, though her lashes tried to flutter shut.

It seemed that she needed more incentive to rest. Romir gripped her shoulders and pressed down firmly, discovered knots of tension and set out to circle them to submission. "Go to sleep."

When the nightmare came, Asrial knew she dreamed, but that knowledge did nothing to change what she dreamed. No matter how much she wished she could change it.

Because it was past.

Immutable.

The nightmare began as it always did: red flashes across the board, the bogey's sudden appearance and rapid approach, the plasma shields' catastrophic failure. The scenes came one after another in rapid succession, matching the rhythm of her bounding heart.

Apprehension choked her, dread a heavy weight in her belly and growing to stellar proportions. It didn't help that she knew what was coming. She wanted to wake up, to escape the nightmare, but she couldn't break its hold.

Nothing stopped the nightmare once it started. She could only watch as it played before her sleeping eyes.

"Stay here. Stay safe." In the dream, Jamyl's black eyes bored into hers, alive with fear and desperation—the knowledge of his coming death. In reality, she must have only glanced at her father, meeting his gaze for no more than a moment, more concerned with breaking the *Castel* out of the pirates' grab net.

She was the pilot. It was her responsibility to guide the ship to safety.

Nasri was running from the main hold, but it was only in the dream. Asrial hadn't seen her mother do that; there was no way she could have witnessed that from the piloting chamber. It was simply her subconscious filling in the details based on Patrol reports. But though she knew that, the nightmare rolled on, and she watched as Nasri grabbed a machete from the freight intended for colonists on Vignis in the Brauten sector.

No!

The hatch squealed in protest, forced open with a torsion jack. Pirates spilled through, a swarm of monsters in the nightmare. Her mother charged them, somehow avoiding streams of stunner fire to force them into desperate battle. Asrial didn't know if that was how it happened—she had only seen the aftermath and the stomach-churning remains of Nasri's body mixed with the pirates'—but that was always how the nightmare played out. Nasri had died of blood loss from her wounds. The nightmare strung scene after gory scene before her eyes, of the pirates overcoming her mother, each one worse and worse. Her imagination had had more than a thousand nights to refine the horror to nauseating, heart-rending perfection.

An explosion shook the *Castel*, the straps of the shock harness snapping taut around her torso. The rumbling thunder should have been impossible in the depths of space, but she heard it—was hearing it again—as she slammed back against her seat, the board jolting under her hands.

The pirates' ship dominated her near space screen, looming above the *Castel* like an yfreet over wounded prey. Her maneuvers failed to break the hold the grab net had on her ship. A boarding tube tied the *Castel* to the other ship, a deadly umbilical that spilled more pirates into the corridor outside the sealed piloting chamber.

Buffeted by the crackle of stunner blasts, shouts, and fighting, she remained at the pilot board, tied there by duty. More explosions.

Mother. Father. Her body was heavy, unresponsive. She couldn't move. She couldn't speak. She couldn't leave her place.

Helpless. Once again, she was helpless. Once again, she could do nothing.

And she hoped. Maybe this time it would be different. Maybe this time it was her turn. Maybe this time she wouldn't survive.

It would almost be a relief.

Then came another explosion—a much louder one that rattled her teeth. She felt the tremors all the way to the bone.

That was the last one. The worst. The one that had freed the *Castel* . . . and killed Jamyl. He'd armed the mine knowing it would open his compartment to space, and him without a vacuum suit. He'd deliberately sacrificed himself to save her.

Old, familiar grief made fresh dragged her down into the heavy darkness.

If only she had died with them . . .

Sixteen

Patient caresses impinged on her consciousness. Slow and gentle, they offered comfort and demanded nothing in return. Just quiet strokes over her hair and shoulder. So nice. She'd been dreaming, about what she couldn't remember, but now she didn't want to wake. The lethargy pervading her body only added to her reluctance.

Except there was only her to get things done.

Asrial pried her eyelids open, her lashes heavy, and stared at an unfamiliar brown wall. With ridges. The *Castel* didn't have a surface like that anywhere.

She wasn't in her cabin?

Her pulse went on overdrive, boosting the rest of her to alertness. *Volsung!* She'd been stunned and abducted, awaiting delivery to some mysterious client. Romir had come to her rescue . . . but had she dreamed the rescue?

Then the wall expanded, rippled. She pressed her fingers against it and found warm, resilient flesh.

"Forgive me. I did not intend to wake you."

Asrial rolled her eyes to the source of the voice: Romir, once again wearing only those loose pants. She was curled up around him, her head on his lap, facing his bare belly, an arm around his waist. She blinked at the sight.

His hand lay on her shoulder, resting lightly, an easy weight. It hadn't been a dream. He'd been stroking her hair.

"You were . . . agitated. I thought to ease your sleep." His thumb wiped away some dampness on her cheek.

Dampness? She'd cried in her sleep? She must have had that nightmare again. Gory scenes came trickling back to haunt her. Definitely the nightmare.

She checked Romir's reaction, but he was looking away, staring at—she glanced over her shoulder—nothing in particular, discreetly ignoring her distress. Uncommon insight, or was he merely treating her the way he would wish to be treated? It was not for lack of sympathy; otherwise he wouldn't have been trying to soothe her.

"I was dreaming." She swiped at her wet lashes and blinked her eyes dry. "Dreaming of pirates."

Romir made a noncommittal sound, stroking her hair with a light hand that said she didn't have to continue. He wouldn't press her for details.

"They caught the *Castel* in Nikralian space." Her heart skipped then picked up speed at the memory. They'd been outsystem, far from the major trade routes, beyond comm range of the Patrol.

Back then, the *Castel* had been a tramp trader, supplying small colonies struggling to get on their feet and systems that couldn't afford a starport. Asrial's parents had brought her up shuttling around the Wainek and Brauten sectors with Lyrel 9 as their home station. She'd learned her piloting skills on the *Castel*'s board.

Their profits had been modest, but her father hadn't minded.

Jamyl had had no wish to compete with larger traders; there was safety in avoiding conglomerate scrutiny.

"They forced their way aboard. We tried to fight them off." It sounded so simple when she said it, so clean and clear-cut, but it wasn't. She'd been at the board as usual; that had been her duty ever since she earned her pilot's license. Jamyl had sealed the pilot chamber as he left. An explosion damaged the pirates' ship and its grab net and broke loose the boarding tube so she could fly the *Castel* free. But in the aftermath, she'd found her mother dead, her throat ripped open, and strangers lying around her just as dead. Nasri had fought to the very end. Her father had been killed in the explosion that allowed Asrial to escape.

"My parents died protecting me."

Useless. She'd been useless, unable to do anything until it was too late.

Nightmare scenes appeared before her mind's eye like projections on a holotube, though nothing so pretty as a standard avatar, nothing so easily dismissed. She couldn't forget; it had been too real.

Flushed with heat, then a sudden chill, Asrial panted. Her head swam, her thoughts disconnected. A roaring filled her ears, her heart pounding like it would leap out of her chest. Her body felt like it would float away.

"Hey!"

Arms embraced her—Romir's. His heat seeped into her, driving away the cold. The press of his body anchored her, drawing her back from the unchangeable past and failure. "Be at ease. There are no pirates. There is no danger without. No one has entered the bay. Your ship is safe. Go back to sleep."

The statement was filled with such certainty that Asrial could not doubt its veracity. Her body was heavy, fatigue a grab net dragging her back to sleep. Closing her eyes, she gave up the fight, equally certain she was safe in his care.

* * *

The next time Asrial woke she was facing the familiar bulkhead of her cabin. No disorienting brown wall this time. She suppressed a twinge of disappointment. Right then, she felt fine. But give her a few ticks in Romir's arms, and she was bound to feel even better.

Then what happened yesterday—was it only yesterday?—came tumbling back, and she realized she hadn't commed Amin about Volsung!

Asrial lunged upright—or tried to. All she managed was a breathless jerk and had to claw her way into sitting up. It looked like her stunner hangover wasn't quite as gone as she'd thought. Just as she achieved vertical, the door of her cabin hissed aside to reveal Romir carrying a tray laden with a bowl and sip tube. No doubt he wanted to feed her up again.

His tight smile contained more than a splash of relief around the eyes. He'd been worried about her. She couldn't fault him, since she'd been worried, too.

She put him off to comm Lyrel 9's admin to lodge a complaint against Volsung. Nothing much was likely to come of it, since station peace hadn't been disrupted. Even if the station admin questioned the Cyrian, it would be his word against hers.

When she cut the link to Lyrel 9, Romir set the tray on the table with a distinct *click* that insisted on her attention. "Eat."

"I have to comm Amin next." Clinging to the edge of the table to steady herself, she started to key in his comm link.

"Eat first. You missed last meal." He thrust a spoon in her direction. The message was clear: food first, comm later.

Asrial complied with ill grace, in no mood to pretend just yet. Her body continued to ache from stunner hangover, but at least now she could sit up on her own—if a shade unsteadily. Her stomach welcomed his offering, finding the normally bland veg noodles surprisingly savory.

As she expected, Amin insisted on seeing her in the flesh, with his own eyes, before accepting that she was safe. Seeing her over the comm wouldn't suffice, since the vid could just as easily use an avatar. Which meant dragging herself down to Lyrel 9's residential levels.

Walking took conscious effort, requiring force of will to pick up her heels. Her muscles protested every step. Her head swam. Blood pounded in her ears as loud and insistent as a station's seal breach alarm; she wouldn't have been surprised if there had been flashing lights behind her eyes. Frigging crap. She really hated stunner hangover.

The effort was necessary. She just had to remind herself of that. Right then, however, death seemed the better choice, preferably soon.

Romir kept a firm grip on her forearm, quietly insistent in his support. She didn't refuse, hoarding her strength for Amin.

Shift change turned the corridors into a crush, boisterous conversations bouncing off utilitarian walls. The crowds pressed in on her, too many, too close for comfort. Scents she didn't normally notice assaulted her nostrils: fuel volatiles, cleaning fluids, hydraulics markers, sweat, spices, Jenin signal musk.

The next junction marked the start of a low-grav zone and welcome relief for her body. Progress slowed inevitably as grounders staggered among the spacers to regain their balance after the abrupt change in gravities. Romir made the transition like a spacer, and she practically floated beside him as gravity suddenly released its net.

Normally she didn't notice the change in grav zones. Every station had them, and spacers got used to them. But in her current state, they made her head reel. By the time they got to Arm 5,

Sector 3, Level R-9, where Amin's quarters were located, only Romir's sure guidance held her on course. The bland gray door of their destination never looked so good before.

Outrage splashed high color across Amin's face the moment he saw her and Romir. "What happened to you?"

"Volsung happened. With a stunner at full power." Asrial tried to avoid going into detail about the rescue, but the screen of half-truths didn't stand up to Amin's determined questioning.

"Asri-*ki*, he simply . . . managed to sneak you out?" By this time, Amin had parked his floater on its stand, leaving him free to give her all his attention. "He traced you to Volsung's ship. Found where you were held. Rescued you. And he did this all by himself. Without anyone noticing."

She couldn't blame him for his suspicions. Ordinarily Romir shouldn't have been able to find and free her so quickly, so quietly, all by himself—unless he'd been in on the abduction in the first place.

Only the truth would put Amin's concerns to rest. But there was no way she could risk Romir's secret getting out.

Romir could not bear to watch more of this farce. Asrial was twisting herself into knots trying to explain without revealing his enslavement. Her distress at shaving the truth with her kinsman was clear for him to see, and still she tried, hiding his shame to protect him.

And in doing so, she was alienating Amin—and by extension, her much-loved family. The other man's face was purple with anger, so flushed Romir feared for his health. If this continued, it could lead to a permanent estrangement.

No more. He could not allow Asrial to sacrifice her family for his sake. He could not inflict more pain on one who sought only to help him.

"Asrial, this is not necessary."

She glanced at him, distress and concern amber bright in that quick look. "I—"

"You!" Amin spun the levitating chair around to glare at him. "This is your doing?"

"I can explain." Romir bowed his head as he opened his weaver's sight and sought the glimmers in the walls for wrongness—intrusion, observation, something that did not belong. The room was safe, devoid of watchers, as far as he could tell.

"Nothing you say can excuse your forcing Captain Dilaryn to lie to me."

"Then perhaps it is just as well that I will not use words." Frighteningly, it was simpler than he thought it would be. He merely eased the grip he had on the image in his mind, eased his resistance to his prison's pull, and . . .

. . . the hand he extended to the furious man turned to mist.

With a gasp of shock, Asrial grabbed his elbow, her short nails digging painfully into him. "Romir!" She leaned into him, her small breasts firm against his back, rising and falling in her alarm.

He reached out to brush his missing hand along the other man's cheek. "This is what Asrial could not tell you."

"You—What are you?" Amin stared at him with wild eyes, the whites around his irises widening as he took in Romir's empty sleeve.

"I am djinn." Romir concentrated on completing his form, envisioning the hand that was gone, the shapes of his fingers, the nails at their tips, his palm—the reality of a hand. The effort was probably unnecessary, since his form took the shape of his original body, but it helped him resist the call of his prison. And as quickly as his hand turned to mist, it reappeared with fingers curled against Amin's cheek.

With a hiss, the other man flinched from him. "Ch-children's tales."

"No, that's how he was able to rescue me so easily. I'm sorry I didn't tell you before, but it wasn't my secret. I hope you can understand." Asrial explained the actual sequence of events that she had taken such care to omit. For the most part, Romir kept silent, leaving her to handle her kinsman, speaking only when she sought clarification.

Finally, she leaned into Romir with a sigh, wrapping her arms around his waist and resting her forehead on his arm. Even seated, she let him support most of her weight, clearly still recovering from the stunner and determined to hide her weakness from her kinsman. "I'm going to free him. Somehow."

"Free him?" Amin echoed in a weak voice, his hands trembling on the arms of his levitating chair. His face was now gray and shiny with sweat. "Free a djinn? A *djinn*."

"There should be a way. I'll find it." Her jaw took on that increasingly familiar tightness of determination.

"This is why you plan to sell the Dilaryn jewels." Amin's eyes were still wide though no longer panicky as he swallowed deep gulps of air.

Romir stared at the top of Asrial's bent head, guilt churning anew. He was the reason for her inventory of the Dilaryn jewels? She intended to sell her inheritance to aid him?

"Only if necessary." Pressing her face into the hollow of Romir's shoulder, Asrial stuffed the twinge of guilt in the back of her heart. That decision could wait.

Amin was taking Romir's revelation better than she'd expected. His temper ebbed as his agile mind turned to picking holes in her plan to free Romir. She already realized most of them, but she listened politely, knowing he did so out of concern for her, while she drew on Romir's warmth and steady strength to push back her weariness.

Their discussion was interrupted by a chime announcing someone in the corridor outside: Inuoie, alone and visibly upset. Amin admitted his friend, his concern shifting focus—to Asrial's short-lived relief.

Bowing his head, the Ruxilian swirled his long fingers through a complex gesture of abject apology, addressing himself to both Amin and her. "We were too late. The slot was empty. According to the records, the *Eikki* undocked at sixth hour and transited as per their revised schedule."

She'd still been asleep at that time, exhausted from stunner hangover. If Romir hadn't found her, she would have been on board and now on her way to that client Volsung mentioned.

Asrial rubbed her forehead, trying to erase the throb of weariness cycling up between her brows. "It doesn't make sense. Why the abduction? Why go to elaborate lengths to get me?" She hadn't told Amin that she'd been the specific target, but he probably suspected it hadn't been some random snatch by slavers. It chilled her to think that she could lose her freedom just because someone was willing to pay hard creds for her.

But why?

"Could it have been related to the auction? This Volsung was a buyer, was he not?" Romir ran his fingers through her hair, restlessly playing with the short strands. The ruffling sensation was oddly soothing.

"We received no demand for ransom. All we knew was that you were not in the hall during the inspection of the relics and had been missing for some time."

Amin's words startled Asrial into opening her eyes. She'd

forgotten about the auction scheduled for later, her abduction and subsequent rescue thrusting it to the back of her mind. "Then the only thing I can think of is my knowledge of Majian ruins. Volsung was acting as the agent for a new collector, after all. Perhaps they suspect I found a new site and there are more relics to be gotten?" That was the only reason that made sense to her. After all, the Cyrian had lured her into his trap with the possibility of a contract for Majian artifacts.

Amin shook his head, his mouth working wordlessly, rage mottling his features. His hands worried the floater's controls to no purpose, and it worried her.

Guilt twinged again. She'd rarely seen her mother's cousin get mad; even when the Paxis credit crunchers had reduced him to that miserly disability pay he hadn't gotten mad. But on this visit he'd lost his temper twice—and both times on her behalf. If he didn't calm down, the stress could take a toll on his already weakened body. She didn't want that.

"Without questioning Volsung, we'll probably never know. Never mind about him. At least he's gone. Just focus on the auction." Asrial took her leave amid Amin's protests for her to wait for her cousins. Staying would only keep him worked up when he ought to relax. Besides which, she wasn't feeling too steady herself and needed to get away before Amin realized she wasn't as recovered as she pretended to be.

Romir was quiet on the way back to the *Castel*, not an unusual state of affairs with him, but the downward tilt to the corner of his mouth said it was more than his customary reserve.

"Something else bothering you?" she asked to distract herself from the effort of walking, not really expecting him to answer. Her body felt three times heavier with much of the extra weight in her head.

"I failed you. I should have dealt with your abductors so they could not have escaped. Time and again, this failure."

Surprise gave her pause. The dark expression on his face was familiar; she'd seen similar ones on hers after Jamyl's and Nasri's deaths. *Time and again?* He wasn't thinking only of her abduction; this self-recrimination went deeper than that.

"I don't know what you're talking about. You saved me—that isn't failure." Ignoring the people around them, she pulled out his weaver's badge, rubbed her thumb across the engraved *Promise*. "This is proof you didn't fail. The people who escaped the Mughelis—the people you saved—survived. My father's people, the Lomidari, have you to thank for their existence."

The blink she got conveyed his doubt. There was no point arguing with him. Mere words wouldn't have worked with her, either, back then; even now she struggled with her own guilt.

Asrial tucked the badge back under her T-top and continued the long trek to the *Castel*, leaving Romir to his thoughts. Speaking of her abduction sent her own thoughts circling back to Volsung.

If the Cyrian had succeeded, Romir would remain as a djinn, since he couldn't just take his prison and run. With her gone, his prison would have eventually recaptured him, trapped him once more, perhaps never to regain even partial freedom. That made it more imperative that they find a way to free him.

Her head throbbed, every beat driving home how very nearly her fears could come to pass. She couldn't afford to wait while the *Castel* was refurbished; the work would take at least half a year and leave her coffers low.

If the promise meant a technique for freeing djinn, then the logical place to search for the promise's fulfillment was Salima. Then, too, if Romir saw for himself that the Lomidari, the descendants of his people, were thriving, that would be good. Anything to ease his unjustified sense of failure.

They had to go to Lomida.

Seventeen

Lomida grew on the primary screen. The sparkle of the wide ice ring that encircled the planet paled in comparison with the insystem traffic surrounding its constellation and the shuttles connecting the stations with the planet. Ships arrived and departed with soothing regularity—bulk carriers, cruise ships, one-man fast couriers, and all sizes in between, plying the space lanes in an orderly procession.

Or so it seemed from a distance.

Asrial knew better. Beneath that placid surface lurked sinister backroom deals, all so profitable and dominated by Dareh conglomerate interests.

She tried to steer clear of Lomida as much as possible. While Jamyl and Nasri were alive, they'd avoided this sector of the Inner Worlds entirely. She hadn't set foot on the planet until after their deaths, and she'd done so then only because a buyer refused to take delivery elsewhere, and even then, she'd gone in stealth and had stayed only long enough to complete the sale.

This was another time she couldn't avoid it.

With grave misgivings, she piloted the *Castel* through local space traffic and into the atmosphere, heading directly for the main starport. This visit posed the best chance of discovering how to free Romir, but Lomida was the planet House Dilaryn had ruled for generations. Although Jainyl Kharym Rashad had been forced to abdicate, the Dareh's victory was an uneasy one. Her father had been forbidden from entering Lomidar space because they feared he would attempt to reclaim the scepter of the *reis.*

Who knew how the Dareh would respond to her sudden appearance and prolonged stay on planet? To this day, decades after the abdication, she steered clear of the Dareh conglomerate, its subsidiaries, and its allies. She could only hope they'd forgotten about her, but how realistic that hope was, she had no way of telling. However, they couldn't avoid Lomida if they were to solve the riddle of the *Promise*, not when their best lead lay in Salima.

In the middle of a vast plain, a lone mountain pierced the horizon, its crown wreathed by clouds—Babbahar. As they neared, the broad shadow at its base resolved into sprawling urbanization: Yasra, their destination.

Asrial had seen vids of the Lomidar capital city, but they'd failed to convey the reality. The local starport was a hub of activity, though not as packed as a major constellation like Eskarion. But accustomed as she was to the lighter traffic of the Rim, the Inner World facility felt too crowded. Ships were parked too close for her comfort. There was just too much.

The smell of the air alone made her shoulders tight, the heavy metallic fumes from so many ships so different from the filtered air of the stations or the wildness of a Rim World planet. Lomida might be her parents' home world, but to her, it would always be the planet that had rejected them, the planet to which they had been forbidden to return, the planet that had threatened to kill them.

It didn't take much to imagine security bods lurking behind the many ship struts, just waiting to pounce. Her father's vehemence whenever conversation touched on Lomida and Dareh interests had left a strong impression, even several years later.

Perhaps she was being unreasonable since she no longer had any relics on board, but with her paranoia waxing high, she activated every last one of her security circuits—primary, secondary, and the multiplicity of backups—until nothing short of a major bomb would get through. Despite those measures, she still couldn't relax, not while on Lomida.

Romir was scrutinizing the other ships as he waited by the grav sled. He looked so different now from when she'd first seen him. The changes weren't limited to his clothes. His stance and demeanor had changed as well. The slight defensive hunch of his shoulders was gone, his back now straight and sure. His expression was more open, letting an occasional smile slip through.

Just the sight of him eased the humming tension in her shoulders. With him by her side, she could believe things would be fine. They could handle whatever life threw at them.

Spirit of space grant that the *Promise* was what she hoped it was.

She studied the map of the city, then programmed their destination into the grav sled's navputer. Compared to star charts, Yasra was far simpler to navigate. The city still bore the evidence of the last time it was reconceived, fanning out from the walls of Salima in an orderly grid. It curved along the western flank of Babbahar in a crescent of towering spires. Much of the industrial sector lay to the south, nearest the starport. The west claimed most of the spires, the buildings mixing businesses and residences for the extremely wealthy. Walkways connected the spires at the upper levels, spiderwebs of glassteel.

And above it all was a dark, whirling cloud of yfreet, scavengers drawn to the wildlife preserve that Salima had devolved to and the refuse piles beyond the industrial zone.

They left the starport, diving into the stream of air traffic headed into Yasra. The navputer threaded the elegant maze of the city, past lavish corporate complexes, finally sweeping into a boulevard that paralleled a high stone wall—the wall that separated Yasra from Salima.

If she hadn't known better, she would have thought the navputer in error. The granite blocks were clean, their lines sharp and fresh. One might be forgiven for believing the wall a recent construct, instead of thousands of years old. That unchanging appearance was part of its mystique.

The last of the Dilaryn domain, Salima was the old capital of Lomida, founded between the arms of Babbahar. Over the centuries, it had come to encompass the mountain, only to be abandoned as the population grew and spread and old knowledge was lost. Now, only wildlife was found there, a supposedly impenetrable preserve along one side of Yasra, the new capital that had sprung up in the plains beyond its wall.

The starport lay on the other side of Salima from most of Yasra, the authorities using the preserve to buffer the city from the noise and danger of the ships landing and launching.

Salima was the only holding that hadn't been stripped from her family when the Dareh forced her father to step down as *reis*. The Lomidari might have accepted the abdication of Jamyl Kharym Rashad, House Dilaryn, for the sake of peace, but they had resisted the violation of tradition, and Salima remained House Dilaryn's.

"No one leaves or enters?" Romir asked after she explained their destination.

"No one lives in Salima. It's been abandoned since before Lomida reached the stars. There are stories that it's haunted."

She'd delighted in her mother's tales of the supposed hauntings, little suspecting she would someday walk the land of her ancestors.

"Haunted?"

"Mysterious lights, apparitions, and so on."

"And we are to enter?" Romir turned wide, wondering eyes to her—so wide they should have fallen out. Teasing her.

"Nothing less."

His laugh was rusty, barely two puffs of air, but all the more precious for it. She glanced aside to hide her smile, inordinately pleased by his reaction.

Air and foot traffic kept to the far side of the boulevard, despite a lack of signs and dividers, maintaining an explicit distance from the wall. Even the sled's navputer observed the invisible boundary.

"According to the maps, there should be a private gate along this section, one large enough to permit the entry of a grav sled." She couldn't see any breaks, however.

"There." Romir pointed at yet another featureless stretch of granite.

Taking back control from the navputer, she set the grav sled on hover, sidling it out of the traffic stream and toward the wall. "Here? I don't see a gate."

"It is private."

Asrial slid him a chiding look. What a time for him to discover a sense of humor. They were drawing attention from pedestrians. "How can you tell?"

"The energies part there."

The energies did indeed flow around a square section on the wall, but unlike the sparkles Romir saw on the walls of the *Castel* and the stations they had visited, this pattern was tantalizingly familiar. "It will open when you are nearer."

"Nearer, eh?" Without hesitation, Asrial caressed the controls, floating their craft where he indicated.

The pattern lit as he expected, a thread of energy reaching out to them. There was no response to him, but when it touched Asrial, another portion of the pattern brightened.

A gate appeared in the wall.

Asrial took them through on a burst of speed, skewing about to face the gate—that was gone. She swore in an undertone, shaking her head in disbelief as her hands danced. "It's like that complex. All the scanners say the wall's solid."

"That complex?"

"On Maj, where I found your prison."

The land around them was silent, as if the wall blocked more than sight and access. Trees lined the wide, grass-choked road Asrial followed, towering high above and letting through only a sprinkling of sunlight into an intimate green world. The road's enormous slabs lay awry, mossy and buckled over trunklike roots. Quite unlike anything he imagined. The garden—if garden it had been—was overgrown, wild, and untamed.

This place was the haven his people had fled to?

From the width of the road, Salima must have supported a sizable population to require so massive a causeway. And yet the construction technique used was primitive. The road had no weaves—unlike the wall and the gate through which they entered.

Again, he was reminded that Asrial had known nothing about djinn and the weaving of power. If the Lomidari were his people as she speculated, the loss of knowledge was troubling.

Why had the people abandoned Salima for outside its walls?

Scarlet flashed between the trees, sudden and fleeting, startling as an explosion. Something besides them moved in this quiet wilderness. Perhaps a bird, if they had birds on this world. He sensed the pulse of life, though he could not see it.

A break in the trees revealed fallen stones; the building they had been part of, a ruin in every sense of the word. Its roof had fallen in, leaving debris to gather within. Trees grew from atop the crumbling walls, their roots digging deep into the joints and prying them wide. In some places, only unnaturally straight lines betrayed the existence of a structure.

Asrial made a sound, as if in pain. She bit her lip but continued on. Clinging to hope despite the evidence before her.

"Is this like the abandoned cities on Maj?"

She shook her head, her attention fixed on her controls. "Weeds wouldn't dare grow in the streets of Maj."

The image her answer conjured disturbed him at a visceral level. That the wildest plants could not defy the Mughelis even thousands of years after his enemy's disappearance!

Silence settled between them as they left the ruin behind. Romir did nothing to break it, leaving Asrial to fly them to her family's palace. It was a faint hope she pursued. Examination under the bright light of reason would likely reduce its embers to ashes.

Doubts nibbled at him. She was wasting her credits and resources on a hopeless search. Even if someone had discovered the means of breaking a djinn's enslavement, what were the odds that the knowledge had survived the passage of time? After thousands of years, what could be there to find?

Surely Asrial had made the same calculations, yet still she pressed on. Such foolish, headstrong determination. But it was typical of this woman who would take a djinn to her bed. His lips tilted upward despite himself.

More ruins appeared in the distance, surmounted by bushes and the skeletons of dead trees, the victims of centuries of abandonment. Some were little more than piles of timber overgrown by vines. The latter presented a strange sight. His people had preferred to build with stone, not wood. Stone and metal held weaves of power better.

They crossed a tumultuous river, the wide bridge spanning it furry with moss and feathery with ferns.

She touched the panel, her expression controlled. "According to the map, we're close. The palace is near the headwaters. We should see it soon."

Romir nodded, hoarding his doubts within. Then they would know—one way or another.

A building emerged above the trees to one side of the road. Straight lines, unadorned granite, a gray needle in a pool of sunlight within the forest. As they got nearer, he saw it was more than that as the rest of the sprawling structure came into view. Like the wall, it stood untouched by time, unstained by moss or the elements. A Parvinese fortress, strong and imposing. Built to defend a battered people. Even from this distance, he could feel the protections woven into its massive stone blocks. The lower levels had smooth granite as walls. No windows pierced their spans, at least none that could be seen from outside.

"Yes!" Asrial whooped, shaking a triumphant fist. "That has to be it!"

He stared in astonishment. Despite the granite wall that enclosed Salima, he had come to expect a ruin, much like the other structures they had passed.

Asrial coaxed more speed from their craft, the gleam in her eyes hunter bright.

The fortress proved even larger than he had thought, its walls backing against the mountain. The river they had crossed had its headwaters within, its channel emerging from a section of granite wall.

"Do you think this is another of those walls?" Asrial pointed ahead where the road ended at another stretch of granite.

Romir nodded. "The pattern is the same."

She slowed only slightly, a small smile escaping her when a gate appeared just before they would have crashed.

They emerged on a narrow platform overlooking a gentle meadow and a paved courtyard that was as different from the land outside as day and night. Flagstones worn by generations of feet and centuries of weather stretched out on both sides.

Asrial's hands danced across the controls, and the craft rose until they were twice the height of the wall, affording them a bird's-eye view of the fortress. A maze of rooftops bewildered the eye, intact and bristling with defensive weaves. In the distance, water spilled down the side of the mountain from several points, sunlight making the spray glitter like crystals.

"Oh." She took it in, her eyes wide. "Where do we start looking?"

Romir shared her dismay. Even a cursory search would take days—and that assumed there was anything to be found. Only gradually did he realize a sense of familiarity about the scene. Something about it nagged him.

The walls were plain, blank stone. The windows in the upper levels were equally utilitarian, bereft of any detail to delight the heart and eye.

So why did he feel he had seen it before, somewhere?

He cast his eyes over the rooftops once more.

It took a while before he understood why it seemed familiar: the layout matched that of the Academe of Daraya, the seat of weaver lore and the most heavily defended institution in his homeland of Parvin. It was the school where he had received his training. As an apprentice weaver, he had had years to learn its every recess and back way. His people must not have had time or energy to design a safehold, so instead had chosen to rebuild the strongest fortress of Parvin in this new world.

If they remained true to the design of the Academe, he knew where to search. "Go there." He pointed into the complex toward a building closer to the mountainside.

"Why there?" Asrial asked even as she maneuvered the craft in accordance with his direction.

He explained his reasoning absently, his attention on the rooftops they flew past, so different yet so similar. A growing sense of certainty filled him the farther they went. His instincts had not steered him wrong. "This is it."

Little distinguished their destination from the other buildings in the complex. It had the same blank stone walls and utilitarian windows as the others with none of the dignity of the main archive, the central repository of weaver lore.

Asrial set their craft down in another weathered courtyard, and they continued on foot to explore.

A cold cloak of disconcertion settled around his shoulders, unpleasant and increasingly oppressive. He had never been here before, had never walked its halls, and yet it was as if he had lived here all his life. He kept turning around, expecting to see something that was not there, that had never been there—a statue, a mosaic, some carving, a fountain—and each time he was disappointed.

Each disappointment weighed on him. This was not the Academe of Daraya all over again, but a plain shroud hung over the forged bones of that great institution. This was a barren place, bereft of life and the little touches of beauty that warmed the heart, speaking of desperation and dire straits that predated its abandonment. A sorry excuse of a Parvinese mausoleum. What had happened to his people after their escape that what should have been the soul of their haven had been left so stark?

The memories of his time at the Academe that woke during

the walk through the empty halls pricked him with melancholy, a longing for the carefree days before the Mugheli invasion when his greatest worry was perfecting his weaves and attaining his master's sash—before he had plumbed the depths of betrayal and killed his own people.

He had thought himself world-wise in his innocence. He had been a fool.

Room after barren room contained nothing to assuage his disappointment. Even the weaves set into the walls were utilitarian, controls for light intensity and heat but none to freshen the air or for beauty—here in what should have been the heart of the Academe.

Night had fallen while they explored, the heavens lit by a strange half-light from the planet's icy ring that drowned the glow over the trees from the city. The outer edge of the ring sparkled with the dazzling color of thousands of rainbows, lending a dreamlike quality to the desolate ruins. A cool wind blew down from the mountain, carrying the pungent smell of tree sap and the clean perfume of askei flowers.

Askei trees, here? A longing for home grabbed him by the throat and refused to let go. Why, after all this time? Its grip was so strong he could not bring himself to speak when Asrial startled at the darkness.

"This late already?" Flicking on a head lamp, she craned her head around. "I hadn't realized," she added with a self-deprecatory laugh devoid of surprise. Clearly she was accustomed to losing track of time while exploring.

In silence, he trailed after her to the courtyard where she had landed their craft. Instead of going to the front, she went to the back.

"I thought we would be returning to the *Castel*."

Smiling, she shook her head. "No point. We haven't found the answer to the *Promise*. It'll be more efficient to just camp here until we're done. Less chance of drawing attention, too."

Attention? He was reminded that she had been worried about spies on Eskarion 14. He had thought her caution due to her cargo, but perhaps she had other enemies. Such as the one who had her abducted?

The rear section yielded a large pack. Curiosity stirring, Romir picked it up when Asrial moved to lift it. The pack was bulky, with some heft to it, but nothing he needed two arms to carry. "Is there anything else you need?"

"That has everything."

He followed her back to where they had ended their explorations. She chose a room, apparently at random, as her campsite, dragging out a thin sleep sack from the pack and spreading it out in the corner farthest from the windows.

It was an austere camp: no heat, a small headlamp for light, the inexplicably functional toilet down the hall for her necessities, the hard stone floor as a bed. All it lacked was a crush of frightened children and moaning casualties for it to be war conditions. So had they camped during the days leading to the escape to Omid.

He could have twisted the glows to life; the weaves were there, their threads bright, ready to be used. But as during the war, the light might draw unwelcome attention.

"Will you be fine?"

Asrial laughed, her eyes glinting in the beam of the head lamp set on the floor at an angle to illuminate most of the room. She pulled something from her belt before sitting down on the sleep sack. "Won't be the first time I camped on-site. Won't be the last. At least there are working facilities."

When unsealed, what she held smelled unpleasantly rich; Romir was suddenly reminded of . . . concentrate rations—the dry, nearly inedible bars that allegedly provided all the nutrients necessary for survival. In the latter days of the war before his capture, he had subsisted on rations.

He stiffened in shock. Why were all these memories stirring? All day bits and pieces of his past had surfaced to bleed anew, tattered rags of a lost life. He willed himself not to breathe to avoid the scent.

It was this place with its similarities to the Academe of Daraya. If only he had not had to rouse those memories. But the reminders of happier times created cracks in the wall he had raised to block out more recent ones of war and betrayal. He could only hope they left this place soon.

"Sleep. I shall keep watch." He took a position beside the sleep sack when Asrial was done with her meal, his back on the wall, his legs stretched out in front of him.

She slid into the sleep sack and lay down, pulling the edge over her. No complaints. No hesitation. An unusual woman. One who did not take care of herself as well as she ought. He was tempted to bundle her in blankets and sit her down for a proper meal. She neglected herself out of consideration for others.

Quiet settled with the darkness, then slowly gave way to night sounds—the rush of the river, branches scratching against the stone walls, the small chirps of some nocturnal creature, the wind whistling through the empty streets.

He was left to stare at the sparkles in the walls—old patterns he had memorized in his boyhood—and wonder at the sequence of events that had left Salima deserted, abandoned by the people who had fled to Omid in hopes of safety and a better life. Why had they left what should have been the heart of the city barren? Free of the Mugheli threat, surely his people had flourished; after all, they had spread throughout the planet and reached the stars.

Nothing he could see with his weaver's sight enlightened him. Nothing hinted at an answer. Everywhere he looked, the patterns of power looked fine—strong and steady. No damage, no trouble, no danger.

So why . . . ?

Some time later, the night sounds were interrupted by a rustle . . . rustle . . . *rustle* from close by. Not leaves on stone, not from outside. Closer. Much closer.

Asrial rolled over and again that rustle: the friction of the thin fabric of the sleep sack. Though she slept, it was a restless sleep.

He touched her cheek and found it cool but dry. Free of tears, thankfully. But when he raised his hand, she grunted, a small sound of displeasure, her head turning . . . in pursuit?

Huh?

She twisted around, wrestling with the sleep sack and kicking the flap away, only to shiver. He could not ignore that. She could fall ill from the cold. Reaching over to cover her, he stilled. Her hand was on his thigh, petting him. His awareness homed in on that point of contact, a low throb starting in his balls.

Was she awake? Was this an invitation to warm the sheets, as she phrased it?

A sigh drifted up and only that. Then she shifted again, crawling closer. Burying her face in his lap, she curled up around him, a hand clutching his waistband. After long moments hearing only her soft breaths, he had to conclude she was asleep. He drew the sleep sack back over her. The rustle disappeared, leaving Romir to listen for night creatures as he waited for the ache in his loins to ease.

He tried to convince himself she only sought his heat, but the smile on her lips tempted him to dream a dangerous dream. He brushed the curls back from her cheeks for a better look at that smile. Impossible hope. It was only her sense of justice that made her want to free him, her soft heart pained by his circumstances. Surely that was all it was.

* * *

Morning came an eternity later. Asrial spent the rest of the night wrapped around him. Whenever his arousal eased, she did something—rolled on his lap, pressed her face against him, petted him—that fanned the flames of desire anew.

But at least she looked rested, her cheeks pink, as she ate another of those detestable rations. If he were guaranteed that outcome each time, he would gladly face a thousand such nights.

They continued their exploration, Asrial persisting in her orderly assault of the archive. Romir made no objection, wanting to put off further comparisons with the Academe of his boyhood for as long as possible. But finally the last of the outer rooms proved unhelpful, leaving only the inner chambers.

Lights activated as they turned into a windowless corridor, warm yellow glows from recesses near the arched ceiling, a response to Asrial's presence. Romir stopped when he realized he had left her behind at the turn. "What?"

Standing with her back to a wall, she pointed wordlessly to the ceiling, her eyes wide and wary, her other hand on the grip of her stunner.

Confused, he frowned at her.

"Why'd they go on? Did you do that?"

"No, they are like the gate in the wall. They detected your presence and responded." His words seemed to drop into a quiet well, echoing in his ears with strange import.

Then the significance struck him. The weaves responded specifically to *Asrial*—without the intervention of a weaver. Just as the gate had opened to her presence.

Why had those long-departed weavers done that?

Romir tucked that question into the back of his mind to ponder on later. The longer they took to explore, the more nights Asrial would spend here. While she might not mind the privations, he intended to do everything in his power to avoid inflicting them on her. She had already sacrificed too much for his sake.

From memory, the windowless corridor gave access to the guarded inner sanctum—provided the original builders had remained true to their inspiration. "In my homeland, this would have been the Archive, the library of Daraya."

More utilitarian walls lined the hallways, their plainness reminiscent of prisons. The rooms that should have contained tapestries and the smaller scrolls of weaver's lore lay empty, bereft even of rotting threads, which could not have been—he could see preservation weaves lying latent on the walls.

Over and over, one question repeated itself in his mind: why?

Asrial walked beside him, her head in constant motion as she studied their stark surroundings. "You'd think there'd be more to find. Even the ruins in Maj had more relics."

She was just as meticulous in her search of the inner rooms. Despite the absence of relics, the archive building was extensive, necessitating another night in Salima.

In the innermost chamber, Romir found the one fixture identical with the original in Daraya: a pedestal carved with stone lacework, its enamels still bright with color. It stood tall, unmarred by time, its design a shocking contrast to the earlier barrenness so that it seemed out of place. The sight made him uneasy for no reason he could fathom. Was this not more in line with what he expected?

"That is what we need." He pointed to the waist-high pedestal and tried not to stare. It looked exactly like the one in memory; he had occasion to use the one in Daraya several times after he had attained his master's sash. He took a deep breath to quiet the dread that fought to rise like a behemoth from the deep—a *kralka*, a mature one with long, venomous tentacles and multiple rows of serrate teeth.

"What does it do?"

"If you would set my badge here." He tapped the cleverly disguised access niche on top, and his finger tingled at the contact as the interface sampled his essence. A live console, as he had expected.

Asrial darted a glance at him, then fumbled under her blouse with surprising awkwardness. He gave her his back to diminish her embarrassment, but the reminder that she wore his badge between her breasts eased his disquiet.

"Here," she said gruffly, thrusting the badge at him.

With a feeling of unreality, he put it on the niche with the design side down. Though he tried not to dwell on those days, he had done something like this before—done it so often his body remembered the motions. Almost by habit, he laid his palm on top, and it locked into place with an audible *click*.

Power licked up. It read his badge, tasting the pattern of his blood and the binding to his essence. He triggered it, weaving power through both badge and niche in the set patterns he had learned with the awarding of his sash.

A soft hum came from the stone lacework as points of white light bloomed around his badge. The light pooled, color rippling in rainbow waves. Finally, it settled into the dark blue of saffir and spilled over, flowing along the stone lacework to limn out the glyph of a sixth skein master on all five sides of the pedestal.

The barren walls flared to life, portions of the stones glowing from within, golden words forming on the blank panels. Patterns in blue, red, green, black, and white formed and re-formed in silent, steady repetition beside the words.

I write in light to hold the knowledge safe, sealed to those of our training.

There are those who believe as the Mughelis do, who wish to be vyzier and master djinn. To protect the people, they say. I cannot believe them. . . .

Horror chilled his heart. Betrayed from within? After all the risks taken, the sacrifices made and lives lost? How could it have come to pass? He staggered back, shaking his head in denial.

"Romir?" Asrial's hand on his back steadied him. "What is it? What's wrong?"

Others counsel caution, that we withhold our teaching. Perhaps it is best if the craft dies with us. If there are no weavers, no one else will be forced to become djinn. But the knowledge of breaking that weave should not be lost. . . .

Was this why Asrial's people retained precious little knowledge of weaving? So little that djinn had been relegated to children's tales?

Whatever the words meant, they didn't look promising. Romir's reaction was like he'd been dealt a mortal blow. She might have looked much the same when the knowledge of her parents' deaths had sunk in. He didn't respond to her question, simply stared at the light script with haunted eyes while slowly shaking his head.

If he were a normal man, Asrial would have worried about him going into shock. But that was impossible in his case. Physically, anyway. Still, his frozen demeanor sent a chill through her. *Useless. Failure.* Old reproaches made familiar by repetition, but they still struck close to the bone. But now was no time for self-indulgent brooding.

Had she been wrong? Was *Promise* a reference to something else altogether? Was there actually no technique to free djinn?

Frigging crap, she hated all these questions and no answers. This was no time for doubts. She shouldn't assume the worst just because of Romir's reaction.

Ignoring the prickling of her arms, Asrial grabbed her comp from her belt and set it to record the text. She'd have to depend on the comp on the *Castel* for a translation. She couldn't ask Romir to read it to her, not right now. That would be like throwing acid on a raw wound.

"Is there more?" She hated to ask, to disturb him in his pain, but they had only so many chances and limited time on Lomida. She couldn't let it go to waste.

Romir responded to the question like a bot, moving only at her prompting. If he was reserved before, he was next to catatonic now. She worked quietly, out of respect for his distress, but her mind churned. What was so terrible that Romir shut down into himself like this?

It was the afternoon of their fourth day in Salima by the time she was willing to concede that there were no more secret messages to be found in that place. She'd recorded what she could. Now she had to get Romir away.

She retraced their route slowly, giving herself time to impress into memory what she could of Salima. This was probably her only chance to see the land of her ancestors.

All too soon, the wall came into view. The gate appeared as soon as the grav sled got within the sled's length to the wall.

They emerged into chaos—lights, parked grav trucks piled high with equipment, so many people standing around as if they didn't have anything better to do. The crowd erupted in voice, shouting and screaming like idiots.

"What the frigging crap—" Asrial swerved wildly, pulling up

to avoid some expensive-looking electronics parked in the middle of the boulevard. The last thing she needed was some idiot filing a lien on the *Castel* to hide his stupidity who found a grounder judge to agree with him.

"Grounders!" She sped away, cursing under her breath.

"They are following." Romir's comment carried less emotion than the *Castel*'s comp, but at least he'd offered it of his own volition. For some reason the sound of his voice, even in monotone, slowed the racing of her heart.

She checked her screens. She hadn't hit anything, but he was right. They were following her, several grav sleds taking to the air after her. They didn't try to catch up with her, but they dogged her tail all the way back to the starport.

Luckily, that was as far as they went. Since nothing more came of the incident, she put it out of her mind.

Until the first vid message, some avatar wanting an interview with the *sraya*. Then another. And another. And another!

With a curse, Asrial blocked incoming communications. *Frigging crap*. All this attention simply because a Dilaryn visited Salima? When nothing happened when they left the *Castel*, she'd thought she was in the clear. She'd started to dismiss her worries as overreaction, to believe that knowledge of her Dilaryn heritage had faded from Lomidar memory, leaving her as just another ordinary Rim rat. But from the barrage of requests for interviews, it was clear that Amin wasn't the only one who viewed her first as sovreine.

Eighteen

Asrial transferred the record of the light text to the comp, working quietly in the hopes of not drawing Romir's attention. After that brief chase back to the *Castel*, he'd lapsed into troubled silence. Whatever information the text contained had hit him like a stunner blast on full. She wanted to know what it was, wanted to understand Romir's pain—and ease it if she could.

It would take a while for the comp to extract the text from the record. While the *Castel*'s comp was capable, it wasn't as advanced as an archeologist's research comp.

Asrial left the work cabin, then blinked at the silence that met her. They were on planet, so none of the usual hums and noises of a properly running ship could be heard. But Romir was nowhere to be seen, either.

The common room was empty, as was the galley. The hold was the same, her footsteps echoing hollowly with only supplies and the grav sled to fill the space. She called his name, but he didn't answer.

She shook her head, denying the horrible possibility. His prison couldn't have claimed him. It was on the ledge the whole time she'd been at the comp.

He was sitting on the floor of her cabin when she entered, the last place she expected to find him. His pose was similar to the first time she'd seen him on the floor, his arms a wall across his knees, except that this time his eyes were blank, as if he'd barricaded all emotion inside.

It hurt to see him that way.

They couldn't stay here where he would be captive to his thoughts. She needed a distraction, something to break the grab net that message in Salima had cast over him.

"Let's leave this for now." Asrial pulled him to his feet, talking the whole time. "All we've seen for two decs is the interior of the *Castel*. We're in no rush to get elsewhere, might was well save the supplies for later and eat something good."

"But—"

"Salima doesn't count." Urging him out wasn't just for his benefit. She did wonder if knowing the sacrifices Romir's people had made to reach Lomida changed her perspective of Lomidari.

"—I have no need to eat."

"Then you can keep me company." Keeping a hand on his arm, she headed for the airlock.

"You . . . are not taking your craft?" Just asking seemed to take a major effort for Romir, but at least he was pulling out of that downward spiral. His back straightened, alertness seeping into his eyes with a force of will.

"The grav sled? Not this time. I'm tired of port food, so I thought we'd look around to see what else is available. Easier to do that walking. Who knows where we'll end up. Let's start there." She pointed to the commercial arcade at the edge of the starport. Besides, if they flew, he wouldn't see much of his people.

Romir wouldn't say anything, but he had to be curious about the fate of the people he'd saved, and the Lomidari were their descendants. She could help him satisfy that curiosity; the cost of an off-ship meal—extortionately high in the Inner Worlds and on planet—was minor compared to that. This would be his only chance, since she had no intention of returning to Lomida in the future. A sudden fear gripped her: unless he remained behind. Here she was plotting a course on the assumption he'd continue crewing with her after he was free. What if he preferred to stay on Lomida?

A port robocab pulled over. The automated transports roved the landing field, serving the shuttles of the passenger liners and the ships that didn't have a grav sled or an aircar. She usually didn't resort to a robocab, preferring the independence of piloting herself, but they were a necessity if one was afoot. The starport was a city in itself, rivaling Yasra in size; it had to be to accommodate all the space traffic. They rode it to the arcade, Asrial now beset by doubts.

Chaos was her first impression of the arcade. It spanned two sides of the starport and was mobbed by a miscellany of races that more than anything proved they were on an Inner World. Even for a spacer like her, standing among this multitude was overwhelming.

Romir caught her arm, pulling her out of the way of a pair of scarred Hagnash shoving through the crowd. "Where do you wish to eat?"

Not here. Most of the people were spacers. "Let's walk around. See what's available."

After a short stroll, the number of spacers petered out to be replaced by just as many grounders, but it still wasn't what she had in mind. She left the arcade for the streets beyond.

Once outside the arcade's walls, the atmosphere changed

immediately. The low buildings along the streets began their steady climb toward the spires in the heart of Yasra. But this close to the starport, they had a good view of the Lomidar capital and its manufactured mountains.

Asrial followed her nose to a small sidewalk eatery that promised fast, cheap food and hearty servings. Authentic Lomidar food—or as authentic as one might get so close to port. She watched Romir as she ate, feasting on the expressions that escaped his restraint as much as on the meal before her.

She'd been right in thinking he needed to see the Lomidari in order to accept his people's survival. It wasn't the same as reuniting with his family, but that would have been impossible, even back in his time.

In light of Romir's pleasure, she didn't regret her decision until later, after they walked around a bit, exploring one of the broad boulevards tucked behind the industrial area surrounding the starport. The deeper they went into Yasra, the more people there were in the streets, as if the open spaces attracted the rowdy throngs. There were as many on a station—probably—but in space the corridors and limited lines of sight hid the reality.

Here, she felt as if a spotlight were focused on them. She wasn't imagining the attention: the grounders turned and stared openly, the ruder ones going so far as to point their fingers—at her. Some dared come closer—into punching range—too close, as though they had no concept of personal space. So much for the myth of Inner World cosmopolitan sophistication.

Only grounders were staring, and not at Romir. *First the chase from Salima, then the barrage of requests for interviews, now this? Don't tell me they recognize my face?*

Glaring at the rude bastards, Asrial forged ahead. *"Keep moving. Don't get pinned down,"* an inner voice trained by years on the Rim whispered in the back of her mind.

Crap, maybe this hadn't been such a good idea, after all. She'd just wanted to pass time while the comp worked on translating the light text she'd recorded, to distract Romir from his shock and show him that the descendants of his people flourished. But they were drawing a crowd. This was more serious than a bunch of Inner World grounder snobs gawking at spacers.

All this interest made her fingers itch for her stunner.

Romir seemed to pick up on her unease, lagging to take a position behind and to her left. He was protecting her again.

The small hairs on the back of her neck stood on end half a beat before the twinge in her gut. What she would give to be able to attribute her concern to paranoia . . .

Of course, life was seldom that easy. If it were, there wouldn't be a man lurking among the bystanders, pretending not to trail them.

She didn't like the look of him. Dressed all in corporate black that failed to conceal the weapons on his person, the grounder moved with an economy of motion that boded trouble—a trained fighter, not simply a brawler. And he wasn't alone.

"What is it?"

Asrial glanced back at Romir, noting the deceptive boredom shuttering his eyes. "We're being followed."

If she hadn't been looking at him, she'd have missed the silver ferocity that flashed beneath his thick, black lashes, an intimation of the man whose memories were dominated by war and enslavement, death and destruction. A man who'd been used as a weapon against his own people. He'd suffered so much. Surely he'd faced more than his fair share of violence.

She could feel the net closing in on them, invisible for the time being but drawing tight. Instinctively, she headed for the starport and safety. But each change in direction found more lurkers all around. And once they realized she'd spotted them, they didn't try too hard to hide their numbers from her.

The men herding them used her scruples against her, the presence of innocent grounders limiting her options. The only way she and Romir could escape was if she were willing to stun people whose only offense was being in the wrong place at the wrong time. She'd hoped they would hesitate to try anything in public, but the muscle that oozed out between the nooks and crannies of the gathering crowd like seeping old hydraulic fluid was obviously corporate hire, not mere port toughs—an expensively outfitted private army and willing to advertise that fact.

Flight had never looked so tempting. "That's far enough." Keeping a hand on her stunner, Asrial checked around for a way out, but they were surrounded with no help forthcoming from the clueless bystanders.

One of the professional muscle gestured sharply at his companions, stopping them in their tracks, as he stepped closer. "Come with us. My principal wishes a word. It should be profitable for both of you," he informed her in an emotionless monotone that told her more than she wanted to know about the situation.

If his delivery wasn't enough, his stone face wiped clean of all expression set her internal alarms flashing red. "Sorry, not for hire. Try the port." She sidestepped, staying out of reach.

Romir pulled her behind him, shielding her with his body. The glance he shot her conveyed an offer to take her away.

"We must insist, *Sraya* Dilaryn."

More men stepped out of the murmuring crowd, heavily armed, their high-power stunners worn openly. Hers could kill if set at full power, fired at point-blank range at a major neural cluster, say the base of the skull at the top of the spinal cord. Theirs looked to be brute force military models that weren't so finicky about aiming.

Frigging crap, they knew who she was—moreover, they had addressed her as a sovreine . . . just like those avatars wanting an interview. Any way she looked at it, that was bad.

Worse, they were corporate muscle! That was *very* bad. It wasn't just her gut screaming at her; her skin desperately wanted to crawl off her arms. She'd been afraid something like this would happen.

Asrial preferred to avoid grounder politics, especially Lomidar politics. Especially after everything she'd heard from her father. And this situation had all the tag marks of politics. If she had her way, she'd run far and fast in the opposite direction. Except it didn't look like that was an option at the moment. These men would be able to find her no matter how fast she ran. After all, she'd eventually have to return to the *Castel.*

On Lomida, she had nowhere else to go. She couldn't leave her ship behind.

Frigging, *freaking* crap. There was no other choice. She had to play along for the moment.

With a sinking feeling of inevitability, she caught Romir's wrist and shook her head minutely. If it were known he was more than an ordinary man, if they knew he was a djinn, who knew what they would do, how far they would go?

If they stole his prison . . .

Besides, she might need his powers later. She felt a twinge of guilt. So much for her high-minded ideals about believing Romir was a man. In a pinch of trouble, here she was, thinking of him as some sort of secret weapon.

Loud speculation rose behind the wall of professional muscle surrounding them. Stone Face ignored it, his mouth moving silently with subvocalized instructions, the result of which was immediately obvious.

A hover limo swooped out of the air traffic, long and black, wide stretches of glass tinted for privacy. Extravagant. It grounded with barely a whisper. A line appeared by the rear compartment, spreading into a door that opened like a mouth.

She'd seen more inviting maws in the Rim, though none that smelled this rich.

Stone Face stood by the door, as mannerly as a court attendant in her mother's stories. But there was no mistaking the demand in his posture: if she didn't enter by her own power, they would force her inside.

Romir stepped to her side, placing his body between her and the rest of the muscle. If she gave the word, he would fight—here in this very public place before countless witnesses, living and electronic.

Unwilling to risk Romir's discovery, Asrial stepped in, sliding to the far side to make space for Romir. Leather gave way under her, petal smooth and yielding, the ultimate of luxury, to slaughter an animal for such an outrageously ordinary purpose—merely because they could.

She crossed her arms, chiding herself for being surprised. This was the Inner Worlds, after all, and Lomida, at that. Carbon silk upholstery would be the exception here.

Romir settled beside her, a solid warmth against her side. He slung an arm around her shoulders, his thoughts unreadable, as he studied the hover limo's ostentatious luxury.

Stone Face followed him inside, taking a seat across from them, and the door sealed shut with a hush behind him. The limo took to the air at his word; obviously he was no mere flunky.

The rapid ascent pressed her deeper into the extravagant seat, making her wonder if the driver harbored illusions of space flight. It certainly felt like it. Faster than she liked they were threading the maze of spires that rose in the heart of Yasra, the limo a dark blotch on flashing glassteel windows—too fast for her to get her bearings. Seen through the hover limo's dark windows, the people on the streets below looked like sand grains borne by artificial rivers and just as powerless against the whims of those who commanded those rivers to flow.

Stone Face kept silent the whole trip, a watchful presence impossible to ignore as his eyes shifted between her and Romir and back thoughtfully. She could see him weighing the connection between them, then identifying weak points and calculating the odds. The brains behind the professional muscle. He probably thought he could use Romir to control her.

Asrial gritted her teeth as the steel weight of understanding sank home: Stone Face would be right, too. If they knew what Romir was and could lay their hands on his prison, she'd do anything they wanted, to save him. Somehow, without her knowing, Romir had wound his way into her heart.

So perhaps she didn't consider him just a secret weapon after all?

The limo landed on a parking deck, the rooftop beside one of the numerous spires that littered Yasra. Her gut clenched, her sense of foreboding ratcheting higher. Most of these spires were owned by one corporation or another. Given who held the power in Lomida, she had a strong suspicion which one owned this particular building.

Several aircars landed around them and discharged a throng of heavily armed professional muscle. She swore silently. She should have known it wouldn't be that easy. She'd gambled that riding in the limo would reduce their numbers, since it could only accommodate so many, but obviously Stone Face had taken that into account in his planning.

Like an oxygen bottle running down, the trap was drawing tighter around her, a circuit closing, whether she wanted it to or not. Their options were few and getting fewer.

When they got out, Stone Face's men surged forward to surround them, shoulder to shoulder, a solid wall of black suits, like a protective detail. They weren't taking any chances. Too bad she couldn't believe they were there to protect them.

The quibbling did little to distract her from their situation. Outnumbered, unless she chose to expose Romir's secret. Definitely outgunned. But hopefully not outwitted.

Right, just keep telling yourself that.

Their entourage swept them through various security checkpoints, their flouting of standard procedures reinforcing Asrial's suspicions of their principal's standing. No mere admin bod could have endorsed such behavior and survived.

Romir kept an arm around her. He said nothing, but the grim look in his eyes announced to one and all that they would have to go through him to get at her. None of the muscle took him up on the challenge.

Stone Face waved them into a small chamber with transparent walls that looked out on the neighboring complex. His men crowded in after, forcing her deep into Romir's embrace if she didn't want contact with them.

Only when the room began to move did Asrial realize they stood in a lift tube. It carried them to the very top, the speed of its ascent blurring the lines of the complex's spires, so fast it reminded her of takeoff in the *Castel*, yet the acceleration felt negligible.

What she would give to be back on her ship, preparing to shake off the dust of this planet forever. So far, nothing good had come of this visit. She didn't expect that to change any time soon.

They came to a smooth stop that belied the rapid ascent. The lack of extreme decel effects pointed to the cunning use of varigrav plates . . . in a lift tube. Only for the elite.

At the top, the doors opened onto opulence designed to awe: wood-paneled walls shone a golden brown, pale carpeting thick enough to sleep on that probably showed every dirty footprint, rarefied air spiced with some vaguely tangy green scent. Expensive vases with deceptively simple floral arrangements filled nooks in the empty, silent corridor—real flowers, no two alike. The extravagance worked, driving home the message of overwhelming power. The muscle spoke in cowed tones that didn't carry far as they spilled out of the lift tube and arrayed themselves around her and Romir.

Walking with the arrogant swagger of a big winner, Stone Face took the lead down the curving corridor, taking them past several unmarked doors to the very end and an imposing door covered by two pairs of guards. The entrance to the yfreet's lair, no doubt.

Still no chance of escape. She and Romir remained surrounded, and making a break for it at this point didn't seem to offer a reasonable chance of success. She ground her teeth in frustration. *Frigging corporate bods and their frigging sense of entitlement!* This was why she'd much rather gad about the Rim instead of settling on one of the Inner Worlds.

"Wait. Before you enter, please hand over your stunner." Despite the polite words, the hand Stone Face extended was clearly a demand.

Asrial stiffened. Disarm herself voluntarily? No way. She couldn't leave herself deliberately helpless, especially among such unquestionably dangerous individuals.

The hand remained extended. "My apologies, *Sraya*, but I cannot allow you to approach my principals armed."

So Stone Face was willing to flout standard procedures only so far? She swore silently. Worse and worse luck.

"They're the ones who asked for this meeting." Her protest drew only subvocal grunts.

One of the guards by the door flexed his shoulders, impatience narrowing his eyes. Though he said nothing, he held himself ready to force the issue.

Romir stepped forward, placing his left hand on top of her right and against her side, circumventing any attempt on her part to draw her stunner. "Defiance will only make them use force."

Cold prickled her arms, dismay curdling her stomach at his

betrayal. Why was he doing this? Why was he helping them disarm her? Surely he had to have a good reason—she had to believe he had a good reason—but she didn't like it.

Stone Face gave Romir a brusque nod of approval, the corners of his thin mouth curving slightly. "You understand the situation. Now give me the stunner. Slowly. Use only two fingers. Don't try anything." Though the harsh tone grated on Asrial's patience, at least he didn't seem to consider Romir a threat.

With his thumb and first finger, Romir extracted the stunner, then surrendered it to Stone Face. Ice filled her veins at the transfer, her heart numb at the turn of events.

She watched helplessly as Stone Face handed her stunner to one of his men, a sinking sensation in her stomach. She wrenched her eyes away to stare at her shaking fist. Her empty holster taunted her. At least it looked empty—it didn't feel that way though. The weight on her hip remained the same, as if it still bore a stunner. What had he done?

One of the door's guards flashed a wrist comp, then nodded his satisfaction at what it displayed. "They're clear now."

At that statement, his partner went through an elaborate show of disengaging the door's security.

It was a struggle to keep the disbelief off her face. The scanners didn't detect anything? What had Romir done? Despite the evidence before her eyes, she didn't believe that he had really disarmed her.

The four guards stood aside with an unctuous air of virtue that made her want to grind their heads into the nearest wall. Once more, Stone Face took the lead as the door to the yfreet's lair split in the middle, parting with unnecessary slowness.

Beyond a field of more thick carpet, the far wall was clear glassteel, the light streaming through making it difficult to see the faces of the three people seated behind a wide, leather-topped table. More muscle propped up the other walls, their corporate black suits conspicuous against the pale wood paneling. Except for that table, the room was mostly empty, a deplorable waste of space that reeked of power and pride. The heavy-handed setup clearly intended to overawe would have disinclined her to entertain an offer from these corporate types, if the peremptory summons hadn't already done so.

Moreover, the vista the wall afforded was one of towering buildings and circling yfreet, reminding her of the complex hidden in the mountains of Maj and the Mughelis who had imprisoned Romir for so long. Despite the passage of thousands of years, there were still those who seemed to associate altitude with power.

Only Stone Face and four others entered the room with them; the rest of his men remained outside. Whether that was good or not was too soon to tell. Those professionals still lay between her and escape. Stone Face himself quickly crossed the carpet, taking one side of the table as his station.

When she reached the center of the room, about an aircar's length from the table, the intensity of the light eased. The effect was likely deliberate—some treatment on the glassteel, rather than her eyes adjusting. It meant that if she wanted a clear view of Stone Face's principals, she had to keep her distance—just right to stand on ceremony and too far for equality.

Asrial hid her shock at their identities.

They were the highest of the Dareh: Malek Bazhir, the president of the entire conglomerate; Nabila Bintanan, the matriarch of House Bintanan, sitting in the middle; and Sekkar Bintanan, her heir. The last people on this planet she wanted to see.

Nineteen

For a woman in her ninth decade, the Bintanan was remarkably well-preserved. The hand of time touched her only lightly: faint lines at the corners of her eyes, the barest creases between her elegant brows, a certain fragility to her gold-washed skin. She looked much as she did in the vid records of Jamyl Kharym Rashad's abdication—like a woman half her age. It must have cost a fortune to chop that many years off her body. Even the skin of her hands was taut and unmarked.

Though he wasn't as old as the Bintanan, Bazhir's features wore a similar pampered hauteur. His eyes held the cold disdain of one who saw lesser mortals as pawns in a game. Here was a man who assessed people by what they could do for him.

The heir looked to be Asrial's age, though she knew better. He'd attained his majority before her birth. He'd stood beside the Bintanan and Bazhir on the stage when her father had announced his abdication.

Of the three, the woman appeared to be the leader—an intricate earring dangled from her left lobe, marking her as a sovreine. A recent ennoblement. Asrial might avoid grounder politics, but she kept track of the people responsible for her father's downfall. Up to the time of Jamyl's and Nasri's deaths, the Bintanan hadn't worn the trappings of a sovreine.

She shouldn't have been surprised by their identities or elevation. What else could be expected from those who arrogated the authority of a *reis*? Who else would have been so interested in an otherwise no-account Rim rat like her in an Inner World?

All the attention at the starport made sense now. The Lomidari hadn't been staring at an anonymous spacer but at the scion of House Dilaryn. If she didn't claim a sovreine's dignity, she'd surrender a potentially useful weapon in this confrontation, accepting a handicap to no purpose.

"The *sraya*, Asrial Dilaryn," Stone Face announced—to Asrial's shock, such politeness not what she'd expected from her enemies.

She continued forward, hoping they'd taken her hesitation for protocol, not weakness. If she was to have a chance at escape, she had to fly this course with utmost care.

Without prompting, Romir dragged a chair over to the table, playing retainer with aplomb. When she sat down, he took a station by her shoulder, lending his pride to her consequence. His support came as a relief after he'd helped disarm her.

She pretended to take it in stride, narrowing her eyes against the sunlight's glare to focus on the Bintanan. "What is this about?"

The older woman kept her hands folded together on top of the table, her self-control absolute with not even a twitch of a finger to betray her age, space her. "You know who we are."

To her misfortune. Asrial grimaced at their arrogance. Had the three of them sat like this when they'd confronted her father to force him to abdicate? She could easily imagine the scene.

"We summoned you here to offer you a proposition," the

Bintanan continued without any change in her expression. Her manner exuded confidence; she fully expected Asrial to accept.

"You were seen entering Salima." Bazhir took over control of the audience, tapping the leather top with a stylus. At the peremptory motion, an image appeared in the air above the table, a vid of the granite wall transforming into a gate through which her grav sled disappeared. "And even more publicly, leaving."

Leaning back in her seat, Asrial said nothing, unwilling to give them even that much. She felt her face settle into stiff, formal lines. *Sraya*, the professional muscle had addressed her, the proper address for a sovreine. In this instance, she could not escape her upbringing.

The vid continued, showing men trying to find the gate and encountering only solid granite. Attempts to go over the wall were met with an energy barrier that appeared out of nowhere—no projectors, no generators, no obvious explanation. Like a force wall, except actively hostile. The barrier didn't wait to be hit to attack. Clearly not just anyone could enter Salima. No wonder it remained in Dilaryn hands. Quite possibly the Dareh couldn't have taken it by force.

Only now, knowing about djinn and weaves of power, did she realize that there was more to her mother's stories than simply ancient family history. Those supposed hauntings weren't anything so supernatural. Salima somehow utilized a similar technology—for want of a better term—to the strange force walls in that complex on Maj, so similar that Romir could locate the gate. She shouldn't have been surprised. After all, the working Romir's people had done to travel from Maj to Lomida was essentially a planet-based jump ring. She didn't understand how Salima's defenses worked, yet the wall had responded to her presence, and that was all that mattered.

Bazhir's eyes narrowed, his mouth crinkling with displeasure as she said nothing. And what was there to say? Clearly there was no way she could convince them they were in error, and she refused to volunteer information. When she persisted in her blank stare, the Dareh president finally broke the silence. "You do not deny it."

Asrial shrugged. "What is there to deny?"

The Bintanan snorted, a sudden puff that nonetheless managed to sound elegant. "So troublesome. Enough with this pretense of ignorance. The Lomidari are restless. Your appearance encouraged a small minority of malcontents." The statement didn't carry any emotion—flat, uncaring, a data point.

Pretense of ignorance? They expected her to be as manipulative as they, to act with only her own best interests at heart. That sort of sinister thinking was alien to her, but could she use it against them? She doubted they'd believe she hadn't factored in the political ramifications of her appearance on Lomida when she decided to go to Salima. But she had thought that was in the distant past and forgotten; she'd never considered the possibility that anyone would think she would want to take up the scepter of the *reis*—much less give it great credence. No matter what Nasri might have wished, she had grown up a spacer. She knew nothing about ruling multiple planets and colonies spread across however many galactic sectors, and she didn't care to learn!

"Did it?" Needing a reprieve from those cold faces, Asrial turned her head and her gaze to the line of spires beyond the glassteel. Unlike the blank expression Romir maintained, theirs were rooted in ego, in selfishness, in raising themselves above all others. She could only be glad she hadn't grown up among such people. For the first time, she found herself grateful for her father's abdication.

"You know it did, you ca—"

The Bintanan waved her heir to silence, cutting him off in midsentence. "That is beside the point. Your actions have unnecessarily stirred the Lomidari. You are therefore obliged to correct the situation by showing your visible support for our administration."

Disbelief locked Asrial in her seat.

"Of course, you will be well compensated, sufficient for a life of comfort anywhere in the Inner Worlds." The Bintanan named a figure that would have covered the *Castel*'s upgrade with funds left over, with a prim smile that said she fully expected Asrial to pounce on the offer. Clearly she saw nothing untoward about requesting the support of the daughter of the *reis* she helped depose.

None of the Dareh evinced even the slightest shred of guilt, only the willingness to use their creds to buy their will—to the detriment of the people they wished to rule. Nasri had been right to describe them as yfreet. They may lack the long, snaky necks, the sharp fangs, the tearing claws, the broad, leathery wings, but they were just as vicious as those Lomidar scavengers.

Plasma-hot fury shrank the world to the three barricaded behind privilege and entitlement. Feeling the ground teeter under her boots, she gulped down the words boiling in her gut. She had to keep her wits about her. This meeting was no ordinary trade with goodwill on both sides; something else was happening besides the obvious. "Let me get this straight. You want me to lend the Dilaryn name to the Dareh conglomerate. To bolster its standing with the Lomidari. After you forced my father to abdicate."

Asrial stared into the smooth, self-satisfied face that wore not a single line of toil, remembered the furrows of strain on her mother's brow that came from scrounging for trade contracts and years of worry for her husband and daughter, old before her time. Leaning forward, her weight on her hands flat on the table, she chose her words carefully. "No way in frigging hell."

Fury erupted in the Bintanan's eyes, towering offense at the thwarting of her will. Blood washed the old woman's cheeks with ugly color as skin stretched pale over the knuckles of her shaking fists. She gaped, her wide mouth opening and shutting repeatedly before she found her voice. "You . . . dare?"

Her heir arched a dark, well-shaped brow but said nothing.

Bazhir glared at Asrial, unblinking black eyes frigid with the cold of deep space and just as unforgiving. "You are in no position to reject our proposition." As the president of the entire Dareh conglomerate, he wielded vast influence, especially in Inner World sectors. One word from him was sufficient to destroy many businesses, another reason why she never considered settling for a corporate job after her parents' deaths.

"And you'll do what? Make me disappear? Too many people saw me. If I disappear, how would your restless Lomidari react?"

The Bintanan's florid cheeks went gray, the thin lips white at the edges, confirming her guess.

Asrial nodded in satisfaction. "That's what I thought." It didn't matter that she didn't think she had such influence, only that the Dareh believed it.

She pushed away from the table, wondering how many of the muscle she could take down if it came to shooting. Not enough, she suspected. She was just a Rim rat; against professionals, she didn't stand a chance. That didn't mean she wouldn't try—no way she was helping this carrion-eater stay in power.

At least she didn't have to worry about Romir.

The Bintanan tapped the tips of her fingers together, a sneer creasing her cheeks. "Naive child. You misapprehend your position. We do not need your support, merely your face."

Her face? Understanding came in a flash of chill unease. They meant to steal her identity.

Image programs could do that easily; video and audio could be manipulated to show whatever the programmer wanted. That was the reason buyers attended relic auctions in person or sent representatives—and why people gave more credence to face-to-face meetings.

Asrial inhaled sharply, her heart thundering in her ears, the skin of her arms prickling with cold. The world fell silent. Details leaped at her, preternaturally distinct, just like when she took the *Castel* through a Ring. The quivering tic at the corner of the Bintanan's eye. The sudden, white-knuckled tension of the restless heir. The minute motion of Bazhir's thumb rubbing the leather of the table.

Romir's hand on her shoulder silenced the rash words that sprang to her lips, the tightening of his fingers urging caution. He was right, of course. The less said, the less that could be used against her.

She stood to leave. There was nothing to be gained by wasting more time here. The question was whether she would be able to escape—Romir would have no problem.

"I have not dismissed you."

"Tough. I'm done talking with you." Asrial turned her back on the three, her heart racing at the gamble. She glanced at Romir then the probably locked door, hoping he understood.

The nearest guard smirked. She had the pleasure of seeing that smarmy expression vanish when the door slid aside on silent tracks when she got within arm's reach. Nothing like a great exit to do wonders for a woman's confidence.

Unfortunately, it wouldn't last. Couldn't last. The Bintanan hadn't come this far by turning a blind eye to defiance. Her back itched, anticipating a stunner blast. But she had no intention of rolling over and playing nice with the power-hungry yfreet.

Only the fear of instigating the very fight she still hoped to avoid kept her from drawing her stunner. The longer they put off that confrontation, the better their chances of escape.

"Stop her!"

Desperately aware they were outnumbered, Asrial grabbed for her stunner, praying that she had been right, that Romir had simply obscured it and it was still in her holster. The universe slowed to an endless crawl . . . until a familiar grip met her palm.

Romir's hand bit into her shoulder. He dragged her in front of him, shielding her with his body.

Stunners hummed all around them, angry power on ready. Energy crackled, an electric blue corona reaching for them with glittering, searing fingers.

This was going to hurt.

Her body tensed instinctively, anticipating the neural agony of multiple stunner blasts.

She . . . felt nothing!

They missed?! *Never mind about that. Business first.* She fired back, squeezing off shots as fast as the stunner could manage. Aiming didn't matter—there were that many of them.

Romir held her in place, his tight grip keeping her from diving for cover.

Shouts rose, bewildered, outraged, cut short. More beams crackled their way—but instead of hitting, they fed a ball of violent energy that appeared around them. Whirling, sparkling chaos wrapped them in an electrifying cocoon of safety.

It had to be Romir's doing.

The scorched air made the hairs on her arms stand on end. The ball contracted, fluctuating smaller then larger, then smaller, nearer then farther then nearer. The fluctuations came faster as more beams hit it.

They had to get away—and fast. She didn't know how long Romir could keep it up, but if he faded, the Dareh might realize what he was. In their lust for power, they had deposed her father. What more would they risk to command a djinn?

The hum of the stunners grew to a furious chorus—military-grade stunners, she remembered, lethal at full power. And there were several of them. How much longer could Romir hold out before they overloaded his defense?

And when that defense failed . . .

Twenty

Crackling energy scorched the air as multiple stunners fired, acrid and searing. Asrial returned fire desperately, her eyes tearing at the stench, but she couldn't tell to what effect. Hopefully, Romir's defense wasn't stopping her blasts.

With a wild sizzle, the ball around them exploded. Violent streamers of energy lashed out in all directions, arcing through the room like localized lightning strikes. Targeted lightning strikes. The men surrounding them broke into spasms, flung off their feet by their bodies' response. Bouncing off the walls, they fell, convulsions pounding them against the floor.

"Go!" A push urged her on. "Do not look back."

She went. And didn't look back.

Alarms blared, a deafening cacophony sufficient to wake the dead to the third generation and make them wish they'd died all over again. They were too loud to ignore. Someone had to respond, and sooner or later—probably sooner—more muscle would fill the hall. Throw enough creds at a problem, and someone would pick up the slack. In this case, the Dareh had creds to spare, and they had professionals.

Unless she and Romir stole an aircar, they had to get to the ground and out of the tower to get away. Problem was, they were so high up the only way down—realistically—was the lift tube. Descending on foot while outrunning pursuit would be physically impossible. But the lift tube was a chokepoint: security would be able to isolate them.

The clangor of alarms shut down abruptly, leaving her ears ringing with silence.

"Frigging crap." The only feet Asrial heard were hers as they ran past blank doors. Apprehension tightened her gut. Any moment now more muscle would spill out of those doors. Any moment now.

Hoping no one had thought to deactivate the lift tube, she banged her fist on the call panel. The door slid aside. The chamber was empty, which was a stroke of luck, but when they entered, it didn't move, and she couldn't see any controls to get it moving.

"It should go down, yes?"

"Yes, we need to get to the ground floor."

Romir laid his hand on the wall—and the floor, the entire chamber plummeted.

Asrial grabbed Romir as her stomach was left far behind. "Not this fast!" They were dropping faster than they'd gone up, practically free fall. She didn't mind a spot of zero grav, but the landing was a different matter: from this height, all that would be left of her was a bloody smear; she probably wouldn't even bounce. Her skin crawled, and it had nothing to do with the wind from their passage. She screwed her eyes shut to block the sight of spires, floors, lines blurring past. *Spirit of space!* As a pilot, she'd have preferred death by plasma shield failure or just not exiting from Jump.

He put an arm around her. "Worry not."

Easy for him to say! He'd just turn to mist.

Air thickened perceivably. More than clouds. More than steam. An invisible mass almost thick enough to chew. It wrapped her body in a blanket of heaviness.

Their descent slowed. She would have attributed it to terminal velocity, except the blurs through the lift tube's walls regained their distinctness. Blobs in the nearby spires were recognizable as people.

Until the floor under her boots supported her weight again.

A door slid into view, and they finally came to a stop. Asrial froze, incredulous at her survival. "How?"

"Remember the spires on Maj?"

Her brain fumbled for relevance for half a heartbeat—what did Maj have to do with it?—before memory clicked in. Vyziers used djinn to bear them up and down their spires. His confidence was because this hadn't been the first time he'd borne someone that way.

Guilt dug hard spikes into her back. Now was no time for distraction. They weren't out of Dareh hands yet.

Romir released her and turned to the door.

"Wait." She checked her stunner automatically. Since she'd been firing at full power, she wasn't surprised to see its charge read more than halfway to low. She replaced the charge with a fresh pack, then holding the stunner at low ready, nodded at Romir to continue. "All right."

The door opened into silence and surreal normalcy. No deafening alarms. No one in sight. The lobby was empty, though she imagined there were security cams pointed at them. With the Dareh bosses on site, security had to be tight.

Romir caught her arm before she'd taken more than a step forward, then slid in front of her. "Allow me." It galled her to hide behind him, but he was better able to withstand a stunner blast.

Nothing happened when he showed himself, and Asrial quickly followed him out, half-afraid the lift tube would head back up. How much longer did they have?

Not much time at all, it turned out.

He stopped without warning, taking her by surprise—so sudden that she bumped into his back and bounced off. She would have fallen, if she hadn't grabbed his belt, but she had no cause for complaint.

Guards spilled out of a side door, shoulders stiff, masks of urgency tight across their faces, as they rushed to the entrance lobby.

Crap, crap, crap, and frigging crap. Romir could still escape, but there was no way she was walking out the front door now, not without a fight.

Asrial tugged on his sleeve and tipped her head to indicate the opposite direction. There had to be more than one way out of this place—if it was anything like Lyrel 9, there would be all sorts of access corridors for service deliveries and the like. Those in power preferred to keep the maintenance crews out of sight.

Following her lead, Romir walked briskly, keeping his body between her and potential discovery.

"Can you do something about the security cams without putting them out of commission?" The cams going blank would be almost as sure a giveaway of their presence as them being spotted. She didn't hope for much. Unlike on Eskarion, they needed to avoid detection.

Romir's eyes narrowed as he studied their surroundings. "Ah, easily solved." The look he slid her said he understood her concern, the harsh light in his eyes reminding her that most of the memories he retained were of war. "I cannot fool the system, but taking down cams on multiple levels should make locating us more difficult."

"Do it."

"Done."

Despite Romir's reply, there was nothing obtrusive—like sparks or smoke or explosions—though that might have provided some reassurance; the security cams simply stopped moving. She had to trust that he had dealt with them the same as he dealt with the locks.

She took the next door with more caution. Dressed as they were in spacer gear, there was no way anyone would believe they were authorized personnel.

This corridor was narrower, and the walls lacked the gloss of extreme wealth. They were out of the public area and headed deeper into the maze. Now if only she could find an exit. The walls were unhelpfully devoid of signs. Obviously people were expected to know were they where and how to get to wherever they were supposed to go.

Asrial followed her ears to the muted throb of equipment. Heavy equipment meant maintenance requirements and, therefore, access corridors—or so she hoped. She studied the floor, looking for signs of hard use to give their flight direction. Her arms prickled, tension drawing her shoulders tighter the longer they walked as she waited for Stone Face's men to make an appearance.

"This way." Romir waved at a door that obediently opened onto a narrow, raised walkway overlooking a busy delivery dock. Bots buzzed around the dock floor, unloading, sorting, stacking barrels and crates. The scene looked so ordinary she stumbled to a halt to stare, half expecting to find herself in the bay of one of the stations she frequented.

Wishful thinking, of course.

Here the security cams were more conspicuous—white, waving blobs that dotted the overhead like oversize Cyrian optic hair bleached of all color—and likely still online since they were in constant motion.

A heavy gate rose just long enough to admit a laden cargo bot. A different gate allowed the empty ones to leave the dock.

Leaning over the rail, Romir stared at the second gate. "I can get you through." It looked simple enough, but the walkway was higher than she could safely drop; he'd have to carry her down to the dock floor first.

She grabbed the rail with both hands, afraid he would lift her right then and there. "Don't! You mustn't."

He'd done more than enough. If he tapped more of his djinn powers, the Dareh would know what Romir was. She couldn't risk it. They had to find another exit.

"Why?"

Asrial drew him away from the rail and jerked her chin at one of the cams dangling from the wall below the walkway. "We can't take the risk. You can't be sure you got all of them. What we need is one of the personnel exits."

There was still no sign of pursuit, though surely the muscle would get their act together and catch up soon. The Dareh would be out for blood after the shambles she and Romir had made of that meeting room on the topmost level. It was imperative they get out of the complex.

The corner of Romir's jaw twitched, but if he wanted to argue, he didn't act on the urge. He swept the doors leading off the walkway with a searching glance, his gaze distant as if seeing something beneath the surface.

His head jerked, one hand slashing up to point. "There. That way. Hurry, they are coming." He propelled her forward with an arm on her waist.

Abandoning stealth, she sprinted for the door he indicated, the walkway jangling underfoot. Just as they made it through, a barrage of pounding feet erupted on the dock floor, accompanied by terse exclamations and the rattle of shock sticks.

* * *

Romir plucked at the strands of power and gave them a slight twist, sealing the door to slow the enemy. Anyone chasing them on the walkway would have to break down the door to get through.

Imprison Asrial, would they? Pursue her like some discarded pleasure slave to be hunted down, would they? They would pay for this outrage. He would make sure of it.

Fury rampaged in his heart, the confrontation resurrecting memories of desperate battles, of friends and family dying beside him, of his rage and helplessness in the hands of the Mughelis. His hands moved of their own accord, adding a special knot to the gleaming threads of the door, a nasty shock for those who would threaten Asrial.

She ran ahead, keeping her head down and her stunner at the ready, wary as ever. She was a strong woman, yet one who flinched at using his djinn abilities to their fullest.

No matter. He chose to put those abilities to use, searching the threads of power for the exit she sought. The strands glimmered in his weaver's sight, denser around solid matter, brighter around electronics, pulsing with the heartbeat of the universe.

There.

Stretching out his will, Romir tweaked the threads he needed, and a small door slid aside.

The door gave onto an unassuming alley devoid of any touches of beauty: blank walls gray with paint and brown from dust, lacking even the most utilitarian of signs. A side entrance for the insignificant and anonymous. The alley was almost as bad as the mists of his prison. Squeezed between two complexes, it was shadowed by the spires, a steady wind whistling through it and rattling random pieces of trash in dizzy swirls. It was good they would not remain there for long. But more importantly, there was no one else in the alley.

He secured the door behind them.

Asrial staggered to a halt and raised her head to inhale deeply. He could almost see her tension escaping on the puff of air she expelled. She straightened immediately, allowing herself only a moment of weakness.

Romir had eyes only for her. She did not seem to have suffered from that cowardly attack. He must have succeeded in keeping the energies of the stunner blasts from touching her. Her apparent well-being did little to soothe his fury. He could still hear the crackle of power singeing the air, could still see the violent blue white streaks reaching for Asrial, could still taste the eternity of horror at the attack upon her. If his form had allowed it, he likely would have thrown up in the aftermath of relief.

He struggled for control. He had to hoard his strength for her time of need. He could feel his prison tugging at him, its pull much stronger than when they left the *Castel.*

"How're you doing?" She plucked at his sleeve, a slight tug to get his attention that contradicted the long, searching look she gave him, her brown eyes so full of solicitude. Again she wasted her concern on him when she should be worrying about herself.

"That was nothing. There is no need to worry." Romir took her hand and pressed a grateful kiss into her palm.

***Nothing?* He'd stopped** stunner blasts without twitching a finger. Not satisfied with stopping them, he'd somehow gathered them up and sent the whole ball of blazing energy back with interest. What was he capable of that he dismissed what he'd done so casually? The other times he'd flexed his power, he'd only defended her, not attacked.

The thought of what might happen if the Dareh got their hands on his prison chilled Asrial. Now, more than ever, it was imperative they not learn what Romir was.

She curled her fingers around the warm thrill of his kiss, promising herself a leisurely resumption once they were somewhere more secure. They had to get moving.

A stronger, downward gust of wind blew through the alley, heavy with metallic fumes and the hot exhalations of the city. Warned by the change in pressure, Asrial looked up.

An aircar swooped into the narrow space to land beside them, a small, gray craft, nondescript and unpretentious, nothing like the hover limo of the Dareh. Romir stepped forward, shielding her again. A window hummed open, sliding aside to reveal a long-faced Lomidari, a grounder by the brownness of his skin and not Dareh muscle by the lack of outrage in his expression. "*Sraya* Dilaryn."

Not again. "Who are you?" She held her stunner pointed down by her thigh, hiding its presence.

"A friend."

Twenty-one

A friend? Asrial rather doubted that, but she didn't bother arguing the point. The sooner he left, the sooner they could get off the streets. Standing here was just an invitation for the Dareh to scoop them up again. And if there was a next time, she'd bet good creds they wouldn't be polite.

Leaning out the window, the grounder peered at her, taking in her sweaty state, the stunner she had yet to holster, and Romir's aggressive posture. "I can bring you to the spaceport, if that's where you want to go."

Not only did he know who she was, he knew about the *Castel*, which was more than she could say about him. The balance of power favored this nameless "friend," but they weren't exactly flush with options if she was to avoid the Dareh.

Asrial glanced at Romir.

"I am here." The gleam in his silver eyes was a promise of protection, steadfast and confident, inviting her to rely on him. But he'd exerted so much power already. He could fade at any time.

His resistance to his prison was getting stronger, but how long could his strength last?

The thought of chasing a blurry Romir through the busy streets of Yasra, always one step too late, made her heart seize. She bit her lip. They had no time to waste on questions and reassurance. Though she loathed to trust in luck to see her safe, given a choice between sure capture by the Dareh and the clutches of a potential enemy, she knew what she preferred—and it wasn't the yfreet of her childhood. "Very well. To the spaceport."

The rear panel rose, sliding along the aircar's roof and giving access inside. Romir entered first, watchful as always. There were two couches along the sides of the aircar, facing each other. The grounder sat on the nearer one, a leg hitched up, so he could look out the window, disturbing the somber elegance of his teal blue suit with its gold trim. Asrial waved Romir to the other couch and joined him there.

At a flick of the grounder's finger, the door hissed closed. Another flick, and the aircar rose. He programmed their route into the autopilot, then straightened to face them—no, to face her. He barely blinked at Romir after that first long look.

As they sped toward the street, a loud explosion shook the alley, sudden thunder on a clear day. Swearing in a monotone, the grounder tapped the board, and the aircar bucked on a jolt of acceleration.

Several men lurched into sight, bloodied and shaken, one and all. The muscle didn't look too professional now. Asrial didn't bother trying to suppress a smirk of glee before turning her attention from this newest development.

Lucky for her this "friend" just happened to be there. Or was it? She didn't believe in serendipity, not when her freedom was at stake. Her gut said he'd been waiting for her, waiting for a chance to get to her.

The question was, why?

She sat back on the couch, prepared to wait. She probably should be racking her brain for answers, but Romir's warmth by her side infected her with his calm. Some might think it overconfidence, but she was certain this grounder wanted her alive. It helped that her stunner was in hand, charged and ready. That being the case, she could shoot her way out of this situation; and even if she couldn't, Romir would be able to handle it.

Though she kept an eye out, there was no further pursuit. The airspace above the parking deck remained calm, with no sudden departures. The muscle didn't stay in the alley for long, retreating into the complex in some disorder. The lack of pursuit seemed strange, and she said so.

"If the Dareh did that, that would be an open invitation to their enemies. To think two people slipped through their security and escaped Stratos Tower; they must have incompetents in charge." Their nameless friend glanced at the stunner she still held, the ghost of a smile flitting across his dark face. "There's no need for that now."

She set it on her lap, aimed at no one in particular. The feel of its grip in her hand was comforting; if that made her look menacing, then all the better. He might think twice before betraying them. "I think I'm the best judge for that."

The grounder bent his head, gracefully conceding the point—like a courtier in her mother's stories. The observation made her arms prickle.

In some ways, he looked like Romir: the brown skin, the long face, something about the shape of his features. But weren't grounders all dark from UV exposure? Perhaps she was just seeing similarities that weren't there, looking for proof of the link between Romir's people and the Lomidari?

Or maybe she just wanted a reason to trust the grounder . . . because he was helping them. Helping her. For now.

If she was, she had to be more cautious, though it went against her nature. That tendency to trust could be used against her. She had to remember what was at stake.

Now that they had leisure, she bypassed a demand for his identity—with her ignorance of local politics, she probably wouldn't recognize his name, even if he answered her honestly—for the more important question. "Why did you help us?"

He crossed his legs and tapped his fingers on his knee, a quizzical look flashing across his features, as if the answer to her question were obvious. "I thought it would benefit the both of us."

Not unlike the Bintanan's original proposition. That would have been mutually "beneficial," too. It didn't tell her anything.

Asrial studied the calm face across from her, wondering if he would lie. "Are you with the Dareh?" Would someone among the Dareh whisk her away from their headquarters only to hold her captive for a later date? If he were simply a supporter of the Bintanan, wouldn't he have held her until Dareh security personnel arrived? But who understood the intricacies of Lomidar politics? Certainly not her.

Brown eyes flared wide with seemingly genuine surprise under heavy, arched brows. "The gods forfend! *I* wouldn't have let you leave."

How diplomatic. Such soft words, as though he didn't suspect they'd fought their way out. He couldn't have overlooked the muscle chasing them, but little did he know the extent of their resistance. They'd left the Dareh in confusion. Her mouth crooked in an uneven smile. "We didn't ask for permission."

The grounder's eyes narrowed, bright with speculation. "The comm bands are silent, but I imagine the Dareh—or more accurately, the Bintanan—isn't happy with your refusal. They're not known for their generosity to those who oppose their will."

That still didn't tell her anything about his affiliation. Could she trust him to get her to the *Castel*, or was she leading Romir into another trap? She cursed inwardly, frustration getting the better of her. How simple life would be if she hadn't been born sovreine. "Refusal? You're that certain of me?"

"I truly doubt Dareh security would be chasing you if you'd accepted their offer." Their nameless friend reached aside casually and entered an adjustment in the aircar's board. "I wouldn't have found you as I had if that were the case."

Asrial didn't like what she saw on the routing display. "We're not headed for the spaceport."

He nodded, unabashed by her discovery. "My apologies, but a direct route would surely draw Dareh attention."

A plausible excuse. Still, she raised her stunner. She didn't aim it at him, but the threat was clear.

A sidelong look from the grounder acknowledged it. He bent his head again in a formal bow—more courtier manners. "Pardon my impudence, *Sraya*, but I thought to seize this opportunity to approach you on behalf of another party."

That was more like it. She hadn't believed he'd offered his help out of the goodness of his heart. The tension in her gut eased, now that she knew the price for his aid. "Another party?"

"Dareh policies are designed for the benefit of the corporation and its allies. The Lomidari are left to the whims of the Bintanan—she who would call herself sovreine. You could help change that. Certain people believe the Dareh are wrong. Many people," he added, staring at her intently. "With your support, there would be more. Enough to force the Dareh to recognize our concerns."

Did he think she would welcome his proposal just because they opposed the Dareh? Asrial suppressed a smile.

"There may be two sides to a cred, but if nine parties were to sit down at a table, there would be sixty-four sides to their discussion." Jamyl had been fond of that saying. Opposition to the Dareh didn't necessarily make this other party better for the Lomidari than the Bintanan. Like flying through a rock field, danger came from different vectors that changed over time: there was never a single, safe constant.

"Why me? I've never had anything to do with Lomida." It didn't make sense. So what if she'd been born a sovreine? That accident of birth had nothing to do with capability. She was a Rim rat. Yet even the Dareh treated her as if she were someone important, someone whose mere presence could rally Lomidari to their cause. Both sides simply took it for granted that she had such influence.

"You are House Dilaryn . . . and the rightful *reis*. You were able to enter Salima. Your entry and subsequent exit confirmed your heritage—in full view of all Lomida, in fact." The grounder gave her a thin smile as he leaned forward, propping his elbows on his thighs. "The coverage was live. The Dareh couldn't stop it."

Shocked by the matter-of-fact explanation, she gaped at the grounder. "Frigging crap. That's got nothing to do with anything." Calling her the rightful *reis*? What was with him?

"Only a sovreine could open the gate to Salima. No matter how loudly the Bintanan might proclaim her ennoblement, she could not force her will upon the walls of Salima." House Dilaryn's hereditary domain was considered the final refuge for the Lomidari—a sacred trust—and the main reason the Dareh couldn't strip it from her family upon her father's abdication.

"*Sraya* Dilaryn, our movement can return you to your rightful place." The grounder presented such an earnest face, his dark eyes blazing with sincerity, that she couldn't help feeling cynical. Naturally, after a plea to save the Lomidari from themselves, they would try to appeal to her nonexistent ambition. It only confirmed her suspicions that they knew nothing about her or her priorities. Even if she could stomach turning grounder, getting involved in Lomidar politics wouldn't pay Amin's medical expenses. Worse, doing away with his job as her agent would deal his pride a deadly blow.

She arched one brow in disbelief, slow and deliberate, the stunner in her hand a reassuring weight. Jamyl had stepped down to spare Lomida an internecine war—and that had been when he'd enjoyed broad popular support. "As a puppet, to be put on display and paraded when needed?"

"Of course not! You are sovreine—a true sovreine, not that bastard excuse who rules from the Tower—the daughter of the *reis*. You would rule in your own name."

"You offer this so freely," Romir said, his face as unreadable as the granite wall around Salima. She had to wonder what he made of this all. Lomida was the world his people had escaped to; that made the Lomidari his people. He'd sacrificed his freedom for theirs. "*Some of us had to stay behind.*" She didn't doubt that he'd volunteered. If he hadn't anchored the portal, he would have been safe. After millennia of captivity, did he have an emotional investment in the Lomidari?

The grounder frowned at Romir, puzzlement clouding his brown eyes. Apparently he'd initially dismissed him as mere crew. Now she could see questions forming as he gave more thought to Romir's presence. "Who're you?"

"You do not know?"

The frown deepened, another crack in the grounder's confidence. "We don't have a dossier on you."

Romir spread his hands. "Then I am no one important."

His soft answer only drew a sharper stare, calculations clicking behind that intent gaze. "Some might think so, but I'm not buying." The Lomidari ran his fingers along the seam of his pants slowly, repeatedly, as though the motion would coax some wary insight to his hand. "You look Lomidari, but you're not in any database—as Romir Gadaña or any other alias. You're not blood, but you accompanied the Dilaryn into Salima. You're unarmed, you're not muscle, yet there you sit ready to give your life for the *sraya*. I suspect you are important."

The shift in focus to Romir made her neck itch, the stinging bite of uncertainty nearly a physical thing, and she couldn't do anything to alleviate the sensation; right then even scratching would be an unnecessary display of weakness.

Narrowing her eyes at the grounder, Asrial willed his attention back to her. "Who he is makes no difference to my decision. I'll tell you the same as I told the Bintanan: no way in frigging hell."

Large hands fisted and opened, fisted and opened, then clenched on tense knees, knuckles going pale—so pale that her trigger finger itched. Any sudden motion on the grounder's part, and she intended to stun first and apologize later, if apologies were necessary. But he did one better than the Bintanan: no threats were forthcoming.

"Please reconsider." His eyes blazed, erupting with livid frustration. "They tie us up with regulations that only benefit the Dareh. Nonaffiliated businesses are losing out to the conglomerates and their allies. They're strangling us, and it's not even on purpose; they're doing it to defeat non-Lomidar interests. Our memories are not so short that we've forgotten how it was under House Dilaryn, when we had a *reis*. With you to lead us, Lomida could be that shining trust once more."

Bold words. He sounded sincere, but the Spirit of space only knew how much truth it held. She knew nothing about their "movement" and had no intention of throwing her support behind them simply because they opposed the Dareh.

Her to lead them? He was either bordering on desperation or thought her naive.

Her, turn grounder? She couldn't imagine tying herself to one planet when the vastness of space awaited her, much less to a planet of turbulent politics that had already spat out her parents. She had a greater responsibility to Amin and his family; at least that was something within her control.

"Politics is for the insane. I'm a spacer, a Rim rat. I know nothing of Lomida and have no wish to rule it. That would be a direct course to disaster." Asrial grimaced. It was only the truth, but she felt as if she'd crashed the floater of a lamed man. "No, we're lifting as soon as possible."

Their nameless friend's face went blank, wiped clean of all expression. "As you wish, *Sraya*." He bowed his head in seeming acceptance of her decision.

That was a sight easier than the Dareh. Maybe too easy?

The aircar landed. To her surprise, they were at the starport, beside the *Castel*. She'd half expected to be dumped in the middle of Yasra for her refusal. Or perhaps their nameless friend wanted her to think his side was better than the Dareh?

Asrial, you're a cynical jill.

Twenty-two

Asrial slumped against the hatch, relieved to shut out all the Lomidar insanity. What a wild ride. After that spectacular escape, they had to leave—before the Dareh schemed up a plan to take her or the *Castel* into custody. Now she truly understood at a visceral level why Jamyl and Nasri had avoided this crazy planet. If she never visited this sector of space again, it would be no great loss.

Strong arms drew her up to lean into a hard chest. The muscles under her cheek felt hot and solid, only the lack of a heartbeat betrayed Romir for djinn—and a powerful one, to judge by the stunner blasts he'd stopped and turned back on the Dareh.

"Are you sure you're fine?"

"My prison does not draw me so strongly. Perhaps I am developing some resistance."

She studied his features. The lack of tension about his eyes and mouth supported his claim. After everything he'd done, she expected him to be struggling against mist. Worry drained on a surge of relief, flowing from her tight shoulders, down her spine, and through her trembling knees, leaving her clinging to Romir.

Embarrassment threatened to weld her feet to the deck. What had happened to the independent Rim rat content to explore ancient ruins all alone, relying on only her own strength and wits? To the strong woman working desperately not to be a burden to Amin and his family? One run-in with the Dareh, and she was clinging like some spineless jill.

"That's good. In fact, that's great." She retreated to the piloting chamber before she made a bigger fool of herself. Surely Romir had done enough earlier, protecting her from the stunner blasts.

A green light blinked on the board, indicating a completed task. Asrial frowned at it in puzzlement. What task was that? Evading the Dareh's invitation, Romir's astonishing display of power, then that amazing offer from their nameless friend dominated her thoughts, forcing everything else out.

Eager to have something normal to handle, she activated the comp. Words filled the screen. It took her a moment to realize what they were: the translation of the light text. She'd left the comp working on it.

Her eagerness quickly melted into pity. The preface alone made her heart ache for Romir, cut off as he was from everything familiar, lost to his people.

> Writing in light to safeguard secret wisdom / lore of our instruction . . . from adherents of Mougals who want to ???? command djinn. . . .
>
> Safer advice is not teaching. Best course may be if skill ends in our generation. If there are no weavers, no one else will be

???? djinn. But method / technique of unraveling that weave should not be cast away. . . .

The translation was awkward and left much to be desired. But if she understood the preface correctly, despite the sacrifices Romir and his associates had accepted to save his people, sympathizers of their enemy had managed to gain influence among the survivors—sufficient influence to force them to give up this weaving. That discovery would've been enough to scour the hearts of lesser men. But she couldn't think about that now. What was more important was the technique of unraveling it hinted at.

Asrial buried her face in her hands, pressing on her eyes to force back the tears that welled up despite herself. What was up with that? The means for freeing Romir lay before her. She didn't have time to indulge her weakness. But still, when she opened her eyes, the tears leaked through, blurring the text on the screen.

In fount of life, waters from which hope / future / existence sprang forth.

Anoint body to ????

Scrubbing her cheeks dry, Asrial stared at the cryptic words in puzzlement. If that promise did indeed relate to freeing djinn, it seemed they didn't want to make understanding it easy. The fount of life? What body was supposed to be anointed? To what purpose? The rest of the line hadn't been translated—likely a deficiency in the comp's vocabulary. That was probably the same reason why the translation listed hope, future, and existence in the first line: the comp couldn't determine the appropriate reading.

A second pass offered no clarification. She forced her eyes past what she'd already read—perhaps the rest of the translation would help . . .

Summoned by ???? proof of passion, proof of pleasure, proof of life.

Unravel ???? unnatural weave.

By ???? return djinn's sundered existence to proper skein.

Then had to throttle back the excitement that sent her heart tripping along her ribs. Unravel the unnatural weave? Return the djinn's sundered existence to its proper skein?

The translation was clearly faulty, skipping over several words. But even a manual search through Nasri's library didn't produce definitions for those words.

Hope struggled with caution, impatience at her cowardice playing the deciding hand. If this light text with its offer of freedom was the promise entrusted to generations of Dilaryns, she couldn't turn aside. That way lay false kindness.

There was no avoiding it. She had to ask Romir for a proper translation. If the message did hold the key to freeing him, she couldn't let her qualms about his reaction to the light text stop her. Perhaps away from Salima and seeing the text on the comp's screen would mitigate its impact.

Steeling her nerves, she marched into the galley and stopped dead at the sight of Romir setting food on the dining counter. She stared. It was just a meal kit heated up, but he'd garnished the meat portion with shredded leaves that had to have come from hydroponics. "I thought you didn't eat."

"This is for you." He added another plate. "You have not eaten, and you need your strength after that skirmish."

Skirmish? Those thugs had used military-grade stunners, and he called it a skirmish? There was a distinct disconnect between their perspectives.

Her stomach chose that moment to agree with him—loudly. All that tension and running around had given her an appetite. Now that she thought about it, her body felt hollow, brittle, like over-stressed metal, as though the slightest additional pressure would crack her. No wonder her thoughts were going in circles.

"Eat." Romir nudged her toward one of the benches, suddenly demanding.

She sat obediently and proceeded to stuff food into her mouth. Her stomach gave another growl, pouncing on the smell of spiced vat meat as if she hadn't eaten in days instead of just that afternoon. So much had happened since she'd decided to take Romir sightseeing.

Filling the black hole inside her left little room for talk. The leaves he'd so thoughtfully added were a lost cause, barely skimming her tongue; maybe next time.

A sip tube of electro juice appeared beside her plate, the seal already cracked and the straw propped up. It landed with a firm thump and the unspoken command that she drink up. Bemused by the change in Romir's behavior, she drank between mouthfuls.

Romir sat across from her, resting his forearms on the table and watching her with the intensity of a buyer caught up in auction fever. He said nothing until the plates were empty and she was sucking down the last of the juice. "Better now?"

"Oh, yes. Much better. Thank you." Asrial studied his face, remembering his shock and the blankness in his eyes on their return from Salima. She'd set out to distract him and succeeded worlds beyond her expectations. But would reminding him of the message bring back his pain? She'd hate to do that. Seeing him hurting made her heart ache; it threatened to make a coward of her.

"Speak."

"That message you found mentions a technique for unraveling that seems specific to djinn—at least that's the way it reads to me. But the translation I have is very rough. I think—" She bit her lip, second thoughts clamoring for attention. A deep, tight breath forced them back. "I think you need to read it for yourself."

His nose flared, the skin across his cheeks went taut, and the corners of his mouth paled. He slumped forward, his weight on his forearms, as if the skids that supported him had been yanked off, then he straightened with visible effort. One might think he'd received bad news instead a hope of freedom. "Why?"

Asrial licked her dry lips, more than half tempted to change her mind. Self-disgust at her indecisiveness finally forced the words out. "There's something about unraveling a weave, but the translation has some gaps."

Romir sighed, the sound heavy with unnamed emotion. "Very well. Lead the way." He accompanied her to the work cabin and the comp console, his thoughts hidden behind bright silver eyes.

As she suspected, he had no difficulty reading the text, reciting in a glib tongue that denied any distress: "In primordial waters, anoint the body with the antipode. Focus the power—no, it would be more accurate to say *life energy*. Focus the life energy through the proof of passion, proof of pleasure, proof of life to unravel—here it goes into how to balance the unraveling energies—the unnatural weave."

She'd made sure to skip the shocking preface, going straight to the section that mentioned the technique of unraveling. Perhaps that had been the right thing to do—at least for her. This time her eyes remained dry, allowing her to concentrate on the message.

Primordial waters? The melodramatic phrasing raised her brows. The *fount of life* was esoteric enough, but at least easier to interpret. These references to primordial waters and antipode were way off her star charts. "Does that mean anything to you?"

He shook his head slowly, apparently as baffled as she. "This does not make sense. I lost my body when I was made djinn. How then can there be a body to anoint?" He pointed to some colorful scrollwork that bordered the text—the shifting patterns of red, blue, green, white, and black that she'd thought to be merely decorative. "Yet these are the weaves for the life energy to be applied to the body and the discussion of unraveling seems too detailed for theory."

Asrial waved her hand, brushing aside what couldn't be answered for the moment. "Assume there is a body. How would that work?"

Propping his hands on his hips, he tilted his head back to stare at nothing, his black hair rippling around his thighs. "If the weave is anchored on the weaver's body, then the weaver's own life energy sustains it. That is why the body is necessary in this case." His words lacked heat, as if the problem were hypothetical, not real. Nothing to do with him. "The resulting weave is very powerful. But it also requires a precise balance. If that tension is disturbed, the weave unravels."

Romir stared at the image of the light text a while longer, still dispassionate, his chest so still it was obvious he wasn't even pretending to breathe. "She must have finally discovered what would disturb that tension. Not just anything will. We spent years on attempts to free the djinn that had fallen into our hands."

He'd obviously locked away his pain to focus on the problem before them. She had to do the same.

"The Tehld said your body—your *body*—was there. Not just not here, but specifically *there*." Asrial pointed, mimicking the awkward stance of the Tehld from memory. "That was before I took your badge out of the storage locker. You said a weaver's badge is made using the blood of the weaver. Could they have meant that?"

"My link to my badge is a fragile thing. Strung out, it is difficult to sense, even for me." Romir glanced at her chest where his badge lay beneath her T-top. Despite the importance of the discussion, her body heated with awareness, her arms prickling with arousal.

Asrial forced herself to ignore her reaction. Now wasn't the time for distraction. "But the only other thing you're linked to is—" She whirled around to stare at the golden brown flask sitting on the work cabin's table. Romir's prison was the one link he was always aware of. From what he'd let drop, its pull was inescapable.

That was his body? The flask's phallic design, the wide base and long, narrow neck, looked even more significant the longer she stared at it.

"Yes, that is the only other thing to which I am linked." He dug stiff fingers into his tat, weary resentment shadowing his eyes and furrowing his brows.

A ponderous silence hunkered down in the cabin, waiting for someone to take control, to plot their next course. That meant she had to say something; despite everything they'd seen, Romir didn't seem to believe they could change his fate.

Thoughts tumbled through her head, bereft of order. The pilot in her struggled to make some sense of it all: Romir's link to his prison, his "deathless" existence, the promise etched on his weaver's badge, the light text . . .

"If I understand it correctly, this djinn condition of yours is some kind of suspended animation." Asrial took the flask between her hands to study it more closely. It was warm to her tingling fingertips, hard like pottery yet with a smooth grain that was unlike any clayware or ceramic she had ever touched, not glassy smooth but more like . . . skin? She shivered inexplicably.

"If this is part of you—your body as the Tehld would have it—then it makes sense that you're drawn back to it." It might explain why touching the flask strengthened the contact with his "master."

Romir inhaled sharply, air hissing between clenched teeth. "But my body was lost long ago."

"You don't know that. Didn't you say all you remember is the pain? How can you be certain your body was lost? Maybe that's why you can feel my touch when I touch it—because I am touching you."

He digested her words in silence, his hands clenched by his thighs. Did he struggle against fear or against hope? After several heartbeats, his fists relaxed. "So a djinn is a weaver trapped in a spirit walk?"

Startled by the sudden tangent, she stared at him, flung into a magnetic storm of incomprehension. Give her a star chart, and she could plot a course to anywhere in the known galaxy. But spirit walks? That sort of thing was whimsy fit for children's tales. When faced with djinn and vyziers and weaves of power, she had to operate on the assumption of truth, but understanding was beyond her. "You're asking me? How would I know?"

Romir gave her a small smile, mostly a twitch of the corners of his mouth and warmth in his eyes. "You are doing quite well, thus far."

Asrial leaned back in her chair, propped her heels on the edge of the comp, and folded her hands on her belly. "Well, this is as far as seat-of-the-pants goes. You're the expert here." Everything she knew about weaves, suspended animation, and spirit walks could be crammed on the tip of a laser cutter. From here on out, she might as well be flying blind. Knowing the perils of space as she did, the prospect held no appeal.

"Your reasoning has merit. The only object that remains with a djinn is his prison. If she was able to free the djinn in her keeping with this technique, then it may well be that the prison is the body. Those djinn had nothing else when they came into our hands."

Elation blanked her thoughts for a moment.

One step forward.

She pressed a hand to her chest, urging her racing heart to stay in place. "So we have your body. What we need next are these proofs and the fount of life."

"Passion, pleasure, life. An unnatural weave," Romir murmured, rubbing his fist on his chin. Standing there lost in thought, he looked more like a scholar than a port tough or a pleasure bod, despite the fine array of muscle he flexed. "The contradiction of life in this sense, then, would not be death but undeath. So obvious in hindsight."

Asrial waited, content to let him pilot his course at his leisure. Something inside her melted at seeing this unexpected side of her lover.

Finally he nodded, once and sharply. "It is just one proof: the evidence of orgasm."

"Eh?"

"For a man, that could only be his seed. For a woman, that would be . . . the cream of her body?" A thoughtful hum accompanied the working of his jaw. "Yes, the cream of her body would satisfy the requirements of passion, pleasure, and life."

Her cheeks heated, making her feel awkward all of a sudden. She hadn't thought anything could embarrass her so easily, but apparently a clinical discussion of the by-products of orgasm did just that.

"Is there a problem?"

"None whatsoever. Never mind that." Asrial scrubbed her cheeks, tempted to cover her face so Romir couldn't see her. She snuck a glance at her lover from under her lashes. Standing there in pensive silence, he didn't seem to have any problem with the topic. Not having a heartbeat probably helped.

"How about the fount of life?" *Primordial waters* was just too vague for direction, so she opted for the other reading. "Could that be the spring in Salima that's the source of the river? It's the only body of water on Lomida that's associated with the original settlers."

"You mean refugees," he corrected her calmly, betraying not even a jot of his previous distress.

Relieved to see him flying a sure course despite the reminder of his loss, she let it pass. If he wanted to pretend they weren't speaking of people he'd known, she'd respect his wishes.

"It is a possibility." Romir stared at the image of the light text, reading through it again. "The message contains no equivocation, no hedging nor shaving of meaning as to the expected results. To be so certain of the efficacy of this technique, they must have tested it successfully—here on Lomida. If that spring is the only source of water in Salima, it is likely they used its water in unraveling the weave."

"So that's what we have to do, too."

He turned to her, his face once again wearing an expression of scholarly dispassion. "But did you not say that we were to lift as soon as possible?"

"We can't leave just yet. If the fount of life is the spring in Salima, this might be our only chance to free you." They might not be allowed to return to Lomida, not after she'd defied the Dareh.

Excitement quivered in her belly like the *Castel* preparing to throw off gravity's shackles for the stars. Suddenly, freeing Romir wasn't the ultimately futile dream it had seemed at the start. They had the means to break his curse.

Twenty-three

They waited for the sun to set and the night to come to life. The lights of Yasra filled the shadows in a blinking, twinkling, flashing display of wealth and plenty. Lights outlined the tall spires of the city, drew stylized pictures across their faces, brandished ephemeral banners both garish and tastefully subdued.

Pretty in a way. Quite unlike the Rim Worlds, most of which didn't waste energy advertising with lights. The lavish display reminded Asrial more of station commercial districts, except for the silence, the long sightlines, and the open sky.

The delay preyed on her nerves, every second raising the specter of Dareh retribution. Surely the Bintanan wouldn't leave her defiance unpunished. If they had been willing to simply be the power behind the *reis*, they wouldn't have forced her father to abdicate.

In the interest of stealth, they boarded the grav sled in the hold, instead of outside the ship, opening the hatch only long enough to exit and flying off as soon as she'd confirmed the hatch was sealed and her security system back online. Their run-in with the Dareh had served to emphasize the necessity of her precautions.

Yasra's boulevards slid by in a haze of flashing lights and air-cars. Even this late in the night, the city pulsed with life. Once they were through the gate and inside Salima, Asrial threw caution out the airlock and gave in to the throbbing impatience in her veins that demanded speed. She didn't bother looking at the ruins, aiming the grav sled straight for the palace and the source of the river. Who knew what the Dareh would do if they learned she'd returned to Salima. This second visit would probably reinforce any suspicions they had about her intending to reclaim the scepter of the *reis*, viewing her as a threat to their rule. The best way to avoid another run-in was speed. The sooner they were done, the less time the Dareh would have to set a trap for them on the return trip to the *Castel*.

Her heart thundered in her ears, outpacing the grav sled. *Soon now, soon now, soon now,* it seemed to chant. It couldn't be soon enough.

Romir stared back the way they had come, the clues falling into place with hindsight. "It makes sense now."

"What does?" Though she asked, Asrial did not look up from the controls of the craft, her gaze shuttling among the glasses on the panel without rest.

"Why the lights in the archive and the gate responded to your presence. They tied the defense of Salima to the Dilaryn bloodline, so that even after weavers are no more, the people could still retreat to Salima. I suspect there are other weaves here that would respond to you as well." The additional sacrifice, after all they had lost, must have been heart-wrenching.

Her only reply was an abstracted hum, which was all his speculation was worth. In this age of travel across the abyss between worlds, these people no longer needed such a haven. Despite the loss of weaver lore, they had attained the stars.

He left her to her flying. As much as he wanted a distraction, neither of them could afford one.

Trees flashed in the light from the ice ring arching through the Lomidar night sky above the western horizon, their soaring tops outlined against the splatter of silver. Bright glimmers skimmed the night's light-washed gloom, starships commencing their voyage through the abyss between worlds. The beauty of the glittering heavens was lost to Romir, concerned as he was about detection. This world had so many more ways to spy upon others. The added light could only aid Asrial's enemies.

He could not rely on the defenses left by those long-departed weavers; they could not have imagined the wonders of the present day. If they had also copied the defenses of the Academe of Daraya along with the institution's layout, he most certainly could not afford to trust Asrial's safety to the weaves.

After all, even the Academe had fallen.

Dappled creatures lurked beneath the rustling leaves, taking fright at the grav sled's swift and silent passage. Consigned to patience while Asrial flew them to their destination, Romir found himself in sympathy with those creatures.

He did not understand the trepidation in his heart. It was not the fear of capture by those who hunted the woman he loved that afflicted him. Nor was it the dread that freedom would be snatched away. Freedom lay within his grasp. Had he not dreamed and yearned to escape this damned existence? Why then did fear stiffen his limbs?

The answer evaded him, slipping through his fingers like the gray fog of his prison. All he knew was that his heart quailed the farther they flew.

Beside him, Asrial said nothing, her attention given entirely to the controls of the craft. If she feared, she hid it well, guiding the grav sled along the moss-covered track without hesitation. She did not slow when the black needle of the fortress's silhouette cut the silver arch in the sky, nor for its gate, baring her teeth in a fierce smile as they cleared that barrier. Only when she reached the extent of their earlier exploration did she speak. "Where now?"

He guided her to a gate that gave access to the interior meadow and the spring that was their destination. It was a struggle to keep his voice even and not betray his rootless trepidation. Why this sudden cowardice?

They came upon a lush glade nestled against the mountainside, serene and pristine, the grass flowing to the spring's basin. She landed them at the water's edge, as gentle as a feather settling down.

Moist, warm air and singing water greeted them—so ordinary and, if he was honest, something of a disappointment. The way his heart quailed, they should have been surrounded by flocks of ravenous yfreet and a gross of vyziers. But there was nothing to menace them, not even one of the black-clad men who served Asrial's enemy.

He would have laughed at his foolishness, if the heaviness in his heart had not remained.

Asrial lifted the flask from the buffered storage compartment with great care. Now that they were here, her heart was lodged in her throat, its rapid beat a disconcerting flutter. Her knees threatened to buckle and dump her on her backside. As if she didn't have enough to worry about with the half-light and the wet rocks.

She cursed silently. She regularly risked burn-up on entries—in fact, she enjoyed the danger. She'd walked the darker sides of many

Rim Worlds. She'd had her share of close calls. This time, failure didn't mean possible death, so why did her hands sweat like a student pilot's on her first board?

Romir was silent, watching the skies for danger, keeping his distance from his prison—and therefore from her. That distance felt wrong. Here they were, on the brink of freeing him, but it was like she walked alone.

Not for long. She clutched that hope close to her heart. If she succeeded, the constant threat to his freedom would be gone. No longer would she fear his disappearance into his prison. She would have him by her side without fear. The hope sustained her through the silent walk.

Large rocks dammed the spring, a maze of boulders bordering a dark pool. The lack of color lent the scene an air of mystery enhanced by the strangeness of the sounds around them. Though they stood in an Inner World, she couldn't hear any of the clicks, thumps, or hums of technology.

Romir extended his bent arm, a silent yet graceful offer to steady her. She took it, accepting his support despite her ingrained reluctance. This was no time to cling to independence.

They couldn't risk anything happening to the flask—his body. Though it had survived the passage of centuries, she shouldn't forget that it appeared a prime example of Majian pottery—the only one of its kind intact. She couldn't help but wonder if the other examples—all shards—had been the bodies of djinn. The thought of coming this far only to slip and shatter the flask sent ice through her veins.

"If the flask shatters, the djinn can no longer be summoned. . . . The best guess is the djinn is lost in the mists—or perhaps he dies."

She wanted to free Romir—but not through death!

Up close, the rush of water spilling over the rocks made hearing difficult. Cradling Romir's prison in one arm, Asrial descended the stones to the basin. With her other hand, she gripped his forearm. The stones were wet and slippery and threw strange shadows in the light of her head lamp. The pool seemed clouded with mystery, starlight and ringlight picking out silver points on its dancing surface and making the water look blacker.

Perhaps they should have waited for the sun to rise, but she didn't want any witnesses to the rite. The Dareh's threat was a constant worry, inescapable while she and Romir remained on Lomida. Waiting for dawn would mean exposing Romir's prison to possible scrutiny—and capture.

Her arm tightened around the precious flask. They had to get this done.

Asrial set the flask in a secure niche in the mossy rocks, then took off her boots to dip a toe into the burbling pool. Though the water came straight from the mountainside, it was surprisingly warm, not cold at all. It made it easier to strip off her clothes and enter the pool. If she'd been the superstitious sort, she might have thought it auspicious. As it was, she just thanked the Spirit of space that her teeth wouldn't be chattering like loose contacts.

A weight settled on her shoulders—apprehension, nerves, anticipation, a mix of all three. Her heart thundered in her ears. Time seemed to slow, almost as if the universe itself held its breath.

Mustering her resolve, she picked up Romir's prison, wondering how Lomidar water would break the weave that kept him a djinn. When Romir tried to explain about weaves, it had sounded like children's tales—or advanced tech so bleeding-edge it might as well have been one of her mother's stories. She only knew that they worked because she'd seen it for herself.

But suspended animation . . .

She hugged the flask, the etching rough against her breasts but warm. Somehow, it felt alive, not some inanimate artwork made to be admired. A part of Romir? Romir's true body? For some reason, it helped to think of it that way—not as an object of contempt or horror but something to be cherished.

Springwater splashed around her, seductive in its warm wetness. Flowing over the slopes of her breasts. Dripping down between her thighs. Coaxing her body to readiness. As if the elements conspired to aid her.

Her breath turned choppy, the night air thick in her throat. Her breasts swelled, her skin too tight. Her nipples hardened to aching points.

Asrial waded deeper into the pool until the water reached the tops of her thighs. She could feel its warmth stirring her curls, its dancing surface lapping against her swelling clit. Pure seduction.

Water splashed on the flask in her arms, the spray wetting her cheeks and trickling down her throat. The sensation was similar to Romir's licking her there—light, fleeting, almost an imagined warmth. With her fingers, she followed the water's trail over her breasts and down her body, building on the sensual awareness left in its wake.

The flask turned out to be an awkward burden as she set out to pleasure herself. It was so bulky that despite its shape she couldn't really use it like a pleasure wand. Juggling it from hand to hand didn't work, but she didn't want to put it aside for fear she'd forget her purpose. However, using only one hand was time-consuming—and distracting.

Proof of passion, proof of pleasure was what was required, according to the light text, to anoint Romir's . . . body with the cream of her orgasm. Her cheeks heated at the reminder.

She'd thought she could do it alone, had expected it would be just like countless times she'd pleasured herself. But getting aroused all alone while he watched was too embarrassing. Though the desire was there, she couldn't take it further.

"Help me." Asrial extended a hand to the shadowy form standing guard at the pool's edge.

Romir's clothes vanished as he entered the water. He stood before her naked, the light from the ice ring spangling his body with silver, like some heroic statue in a Majian ruin. Only the tat on the ball of his left shoulder marred the image, as though some monster had taken a bite out of him.

Though they had been lovers for some time already, his approach was hesitant, almost reluctant—cautious, though she wasn't certain what gave that impression. He moved behind her, his hands coming to rest on her shoulders.

"I cannot touch you as I would." He pushed back the wet hair clinging to her cheek and pressed his lips to the hollow behind her ear. The sly touch of his tongue toying with her lobe sent a quiver of surprise sizzling down her spine. He may not be able to touch her as he pleased, but that didn't seem to limit him.

Asrial moaned. That one lick had done more to arouse her than her own efforts. "You're good."

He seemed to take her words as a challenge. With just his mouth, he dissolved her self-consciousness, nibbling on her nape and shoulders and ears. He sucked her lobes, and she felt it between her thighs and in the center of her being.

His erection pressed against the small of her back, hot and thick, ready to take her. She reached behind, taking him in her palm. The heft of him, the heaviness of his balls, just the feel of him made her melt with longing, desire a throbbing emptiness demanding to be filled. Squeezing him, she arched back and rubbed herself against him in deliberate invitation.

Romir caught her wrist, his hold gentle yet implacable. "It is dangerous. You are too exposed here."

Even here in the safety of Salima, he sought to protect her.

From what? The grav sled's sensors hadn't detected any wildlife nearby. From the Dareh? "But—"

"No." Turning a deaf ear to her arguments, he parted her folds, his long fingers gliding over her sensitive flesh in possessive strokes. Over and over. Sending electric sparks shooting through her nerves—and he hadn't even entered her yet.

When he sent his fingers deeper, she was more than ready for it. Her body craved his touch, yearned for a more thorough possession. She wanted him inside her, stretching the tender flesh that ached for him.

Under his hands, pleasure grew, swelled, rose to shuddering heights. Her heart thundered like the thrusters of a ship about to launch. Her knees threatened to fold from under her.

Her fingers twined with his as they dipped between her wet folds. The intimacy of their united touch sent sensual awareness blazing into overdrive, her body shuddering with plasma-hot desire.

It was too much to bear. Carnal hunger erupted in a blast of pure rapture. She clenched her thighs against the spasm of raw sensation as she melted over their joined hands.

Spirit of space, she nearly forgot what they were about. Only the tightness of Romir's embrace kept her on her feet and her mind on their purpose.

Holding her breath, she touched her slick fingers to the flask, smeared her cream over the dark etching. This was it: the final step.

Pleasure swirled under his skin, an insidious seduction singing from his djinn mark, digging tiny hooks into his essence, wrapping slender coils around his will, and weaving a net of sensation to undermine his resistance. Treacherous delight tugged at him, trying to draw him back to his prison.

No, he could not give in.

Romir fought its call, focusing all his thoughts upon Asrial. He could not leave her unprotected, not here in the heart of enemy territory. No fortress was invincible, not the Academe of Daraya, certainly not this barren imitation. And after the violence of the day, it was clear that Asrial's enemies were the sort to insist on revenge. Her safety rested on his vigilance, on his strength.

His heart railed against further betrayal. *Please, not again.* He could not stand to fail yet another person important to him.

Power and patterns. He had to remember his part. The body was anointed, now he had to focus the life energy through the antipode. Weaving took all of his concentration.

Need clawed him, insistent, domineering. The splashing waters only magnified the clamor to return to his prison—no, to his body. But to abandon Asrial when she was at her most vulnerable . . .

He could not do it. Could not give in. Would not give in. Not while he had the strength to resist.

But still the carnal temptation called to him, his djinn mark singing its song of submission, promising a false ecstasy to sate his senses and release from the hunger besetting him. The coils spread through his being, multiplying and propagating the longer Asrial held the flask to herself and caressed it.

"Nothing's happening." The panic leaking into Asrial's voice rent the net of seduction on his senses. "Nothing's happening." She turned frantic eyes to him. "Shouldn't there be something already?"

Fighting to throw off the snare of his prison, Romir shook his head. She was correct. The antipode should be putting great stresses on the unnatural weave. If it were to unravel, the effect would have been immediate, like the snapping of an overly tight string—that explosive release of energies was what he was supposed to control. But no matter how he looked, there was no change to the weave of his imprisonment. "Nothing has changed. The weave is as strong as ever."

Asrial burst into tears. She who had faced kidnapping and deadly attacks without flinching shed tears over this one failure. Over him.

Romir cradled her to himself, her distress hurting more than the disappointment. "No, do not cry, *biba*." The endearment fell from his lips with unthinking—unthinkable—ease. "It was not meant to be."

"I thought we had it. I was so sure." Scalding tears dripped off her chin to land on his chest. He felt each one, a painful sweetness searing his heart.

Twenty-four

The grav sled's cabin loomed around Asrial, strangely large and hollow as she huddled in the front seat. Unlike the other times, she hadn't packed any equipment or supplies. All it had now was Romir's prison, tucked away in the rear compartment. Just like her heart, echoing in emptiness, barren of hope.

What now?

She'd pinned her hopes on this one desperate attempt. With this failure, she was left adrift, unable to plot a course forward. She'd been so sure it would work that she hadn't given a thought to the alternative. Now she couldn't think. Her head throbbed. Her eyes were hot, swollen from crying.

She was drained. Since Romir somehow got her dressed and back to the grav sled, she hadn't been able to muster the will to move. What did it matter? She had nowhere to go, no idea what to do. Hollow. Brittle. Fragile.

Romir pulled her onto his lap, his tight embrace unexpected—and an unexpected comfort. For the longest time, he did nothing but hold her—and she was content with that, floating in a world of silence. No demands that might shatter her. Then with a finger under her chin, he tipped her head back and kissed her, sharing heat and tongues, soft and slow, a curiously innocent exchange despite the intimacy of the contact. Not carnal hunger but the need to express sympathy.

Guilt hit her—hard. He was the one trapped, yet he was consoling her. She couldn't believe she'd cried in front of him.

"It is for the best." The sad smile on his lips conveyed no blame, only brave acceptance of his continued imprisonment.

Asrial couldn't accept it, refused to accept it. She pulled away, shaking her head. "No, it isn't. I must have done something wrong. The technique works. You said so yourself: no equivocation, no hedging nor shaving of meaning. They must've tested it successfully to have phrased it so. The problem is in the execution. I didn't do it properly."

She rubbed her forehead, trying to jump-start her brain. That was right. The technique to free djinn had to have worked. She shouldn't give up so quickly. There was still hope, still a chance they could free Romir.

He stared at her, his smoky gaze fathomless, as though weighing something in her she couldn't see. "Then we need to know what was wrong."

"Let's start from the translation." She took out her comp from her jacket pocket, linked it to the grav sled's board, and pulled up the vid of the light text. "Umm . . ."

Romir drew her back under his arm, sharing his heat and strength with her as he checked off sections in the vid. "The antipode had been correctly applied and the life energy focused. Balancing the energies only comes into play with the unraveling of the weave, to return the djinn's life energy to its proper skein. That leaves only one condition under contention."

Fount versus primordial waters.

Averting her gaze, Asrial bit her lip in consternation. She'd been quick to opt for the *fount* reading because it was simpler, easier to interpret, the meaning seemingly obvious. Her nails dug into her palms when she clenched her hands. The pain helped to focus her thoughts. "If the fount isn't the spring, then maybe it wasn't *fount* in the first place? If the correct reading is *primordial waters*, then it's no wonder it didn't work."

"Primordial waters are generally believed to be seas, not springs," Romir pointed out with scholarly dispassion. "But there are no seas near Salima, so your interpretation is valid."

"But that's the main difference between the comp's translation and yours." She thumped the board in frustration; maybe the impact would knock some inspiration loose.

He took a fist into his hands and pried her fingers open. "Take more care. Injuring yourself will not help anyone."

The nails had broken the skin, cutting bloody crescents into her palms. She licked the blood away, making a face at the salty metallic taste. Her heart stumbled. *Salty metallic taste*.

"What makes seawater different from lake water or any other water—like fresh water, distilled water? The dissolved salts, right?" It felt like she was on the proper course there. "If it's the salts, then wouldn't the composition and proportions of the ions matter?"

Romir's response was a thoughtful, noncommittal hum.

She rubbed the marks on her palm, wondering if the excitement she felt was premature. "The seawater of Maj is probably significantly different from the water in Salima."

"Perhaps there is something in what you say. We sought a world that could support us. But it was not—and could not—be identical to our home world."

Maj was the planet where Romir's people—her father's people—had evolved . . . *been given life*. "Could—somehow—could the primordial waters used to free djinn be from a Majian sea? Or at least Majian seawater?"

Couldn't it? Romir's people hadn't simply escaped; they had planned an evacuation. Romir had expected to see scrolls and tapestries taken from the Academe of Daraya. Who knew what else weavers might have considered important enough to pack?

"I do not know what was brought over. Could someone have brought over seawater from our home world? Perhaps. It is not beyond the realm of possibility. I only knew a small fraction of the people who escaped and less about what they had."

Asrial could imagine the chaos at that time, her experiences at various Rim World star ports and jump rings filling in the details: the shouted orders, the frantic search for connections, the jockeying for position, the rush to transit, the dust, the fear, the exhaustion.

"It would explain why the cipher for *primordial waters* was used for *fount* when that is a less common phrasing. If the seawater was brought over, then it was likely contained in a fount. Both meanings would apply." Romir's eyes glittered, enthusiasm and enjoyment of the scholarly discussion bringing out the silver amid the gray. She recognized the signs; Nasri had been much the same when her interest took flight.

Asrial smiled, her spirits buoyed by fresh hope. They still had a chance—one that didn't require them to remain on Lomida.

It was time to return to the *Castel.*

A rumble from the distant hot pads shook the early morning as a ship took off, flaring thrusters a blinding glare against the dark horizon—nothing unusual for a starport. Lomidar authorities had no block-off periods for landings and liftoffs.

Asrial ignored the noise, more concerned about what didn't belong. No one had followed them from Salima, but that was no guarantee of safety. The Dareh would know to search for her at the starport. It wouldn't take a genius to plan an ambush.

The first thing that caught her eye when she banked the grav sled into the lane of her ship was a nondescript aircar sitting beside the *Castel*'s right front skid. Her gut tightened, her recent failure putting an edge to her paranoia. But she didn't see anything else in the surrounding shadows that shouldn't be there: the ships in neighboring slots had their hatches sealed; no one loitered about; no suspicious objects had piled up since their departure for Salima that evening. Besides the aircar, there was nothing within stunner range that might hide attackers.

Her nerves still twinged. The Dareh had professionals and military hardware. Their definition of stunner range might be much farther than hers.

As she brought the grav sled closer, the aircar's front panel slid open, disgorging their nameless friend and another grounder, a much older man, one who held himself with the dignity of rank and age. She'd made a point to know the principals of the Dareh conglomerate and its allies, those who had proved themselves a danger to the now sadly diminished House Dilaryn; this man was no one she recognized.

Someone local, then.

She clenched her teeth, in no mood for another go-around about Lomidar politics.

"Asrial?" Romir's open concern injected glassteel into her spine. After the way she'd broken down, he'd worry more if she didn't meet their visitors—and she wouldn't be able to face herself if she turned coward now.

Besides, while she so desperately wanted to see this planet receding on the aft display, there was one thing left to be done: a spot of petty revenge, one their nameless friend might be willing to help her with, now that she thought about it.

"I'm fine."

The two grounders stayed in the shadow of the aircar as she landed the grav sled close to the cargo hatch. Cautious of them.

Romir held up a commanding hand while he peered around, probably using that weaver's sight of his. "There are no other watchers that I can see. Do you wish to speak with them?"

She stared at the waiting grounders, wrestling with the urge to just take off. Go. *Go!* Her heart shivered, the need to escape, to kick the dust of this world off her boots and launch the *Castel* toward the Rim, safety, and freedom rushing through her veins on a flood of fear.

Sooner or later the chaos they'd created would clear up, and the Dareh would get their bearings. Once that happened, there was no question whom the Dareh would go after, and the obvious place to start looking for her was the *Castel*. They had to get out before it was too late. Every second they delayed on planet was one more second the Dareh could use to keep her insystem. The longer they remained in Lomidar space, the greater the risk of capture.

Yet her hands didn't move, her fingers frozen. It would be so simple to trigger the hatch and fly straight into the hold. But something held her back. Call it pride, recklessness, stupidity, what have you—she couldn't let the Bintanan get away with trying to control her. So long as she didn't take a stand, the Dareh could twist her meeting with them to suit their purposes.

And if she was honest, that near capture and the threat of having her identity stolen by the very people responsible for her father's downfall scared her to the soles of her boots. She didn't deal well with being scared. Frankly, it pissed her off.

"I have to." Even with that admission, she hesitated a beat longer before she released the grav sled's canopy and left its dubious protection. Despite Romir's presence beside her, she drew her stunner, its familiar heft additional reassurance.

Displaying empty hands, their nameless friend stepped forward. "*Sraya* Dilaryn, a senior member of my party wishes to speak with you. Is there some place we could go . . . ?"

"Here's fine. Make it fast." She didn't want to leave the *Castel* now that they'd gotten back but didn't want to let these strangers aboard, either.

The older grounder joined his companion and waved his assent. Pressing his spread hand to his chest, he gave her a formal court bow of introduction. "I am Khodi." He looked at her expectantly as he completed his bow. Apparently she was supposed to react.

Frigging crap. If she accepted his bow properly and it was recorded, who knew how it would be twisted. No amount of sound jamming would block that communication. Worse, his use of a single name in addition to court manners implied he was the head of a high house. House Khodi?

Asrial shrugged instead. "I'm sorry, I don't recognize your name."

"But you met with my nephew Firuz." He gestured to the younger grounder, their nameless friend, standing beside him.

"Perhaps. He didn't introduce himself."

Firuz gave her a practiced bow and a long string of names denoting house, rank, birth order, and affiliation, besides his personal names. Definitely high house.

She suppressed a shudder, choosing instead to stare at Khodi. The broad welcome on his face looked genuine; she didn't trust it. "Why the smile?"

Despite her open suspicion, there was no change to his expression. "When I last saw you, you were so small. Now, you look so very much like your mother when she was your age."

The comment gave her pause. He'd known Nasri? And so what if he had? Did he think to manipulate her so easily? Her teeth ached at the sudden clenching of her jaw. She hated thinking this way, looking for hidden motives and suspecting every kindness.

Impatience stirring, Asrial glanced around. She was confident that Romir was on guard against another attack, but the habits of a lifetime made her check for herself. "Is that all?"

Firuz's lips thinned, the muscles in the corner of his mouth twitching. But he said nothing, leaving Khodi to answer.

The older grounder cleared his throat. "Forgive the digression. I came to ask you to reconsider. In the past, we were too weak. We wanted to move sooner, to restore your father to his rightful place, but the time was not right. Now we are in a position to act."

"You want me to believe you spent several years in preparation without even asking me if I'm interested?" She crossed her arms, even more disinclined to agree. A warm wind ruffled her curls, carrying with it the acrid smell of hydraulic fluid and scorched ceramics.

"I promised Nasri-*dai* we would not contact you until we were certain of winning."

Again, a reference to her mother, this time with the unfamiliar suffix denoting the consort of the *reis*. More court manners. "What?"

Khodi nodded, speaking quickly. "Jamyl Kharym Rashad abdicated to prevent a bloody war that would have left Lomida in shambles, easy prey for pirates and raiders. It would've been a disaster. The Dareh had enough supporters who wanted self-determination, so he stepped down. But your noble mother favored our proposal."

Asrial's eyes narrowed. If Nasri had felt that way, she'd never said so in Asrial's hearing. "I'm not my mother. I've lived most of my life away from here. Lomida hadn't had a *reis* during that time. Don't you think it's time you gave up that outdated institution? Let the Lomidari decide their own fate." It would have happened eventually; that was what her father had believed. He'd seen the abandonment of Salima as one of the signs of the estrangement from the *reis*.

"Never in our long history have we not had a *reis* to lead us. Until your father," Firuz objected, slashing the air with his hand.

She glanced at Romir. "Hardly." The Parvinese hadn't had a *reis*; it was a position that had been created after the establishment of Salima. But she wasn't about to say that. She wasn't interested in prolonging a pointless debate.

Romir stepped forward, imposing himself between them.

At that, Khodi extended a plaintive hand. "Hear us out, *Sraya*. Rumors are that House Bintanan is in disarray. Something happened yesterday, when you were at the Tower. This improves our chances of success. We have the numbers and the money; now, we have the perfect opportunity. The Lomidari will support you."

So that's why no one's tried to seize the Castel*?* She hadn't stopped to look but suspected the muscle hadn't absorbed all the stunner energy Romir unleashed. If some of that had spilled over to the Bintanan or her heir, the various factions within Dareh would be maneuvering for advantage.

Khodi was right. The Dareh would be divided, weakened. Now would be the perfect time to overthrow them. But still—

"My answer remains the same."

"Then why did you agree to speak with us a second time?"

She smiled, feeling herself on firmer ground. "I need you to do something."

In the end, the briefing had probably been unnecessary. But she'd done it anyway, wanting to do everything she could to ensure the Dareh couldn't repackage her "visit" into an expression of support for Dareh. Someone skilled in vid manipulation might be able to extract something that would read as acceptance of Dareh. While an association with Khodi was inevitable since she'd used his connections to invite the so-called reporters, it was better than the alternative.

Romir had objected to Khodi's initial suggestion of using one of the starport's function halls. Given how easily Dareh muscle had scooped them up, she couldn't fault Romir for his stance. The hold of the *Castel* ended up packed with unfamiliar equipment and people, both real and avatars projected in holotubes, the latter looking like substantial ghosts trapped in the clear cylinders.

She'd suffered the invasion in silence. The more there were, the better the likelihood of her message getting out. She could only hope that one of those avatars would give an accurate account.

Twist that, Bintanan!

Her statement should throw a wrench in the drives of the Bintanan. Let the Lomidari decide their future without including her in the equation. That was how her father would have wanted it.

All she wanted to do was free Romir. If only the Dareh would leave her alone.

Twenty-five

The universe spasmed in that familiar, nerve-ruffling, stomach-twisting sensation of falling yet not falling of transit. Asrial landed back inside her skin on the Rim side of the Eskarion Ring, shock harness snugged to her body, the lumps and scars of the old pilot's seat chafing the usual places.

The *Castel*'s board lay before her, all indication lights showing green. The glory of the Dagaerin Field replaced the dim stars in the Trinami Cluster in the upper left screen. At the sight, some of the tension on her shoulders was off-loaded.

Beside her, Romir sighed, the soft sound resonant with delight. Leaning back in his seat, he stretched, corded muscles flexing and bunching in leisurely distraction.

She shared his relief. Despite her fears, they hadn't had any trouble lifting off from Lomida nor in the decs since they crossed the Danar and Cyri sectors of the Inner Worlds to the Eskarion constellation. She'd covered the distance in record time, pushing herself to her limits, relying on the autopilot only when Romir insisted she eat and sleep.

Out in the Rim, farther from Dareh influence, she felt more at ease. It might be a false safety, but she was a Rim rat, and if she had territory, it was the Rim. The confrontation with the Bintanan had only served to bring that understanding to the forefront: she might have been born sovreine, but she chose to be a Rim rat.

She quickly guided the *Castel* out of the emergence zone to make way for the ships transiting after her, docking at Eskarion 17 just long enough to resupply. Impatience and uncertainty were constant companions, vying for the forefront of her thoughts. Hope clung as well. The last decs had shown her how life could be with Romir, his quiet care, the contrast in his perspective from hers, his occasional intractability . . . his careful lovemaking.

A dec from Eskarion space, one of the harsh realities of Rim travel raised its head. This deep between the stars and given the variables involved in Jump, a chance encounter with another ship was unlikely, especially since her route didn't take them to one of the more popular stations.

Yet the nav screen was reporting a trailer bogey at the edge of detection range, one too large for a fast courier and too small and fast for a cargo ship. And there it remained a few hours later—too long for coincidence and her peace of mind. Most ships of that size could have recharged their drive and jumped in that time.

And it was closing the distance.

Asrial left the autopilot in control as she flicked through function lists to refine the take from the *Castel*'s sensors. Her mind raced, weighing the options: trader, freighter . . . pirate?

Her lungs seized, her heart skipping, at the latter. *Spirit of space forfend.*

A large hand appeared beside hers, then a fall of black hair, as Romir leaned down to stare at the sensor display. "What is wrong?"

She tapped the ominous bogey on the screen. "That's what's wrong. Could be trouble." Probably *was* trouble. She couldn't think of any reason a trader or freighter would be on this course. There were no major magnetic rifts or stellar storms to justify a detour. The only systems in this vector were long dead or abandoned or had never developed any sentient life; even the colonies of free miners and solos lay elsewhere.

"It'll take hours for whatever that is to catch up, but the jump drive also needs hours to recharge. Best to prepare for the worst." Eager to be about the preparations, Asrial sprang to her feet, adrenaline speeding her motions and infecting the ordinary hums and rumbles of the *Castel* with sinister portent.

The shields had first priority. The generators had to be at 100 percent, and checking those couldn't be done from the board. They couldn't afford even minor shield failure.

Romir's quiet help made the work easier. He could pinpoint system problems and weaknesses faster than her test probes.

Despite the direness of their situation, Asrial found herself smiling. She couldn't think of anyone else she'd prefer to have by her side when she faced danger. He made suggestions. He didn't question her decision to fight. He did what he could to support her in her tasks. The perfect partner for her. All she wanted was the chance to see what they could make of a future together.

While she dealt with another unreliable circuit, Romir waited, leaning against a bulkhead, bare-chested as usual, his crossed arms blocking part of that distracting display. "You are a strange woman," he murmured, a furrow between his slashing brows.

"How so?" she asked, though his comment had been soft enough that she could have pretended not to have heard without being rude. She gave the micro wrench a final tap to make sure the replacement relay was properly seated. The pile of spares on the dolly taunted her. Time was running out, but she had to force herself to go slow. Better to do it right the first time than have something fail because she was rushing too much.

"You seem to be enjoying yourself."

She ducked her head. "I'd probably be scared witless if I were alone."

"No, you would not. Scared perhaps, but never witless." The tenderness in the smile he turned to her made Asrial's heart skip and stumble, the emotion and its open expression taking her by surprise. Seeing it hardened her determination to fight.

Hours later, she'd completed what repairs she could, which was less than she preferred, constrained as she was by time and supplies. They returned to the piloting chamber to find that the bogey had halved the distance between the ships.

She studied the nav screen and the sensor take a while longer, hoping for a break. Built along the blocky lines typical of Hagnash ships, the bogey wasn't designed for atmospheric entry. It was larger than the *Castel*, more the size of a freighter, but clearly faster than a freighter to have caught up this quickly.

Still no ident code. The bogey wasn't broadcasting a call signal. "Unidentified ship, this is the *Castel*. Your approach is in violation of safety protocols." In deep space, there was no good reason for two ships under power to pass within a quarter of a light-second of each other.

Time stretched out without change. There was no response, and the ship continued to maneuver steadily and smoothly closer. Definitely under control, not autopilot. That ruled out damage, and a legal AI would have had to answer to her comm. Therefore, she had to conclude the bogey was hostile. "Pirates."

"Can you outrun them?"

"If I could've, I'd've done it sooner. Using the thrusters will divert power from the jump drive. We need that powered up as soon as possible. The only sure escape is Jumping. They can't follow us if we Jump." There were too many factors to make tracking a ship through Jump anything but a game of chance.

The pirates had to have been lying in wait to have found them—though hunting in this area of space didn't make any sense. It wasn't a major—or even a minor—shipping route. It offered only slim pickings for pirates. Relic raiders, on the other hand, knew better than to target ships headed deeper into the Rim when holds would be empty—and most of them wouldn't bother with a ship as small as the *Castel*.

Asrial stared at the steadily dwindling separation between her ship and the bogey, an acrid taste coating the back of her throat. They wouldn't make it. The pirates would get to strike range before the jump drive was fully charged. She'd sworn she'd never let herself be captured again, but all the *Castel* had were point defense lasers and shields.

Strike range came far sooner than she anticipated. With still an hour to go before the jump drive was fully charged, the bogey fired hypertorps. She swore, channeling her frustration into creative curses. *Frigging crap* didn't do justice to their situation. Definitely pirates, then. Hypertorps were used to wear down shield capability. No honest trader carried that sort of military hardware.

Her stomach lurched as she activated the lasers. Those would divert more power from the jump drive, but if the shields dropped below 40 percent, the pirates could use a grab net to lock on to the *Castel*—then they could force their way aboard.

A hiss drew her attention to Romir, who had twisted in his seat to face the rear, a cold, baleful light in his eyes. He glared at the bulkhead—no, at something beyond it she couldn't see. "That ship is the one that tried to steal you."

Volsung?

She hadn't gotten a good look at the Cyrian's ship when Romir rescued her. The *Eikki* had been large enough to require an outside slot, but she didn't remember any details beyond an imposing darkness that blocked out the stars. But if it was Volsung chasing them, did that mean his objective remained the same: her?

"The client's paying good credits to get her alive and unharmed." The Cyrian's words had been laser-etched into her memory. A wealthy client to afford the earnest for the bidding and now contraband military hardware. She couldn't help but make a connection to the Dareh's recent interest in her. Who else would go to such an extent for a Rim rat?

"You misapprehend your position. We do not need your support, merely your face." Ordering her abduction wouldn't be beyond the Bintanan.

The roiling of her gut worsened. Asrial shook her head. The whys and wherefores had to wait. She had to buy time for the jump drive to finish charging. But if capturing her was the objective, then Volsung would probably—probably—hold off on more forceful maneuvers that could kill her. Surely that gave her an edge, something to work with?

She took over control of the *Castel* from the autopilot, a chill prickling her arms. Never again would a pirate board her ship—she'd die before she let it happen.

Romir watched, mired in helplessness, while Asrial played her hands across the panel, mustering the *Castel*'s defenses. Her concentration was absolute, a rock-solid determination to deny victory to her enemy.

How strange this battle was, so silent, unlike those he had fought against the Mughelis. It lacked the sizzle and crackle of opposing weaves, the cries of pain and shouted orders, the harsh gasps of effort, the stench of sweat and blood and burning flesh. Even the starship's lurching contributed to the disconnect, since nothing he could see could account for the sudden shifts in weight. The chamber was motionless, quiet, and cool, with the slightest scent of greenery from the plant room. Only finger taps and clicks of the controls and an occasional scathing murmur broke the silence. That serenity made the battle seem more like a child's game with little at stake instead of a race to freedom.

Red bloomed across the panel, an explosion of garish brightness that could not be good.

"Aft shields down to seventy percent—repeat, seven-zero percent." The emotionless warning issued from thc air around them, the ship comp Asrial had occasion to address in the past.

Asrial *tsk*ed, her jaw tensing.

He fought down a smile of relief at the report. Here was something he could do to help. He thrust his awareness toward the failing shields, leaving a corner of his mind to maintain the form in his seat. Becoming mist would be easier, but it would frighten Asrial at a time when distraction could be fatal.

The flows of energy from the vortex in the *Castel*'s heart fluctuated in his weaver's sight, the feed to the shields thinning noticeably as if worn. As he watched, threads of light frayed and winked out.

Romir gestured, manipulating the energies to his will, weaving patches onto the feed to the foundering shields. They were temporary fixes at best—Asrial would still need to replace the damaged parts—but perhaps they would buy her the chance to make those repairs.

With his awareness focused beyond the chamber, he became conscious of the *Castel* twisting in flight like a wounded yfreet, lances of energy shooting from its skin. They struck insanely swift missiles swimming through the abyss between worlds, shattering them into brilliant shards that splattered against the *Castel*'s shields like so much mud.

But even mud could sting. As he watched, a portion of the already weakened shields faltered once more, and not even his weaves could restore them all.

When he returned his awareness to Asrial's side, she was growling at what the glasses showed her. "They're matching our trajectory and velocity."

More lights flashed on the panel, their insistent repetition surely of import. Romir frowned at them, wondering what they signified. His ignorance pressed at him; there was so much he knew nothing of, and that failing could mean defeat in this particular battle.

"Proximity alarms," Asrial said, pointing at a set of flashing lights without looking away from the controls. In the middle of battle, she had noticed his confusion and taken time to explain—distracting her from what was important, hindering her efforts against the enemy.

Romir dug his fingers into the arms of his seat, frustration flailing him for doing so little. He had to help Asrial somehow, aid her in her struggle. He was not helpless. He may not fully understand how she flew the *Castel*, but he did know energy. He could sense the enemy's power, could see the lines with his weaver's sight. Surely he could do something more than patching the shields, could find some way to attack the other starship.

"Aft shields down to thirty-four percent—repeat, three-four percent."

A flare of energy jolted his awareness, coming from beyond the ship. The enemy?

"Grab net. The bastards intend to board." Asrial muttered a scathing curse, her teeth bared in a ferocious snarl. "Not again, damn you to the ends of space. Not. Again."

Not again? This had happened before?

She was remembering her parents, Romir realized. They had been killed by pirates, and she blamed herself for their deaths—or perhaps for surviving when they had died.

The lights on the panel blinked amber and red, their ominous flashing painting Asrial's face like flames. The dire expression they revealed boded ill for the pirates. But with the *Castel* caught in the enemy's talons, the avenues for resistance were limited.

Her chest rose and fell with unspoken emotion. Despite the coolness of the chamber, sweat trickled down her neck and gleamed on her arms. She punched ciphers on her panel in rapid succession, the abrupt motions edged with urgency. With desperation?

Romir had a sick feeling of history repeating itself. He, too, had rued surviving his companions. Was Asrial determined to embrace the path he had failed to take?

His impotence battered him, an old torment renewed. Once again he was standing aside, forced to watch while disaster unfolded before him.

Not this time. Not Asrial! There had to be something he could do to save her.

Something . . .

Romir thrust his awareness beyond the walls of the *Castel* to see for himself the trap the enemy had sprung.

In the abyss between worlds, the threads of creation shone bright against the emptiness. Energy extended from the other starship, furious strands spread wide to hold the *Castel* between two jaws.

But he saw more than that.

The vortex of primal energies in the heart of the *Castel* bloomed, roaring hungrily against its restraints. Power to challenge even a djinn. It beat against his senses, portent and potential both, wound into a single skein promising . . .

Hope hovered before him, blazing hot and chill with peril, waiting for him to stretch out his hand and grasp it. There was a way . . . if he was willing to pay the price.

"Can you Jump?"

"While tangled in a grab net, with no destination set?" Asrial shot him a wide-eyed stare across her shoulder. "The power levels—"

"Do it anyway."

Trust me!

The *Castel* shuddered around them, the proximity alarms on her panel continued their malevolent flashing.

Her jaw firmed with decision. "Whatever you're planning, get ready." She slammed her hand on the square that initiated Jump, despite its steady red ring.

Twenty-six

In the heartbeat before the *Castel* entered the portal, Romir took control of the weave, mustering every drop of his essence to bend it to his will. Primal energies roared through him, the threads of creation unraveling into a myriad colors, as he altered the flows. He reshaped the portal into a Heigen cloak around the *Castel*, a cocoon to protect it against the enemy's pincers of power.

Without need to breathe or to keep a heart pumping, he could manage the feat by himself. This was the reason the Mughelis created djinn—the perfect shuttles to weave their will. If he were not djinn, his expenditure of power would have been fatal, and still he would have failed.

Now, the vortex in the heart of the *Castel* sang to him, and he rejoiced in the boundless energy at his command. The threads blazed in his weaver's sight. With a twist of his hands, he expanded the cloak, driving it into the pincers.

The attack shattered, unable to contain the flash flood of power. Out of the chaos of flaring energies, he gathered the flows of the enemy's pincers and channeled them all back up their track, the path of lesser resistance.

Back to the ship that wove them.

The *Castel* bucked around them. His seat straps snugged tight, the sudden sensation snapping his awareness back to the pilot chamber and Asrial.

"Crap! What did you do?" She gaped, her eyes and mouth wide, her arms frozen in mid-reach.

The glass showed an explosion from the enemy's ship. It veered away and fell behind. Tumbling through the abyss like an injured yfreet, it broke up.

His prison yanked on his essence, sucking it down through the black star of the djinn. Pain clawed his shoulder, the chain snapping taut. He had spent his strength; nothing was left to resist. That was the price of weaving that much power.

But he had not failed Asrial.

As he faded to mist, he clung to that certainty.

They hadn't Jumped. In violation of all safety protocols, she'd activated the jump drive while within close proximity of another ship and still caught in the grab net. Without allowing the drive time to power up to Jump levels. Without proper calculations. Without a set destination.

They should have been lost in Jump.

But despite all reason, they were in normal space.

They were alive.

Gulping air, Asrial stared at her primary display and the image of the disintegrating pirate ship. Her greatest nightmare vanquished. Over in the space of a heartbeat. No endless battle while she sat trapped at her board.

Impossible.

Somehow Romir had used the jump drive as a weapon.

She powered down the drive, activating the autopilot and releasing her shock harness with trembling hands. Her heart beat so fast it felt like it would tumble out of her chest. They were safe!

With a crazed smile, she spun to Romir.

Elation turned to shock. His seat was empty, only a shimmer of mist quickly fading filled its space.

"Romir!" Without thinking, Asrial threw herself out of her seat, toward the indistinct form of her lover. Safety be damned.

Fending off the pirates must have taken all his power. He'd protected her—at the risk of losing his independence.

The mist fought to escape her, swirling between her fingers like sentient fog, like the specter of failure come to life.

No! She couldn't lose him now. Not when they were so close.

Asrial clung to him, pressing her body wherever she could touch him. Heat answered her, the only indication she had of his presence. She could barely see him. This was her worst fear made real—and this time he didn't seem to be struggling against his prison!

She reached up to where his head should be, straining to see his face. Only the barest mirage was there—heat illusion, her eyes playing tricks on her. It couldn't be! "Romir, fight it! Stay with me."

Resistance met her grasping hand, a hint of thick hair. She tangled her fingers in it. Sensation, pleasure—those were what anchored Romir's freedom at her side. She had to try.

With her free hand, she fumbled for his neck, his jaw, trying to hold him in place for a kiss. Pressure against her mouth, firm and searching, told her he reciprocated. She opened herself to it, feeling something slide across her lips, seeking entrance. She poured her heart into the kiss, desperation heightening her senses.

Please. Spirit of space, don't take him from me.

With her eyes closed, she could imagine Romir was still with her, still in her arms, that his hard body still strained against hers. She could feel his chest against her breasts, his thighs between her calves, the bold ridge of his erection against her mound.

"Ha!" The harsh sound by her ear jerked her eyes open. Golden brown skin filled her gaze, looking every bit as solid as her own, with not a speck of otherworldly shimmer. She could see black hair, a strong jaw, taut muscle, the hollow of his throat. The cords of his throat worked as she stared. "I am here."

Gasping in relief, Asrial covered his face with desperate kisses, gloried in the passionate ones she got in return. He really was in her arms!

She hid her face against Romir's neck. Fear made her weak. Tears spilled over, painting her cheeks with heat and wetness. *Too close. That was too close.*

Romir's tight embrace drove the air from her lungs. He pulled her down to straddle his lap, holding her as though he would never let her go. She didn't want him to let her go.

His heat filled her arms. Hard muscle pressed against her thighs and calves, against her cheek and breasts. Beloved heat. Her lover's.

Gradually the reality of his survival sank in. She trembled, her body burning, needing more intimate contact, but there was no time for that. *Right*. She had to check the *Castel* for damage. They couldn't Jump until she was sure the drive was stable. And just because she'd seen an explosion from the *Eikki* didn't mean the pirates no longer posed a danger.

Enough of the weepy jill. She had a ship to fly.

Asrial wiped her cheeks free of tears, though she couldn't do anything about those trickling down his chest without drawing attention to them. She pulled away reluctantly, her eyes clinging to Romir as she slid off his lap and got her feet back under her. "Will you be safe like this?"

With a weak smile, Romir stood up and cupped her face. "I will stay near." And true to his word, after she returned to her seat, he rested his folded arms on her seat back. His mouth was just a breath away from her shoulder and neck—and she knew that for a fact because he closed the distance more than once. She didn't know if he needed the contact, but the gentle friction certainly reassured her.

Though it had felt like forever, she hadn't been away from the pilot board that long. The pirate ship was still well within near distance range of the *Castel*'s sensors.

She checked the screens a second time. Their readouts remained the same. The *Eikki*'s uncontrolled tumble was unchanged. No thrusters were firing. No deceleration nor change in vector was detected. No communication was received. The gap between the ships continued to open.

"We're in the clear." For the first time since she noticed the bogey, she took an easy breath. The pirates weren't coming back, not with their apparent damage. They wouldn't be able to catch up with the *Castel* again.

A longer look made her conscience itch. Was the damage so severe the pirates couldn't bring it back under control? If they couldn't, they'd be trapped on the *Eikki*, continuing on that vector forever. Until supplies ran out or life support failed.

Asrial shuddered at the thought, the skin on her arms prickling. They were pirates and had nearly succeeded in boarding her, but she wouldn't have wished such a fate on her worst enemy. It was a slow and ugly death.

Romir crossed his arms over her chest, his chin on her shoulder. "You are troubled."

She leaned into him, taking comfort from his solid presence. This time was different. Unlike the other pirate attack, she wasn't the lone survivor. "That could have been us, the *Castel*."

"They deserve it."

A slight course correction increased their divergence from the *Eikki*'s tumbling track. Asrial smiled at the result: one less detail to worry about. She turned her attention to damage control. As expected, the explosion that broke the grab net had strained the *Castel*'s systems. The port side had taken the worst damage. Shields there were down to 15 percent—hopefully it was nothing she couldn't fix. She needed those shields for entry when they got to Maj.

Hull integrity was compromised, several sections glowing red and amber on the schematics. Even the corridors showed possible breaches. Damage control automatically sealed the affected holds; the *Castel* could still Jump, but she'd need a shipyard before she could use those holds again. Repairs to those were beyond her capabilities.

The magnitude of the job they faced was daunting. "This will take days, decs even, if we do it ourselves."

"I am not going anywhere." Romir affirmed his promise with a warm kiss on the side of her neck. "Not without you."

Confident that the *Castel* was secure, Romir sat in silence while Asrial queried the ciphers on her panel. The heart of the starship was intact, but even if he told her it had not suffered any serious damage, she would want confirmation.

He watched her gladly, amazed that he could do so. He had been so sure that that time would be the last when he succumbed to his prison's call. But though he was confident he would remain free for now, he kept his arms around her. He needed that contact, the sturdy warmth of her body, the spicy scent of her hair, the tickle of her curls.

Asrial finally leaned away from her panel, tipping her head back to smile up at him. Satisfaction lit her brown eyes and eased the lines of strain on her face. "Slight change in plans: I have to inform the Patrol about the pirates. I don't think the *Eikki*'s in any condition to get anywhere without assistance."

"You are too kindhearted."

Waving a limp hand, she brushed aside his comment. "Not really. You'll notice I don't plan on assisting them myself."

Romir smiled, keeping his opinion to himself. His *biba* was too kind for her own good. Witness the care she had given him, a nameless djinn foisted on her by circumstances. A more cautious woman would have left him to his prison and sold it to be rid of him—but not Asrial.

Her next words only confirmed it. "So, Nudra 4 to report the attempted jacking to the Interstellar Patrol and repairs to the *Castel*. Then next stop: Maj."

"You should rest."

A doubtful hum met his suggestion. Asrial twisted around in his embrace and looped her arms around his neck, warm concern shadowing her eyes. "First things first."

She drew his head down for a searching kiss, her tongue sliding into his mouth to lick and linger, to tease and tempt. Such fervent intimacies and the spice that was uniquely Asrial. His entire being leaped to the carnal summons in a flash of delicious sensation.

The tight clasp of her soft lips around his tongue sent sweet lightning streaking through Romir. Heat and wanting, the response she elicited from him felt as new and as precious as the first time he had touched her. He sank into her kiss, surrendering all to her possession as she sucked his tongue and stroked him with hers. Strong and urgent, the seductive caresses consumed him, waking the scorching passion in his heart that burned only for her. That first kiss strung out into kisses, deep and lush and poignant with yearning, neither of them willing to release the other, the fear of loss too recent, the need to touch too strong.

Asrial arched up, the soft mounds of her breasts pillowed against him, their hard tips painting lines of fiery awareness across his chest. She filled his arms so perfectly, as though she had always been meant to be there, the same way she filled his heart.

Sensation piled upon sensation, magnifying the hunger boiling in his loins, winding molten threads of desire through his limbs. She knew him so well, knew how to touch him to best effect and fight the call of his prison, the call that even now dragged on him like an anchor.

Long, blissful moments passed in that sensual exchange of lick and thrust, glide and suck before Asrial broke off to whisper, "I was so scared. You disappeared." She ducked her head, but not before he saw tears welling up in her eyes.

"I am here. I will always be here," Romir promised her recklessly, spurred by the hot wetness trickling over his chest and the desperate strength with which her fingers gripped his shoulders. So rarely did she speak of her own needs, her fears, for her to speak of them now hinted at a depth of ice-edged horror he had not suspected.

Bending down, he captured her mouth to resume the quest for pleasure, to reassure her of his continued presence—and to reassure himself as well. Asrial was safe. That was all that was important. His strength had been sufficient to protect her this time.

As desire resurged to sweep all concerns away, one faint thought lingered: it had not simply been a weaver's strength that had broken her enemy's trap but . . .

Djinn strength.

Twenty-seven

Their descent into Maj transpired with a feeling of surreality. Once more, glowing clouds parted to reveal dark blue water and an edge of land. Only this time she had the luxury of admiring the view. Though guiding the *Castel* down took most of her attention, this time, her approach was slower, her destination closer. The coast, not the mountains. Lucky for her, since it put less strain on the plasma shields. They'd stopped at Nudra 4 just long enough to get the worst damage fixed. The *Castel* was now reasonably intact, but its systems were running at less than nominal—even the shields were up to only 78 percent.

Asrial flew the *Castel* parallel to the coast in search of a good landing spot, one with easy access to the ocean.

Romir leaned toward the screen with hungry eyes, reminding her of the other difference from her last visit to Maj: this time she wasn't alone. "This is not as I remember my home."

"Has it changed that much?"

"It is peaceful." Indeed, it was . . . and they were the only people on Maj. What an indictment of the Mughelis.

The desolation in Romir's voice told her more than words that it would be best not to seek more detail. She'd refrained from asking before, reluctant to stir painful memories and remind him of the woman he'd lost; now she vowed to leave it be. Nothing good would come of dwelling in the past.

A good spot appeared—a broad sweep of relatively flat sand with sufficient space for the *Castel*, an easy slope, and gentle waves. She set down, her heart pounding with more than the usual excitement of a fast entry. The antigrav held up, allowing the *Castel* to land with barely a shudder.

Asrial pressed the release for the shock harness and turned to Romir. "Ready?"

He stood with his hands on the secondary board, head bowed, the curtain of his hair concealing his expression. "You should not do this."

Surprise froze her in her seat. She couldn't believe her ears. "*What?* I thought you wanted to be free. What happened to change your mind?" His enslavement was an abomination. How could he now want to remain a djinn?

"Perhaps I do not deserve to be free. You don't know all that I've done as a djinn." He didn't look at her, his answer delivered in a low monotone heavy with guilt.

Her temper flared, ignited by his unthinking and wrong-minded acceptance of responsibility. "What the Mughelis forced you to do is irrelevant. I know that given a choice, you wouldn't have done any of it, so that's beside the point. Don't hide behind the past."

"I can better protect you in this form." He cupped his right hand over his tat.

"But odds are your prison will pull you back one of these days."

"You can summon me."

"No! That would make me your master."

"I would not mind."

Her heart trembled at the sacrifice he was offering, that he was willing to make—for her. Tears filled her eyes and choked her throat, making it difficult to speak. "If anything happens to me, if someone were to steal your prison, you'd be trapped forever." She forced the words out, breathing through her nose so the tears wouldn't spill over.

Jumping to her feet, she glared at him. "I won't risk it."

Romir finally turned to face her, his expression haunted. "But—"

"I won't." Asrial fled the piloting chamber before she embarrassed herself by crying. Fighting for composure, she prepared as though this were just another strike instead of the most important undertaking of her life, trying to be methodical in her approach though her sight blurred with irritating regularity. Stunner, spare charge, med kit, comp. No need for the lamp or tool kit. She added towels and—on a spark of desperate optimism—the jumpsuit in Romir's size that she'd bought on Eskarion 5 while waiting to transit to the Rim.

She'd reached the work cabin before he joined her. He said nothing when she picked up his prison, walking by her side to the hatch. She cradled the flask against her chest, half-afraid he would try to stop her.

A steady breeze blew across the *Castel*, carrying the smell of hot metal from the cooling hull overlaid by those of unfamiliar vegetation and seawater. It tickled her nostrils, acrid and comforting after numerous safe landings, and was slowly left behind as they descended the slope to the shore.

Their approach couldn't be more different from that time in Salima: in broad daylight instead of the stealth of night; on foot, not by grav sled; sparse shrubs, not meadow and thick moss; heat instead of coolness.

Heat and humidity quickly turned her sweaty, her curls rioting and clinging to her cheeks. The sand scorched her feet through her boots, swishing as it shifted under her weight—and only hers. Romir's steps were silent as always. Insubstantial. As though he weren't there.

The desolate dunes flowed down to the ocean, to the sparkling waves ruffled by the restless wind. The rhythmic ebb and rush soothed. No wings broke the sky, and the scan of the water had returned a safe reading. A lone tree near the shore offered dappled shade, its gnarled roots attesting to a long history of resisting sun and surf.

Asrial set her precious load at the foot of the tree, above the line of wet sand, then released the seals of her boots. Sitting on a towel, she pulled off her boots, then her socks. The sand felt strange to her bare soles, not quite powder but not grit. Pushing her pants down, she undressed slowly, discomfited at baring skin under this alien sun, in this alien world, even if it was the world the Lomidari originally came from.

"Do not do this, *biba*." Romir knelt beside her, casting her in deeper shadow. With stiff fingers, he tipped her chin back, forcing her to look at him. "My freedom is not worth the loss in power. I could not have done what I did to the pirates were I not djinn."

Again, his first concern was her safety. The calm look on his face said he'd made his peace with his decision. His selflessness sent a pang through her heart. She couldn't accept it.

She shook her head, her wet curls stinging her cheeks. "I couldn't save my parents. I can't heal Amin. I can't bear to leave you trapped."

His silver eyes darkened to stormy frustration as he gripped her upper arms, his jaw set in a hard line. "I do not want this. You violate my choice if you do this."

Asrial stared at Romir, stricken by his implacable refusal. Freeing him would mean losing his love? Did he see it that way? Would pressing on in spite of his objection be a betrayal, treating him as if he were no more than a djinn? "I—I want a normal life with you. To have your children. To grow old with you."

He reared back, his fingers no longer biting into her skin. White showed in his eyes, their pupils thin, smoky rings. "You—"

She cupped her breasts, conscious of the transience of health despite medical advances. "I'll grow old, or I might get sick or injured like Amin. If that happens and I lose this body that helps you stay free, I don't want to lose you to your prison. I can't bear for that to happen, not if I could've stopped it. Let me try." Tears spilled over, etching hot lines of wetness down her cheeks. Straining to read his face in the shifting shadows, she ignored them. Air came in short gasps that hurt her chest; she couldn't seem to breathe properly.

"You—" Romir pulled her into his embrace, pressing her face to his chest, holding her tight. His shudders shook her, his heat branding him into her senses. "*Biba*, you shame me."

Hope flickered to uncertain life. "Then . . . ?"

"I want that, too."

Relief sent more tears splashing down. He kissed them off her cheeks, murmuring soft words she didn't understand. But she didn't need to understand; his voice simply augmented the tenderness behind each gentle kiss. This was the man she wanted beside her for the rest of her life.

Finding a tremulous smile from somewhere, Asrial pulled out of his embrace. "So let's do this."

Romir released her slowly, his hands lingering as they slid down her sides. “Very well.” He finally stepped back and out of reach, spreading his arms as if to say he wasn’t stopping her.

She finished undressing, leaving her folded clothes among the tree’s roots.

When she picked up the flask once more, she nearly dropped it in shock. It might have been her imagination playing tricks on her, but the flask felt vibrant against her bare breasts—almost as if it were living flesh.

Wet sand crunched underfoot, crept between her toes with rough insistence. An alien sensation.

Trepidation dragging on her heels, her feet slowed, then stopped, without her willing. She had no other options if she failed again. This long shot offered the only hope of success. The Majian texts she had access to didn’t make any mention of “waters of life,” and Romir didn’t remember any place on Maj that might be relevant. This place seemed as good as any other sea.

But what if she was wrong?

Her nerve wavered. Suddenly she was in no hurry to make her attempt. So long as she hadn’t tried, there was still a chance of freeing Romir. She could still dream of a life together. Pain had her opening her hand; short red crescents marked her palm where her nails had bitten into the skin all unthinking.

Pure foolishness.

This had to work. She couldn’t bear the thought of failing Romir again.

The water was warm, its taste laden with strange salts. The waves lapping against her naked body and the gritty sand under her legs made her uneasy, the sensations unlike anything she’d experienced before. Sitting here, under Maj’s bright sun, clad in nothing but sweat felt unnatural. Dangerous.

Romir kept pace with her, entering the water when she did, coming to a halt when she did, doing nothing to impede her advance. He took his cue from her, an undemanding presence, all quiet patience and encouragement now that he'd ceded his will to her choice.

She stopped before the water was halfway up her calves, its pale green clarity revealing forms in the wave-rippled sand farther out that she didn't want to disturb. Surely this was deep enough?

Asrial struggled to draw a calming breath as her heart threatened to launch itself from her tight chest. She choked on a laugh. "All of a sudden, I'm scared. How foolish is that?" It was an effort to force the words out.

"Take your time. I have been djinn for centuries. A few more moments do not matter," Romir murmured into her ear. He embraced her from behind, wrapping his arms around her waist, a band of male strength she'd come to depend on. His touch dislodged a weight on her heart, the heaviness from the dissension between them vanishing like launch steam on a hot day, thick clouds shredding into wisps.

She took an easier breath, leaning into his support, and smiled as his embrace tightened, pressing his ready erection into the crease of her backside—if she needed more proof of his willingness, there it was. Together, they could do this. She had to believe that.

"Thank you. I'm fine now." She arched her back, deliberately teasing the hard, very male ridge branding itself into her flesh. With the flask in her hands, she had to rely on other means for foreplay.

"Good." Releasing her, he reciprocated, his large hands rising to cup her breasts and covering them completely, his hold possessive.

Asrial could feel herself melting inside in anticipation, her body confident of what had to follow, as sure as stellar winds in deep space.

Romir didn't disappoint. So gentle, so tender, a courtier in his exquisite care of her. He made love to her, fondling her eager breasts, his fingers brushing her nipples in slow circles, coaxing them to aching points. He planted soft, searching kisses along her shoulders, his tongue tracing delicate patterns on her skin. Flickering, fleeting, teasing, the contact ignited a fire in her core, hot and greedy, a hunger that only he could satisfy.

Wild, sweet seduction.

"Biba," he crooned, his breath ruffling the soft hairs of her nape, his tone making an endearment of the strange word. He nibbled on the meat of her shoulder—and lightning blazed down her spine and along her nerves, crackling, sizzling, a shock to the system.

Before the onslaught of delight, her knees gave way. "Oh!"

He caught her with a soft laugh, easing her into the water with only a small splash and settling her on his lap. His crossed legs made an unusual seat, a steady strength beneath her, his chest hot against her back, his erection just as hot against her backside. He surrounded her, protecting her from the sea's more energetic waves.

The new position didn't slow his seduction. Romir's hands, his mouth, his smooth chest, his stubbled jaw—his whole body—stroked her with artful intent. He took full advantage of the fact that she couldn't use her hands. A lick and nibble here, a squeeze and caress there, the subtle slide of his hair hanging loose and wet across her breasts, the rocking of his hips. He murmured toe-curling promises as he nibbled on her ear, telling her how he intended to make love to her, vowing not to rest until she was boneless from satiation.

Her heart skipped, her body heating with anticipation. Need unfurled, a crimson flower blooming under his exquisite care. When Romir decided to support her decision, he didn't stop at half measures. She couldn't resist his persuasion—and had no wish to.

The sea joined in. The waves topped her thighs, splashing around them and washing over their legs with almost sentient insistence. Pleasure whispered through her in blissful little quivers and riotous wisps of sweet sensation, triggered by his play. Light dazzled her, thousands of stars adorning the waves. Like a dream.

But this was real.

And their purpose here was more important than simple pleasure.

She dropped her gaze to Romir's prison, the focus of their hopes for a future together. It looked unchanged, still that distinctive golden brown prized by collectors of Majian artifacts, still with that dark, elaborate etching around its base, still retaining the shape of a stylized phallus.

The previous failure hovered in the back of her mind. How would they be able to tell if this attempt was successful?

Twenty-eight

Romir's caresses grew bolder, his fingers gliding over the tender skin of her inner hips and between her legs, combing through her curls. He ground his palm on her aching mound, but the hard pressure did little to ease her growing hunger, setting off flares of desire along her nerves.

"Touch me." Her voice broke, needy to her ears, but that didn't matter, only that he fill the melting emptiness he'd awakened inside her.

"*Biba.*" Whispering a kiss along her neck, he parted her folds, using a thumb to rub and circle her clit. His fingers pressed into her, probing, filling, delighting. So deep. Two . . . three of them. He knew just how to drive her wild.

The flask warmed in her hands, almost as though it invited her touch. Though she knew Romir disliked her touching his prison, she couldn't stop herself from running its neck between her breasts. It didn't feel like pottery at all. Its warmth seemed to beat against her palms, an insistent, rhythmic beat—like a rapid pulse. It felt alive, though that should have been impossible.

She rubbed it over herself, inhaling sharply as her nipples throbbed at the contact. The electric spark leaped from her breasts, zinging to the center of her being. It was almost like a pleasure wand, inflaming her desire.

A groan rumbled behind her, half protest, half incitement, and all male hunger. Romir was chanting her name, she realized belatedly. The hoarseness in his voice sent a thrill through her, the strength of his desire for her more arousing than any toy she could buy.

Spirit of space, this had to work. She wanted to spend the rest of her life with him.

"No more, *biba*. I must have control for the moment." Asrial barely recognized the guttural growl as his, so deep did it sound, as though torn from his bones.

"But after you're free, I want you to make love to me hard and fast."

"Of course. As often as you wish." The grunted promise resonated deep within her, evoking a heart-pounding vision of the future hovering within reach.

Locking his hands around her thighs, Romir raised her nearly out of the water, spreading her legs wide as his hard length slid down her backside in a heated caress, a brush of velvet strength that made her quiver. Then he brought her back down. The blunt tip of him pressed into her, the broad head stretching her welcoming flesh.

He entered her slowly. Breathtakingly slow. So slow she had time to count her heartbeats. Then he was completely in, and she could breathe again.

The sensation of him filling her, stretching her to overflowing, was a glory she could never tire of. Perfect union. The gentle nudge of him against her womb was a sweetness unlike any other, silent reassurance that they were together.

Romir started to move, rocking her once more. This time Asrial didn't protest. They could not afford haste. This was no race to the finish where she could lose herself to sensation. She had to remember their purpose.

The sea's steady murmur mingled with Romir's growls of praise and her own gasps. The waves splashing over them magnified the delight of his caresses.

She rolled her hips, her breath catching at the feel of Romir swirling deep inside, the ridge of his head rasping against her delicate muscles. Her hunger rose with each velvet nudge, spiraling higher and ever higher.

Needing to touch Romir, to feel more of him than just his thickness inside her, she reached down with one hand, finding a lean hip with which to anchor herself as she ground down against him. Together. They were together.

Desire gathered, spinning out to a precarious edge, the coiled hunger inside her nearly at the breaking point.

"Yes, just so. Give me your passion, *biba*."

Then it began—

A slow, sweet slide to breathless ecstasy.

Rapture broke, spilling through her veins in a thunderous bloom of pure sensation. Closing her eyes to shut out the endless expanse of water dancing before her, Asrial sagged against Romir, her head coming to rest on his shoulder, too heavy for her neck. Without the light-gilt waves to distract her, the feeling of fullness intensified, the sheer bliss of it forcing the air from her lungs.

She could only hope it was an omen of things to come.

Waves washed over them, salty with the memories of unseen shores. Romir allowed the steady rhythm to rock them, the sensual friction triggering another string of tiny sparks along his length as Asrial quivered around him.

Curls the color of old askeiwood clung to his skin, damp from the spray and Asrial's sweat. They tickled, teasing him with possessive caresses that grew wilder as she tossed her head.

Her open passion seduced—the flush on her usually pale cheeks, the dark pink of her full lips, the color across the slopes of her breasts, and the darker pink of her drawn nipples all announced without shame her desire for him. She called to him, and he could not help but respond.

Need lashed him with pinpricks of wanting, a carnal hunger honed to a cutting edge that could not be satisfied—for the last time, if they succeeded.

His name drifted into the air on a husky moan that resonated through his essence, gratification spearing him with elation. Clutching his prison to her hard-tipped breasts, Asrial panted, her breath caressing its surface. Moist heat curled through him from the black star on his shoulder, seductive coils urging him to submit.

And this time, he dared not resist.

Careful not to touch the flask, Romir stroked the sides of her breasts, the firm mounds tempting him to take her in hand. He sucked on the tender lobe of her ear to draw out her release.

Asrial gasped, throwing her head back as she rocked in his lap. Her wet flesh squeezed his length yet again, fluttering around him with those sweet, seductive ripples that honed the familiar edge of desire to razor sharpness. "Good . . . you feel so good."

He reached between her legs, found the entrance of her body stretched around him and the hard nub veiled by her curls. Her dew flowed over him, easing his thrusts as he rocked under her. More slicked his fingers as he circled her nub, drawing another cry of delight from Asrial and another wave of ripples.

Proof of passion, proof of pleasure, proof of life . . .

Yes, this was it. Now was the time.

She groaned his name, her short nails digging into his hip.

"Here." Romir cupped her hand, guided her to their joined flesh. She had to be the one to do it, to take her cream and anoint his prison. "Take the next step."

Delight scorched him in a blast of heat as her fingers scraped him—scraped both of them—her nails adding sensation upon sensation. He shivered at the contact, something inside him welcoming the possessive friction. The unspoken claim on his body as hers. For always.

Closing his eyes against the distraction, he mustered his will. He had to shake his head to clear it of the carnal hunger fogging his thoughts. What else was there?

Patterns . . . there had been patterns in the message. The threads needed to bring power to bear to unravel the djinn weave.

As Asrial smeared her cream across the flask, he plucked the threads of power—blue, red, green, black, white—and started to weave, focusing on the proof of her passion, on the pattern of life it carried and its link to her essence. He understood now the insidious logic of the Mughelis. Unraveling the djinn weave required the master's deliberate cooperation. No djinn could have unraveled it working alone.

Pleasure sang through the black star, the djinn mark sinking its hooks deeper into Romir, ready to draw him back. He surrendered to the sensations as he continued to weave. This time, he did not fight the call of his prison, embracing necessity in willing sacrifice. If he returned to the gray mists, then so be it. He would serve his *biba* to the best of his ability—in any form—in any way she wanted.

Light faded, flattened. The sparkles on the water around them disappeared into gray mists.

* * *

Heat bloomed under her slick fingers—first warm, then hot, hotter, and increasingly hotter. Asrial's heart skipped a beat. Something was happening! It hadn't been like this in Salima.

She landed with a splash and flailed for balance. Her body clenched, aching at the sudden emptiness inside her. Romir was gone—his chest no longer supported her, his legs no longer cradled her. But that wasn't all. His prison filled with mist and starlight, the glow growing brighter with every beat of her heart. The flask shimmered, turning transparent, the indigo tracery thinning beneath her fingers.

Asrial gasped, tenuous hope and desperate fear twisting into an involuted knot, wrapping around her heart until it wouldn't beat. Waiting . . .

The flask vanished in a soundless explosion, brilliant sparkles of color whirling madly into nothingness.

Leaving—

A naked man sprawled between her thighs, warm and heavy, pressing her into the surf. Shadowed cheeks scraped her breasts. His head jerked up, revealing—

Brilliant silver eyes.

Romir!

Incredulous, Asrial framed his head between her hands, rejoicing in the rasp of his stubble against her palms. "It worked?"

"I think . . . yes!" Groaning her name, he pulled her into his arms for a searching kiss. His tongue danced over hers with a playfulness he'd never shown before, teasing her until she had to catch him and suck. The hot taste was really him; she wasn't imagining it.

Tears of joy spilled down her cheeks, and he kissed them away tenderly, brushing firm lips over her eyes, her forehead, her neck.

Then he licked the base of her throat, and desire reawakened. Her earlier hunger sprang back to life, her body throbbing with need.

"I need you. Come to me."

Romir mounted her, his hardness cloaked in gentleness, a blunt pressure, hot and steady, stretching her delicate flesh. They gasped at the intimate contact, sharing one breath, one thought, as he worked himself deeper. Ever deeper.

She clung to his shoulders, his wet hair tangling with her fingers. Incredulous at his renewed possession, she arched into his thrust. "Yes, oh, yes! You feel so good." She could feel his length throbbing inside her.

Throbbing . . .

He stared into her eyes, a dark flush staining his cheeks as he gripped her shoulders, anchoring her for his taking. "I do not know if I can control myself."

Asrial laughed, relief and happiness bubbling over in a frothy brew. "Don't hold back. Hard and fast, remember? You promised."

Before she'd finished speaking, Romir was moving, lunging, pounding into her with short, powerful thrusts that drove cries of delight from her. He'd never let go quite like this before, almost furious in his lovemaking.

With the hard-packed sand beneath her and the waves adding their splashes, it was all she could do to hold on. He swept her back up the dizzying heights of pleasure, need flaring bright and plasma hot. He moved over her, into her, relentless in his desire until the promise of rapture hovered temptingly near.

Romir shuddered in her arms, his gasps hoarse above her, his eyes wild. "Asrial—I—"

Need shook her. Her earlier release had sensitized her so that it didn't take as much to get her to the peak. But she had to hold on.

She'd had an orgasm already. This time was his. She wanted to give him this much and more.

"Don't wait." Clamping her thighs around him, she squeezed him with her aching inner muscles.

"I—*ah!*"

Heat bathed her inner flesh, straining her control. She felt him jerk inside her as he surrendered to the moment, his release a strong pulse that resonated throughout her body. For the first time, he'd finished!

The shock on Romir's face at his release was worth the wait and all her restraint. The rapture transformed his features, such incredulous joy that she could never have imagined from him. The edge of pain and desperation that had become a familiar sight during their lovemaking vanished beneath a flush of distilled ecstasy.

Elation overwhelmed her. He was free! No longer djinn. No longer bound to that unnatural existence. Free to choose. Free to stand by her side.

Finally, Asrial gave in to carnal hunger, need splintering, erupting in a thousand blistering shards of singing pleasure. It blew through her in an endless moment of ecstasy. Rapture sent her soaring through the heavens, gravity be damned.

On and on. It stretched out, spinning through air and light and heat . . .

When Asrial came back to herself, she lay sprawled across Romir, still joined with him in intimate union. The water was higher, its waves wafting his hair across her back in fleeting, teasing caresses. His heart thundered under her ear, fast and insistent, a sound she'd never felt before, his chest like a drum resonating to his rapture.

Everything felt like a dream.

Was Romir truly free? Truly hers?

Twenty-nine

Romir gasped, salt stinging the back of his throat. Despite the weight on his chest, he felt as though he might float away on the next wave. He could not remember ever feeling this way before—so light, such a sense of liberation. And all because of one woman.

Propping herself up on an elbow, Asrial leaned over him, studying him with hungry eyes. She was beautiful in the manner of a hunting *shera* with an intensity of purpose that made her outshine those perfect constructs she called avatars. The thought of her displaying that fierceness in the defense of the children she wanted—their children—made his heart melt all over again. The intensity of his reaction had him dropping his eyes while he sought to untangle the skein of his thoughts. "What is it?"

"I can't get enough of you." Her hands stroking his sides gave credence to her unblushing statement, lingering over the sensitive skin around his hipbones to devastating effect. Lightning streaked down his length and up his spine.

He could not get enough of her, either. But more would have to wait. Her shoulders were turning pink, her spacer paleness so vulnerable to the harsh sunlight. "Shall we move to the shade?"

"What?"

"You should not expose yourself to the sun for so long." It would be a pity to mar the silken expanse of her back. He would prefer to press kisses there rather than medication.

Arm in arm, they stumbled to the tree, the playful waves making a steady pace difficult. His legs had never felt so weak, as if all his strength had pooled in his groin. Sensations pressed on him: sand between his toes, the warm wind drying the seawater on his skin, his wet hair clinging to his back, Asrial's soft body against his side.

His knees gave out once they achieved the tree's protection. Thankfully, there were no stones in the dry sand that cushioned his landing. Pulled off balance, Asrial dropped into his lap, her joyous laughter making his heart skip a beat.

"This is embarrassing. I am so weak."

An amused snort contradicted him. "Doesn't look that way from where I'm sitting." Bold fingers traced his length and measured his girth, trailing sparks of delight in their wake and fanning the embers of carnal desire. His nerves sang their anticipation, fluttering and aching and all but cheering.

Gathering his long, wet hair over his shoulder and out from under him, Romir groaned. *"Biba."*

"What does that mean?"

"Beloved." His heart took wing, awash with the freedom to share his feelings without fear they would be used against him. To stand by her side—by his choice—was a future he had never dared to imagine.

She stared at him, her mouth hanging open, at a loss for words.

Romir had to laugh at her bewildered expression. After everything they had said and shared and gone through, she still doubted his feelings for her?

"I love you. I love you with every breath I take. I will love you until the day I die." Perhaps only time would convince her. But at least now they would have that time.

Asrial blushed, a delightful shyness he had not expected in so confident a woman. "We just freed you. Don't talk about dying so casually."

"Then make love with me." Bending down, he kissed her, treasuring the softness of her lips, the salt of the sea mingling with the taste that was uniquely Asrial. Her tender reception as she wrapped her arms around his neck confirmed them as lovers, joined heart to heart. There was a rightness to their unhurried exchange. The lazy kisses celebrated the absence of an emergency: no longer did the threat of recapture by his prison fuel their lovemaking.

All too soon carnal hunger awakened, roused by her proximity, by the hard tips of her breasts insistently poking him in the chest, by her hip pressed against his stirring shaft, by the musk of their mutual desire. Straddling his hips, she guided him to the entrance of her body, her small hands squeezing his shaft with delicate strength.

His heart skipped when his head grazed her wet folds. There were no waves now to disguise that first intimate contact, and his heightened awareness made his skin feel too tight to contain him. The heated clasp of her body as she slid around him sent his heart scrambling for his throat. He struggled not to spill his seed so soon.

Asrial gave a surprised laugh. "I can see your pulse." She planted a kiss on the betraying flutter, followed by a quick lick that sent a sudden shiver winging down his spine and straining his control.

Romir smiled, sharing her delight, hoping he could hold back.

There would be more discoveries as he adjusted back to life as a man. He looked forward to sharing them with her.

He leaned against the tree's roots for support and thrust up, chasing Asrial as she rose off him. He caught her hips to him, reveling in the freedom to make his own demands. "I cannot get enough of you."

She took his mouth in a deep kiss that did little to soothe his rising hunger. "I'm not going anywhere. I want you. I love you. More than anything in this universe."

Her fervent words snapped the leash of his control. How could he hold back when she said something like that? He moved then, no longer able to contain himself. The need to cherish Asrial filled him with a bone-deep—no, a soul-deep—hunger. He channeled everything he felt into his motions and his inevitable release.

Romir was so hard and hot inside her, all male strength, and yet so vulnerable as he surrendered to pleasure. She couldn't get enough. The need to have him—all of him—was a craving in her blood, a yearning programmed into her cells. It frightened her that she could want him this much. But not having him would be even worse. She could face anything but that.

Asrial buried her face in the damp hair veiling Romir's chest. This second time was even better, allowing her to savor the heat of his release inside her, the jerks of pulsing pleasure stretching her delicate flesh.

An eternity passed in racing heartbeats and breathless sighs before she managed to raise her head.

In the dappled light, his left shoulder was an even golden brown, devoid of the indigo ink that had marked him as djinn. She pressed a kiss on the unblemished skin, feeling only smoothness under her lips, salty slick with sweat and smelling all male.

She looked forward to learning more of Romir the man.

Hard arms tightened around her, squeezing the air from her lungs. Romir stared up at her, an incredulous smile on his lips, the lines of strain drawn on his face gone. "I love you."

The fierce avowal sent a thrill winging through Asrial, her heart stumbling with joy. "I know you do." She gave him a tremulous smile, fighting back tears. "I love you, too."

A growl sounded between them, low, loud, and long. Romir's eyes flared wide in startlement. He stared at his belly when the sound repeated, his brow furrowing.

"What is it?"

"I am . . . hungry?"

Asrial burst into relieved laughter at the perplexity in his voice. That mundane growl confirmed their success better than even the disappearance of his tat could. When she recovered her composure, she kissed him, savoring the firm pressure of his response. "There's food on the *Castel*."

The prospect of watching him eat filled her with inordinate happiness. Spirit of space grant that it would be the first of better things to come.

Epilogue

Asrial found Romir in the hold, making passes with his hands over the gleaming new hatch, doing what he called his weavings. She still didn't quite grasp how he did it, but faint sparkles hinted at arcane modifications she couldn't see.

Her husband looked so different with his hair cut close to his head. She still missed those long tresses flowing over her body, but she understood the reason for the change. The long hair had been a reminder of his enslavement, one he'd been eager to discard.

That wasn't the only difference. He no longer went around bare-chested. The shirt he wore hid the cords and slabs of muscle she'd delighted in ogling. His loose pants had been replaced with carbon silk like hers. Except for the darkness of his skin, he looked every bit a spacer.

He also stood differently, less wary, more certain. While Amin had come to tolerate Romir's presence in her life, the rest of her family had welcomed him with open arms. Their acceptance was responsible for some of the ease in the set of his shoulders.

As if he'd felt her gaze, Romir looked up, and the love and devotion blazing in his eyes made her blush. She hadn't done anything to deserve such ardor.

She cleared her throat. "Problem?"

The pirates that attempted to jack the *Castel* turned out to be members of a notorious gang with hefty prices on their heads. The Interstellar Patrol judged that the *Castel*'s actions had been instrumental in their arrest. Though most of Volsung's crew had been dead, the Patrol hadn't quibbled about paying out. The reward money allowed her to refurbish her ship without selling the Dilaryn jewels. They'd taken delivery of the upgraded *Castel* just that morning. If he'd noticed something wrong, there was still time to get it fixed.

"Not any longer. There was a roughness in the energies of the door. It is gone now. There is no need to delay our departure."

"Are you certain you want to return to the Rim? We can probably find something in the Inner Worlds, you know." They were partners now; she wasn't about to dictate their course according to her convenience.

Unspoken was the possibility of visiting Lomida. The latest reports to reach Lyrel 9 claimed House Bintanan lay in disarray after the tragic deaths of its matriarch and her heir in a hover limo crash. A credible enough story, but since Bazhir, the president of Dareh, had supposedly been incapacitated in the same accident, Asrial suspected it wasn't as simple as that.

However, since a reputation for weakness and instability was anathema to House Bintanan, she was inclined to give some credence to claims that the Dareh's plasteel grip on the planet was weakening. Other reports hinted at covert action by Khodi's faction. Perhaps they could risk a quick visit.

A smile lit Romir's eyes and quickly spread to his mouth. "I have no wish to be parted from you. It is enough to know my people flourish."

He drew her into his arms in a warm embrace and into an even warmer kiss. His mouth claimed hers, his tongue thrusting deep and stroking hers with velvet insistence. "I would prefer to focus our energies on expanding House Dilaryn."

Her body heated, melting in readiness. "Want to warm the sheets? There's no need to deprive ourselves."